ONCE WE HAD A COUNTRY

Robert McGill

Jonathan Cape
London

For Reecia, who's been there

Published by Jonathan Cape 2014

2 4 6 8 10 9 7 5 3 1

First published in Canada in 2013 by
Alfred A. Knopf, Canada

First published in Great Britain in 2014 by
Jonathan Cape
Random House, 20 Vauxhall Bridge Road,
London SW1V 2SA

www.vintage-books.co.uk

Addresses for companies within The Random House Group Limited can be found at:
www.randomhouse.co.uk/offices.htm

The Random House Group Limited Reg. No. 954009

A CIP catalogue record for this book is available from the British Library

ISBN 9780224094160

The Random House Group Limited supports the Forest Stewardship Council® (FSC®),
the leading international forest-certification organisation. Our books
carrying the FSC label are printed on FSC®-certified paper. FSC is the only
forest-certification scheme supported by the leading environmental organisations,
including Greenpeace. Our paper procurement policy can be found at:
www.randomhouse.co.uk/environment

Printed and bound by CPI Group (UK) Ltd, Croydon, CR0 4YY

"Do you know," said the youth, "that your eyes are closed and at rest, and that they see nothing?" "I know it," he replied. "Then what," said the youth, "are the eyes with which you see me?"

—AUGUSTINE, LETTER 159

They were reaching out their arms in love for the far shore.

—GEORGE GRANT, *Lament for a Nation*

part 1

COME HOME, AMERICA

IN THE JUNGLE, Gordon tends a fire beside Yia Pao, the young potter whose soul he hopes to save. It is 1972, the rainy season in Laos, and the two of them shouldn't be here. Nobody should. Although they are barely a mile from the refugee camp, without knowing it they have crossed into a free-strike zone. The lines keep shifting because the Communists keep gaining ground, but the Royal Lao and American generals don't bother making announcements when the boundaries are redrawn. Instead, they simply order their warplanes to treat anybody on the ground as the enemy. Everyone becomes a target.

Nestled in the fire are three figures, each less than a foot high and made of clay, each one smiling. Gordon tells Yia Pao about the saints the little statues are meant to resemble, how this one was pierced by arrows, that one blinded with a rod. Through the heat and smoke, the little bodies glow red, seeming to be possessed of an inner light. Eventually Yia Pao shifts them with a branch to let them cool and says he hopes Gordon will be satisfied. The potter did his best to make the statues like the holy people his new friend has described, but Yia Pao has never seen a saint himself, and this method of firing them is more primitive than he'd like. In his village, before the bombing, he had a proper kiln. It's another of the things he mourns.

A crack comes from the firepit, and one of the little statues hops in place, then shudders. Cursing in his own language, Yia Pao kicks the saint with his boot, spraying ash and exposing a long fracture along the figure's side. He says this can happen when there's no way to control the temperature. Gordon murmurs his understanding and joins him in a vigil over the statues that remain, as if watching alone might keep them intact. Once the fire has died, Yia Pao says it should be all right to let them cool on their own, so the two men turn back for the camp.

At first, Gordon follows Yia Pao down the muddy trail in silence, wearing a troubled look. Then he starts to speak of what it must be like for Yia Pao to be a widower and a father. Gordon says childbirth rather than a B-52 took his own wife from him, and the loss was over twenty years ago, but when it happened he wasn't much older than Yia Pao is now, so he might understand something of how these last eight months have been. He knows about the grief and loneliness, the times when even the sight of your newborn child brings you no comfort but is only a reminder of the loss. He knows about wanting to join your loved one in that other world. Perhaps, he says, it isn't a coincidence that he and Yia Pao met. Their friendship could be the work of God, a way to provide both of them with solace.

At this, the younger man lets out a soft laugh. "Don't look for God in Laos," he says, "or soon you'll lose your faith."

Thick grey clouds swirl lowly overhead, churning through the mountains like a spring flood. A dense canopy of leaves and branches absorbs most of the light so that it's hard to make out the tattered grubbiness of Yia Pao's shirt and pants. A red bandana around Gordon's neck is the only vivid colour to be seen. He has a salt-and-pepper beard that contrasts with Yia Pao's smooth cheeks, and he stands half a foot higher than his companion, outweighing him by perhaps a hundred pounds, labouring as they cross the uneven terrain. From somewhere in the distance comes a murmur that could be thunder or the sound of falling bombs.

By the time the two of them reach the landing strip, a beam of sunlight has punched through the clouds to shine upon the camp on the far side, making the white tents shimmer. There are over sixty of them, and from half a mile away they seem immaculate. The airstrip is sodden, streaked with long ruts that vanish fifty yards before the treeline, as if the plane that left them was swallowed by a great beast. Enough time has passed since the last landing that the ruts are scabbing over with grass.

The men have made it halfway across the field when they hear a gunshot. A water buffalo nearby stops its grazing to look up, while Yia Pao squints at the tents ahead, then raises a finger to his lips and points toward the jungle. The two men run for the treeline, Yia Pao crouching with his eyes down, Gordon still focused on the tents. He's sweating and panting by the time they reach the forest.

A moment later, three men emerge from the camp, two of them white, the other Lao, none in uniform but all with rifles slung over their backs. They look unhurried as they walk across the landing strip in the direction of the trail leading to the firepit. Yia Pao and Gordon wait until the group is out of sight, then make their way toward the camp without leaving the cover of the trees.

When they reach the tents, there's nobody in sight, but they can hear a woman screaming. They run toward her voice, scattering chickens underfoot. The screaming grows in volume and intensity until suddenly they're upon her, an old Hmong woman lying in the mud. The French priest is kneeling by her side in his stained shirt and pristine collar, his hand cradling her head and his surplice wrapped around her arm, the blood already soaking through.

"They were looking for you, Yia Pao," says the priest in English. His tone is flat, his eyes accusing. "She wouldn't tell them where you'd gone, so they shot her."

"And then she told," says Yia Pao grimly. He speaks to her in the Hmong language, uttering words that could be an apology or a reproach.

"If she didn't tell, they would have killed us all," says the priest. "I recognized their leader. Everyone knows that devil. He fights for nobody, he steals from the opium growers and murders for pleasure. He and his men ransacked your tent. What did you take from them to bring him upon us?"

Yia Pao doesn't reply. Instead, he thinks for a minute while the old woman moans.

"I will leave before they return," he says, surveying the camp. "Where is the girl who looks after my son?"

"She took him to the river an hour ago," says the priest. "There's a group there washing clothes." Yia Pao is about to set off when the priest's voice pulls him up short. "Those men arrived by boat. There could be more of them near the water. Do they know you have a son?" Yia Pao shakes his head. "Then leave him with us. He'll be cared for."

"I have no other child."

"Don't be a fool. I'll tell them you have fled to Ban Den Muong. You must run, Yia Pao. You cannot take a baby with you."

The young man doesn't move. After a few seconds, it's Gordon who speaks.

"Go to the waterfall," he tells Yia Pao. "You know the one. Wait for me there, and I'll bring Xang to you." When the priest protests, Gordon says, "They aren't looking for me. If they're at the river, I'll be all right."

"You think they won't notice an American snatching a baby? They'll kill you"—the priest snaps his fingers—"*comme ça.*"

Gordon's eyes are wild and shining.

"I know you wish to give yourself to God," says the priest, "but you have a child of your own. Think of her. You came to be a missionary, not a sacrifice."

"Maggie's all grown up," Gordon says. "She doesn't need me anymore." Clapping Yia Pao on the shoulder, he says, "I'll get Xang to you."

"I'll come too," says Yia Pao, grabbing hold of Gordon's sleeve, but the other man shrugs him off and starts away. By the time he has passed through the tents to the far side of the camp and reached the river trail, it has begun to rain.

I

Everything will be fine because they don't have any-thing to hide. That's what Fletcher has told her as they wait in line at the border. When he finally steers the camper van up to the booth, though, Maggie notices his hands trembling. The uniform of the guard who greets them is dark at the armpits, and the man looks miserable in the heat.

"Where are you two headed?" he asks.

"Virgil," replies Fletcher. "Well, a farm near Virgil." He passes their papers through the open window, but he lets go too soon and they tumble to the ground. "Sorry," he says, reaching for the door handle.

"Stay in the vehicle." With a look of disgust, the guard bends to retrieve the documents, then steps back into the booth. Maggie sees sweat beading on Fletcher's forehead.

"You're doing really well," she whispers. He starts to laugh, covers his mouth, sits up straight when the guard steps out again.

"Fletcher Morgan," says the guard, reading from the page in his hand. He glances up to take in Fletcher's shaggy blond hair, his tea-shade glasses, and his thin line of moustache. "You a draft dodger?"

Maggie holds her breath. They've been told border guards aren't supposed to ask that.

Fletcher shakes his head. "We're coming up here to work."

"For the Morgan Sugar Company," says the guard, looking back at the page. "Your father own it or something?" He asks the question wryly but turns serious when Fletcher nods. "So he's helping you avoid the draft, then."

"I haven't been drafted. I was a student, and then—"

"Park over there." The guard points to a small concrete building nearby. "Stay in the vehicle. Someone will be with you."

"Officer, is anything wrong?" Maggie asks.

"Just wait in the vehicle," he replies.

"I don't get it," says Fletcher when they've pulled away from the booth. "You think it's because I dropped the papers?"

"Don't be silly," she tells him. She's thinking it probably is.

For twenty minutes they wait in the parked camper while the radio plays Neil Young and Jefferson Airplane and songs by Canadian bands they've never heard of. Finally, Fletcher says he's going to find out what's happening, kisses her on the cheek, and leaves the van.

As soon as he vanishes inside the building, she's struck by the feeling that the whole thing is a mistake. What will happen when the immigration people start asking questions and Fletcher says his father has given him a cherry farm to run? What if he tells them that he's a law school dropout and that Maggie quit teaching school before her first year even ended? What if he admits that his father isn't much impressed by their plan to try communal living but he's agreed to put them and a few friends on the payroll for a while if it means getting Fletcher clear of the draft? It will be the first commune in history to be underwritten by a corporation. No, the immigration people will never buy it.

A knock at the window makes her jump. She turns to see two men in uniforms standing beside the camper.

"Could you step out of the vehicle, miss?" says the taller one. He has pop eyes and a mouth that stays open like a fish. The other man's features are doughy, his skin bright pink in the heat.

Leaving the camper for the building's shade, Maggie watches them open the side door and start removing boxes. It takes her a moment to realize they're going to unpack everything.

"Do you have to do that?" she calls out. "I have a list of what we've brought." It took her hours to write it up. All this week, whenever she felt herself growing anxious about the unseen house in another country, checking over the list brought a certain comfort. She starts toward the camper to retrieve it.

"We don't need a list," says the pop-eyed man. "Just stay where you are."

As he and his partner go on unloading and opening boxes, she finds herself anticipating what's in each one and realizes she knows the contents almost by heart. There are clothes and boots and cleaning supplies, a tool box, a toaster, a hair dryer, a roll of toilet paper. There are three cartons of Lucky Strikes and five jars of Nescafé. There are two spoons, two knives, and two forks, a little ark of utensils, even though Fletcher thinks they could be feeding sixty people in a couple of years. There's also the Super 8-millimetre camera her father gave her. She watches the pop-eyed man lift it from its shoulder bag and turn it over in his hands with a quizzical, chimp-like expression.

"It makes movies," she says, not meaning to sound as impertinent as she does. The man scowls at her and she doesn't speak further, but she wants to warn him to be careful with the thing. She has decided that if she and Fletcher are really serious about the farm, if they're going to turn it into a success, they should have a record of the proceedings. When she told Fletcher, she was embarrassed by her own enthusiasm for the idea, but he liked it so much he bought an editing machine and audio recorder too.

From inside the camper comes a long, loud ripping sound. She looks over to see the man with the doughy face using a box cutter to slice into the vinyl of the driver's seat.

"What are you doing?" she shouts, stepping toward him.

"Stay by the building, ma'am," he says. "We're author-ized to do this when necessary."

"But it isn't necessary. There's nothing to find."

"Ma'am, you need to let us do our job."

There's no sign of Fletcher. She should go and find him, let him know what's happening to his van, but the doughy-faced man has resumed cutting into the seat and she feels obliged to bear witness to what he's doing.

As she watches, she remembers Fletcher's trembling hands. What if there really is something hidden in the vehicle? She's been with him six months. In some ways they still don't know each other. When she tries to picture him sneaking out last night and stashing drugs in the spare tire, though, she can't do it. He hates taking risks. It's why leaving the States is a bigger deal for him than for her. He's losing all the security of home.

Thirty yards away, cars depart from the nearest guard booth one by one. A little boy in the back of a sedan presses his face to the window, watching the two men unload the camper. They must search vehicles out in the open like this to make it more humiliating, to let everyone see what can happen.

When Fletcher exits the building, the man with the box cutters has finished tearing into the seats and is conferring with his partner.

"What the hell's going on?" says Fletcher.

Before Maggie can speak, the pop-eyed man approaches them. "You're free to go," he says.

"What about the seats?" says Fletcher.

"You'll have to talk with someone in the office."

Fletcher asks Maggie to wait and storms back inside while the two men walk off in the opposite direction, leaving the unpacked boxes on the asphalt. Maggie sighs and starts to reload them. Ten minutes pass before Fletcher returns, fuming.

It isn't the beginning she imagined. She thought crossing over would feel exhilarating. She imagined they might enter at Niagara Falls. Fifteen years have passed since the time her father took her there, but she still remembers the bellow and crash of the water, the jagged rocks and hovering rainbow. Today, when she woke up in the passenger seat and realized Fletcher had opted for the Lewiston bridge instead, she couldn't help feeling disappointed. But then, she'd never voiced her preference, so how was he to know? He's the first lover she has ever had. Sometimes she worries about putting too much faith in him.

As they finish repacking the camper, she doesn't ask what happened in the building and he doesn't tell her; he only seems impatient to get on the road again. It's enough to allow a shade of doubt back into her mind. No, she's paranoid. But once they're driving away, she turns to him and says in a breezy tone, "You didn't actually hide anything in the camper, right?"

He shoots her a look of disbelief.

"It would have been funny if you had, that's all," she says, giving a little laugh. He doesn't respond, and she feels the seat's ripped vinyl digging into her back.

"The man inside told me it could have been worse," says Fletcher. "He said sometimes when they do inspections they take apart the engine too."

She decides not to ask him who'll pay for the seats to be repaired. They drive on in silence. Then, a few miles down the road, he says, "When we get to the farm, don't tell Brid what happened, all right?"

Maggie frowns. "Why not?"

"It was a hard sell getting her to come up here. You know how she feels about cops. I don't want her taking against the place."

"But she'll see what they did to the seats."

"Oh. I guess that's right."

She dislikes seeming to correct him. His face always gains such a downhearted expression when she does. It happened one time after he pronounced "peony" the wrong way and she mentioned it didn't rhyme with "macaroni." In March, after he told his father about dropping out of law school, he wore the same chastened expression for a month. Now she studies the shape of his eyes, his mouth, willing him not to take things personally. He holds still, apparently aware of her gaze, until finally he starts to squirm and laugh as if her eyes are tickling him.

On a whim, she slides her fingers into his lap.

"Why hello there," he murmurs. But she can tell he isn't into it.

"You okay?" she says, drawing back her hand.

"Sure. Still a bit wound up, I guess." He reaches over to squeeze her leg. "It's only a few more miles. If Brid and Pauline aren't there yet . . ." He flashes her a grin.

"Oh, really," she says, brightening. "Tell me more."

"Maggie, I'm a gentleman," he says, feigning indignation.

"Then tell me what it will be like on the farm," she says. She doesn't want him stewing over what happened at the border.

"Aw, we've talked about things plenty, haven't we?"

"I want to hear it again."

He takes a breath and smiles. "Well, it's going to be amazing. Up here, there won't be any war or election, and we'll get to make the rules ourselves. At first, we'll help Brid and Wale look after Pauline—it'll be four parents for one kid. Then, after Dimitri and Rhea turn up with their boys—" He breaks off. "You know all this. You really want to hear it?"

She nods, but she has a thought. "Wait a second. Let me get the movie camera and the tape recorder."

He looks surprised. "Now? We aren't even there yet."

She's thinking that the border wasn't the right way to start, but maybe with the camera they can have a second chance.

"Pull over," she says. "It won't take more than a minute."

"The turnoff's only a mile away."

"Yeah, but I want to get started right now."

The first shot follows the camper van down a country road as its tires swim through the heat haze. Next, the camera gazes out from the passenger-side window, capturing clusters of bungalows, rows of grapevines and peach trees with the sun strobing between them. The scene is tranquil but the camera shaky. There's the low thrum of the vehicle's engine and, from outside the frame, the sound of Fletcher's voice.

"America's too far gone to save," he says. "The land's polluted and the politicians are corrupt. They send the army to slaughter kids halfway around the world, then order up the National Guard when people protest. In this country we'll do things differently. We'll live peacefully and fairly. We'll get people from all over, people who want to escape the city, who are sick of the crime, the rat race, who want their children to breathe clean air. The farm will let us provide for ourselves. We'll grow our own food and sell what we don't eat. Eventually we'll make enough money to buy the place. It'll be a life we could never have in Boston. We'll be a model for everyone."

The camera pans away from the landscape and across the dashboard before settling on his face. When he turns toward the lens, he crosses his eyes and blows a kiss. There's the sound of some unseen object bumping against the microphone.

"How was that?" he says. "Hey, why don't you drive and I'll film you?"

"It's okay," says Maggie. "Let's keep on the way we are. I'm just getting the hang of it."

She films him until they leave the highway for a gravel road. Then she puts away the camera, wanting to see properly what's ahead. There's only one other house along the half-mile stretch, a mobile home with a gated lane. Soon afterward they reach a dead end and the driveway to the farmhouse. The building is red brick with gabled dormers and a broad porch. An overgrown lawn sprawls in all directions. Fifty yards behind the house, countless rows of cherry trees begin.

"Fletcher, it's gorgeous," she says, and he beams.

Once he has brought the camper to a stop, they exit on their separate sides, Fletcher stretching out his long legs, Maggie pulling her dress away from her body where it clings. For a time they stand there looking at the house. Then they exchange a loud, playful kiss and start up the porch stairs. At the door, he pats under the welcome mat, but there's nothing to be found.

"Maybe Brid and Pauline got here ahead of us," he says.

"There's no car," she points out. "Wale, maybe?"

He hollers Wale's name. No one answers, so he goes around behind the house while Maggie lights a cigarette and retreats down the steps to take in the place again. The roof is missing a few shingles, and the eavestrough is held up at one end by a loop of wire. In the middle of the lawn, an old wooden sign reads *Harroway Orchards*. At the entrance to the driveway there's a mailbox on a post, and beside it stands something obscured by the shadow of a tree. When she looks closer, she realizes it's a man. Tentatively she waves at him, but he doesn't seem to notice her, only starts along the gravel road toward the highway.

From behind the house, there's the sound of breaking glass. Fletcher doesn't respond to her calling, so she stamps out her cigarette and starts after him. A moment later the porch door rattles open and there he is, licking a cut on his hand.

"First order of business," he announces, "replace the back window."

When she goes to examine his wound, he dips and catches her just above the knees, lifts her off her feet, and heads for the door.

"It's not like we got married," she says, laughing. With a grunt, he carries her across the jamb and sets her down.

Inside, the foyer is dim and cramped. On the left, a wide staircase leads to the second floor; on the right, there's a corridor with a few nails protruding from the walls. He starts searching for a light switch, but she takes his hand with a wink and leads him upstairs. Pink roses stare from the wallpaper as they ascend. At the top, Fletcher takes delight in pointing out the hardwood floor, the rectangles of natural light falling from open doorways.

As he pulls her into the first room, there's the smell of stale booze and something burnt. Then she sees the mattress in the corner. It's scorched in the middle and stained at the far end. A pile of sheets lies beside it, singed and streaked with ash. The only other furniture in the room is a dresser that has been emptied of its drawers, which sit on the floor filled with food wrappers, empty beer bottles, and cigarette butts.

"Was it like this when you checked out the place?" she asks. Maybe she should have taken the time off work to come up with him after all.

He shakes his head. "Somebody must have found the key. Probably just some kids." With an anxious look, he starts for the hallway.

"Where are you going?"

"To check the other rooms. If they trashed the house—"

"Hey, we'll manage." She grabs his hand to pull him

back. "You said it was a fixer-upper, right?" If the whole place is in bad shape, he'll want to clean it up right away, and then there won't be time for the two of them.

She gives him a long kiss. When she feels his hesitation, she kisses him again.

"Brid and Pauline will be here soon—" he says.

"Exactly," she replies. "We don't have much time."

He slips a hand under her dress; she reaches for his belt. A shoe comes off, then his glasses. Once his jeans are around his knees, she draws away.

"What is it?" he asks.

"Turn the mattress over." She removes her bra from beneath her dress and tosses it at him. "I'll be back in a second with sheets."

In the camper, she consults her packing list, then finds the bedding in the box assigned to it. When she returns to the bedroom, Fletcher's lying naked on his stomach across the mattress, the afternoon light filtered by blinds. She spreads a sheet over him like a fisherman casting a net. It billows and parachutes onto him, pushing the air across his skin, making all the little hairs along his arms and legs stand on end before the fabric settles. The blinds move in and out against the window screens.

Lying beside him afterward, she remembers another time, another shabby house in the early summer sunlight. Eight years old, she enters the living room clothed head to toe in white, her dress wrinkled from the ride home, the knee-high stockings starting to itch and her father across the room in his easy chair, watching television. Over the carpet she runs to him, the veil scrunched in her hand, torn off as soon as she escaped Gran's station wagon. Maggie launches herself onto his lap and turns herself around so they can stare at the set together.

"How'd it go, little girl?" he asks. "Say your lines all right?"

She nods and kicks off her shoes, then starts to recite the words again under her breath. He lets her go on awhile before shushing her, and they both fall into the rapture of the screen.

"One day will you come to church with us?" she asks after a time.

"You know the answer to that." He sounds pained and says no more. Her father has told her he went to Mass every week when he was a boy so now he doesn't have to go. That's how it works, he says. Gran was disapproving when Maggie repeated his words, but now that Maggie has taken Communion, perhaps she too will be given a choice. She imagines having to decide and can't make up her mind. If it were only up to her she'd stay home, but her father says it's good that she keeps Gran company, even if he seems sad each Sunday morning when Maggie kisses him goodbye.

"Get your old man a beer?" he says.

Without a word, she jumps down and runs for the fridge. Today, as she received Communion, she was made to understand that something had changed forever. It seems this ritual will remain, though, Maggie bringing him beer and changing the channel when he asks. Sometimes she would prefer a book, but her father never reads. He says books only tell you about the past; it's TV that keeps you up to date. Side by side each evening he and Maggie sit before the set, eating their dinners from foil compartments on trays. When they visit Gran next door, she makes wry comments about scurvy and the Children's Aid, and then Maggie's father buys apples or grapes that sit on the counter gathering dust until the house grows lousy with fruit flies. There are times when Maggie herself wishes for some kind of change in their routine—a friend to stay over, dinner at a restaurant—but her father appears content, though he has no hobbies and doesn't travel, hardly leaves the Syracuse city limits. He never complains about clerking at the Public Works Department. It seems he wants nothing beyond the silent hours of Maggie's company in the living room, and the worst way in which she could betray him would be to ask for more herself. Sitting with him in his easy chair, she puts the veil back on and flips it side to side, watching the television grow clear and shrouded by turns.

It wasn't until her childhood was over that she realized she'd been desperate to get out. Her father must have sensed it sooner, the way he turned against her once she got to college. Then she spent half her money on long-distance calls from Boston, close to tears, trying to make him understand without saying it outright that he shouldn't take it personally, she just didn't want the same things he did. Except now he's in Laos, and what the hell does she know about what he wants? Maybe if she understood his desires she wouldn't be so angry with him.

⁓

When she lies in bed next to Fletcher, he's not so different from how her father used to be. She's pretty sure that nothing would make him happier than for the two of them to remain there for hours. Sometimes she can take pleasure from listening to him as he flatters her with compliments that are, in her eyes, demonstrably untrue. Now, though, as he begins to doze beside her, the prospect of Brid's arrival makes her restless. She can't stop picturing the other rooms, imagining floors littered with used needles and broken glass. Brid won't stand for such things. Even though Fletcher introduced the two of them only a few months ago, Maggie knows enough to realize that. Brid has been Fletcher's friend for years now. She's older than he and Maggie are, almost thirty. She has organized protests and founded a health food co-op, and on top of all that, she's a mother. She'll want the house to be safe for her daughter. Maggie gets out of bed and starts to gather her clothes, hoping that Brid and Pauline have been delayed, that there might still be an hour in which to tackle the worst of whatever's waiting.

The next room along the hallway is unfurnished and undisturbed. Fletcher told her the house's previous occupants left things behind when they moved out last year, but the other bedrooms are mostly barren too. Then, upon entering the bathroom, she smells something putrid. She doesn't have the courage to investigate, so she goes downstairs and checks out the living room. It has a couch, a glass-top coffee table, and an armchair. Empty bottles lie scattered across the floor, and on the wall someone has spray-painted a peace sign.

The kitchen is at the back of the house, hot and airless, with a Formica table and a few chairs. Two of the walls are clad in dingy paper; the others are exposed fieldstone that might be attractive if there were fewer cobwebs hanging from it and the mortar between the stones weren't crumbling. A little ridge of broken bits along the floor looks nearly geological. In the mud room off the back, the window that Fletcher smashed reveals an expanse of grassy yard with a wooden outhouse to one side. Farther on, the cherry trees wave in the breeze as if beckoning her, but she wants to get a start on things before Brid shows up. Maybe she can clean the kitchen at least. When she goes to the sink and tries the tap, it shakes violently, then vomits brown water that eventually runs clear.

With a box of cleaning supplies from the camper, she returns to the kitchen and begins to scrub the counter. After only a few seconds she's brought up short by the faint rotten-egg odour of natural gas. Sniffing around the stovetop, she can't locate the source. She's on her hands and knees, poking her nose behind the oven, when she hears Fletcher enter from the hallway.

"Did you see the mess in the living room?" he says. She backs out and finds him standing there in only his jeans, holding a paper bag from the van. "By the way, don't drink the water. We're supposed to boil everything until the well has been tested."

She frowns and shows him her palms, already dark with grime. "Can you smell gas? There must be a leak."

He takes a whiff of air, then shrugs. "A little gas odour's normal in these old houses."

"We should call somebody. You said Morgan Sugar would cover repairs, right?"

"Sure, if it comes to that. I was hoping we could handle most stuff ourselves."

He rummages through the bag in his hands until he's found a package of licorice sticks. Then he sits at the table and starts eating one of them, gazing meditatively at the ceiling while Maggie opens and shuts cupboard doors with a bang. Whoever lived here last, they haven't just left furniture. There's a Mason jar full of paper clips, along with some dishes that make a set only insofar as every one of them is chipped. The shelves are littered with mouse turds, and the first drawer she opens slides off its rails, then refuses to go back on. Something foul is encased in a bag at the bottom of the freezer, welded to the interior. She squirts disinfectant and gives it a few swipes with a sponge while Fletcher goes on chewing his licorice.

Her head starts to hurt. She should stop and sit down, but a voice in her mind insists that she gave up everything to come to this place. She quit teaching, broke her lease. She let her father go to Laos by himself; she let him call her every name in the book before he left. Also, taking over the farm was her idea. For years she'd heard stories about people dropping out, moving to the countryside, living closer to the land, and it always sounded like something she'd like to try. But she never did anything about it. In high school she didn't even march for civil rights or against the war; she stayed at home with her father and watched the demonstrations on TV. At college in Boston she didn't campaign for Hubert Humphrey, didn't vote. She kept her head down and studied. Fletcher has said it was the same with him back then, always playing it straight. Now they have a house of their own and two hundred acres of fertile earth. They have a chance to catch up with the times, and she doesn't want to miss out.

But her head is throbbing. It's the gas fumes, must be. She slumps against the counter and massages her temples.

"Probably there's no point calling the cops about the mess," says Fletcher. "They'd just bawl us out for leaving the key under the mat." He looks up. "Hey, what's wrong?"

Before he can come over to her, a car horn honks and she starts upright. The floor's filthy; the thing's still stuck to the bottom of the freezer.

"Go," she says, waving him out of the kitchen. "She'll need help." He touches her cheek before he leaves.

She wipes down the kitchen table, then makes her way to the front of the house, smoothing back her hair. Through the screen door she sees slim, blond Brid standing in profile beside her Toyota, eyes hidden behind sunglasses, hands on hips, and shoulder blades jutting behind her like the stumps of wings. Pauline's still in the car, strapped into her safety seat and dandling a doll on her knee, its curly flaxen hair very like that of the girl.

As Maggie steps onto the porch, she hears Brid remark to Fletcher, "You haven't even unpacked the van yet? What have you two been doing?" A smooth blend of innuendo and condemnation.

"Aw shucks," says Fletcher in a fake Southern drawl, slouching with his hands in his pockets.

"What took you so long?" Maggie calls out. "Border trouble?"

"Are you kidding?" Brid replies. "The guards were so polite, it was like I was doing them a favour by entering the country. The holdup was at the grocery store." She points to a clutch of bags in the back of the Toyota. "You know this place has a two-dollar bill?"

Maggie looks over to Fletcher and finds him studying Brid's face, with her bright red lips and her cheeks that for three years have kept their postpartum lustre. Then he realizes Maggie has caught him staring. Losing his slouch, he starts to unload groceries from the car.

"Put those in the kitchen," Maggie tells him, and immediately she feels stupid for saying it.

"Good boy!" Brid adds with a smirk. Fletcher lets out a series of cheerful barks, then disappears inside. "It's important to get them trained early," she says to Maggie. "Otherwise they piss on the rug."

There's no time to respond, to be offended, even to laugh. Brid's too quick for her. Already she's gone around the car to lift Pauline from her safety seat.

"Sweetie, you're so patient!" Brid says to the girl. "There you go, free of your shackles, safe in Canada. Just like who? Remember?"

"The slaves," replies Pauline, her attention elsewhere. When Brid sets her on the ground, she runs across the lawn after a butterfly, dragging her doll by its leg.

"Any sign of Wale?" Brid asks, and Maggie shakes her head.

"Someone took the key from under the mat, though."

"Maybe he got here early, then ran off with it. That would be typical."

"Fletcher thinks it was just some kids," says Maggie. "Besides, I thought Wale wasn't turning up till next week."

"Sure, sure," says Brid. "But with that son of a bitch— well, you never know, do you?" Taking a suitcase in each hand, she starts toward the house and calls out to Pauline, "Honey, leave the bug alone. Let's find Uncle Fletcher."

"Don't let her into the kitchen yet," says Maggie. "There's some kind of gas smell." Seeing Brid's look of alarm, she adds, "Fletcher says it's always like that with old houses. Oh, and he says don't drink the water. We have to boil it until the well's tested."

"I'll talk to him," says Brid coolly.

Maggie feels a shamefaced pleasure at what she's done, knowing this woman won't put up with toxic fumes and polluted wells. She follows her into the house and finds it's over even before she reaches the kitchen. The whole exchange—more of a shouted monologue, really—grows louder as she approaches. She hears Brid say, "Pauline and I are sleeping in the camper until you get it fixed." Then Brid glides back down the hall, trailing Pauline behind her. As they pass, Brid's eyes glint at Maggie with satisfaction.

In the kitchen, Fletcher leans against the counter and Maggie returns to cleaning surfaces.

"I'm going to drive into Virgil," he declares after a while. "See if there's a gas repairman." Maggie pushes her sponge across the table and nods.

After he leaves the room, she hears the thud of cases and boxes being set down in the foyer, along with snatches of conversation between him and Brid. Eventually the camper's engine starts, then fades, and he's gone. There's no sign of Brid and Pauline either, only a quiet that grows thicker with the heat, and a yellow blotch that taunts Maggie from the middle of the floor. On her knees, she scrubs hard at it until she discovers it has crept onto her hands, jaundicing her skin, the blotch not a material thing at all but a macula of light thrown there by a square of stained glass above the mud room door.

Following a sudden inclination, she tosses her sponge into the sink and goes to the foyer. Among the unloaded contents of the van she finds the shoulder bag holding the Super 8 camera. Taking it up to the bedroom she recently occupied with Fletcher, she closes the door behind her, loads a fresh film cartridge, and starts to record, casting the lens methodically about her. The mattress, the pile of sheets, the crack running clear across the plaster ceiling. From the belly of the mechanism comes the soft whirr of film unspooling and respooling, first dark, now etched with light. Beyond this hum there's nothing to indicate that a miracle is taking place, that the device is absorbing the visible world. When the film runs out, she sets the camera on the mattress feeling purged, ready to clean again.

The bedrooms take her over an hour. She has almost finished the last one when Brid appears with a duffle bag in hand.

"The toilet isn't working," she says. "It stinks to high heaven in there."

"There's an outhouse in the backyard," Maggie replies.

"Fletcher better not expect me to tolerate this sort of thing just because I'm on the payroll." Brid pushes her sunglasses up on her nose. "I didn't come for the money. I came to raise Pauline in a nice place."

"I thought you came because the army can't arrest Wale up here."

"Yeah, but I only want him around because Pauline will do better with her dad in the picture."

Brid heads back downstairs, then comes and goes at intervals, carrying boxes and bags with Pauline in tow. Each time she passes, Maggie waits to hear some further grievance, but there's little more said. Maggie has just started in on the dining room when Fletcher returns from Virgil with a box of doughnuts, a load of painting supplies, and the news that it will be two days before someone can drive out to investigate the gas smell.

❧

May 14, 1972
Dear Maggie,

Only a week here and already we have had to relocate the mission. Our new home is a Hmong refugee camp south of Xieng Khouang. Nixon says there's no war in Laos, but we live under the constant threat of Communist raids and American bombs. The rice rots in the paddies because people are too frightened to harvest it. Father Jean tells me to go about as if I'm not afraid, so that everyone will see our trust in the Lord. Standing among the tents with planes strafing nearby is hard on the nerves, but so far we have been spared. With luck this is taken by the Hmong to bespeak the power of Christian faith, and I am hopeful it will draw more of them to Mass.

I have decided it's a good thing you refused to come with me. The camp is crippled by dysentery and tuberculosis. There are children with goiters on their necks like goose eggs, and raw flesh on their scalps that doesn't heal. Some people take opium, but there's also pain of the kind that opium can't treat. No family here is without loss. One of the Hmong who came from Long Chieng with us, a young man named Yia Pao, is working for the Church as a translator after losing his parents, his brothers, and his wife. All he has is a four-month-old son he must raise himself. He's one of the few Hmong I have met who went to school, but what good can that do him here? Little girl, it's worse than anything you and I ever saw on the news about Vietnam.

I am kept busy handing out Aspirin, bandaging wounds, and teaching the children how to pray. Two days ago another American flew in for a few hours to show movies about the free world. The people were spellbound, but the night came and went. Many talk as if their lives have already ended. A few ask if I will take them to the States when I go home. I smile and don't have the heart to say it's impossible. The war makes me more thankful for the Church, which serves no country, and for a God who doesn't take sides.

You'll be leaving Boston soon to cross the border. I hope this letter reaches you before the end of the month while you're still in the States. I would send it to your

new address, but you didn't give it to me. I hope you have
changed your mind about not corresponding. I won't write
again until I have heard from you, as I don't wish to impose.

You said you can't understand my coming here, but if
you saw this place you'd know. Despite everything, it can
be beautiful. Fog covers the mountains at dawn, then is
burnt up by the sun. There are mango and papaya trees,
sugar cane, lotus blossoms in the fish ponds. The people are
generous and hard-working. Their longing for home makes
me think of my distance from America and from you.

With love,
Dad

Unfolded on the bedroom floor beside the mattress, the
letter seems to glow in the moonlight. The mattress where
she lies sags in the middle toward Fletcher's snoring body.
She can't sleep. The room is hot as an oven and it's only the
first night of June. This can't possibly be Canada.

It was a mistake to reread the letter so close to turning
in. She'd found it waiting in her mailbox two days ago when
she returned to give her landlord the keys for her emptied
apartment. She was already late to help Fletcher load the
camper, but she tore open the envelope right there in the
lobby and read what was inside, marvelled at the way her
father had tried to make it sound as if she was missing out.

Now her heart has softened. He sounds so lonely. Maybe
she should write back, or at least she could send the new
address. No, she swore she wouldn't. If she writes, she'll
start thinking about him, and if she does that, she'll just
worry about him all the time. She spent the first eighteen

years of her life putting him before herself, then another five feeling guilty about leaving him in Syracuse. All that time he didn't shy away from insinuating that she'd committed a crime by going to Boston and, later, by leaving the Church. He's no longer the man she remembers; he's what Gran would call a nutter. But then, when it comes to religion, Gran is a nutter too.

Maggie has begun another attempt at sleep when a noise comes from the hallway. It sounds like footsteps. Brid going to the bathroom? But the toilet's broken, and Brid's sleeping in the camper with Pauline. Maggie thinks of waking Fletcher and doesn't. What if she's just hearing things? She rises and goes to the door. There are no lights on in the hall, only the moon coming through a window at the far end.

"Brid?" she whispers.

Trailing her hand against the wall, she makes her way to the next bedroom and fumbles for the light switch. A flood of yellow stabs her eyes. The room is empty. Returning to the dark hallway, she goes on to the next room, her ears pricking at every creak of the floorboards beneath her. Another light switch, another melting of shadows. Nothing there.

Then she hears footsteps, moving toward the stairs. She's unable to call Fletcher's name, can't scream, afraid of revealing herself. Finally she edges into the hallway, which now seems even darker than before. Nobody there. At the top of the stairs, she peers down into blackness.

"Brid?" she says.

Someone is standing at the bottom. The figure doesn't move or speak. Maggie can feel eyes on her. She should call out. She should find the nearest light switch. She turns to look for it, and when she turns back, the figure's gone. For a long time she stares down until she's sure.

In bed, she lies shaking, unsure whether she imagined it all. Eventually Fletcher stirs.

"You okay?" he murmurs.

"I thought I heard someone downstairs." She doesn't want to admit she saw someone too; it wouldn't sound believable.

"Just now?" He starts out of bed, wearing nothing, and heads for the door.

"I looked," she calls after him. "There's nobody." The thought of him going naked through the house in search of phantoms makes the whole thing seem ridiculous.

"It could have been Brid," he says. "Shit, if someone's down there—" He starts to pull on a pair of pants.

"I was probably imagining it."

"Stay here, okay?"

"Okay."

She listens as he descends the stairs. After a few minutes he returns, shaking his head, removes the pants, and slides back into bed.

"I don't want you feeling creeped out," he says, putting his arms around her. "Tomorrow we'll buy a chain for the door. I'll replace the window at the back."

She kisses him, and in a few minutes he's asleep again, snoring while she lies staring at the crack in the ceiling.

Her imagination playing tricks. It had to be. Because for a moment she could have sworn the figure at the bottom of the stairs was her father.

When she wakes up in the morning, Fletcher's still asleep, so she dresses silently. Downstairs, Brid is already at work cleaning the kitchen cupboards, her sunglasses hiding her eyes and offering no reflection, only a depthless surface that eats the light. Pauline sits at the table drawing with crayons on a piece of cardboard.

"How did you sleep?" Maggie asks.

"It was ninety degrees and we were in a van," says Brid. "You figure it out."

"You didn't come into the house last night?"

Brid shakes her head, apparently uninterested in why Maggie would pose such a question. Instead, she asks her if she'll watch Pauline for a while. Brid says the kid's driving her nuts. Pauline abandons her crayoning to observe them both with a stern expression, giving no indication of what she's done to send her mother round the bend. The only thing out of place is a smear of something orange on her cheek, crayon or marmalade. Her curly-haired doll sits slumped beside her.

Maggie looks deep within herself and is unable to dredge up the least desire to babysit. The mere idea of it reminds her too much of the little grade two students she left behind in Boston, their clutching fingers and shrill demands, their expectation that she could make everything right for them simply because she was the adult in the room. But her bladder is full and she can't be bothered inventing excuses.

"Pauline, why don't you and I go outside?" she says, trying to sound keen. The girl doesn't move.

"Go with Auntie Maggs before Mommy has a fit," says Brid.

Pauline drops from her chair and crosses the room to take Maggie's hand. Just before she does, she turns back and returns to the table for her doll. "Come along, Buddy!" she says reprovingly. "Before Mommy has a fit."

Brid has said she named Pauline after her own father, a Harvard professor who, according to Brid, is a second-rate mathematician and a first-rate asshole, and who disowned Brid when Pauline came along. Maggie hasn't yet found the right moment to ask Brid why she would name her daughter after such a person. Certainly Pauline isn't an asshole, at least not yet. It's true she seldom laughs and is prone to tantrums, but you can't really say a three-year-old has a personality, can you? She's only a little bundle of flesh and sensory impressions. The students in Maggie's class were more than twice as old, yet this is how she tried to think of them, not wanting to take against them too much. What age must a child reach before you can start to dislike it legitimately? Nine? Ten? In high school, Maggie once babysat a ten-year-old boy who was definitely a first-rate asshole.

"Keep a close eye on her outside," says Brid. "The orchard's a minefield."

"What do you mean?" asks Maggie.

"You'll see."

The air is wet and heavy as Maggie and Pauline cross the back lawn. In the dank outhouse Maggie sits, trying to imagine she's alone, while Pauline waits on the other side of the door. Finally, Maggie gives up and the two of them make their way farther from the house, until they reach a low, flat building with small windows and a tin roof. The door's locked, and the interior's too dark to reveal itself through the glass. Past it, the cherry orchard begins, the trees looking stunted and unkempt.

On the horizon are low hills crested by radio towers, two of them close together, a third off to the right, either smaller or more distant, she isn't sure. The land is more lushly vegetative than in Boston, and when the sun pushes through the leaves, Maggie feels something rise in her—not contentment, it's too giddy and unsettling; more like a charge of possibility. It's what she felt near the end of April at Fletcher's place, that night he first described the farm to her after checking it out. Finally, she realized, she had a proper reason not to join her father in Laos as he wanted. Ever since Christmas he'd been needling her about her complacency, asking her why she didn't want to see the world and make a difference to people's lives. Now she could tell him she was going to do just that, only with Fletcher instead of him.

As they enter the rows of trees, there's the sound of an engine firing up. When she turns to identify the source, for the first time she notices the fence of corrugated metal eight feet high that runs along one side of the orchard. Piled behind it are the bodies of crushed cars. Somehow, Fletcher forgot to mention that the farm is next to a wrecking yard. A bit farther on, Maggie sees what Brid meant about keeping a close eye: the ground beneath the trees is strewn with automobile parts. There are rear-view mirrors, hubcaps, and tumbleweeds of electrical wire. What force of wind could have carried them here? Maggie begins to pick up the detritus, gathering it into a pile, and Pauline joins her, pleased by the impromptu treasure hunt. Once they have accumulated a small heap, Maggie realizes she wants to film it in the same way she filmed the bedroom.

"Let's go back to the house," she announces. "I have a game we can play."

Pauline deigns to take her hand again, and they head off in the direction they came. When they arrive at the bedroom upstairs, Maggie removes the camera from its bag.

"It makes pictures," she explains. "You know, like with television?"

Pauline looks doubtful and reaches to take the device from her, but Maggie lifts it away. "No, not a toy. Only grown-ups can use it. You know what, though? We'll make pictures of you. I'll be the director and you can be the movie star. Would you like that?"

Pauline seems unsure. When Maggie points the camera at her to demonstrate what she means, the girl hides her face with her hands.

"Later we can show the film to Mommy. Won't that be fun?" Pauline peeks out from between her fingers. "Here's what I'll say," Maggie tells her. *"Lights . . . camera . . . action."*

At the beginning the screen is dark. Then two title cards appear in sequence, crayoned letters on buff cardboard.

PAULINE GARLAND AND MAGGIE DUNNE
PROUDLY PRESENT . . .

. . . A TOUR OF HARROWAY ORCHARDS.

The second card is pulled back to reveal the living room with the peace sign on the wall. Pauline starts to enter the frame but is restrained by Maggie's free hand, which proceeds to move aside an armchair even while she continues to film. On the floor behind the chair is a mound of chewed-up foam. A close-up of the couch shows cigarette burns on the upholstery.

The dining room is next, empty save for a few lawn chairs and a plank lying flat across two sawhorses. Then there's the bathroom with its wallpaper coming off in strips. Pauline steps toward the toilet, lifts the lid, and pulls a face. After that the film cuts to the exterior and shots of car parts in the orchard, followed by one of the outhouse. Its door opens and Pauline emerges holding her nose, pretending to cry. In the left side of the frame a small snake flashes emerald and disappears into the grass.

Another shot studies the low building on the orchard's edge. The camera advances and Pauline runs ahead to the door. Inside is a long room with a lone bare bulb dangling from a cord. Fletcher lies on a bench in the corner with his shirt off. His face is red and puffing, and he arches his back as he pumps a bar across his chest. When he sees the camera, he sets down the bar and gestures with delight to a set of dumbbells on the floor nearby, showing off what he has found. In the next shot he's helping Pauline to lift a dumbbell high above her head.

Back in the house, Pauline stands behind another title card that reads OTHER THINGS THE LAST PEOPLE LEFT BEHIND. It's followed by a series of shots in which she presents items to the camera: a furry vermilion slipper, a half-empty bottle of champagne, the box for a jigsaw puzzle of a Florentine villa. Lastly, she approaches with something in her palm. This time she's crying for real. Maggie's hand reaches from behind the camera, and into it Pauline drops the corpse of a small bird. The hand pulls away, reflexively letting the creature fall. The camera's eye descends too, remaining focused on the body. Then it trails Pauline down the hall into an empty bedroom with boggish green walls. Still sobbing, the girl points to three more birds lying stiff on the windowsill, sparrows broken from beating themselves against the glass, two of them curled within themselves, the wings of the other extended as if in flight. There's a shot of Pauline wiping her eyes, Maggie reaching with her free hand to stop her, then leading her to the bathroom. Pauline looks up to the camera as if taking instructions, steps onto a stool beside the sink, and begins to wash.

2

Hidden in the undergrowth, Gordon watches the riverbank. A rubber dinghy with an outboard motor lies pulled up on the shore, several sets of footprints leading away from it in the brown clay. Nearby stand a pair of men, both Lao, not much more than boys, rifles hanging from their necks. One of them keeps wiping his nose with the back of his hand while kicking a pebble back and forth between his feet. The other stares in all directions with hard eyes and snaps at his companion upon noticing his inattention. The man makes a show of standing alert, then takes up kicking another pebble. In the river, a dozen women have waded up to their waists and are washing clothes, laughing with one another as if the men's presence is no more remarkable than the drops of rain spreading ripples on the water. The only suggestion of anything unusual is the jitter in the women's voices.

A few feet from where Gordon crouches, a Hmong girl of sixteen or seventeen sits on the bank holding Yia Pao's little boy. The baby is asleep, swaddled in a beige blanket. Gordon trembles as his eyes dart between the child and the guards by the boat.

After a time, the man with the hard eyes says something to the girl. His tone is jeering, and she looks up for a moment before dropping her gaze. He speaks to her again, louder this time. The girl sets the child down and stands, takes a hesitant step toward the guard. He speaks more sharply and she takes a few more steps, hands clutching the band of cloth tied around her hips. The women in the water have fallen silent and stopped their work. The other guard speaks to the girl now too, laughing and gesturing for her to come closer. When she doesn't move, he barks at her impatiently. Then an old woman in the river, gaunt and hunched, calls out to rebuke him. The man smiles and turns. The women stiffen as he puts his hand on the butt of his rifle.

A second later, the girl shrieks. The women's gaze shifts back to her, and the guards wheel. She points to the place where she was sitting. The baby is no longer there.

When the girl starts for the trees, the hard-eyed guard cries out an order and she halts. The men turn back to train their rifles on the women, as if they're suspected of some ruse. The old woman pleads, but the hard-eyed guard shakes his head, and the women draw closer together. He fires once into the air, then sits down on the side of the dinghy to light a cigarette, and everyone waits for the return of the other armed men who arrived with him.

The first shot is of Brid on the couch. She's wearing a bikini, the freckles pronounced across her tanned shoulders, while on the soundtrack Pauline can be heard having a conversation with her doll. She sits at her mother's feet, and occasionally the top of her head appears in the frame. As Brid speaks, she keeps her eyes fixed upon her daughter.

"So what do you want me to say?"

"Start with why you came up here," replies Maggie, off-screen.

"Hmm. Well, my family disowned me, and then the co-op shut down, so I was out of work. I thought it might be nice to take a ride on Fletcher's tab awhile."

"His father's tab," corrects Maggie's voice.

"There was also Wale. If he ever gets here, it'll be a safe place for him. Mostly, though, I did it for Pauline. I don't want her living in the States. Before she came along, I was idealistic. I organized, I chanted, I threw bottles at cops. I even called my little kleptomaniac phase an anti-capitalist gesture. Then I turned into a mommy and realized that if some pig cracked my skull open, I was dying for two, you know? The question became, what's best for my little girl?" The camera jounces and moves in on her face. "I used to say breeders are nuts, but now things that seemed corny to me, things like devotion and sacrifice, are just everyday facts." She laughs. "Wait till you've had a kid latched onto those boobs, you'll see. You're not on the pill, are you? You know they invented it to let men fuck women whenever they want, right? Anyhow, I thought the pill was illegal for Catholics."

"I know you don't like Christians—" says Maggie.

"Oh, Catholics are different. You worship a chick. I dig that." Brid laughs again, then grows sombre. "To be honest, I don't think in terms of liking or disliking people. It's more a matter of not letting their neuroses increase my craziness."

In the next scene, Fletcher is lying on his back against the kitchen floor. The camera pulls away to reveal Pauline standing next to him in a pink swimsuit with a ruffle around the waist. At some unseen cue he lays his hands against his chest, palms up, and she steps onto them. His fingers curl around her little feet, her arms go out to balance, and slowly he lifts her until she's suspended in the air, shrieking with pleasure at her ability to manage this feat. Brid sits at the table without her sunglasses, bleary-eyed, clapping duly, but afterward shifting her attention to an unseen place beyond the kitchen window. Finally she turns to confront the lens. A flash of irritation changes to something that could be taken for tenderness, before she resumes her vigil over the girl and man at play.

The letter is the sole piece of correspondence in the mail-box when Maggie checks. At the sight of her name on the envelope in the distinctive characters of her grandmother's typewriter, a jangling current of anxiety starts through her. In the orchard, she lies down among the daisies and Queen Anne's lace to read what's inside.

June 2nd, 1972

Dear Maggie,

As I write this you have begun your life in the north country with that man of yours. Although you may not believe it, I worry about you by the hour. A woman can't help but worry when her granddaughter departs for a foreign land.

I should tell you that recently your Uncle Morley spoke to a friend in Massachusetts familiar with your young man's family. It seems Fletcher Morgan is the black sheep of his clan. Morley was made aware of a particularly distressing tale about certain relations with a wealthy Boston girl whose name you may recognize.

The last time we talked, before you hung up on me, you told me you wanted to help your young man achieve great things. I don't know what great things are possible for someone who has abandoned his country in wartime.

As a girl you were so well behaved, always studying your missal and keeping your father's house. It pains me to think you have been led astray. Although you will think you're grown up now, I must remind you that this is your first steady boyfriend, and it is easy to be swept up by certain feelings. I have told you before that your father made a bad match with your mother—certainly she didn't merit his refusal to remarry after she passed on—and I fear you are your father's child. I must ask you, are you abetting Fletcher's salvation or his debasement? We should

put such questions to ourselves with regard to everyone in
our acquaintance.

You and your father are missed here, Maggie. Each time
I come home from Mass it breaks my heart to see the empty
driveway next door. I was spoiled to have a son nearby all
those years. Now he is gone, and in the month since he
departed I have had only two letters. In both he mentions
not hearing from you and asks how you are doing. Of
course I have had to reply that you're no more interested in
contacting your grandmother than in writing him.

I hope you are willing to read this letter, given that you
at least shared your address with me. Your father informed
me that you didn't do so with him. I wrote back straight
away to provide it—I won't abide such nonsense—but he
replied that he is going to respect your wishes. In some
ways he's a foolish man. I'm proud, at least, that he is
serving God. Whom are you serving, Maggie? I don't wish
to be harsh. I only wish for you to see some plain truths.

Sending love,

Gran

When Maggie has finished, she reads the letter once more
and is astounded all over again by Gran's flawless recti-
tude. Not a single typo. How many drafts did that take?

Until the envelope appeared in the mailbox, the outside
world seemed on the brink of fading away. In their first
week at the farm, the only people to turn up have been the
man who installed the telephone and the locksmith who
added deadbolts to the doors. Everyone else they expected
has let them down. Fletcher's old roommates Roman and

Tony both got jobs in Washington at the last minute, while his cousin Dean called to say he was sorry but he was flying to India; he'd decided the girl in Uttar Pradesh was his soulmate after all. Dimitri and Rhea are still with their boys in Cambridge, claiming a flu outbreak, although Fletcher says it's more likely cold feet. The draft dodgers in Toronto were scheduled to arrive tomorrow for a tree-planting bee, but it's been postponed until the repair-man turns up to deal with the gas smell. Fletcher doesn't know the dodgers personally, only through a friend, and he wants to avoid giving them a bad first impression of the farm.

As for Wale, Brid last talked to him in the middle of May when he was in Thailand, running from the army. He said he'd meet them on the farm in three weeks, never mentioning how he'd get there. At meals they agree he must be lying low until it's safe to travel, but Brid eats little and complains of an upset stomach.

Eventually people will come. They mustn't lose their faith in that. In the meantime, they have thrown them-selves into cleaning, painting, and ripping up carpets. Fletcher talks about orchard longevity, yields per acre, and B.F. Skinner's theories of community planning, while Maggie teases him about his high hopes, which are also hers. This year they'll harvest the cherries and plant trees for other fruits. In three years they'll have a windmill and solar panels to produce their electricity. Maggie likes thinking about such things. It keeps her from dwelling on her father. It's only at night, cocooned in the silence of the countryside, that her mind drifts to him and she finds herself listening for the presence of someone in the hallway.

Now there's the swishing of feet through the grass. She looks up from the letter and sees Brid coming along the lane between the trees in flimsy sandals. She sits down beside Maggie and inquires about what she's reading. When Maggie replies that it's a letter from her grandmother, Brid asks to see it. Maggie can't think of a good reason to say no, so she hands it over and sets about trying to interpret the expressions on Brid's face as she reads. It's hard to do, with those impenetrable sunglasses. There's only the odd arched eyebrow and the quick passing of Brid's tongue over her lips. Finally she passes the page back.

"Wow. I feel for you, sweetheart. Your granny sounds uptight."

This is a surprise. In the six months Maggie has known Brid, compassion isn't something she has learned to associate with her.

"The letter's nothing," Maggie replies. "You should have heard the names she called me on the phone."

"So you're not going to write her back? Not your dad either?"

"No." But she says it without the conviction she'd like. She lies down and waits to be soothed by the world. There's birdsong, shadows flickering, and the traffic of ants who arrive at her arm like commuters at a closed road. Eventually a calm begins to overtake her. Hard to imagine any harm coming to them here, only never-ending summer sunshine. She turns her head and sees Brid at ease too, lying with one hand beneath her neck, fingers stroking the skin there as a lover might.

"So you want to help Fletcher do great things, huh?" says Brid. Maggie has been sufficiently lulled that she's slow to recognize her own words being echoed back at her. "Hey, I just thought of something. By coming up here, you're walking in your old man's footsteps, right? It's some kind of missionary work."

"That's ridiculous," says Maggie.

"So you aren't here to save Fletcher from his parents?"

Maggie grits her teeth. Brid sounds too much like Gran. "I don't think Fletcher needs saving."

"Don't get me wrong," says Brid. "Fletcher's all right. He isn't as bad as your granny thinks, anyhow. He's good with Pauline. You want kids?"

Maggie feels a sudden light-headedness. "We're not even engaged."

"Let me tell you a secret," Brid replies sweetly. "A wedding ring isn't a prerequisite." Maggie blushes, and Brid gives a dismissive wave. "Well, I'm glad he's your type."

Maggie doesn't know what to say. She should be reassured by the implication that Fletcher isn't Brid's type, but it offers no comfort. Brid and Fletcher are close enough that Maggie's tempted to ask her about Gran's reference to the young woman in Boston. Maggie's pretty sure it's Cybil, his previous girlfriend; she knows that relationship was a disaster. What if it wasn't Cybil, though? What if it was Brid? She isn't wealthy, is she? After all, she seems happy enough for Morgan Sugar to pay her way. Maggie ponders Brid's earrings, her perfume, her makeup. Fletcher claims not to like such things on women. No, it's stupid even to think it. Still, sometimes Maggie gets a glimmer of something between them, a shared past to which neither has confessed. Maybe it was a fling, a boozy kiss, or only an advance and a rebuff. She's pretty sure she could handle it if Brid was the one who did the advancing.

Sitting on the floor by her bedroom window with a pad of paper in her lap, Maggie stares at the empty sheet. She writes a sentence, looks off into space, writes another, then sets her pen aside to focus on pushing down her cuticles. Finally she crumples the page and begins afresh, this time with energetic strokes.

> Dear Gran,
>   Think what you like about me, but don't go dragging Fletcher's name through the mud. Perhaps one day you'll be able to accept that he and I have values too, even if they aren't sanctioned by your version of God. Until then, please don't write again unless you have something good to say. I'm past the age of needing to be lectured.
>   Peace and love,
>   Maggie

Sealing the page in an envelope, she tucks it into the waistline of her skirt. Then she grabs a sun hat from the post at the bottom of the staircase, tells Fletcher she's going for a walk, and sets off for Virgil. It's a couple of miles to the village, but the time outdoors might calm her down.

After a minute on the gravel road, she arrives at the gated driveway leading to the wrecking yard and takes in the dilapidated mobile home in front of it, the hardscrabble lawn. The place looks so uncared for that it's hard to say if anyone lives there. No neighbour has stopped by the farmhouse to welcome them, and neither Fletcher nor Brid has suggested going over to say hello. They have only agreed that it's a shame the wrecking yard is there at all, and that at least it doesn't seem to do much business.

Then she notices the girls at the far edge of the lawn, sitting under a maple tree. There's a pair of them hidden there, each perched on a beach towel and wearing a swimsuit, each with skinny legs that look ghostly in the shade. Maggie's on the verge of calling out to them when she sees what they're doing. One of them, red-haired with broad shoulders, is smoking a joint. The other, thin with long black hair, holds a beer bottle. They can't be more than sixteen.

Maggie thinks of carrying on, not saying anything, pretending not to see.

"Good afternoon!" she shouts instead.

The girls freeze. The thin one tries to hide the bottle behind her back. The other lets her hand drop casually to her side and puts on a toothy smile. Maggie walks up to the gate and leans on it, trying to affect an affable pose.

"My name's Maggie," she says, then points in the direction of the farmhouse. "I'm one of your new neighbours."

"My dad's not home," says the thin girl.

"That's all right. I just wanted to introduce myself."

The girls look at each other. Without speaking, they seem to manage some communication between them, and they smile at one another before turning back to her.

"I'm Jane," says the red-haired one.

"I'm June," says the other. "We're twins. But not identical. The other kind."

"Jane and June," repeats Maggie, unable to disguise her disbelief. "How old are you?"

"Ancient," says the red-haired girl, and laughs.

"So you're old enough to be smoking and drinking that stuff," says Maggie. She feels stupid saying it.

"Smoking?" says the red-haired girl. "What's that?"

"What's drinking?" says the other one, pronouncing the word as if for the first time. Raising the beer bottle to her lips, she takes a long slug.

The red-haired girl regards Maggie with a severe expression. "You must be confused. Maybe it's sunstroke. Maybe you've gone senile. How old are you, anyhow? Fifty?"

Maggie feels her face burn. She thinks of telling them she's twenty-four, but she suspects that for them twenty-four might as well be fifty.

"My dad said you people are hippies," says the thin girl.

"They can't be," says the red-haired one. "Hippies aren't so square."

"You going to rat us out?" says the thin one, and the red-haired girl shoots her a disapproving look, as if she has broken the rules by asking a straightforward question.

Maggie shakes her head. "That's not my job."

"Then quit staring and beat it, will you?" says the red-haired girl. She raises the joint to her mouth and puffs, looking Maggie straight in the eye.

Without another word, Maggie starts off toward Virgil again, furious with them and with herself. Bested by a couple of teenagers. They must be the ones who got into the farmhouse, who spray-painted the peace sign on the wall. Maybe the first night it was one of them at the bottom of the stairs. She shouldn't let them carry on like that. She should go back later and talk to the father.

Or maybe they're right. Maybe she's just square.

Curtains of grey sky are gathering on the horizon when she reaches the highway. The wind picks up; lilac bushes buck and toss by the roadside. A gust wrenches her hat from her head, lifts it over a fence, and sends it loping across the pasture beyond. Instead of chasing it, she presses onward.

Eventually she reaches a small church with a steeple and thick stone buttresses. The sign out front says it's Catholic, and she thinks of going in but can't fathom why she would. It begins to rain. Within seconds, torrents of it are bouncing on the asphalt so hard they seem to jet from the earth. With a hand shielding her face, she looks toward the distant roofs of the village, then back at the church. Lightning and thunder explode together. She runs toward the front doors.

Inside, a crucified Christ watches over the altar and a few rows of pews. A pale light penetrates the water streaming down the windows, while a stained glass Saint Francis preaches to the birds, his eyes childlike and angled toward heaven.

At first she remains near the entrance, wringing out her hair and tugging loose her top where it lies against her midriff. Then she passes into the sanctuary, her gaze rising to the dusky ceiling with its rafters and arching ribs. Rumbles of thunder are the only sound. She walks up the aisle, slowly pausing at the altar to cross herself before proceeding past the baptismal font and back down along the far side. The wooden floor is neither painted nor varnished, but the upholstery on the kneelers looks newly plush, and someone has gone row by row through the pews to space the prayer books evenly.

At the confessional along the wall, she stops.

"Father?" she whispers, pushing aside the drape. There's the barest of murmurs from the storm, along with the drip of water from her skirt. She steps inside and kneels. "Bless me, Father, for I have sinned. Father? Is there really no one there?" With her knuckles she raps on the panelled wall.

"Piss off," she says quietly. "Goddamn," she continues with more volume. "Shit-cunt-asshole," she exclaims, then feels idiotic, no better than those girls.

From outside the booth, there's a noise like a door closing. Cocking her head, she calls out a hello. When there's no response, she pulls back the drape and scans the building. All is still. Beginning to shiver, she makes her way toward the front door, stopping at an alcove where a few votive candles stand beside a collection box. She bends over in search of something with which to light them. As she does, a voice booms out.

"You, girl! Get away from this!" A thin, balding man in a cassock is hurrying toward her. He looks almost forty, with thick, angry eyebrows. "You have no shame?" His accent is clipped, Eastern European. He turns and shouts,

"Lenka, call police station." A woman with a beehive piled atop her head has appeared in a side door by the altar and gives the barest of nods.

The priest reaches for Maggie and grabs her by the arm. Instinctively, she tries to wrench loose of his grip.

"What did I do?" she cries.

"You know what you do."

"I don't know! I really don't!" Her skin's still wet and she slips away. Reaching to seize her, he fastens onto a strap of her top. It rips loudly, freezing them both. Then he lets go and steps back.

"I only came in here to pray," she says, holding the strap in place with one hand. "It was raining!" But when she turns to go, he blocks the door.

"Where do you come from?" he asks. "You are one of the draft dodgers at Harroway." He speaks these words carefully, whether out of some difficulty in pronouncing them or with a particular disdain for such people, it isn't clear.

"Who told you that?" she demands.

"The man with you," replies the priest with a tight smile. "He speaks to storekeepers in Virgil. This place is the same as everywhere, people like the gossip."

"We're not draft dodgers," she says. "We're working for the Morgan Sugar Company."

The priest seems uninterested in this distinction.

"Stealing is serious thing." He raises a handkerchief to wipe the sweat from his brow. "Authorities send you back to U.S.A."

"Father, it's a misunderstanding. I'm Catholic, really! My dad's a missionary." The priest's face remains stern.

"Oh, never mind!" With her free arm she gestures toward the alcove. "Tell me what I was stealing. Candles?"

"You hide something behind your back."

Reaching around, she pulls out her letter. The ink has bled so that the name and address are illegible. As she goes to offer it for his inspection, the wet paper wilts in her hand.

"For my grandmother," she says.

He doesn't take the letter from her. Instead, he gains a frustrated, almost disappointed look. "Three times this year they break into collection box," he mutters. "You must understand." Turning away, he walks down the aisle, glowers at the woman with the beehive as he passes her, and disappears into the other room.

The woman approaches Maggie with halting steps. "I apologize for my brother," she says in the same accent as the priest's. She has a slender white neck and pale lips almost indistinguishable from her skin. "You startle him. This parish is very little, yes? Friday mornings nobody comes; church for him is like part of rectory." She turns her palms outward to indicate that this is unfortunate but not to be helped. "You are from U.S.A.?" Maggie nods. "My brother and I, we are from Czechoslovakia. You are Catholic? You will come to Mass? Oh, but look!" All at once she seems to have noticed that Maggie's hand is holding the strap of her top. "From him? Is terrible, he will apologize. Stay here, I get pin for you."

Without awaiting a response, she goes down the aisle and vanishes through the door. From the other room comes the noise of her and the priest arguing. Maggie listens awhile, then hastens away. Across the church's front lawn she goes, splashing through the soaked grass like a child let out from school. The rain has stopped and the road glistens. She runs along it in the direction of the farmhouse, dogged by the wet slap of her sandals, one hand holding her top's broken strap while the other is clenched around the water-logged letter to her grandmother. After a time she realizes there's no point carrying the thing, it's ruined, she'll have to rewrite it, so she squeezes the envelope into a ball and throws it into the ditch. It floats away on the runoff and seconds later disappears into a culvert.

The first confession she ever made was to murdering her mother by being born. For some reason Maggie's father blamed himself for the death, but Maggie was the one who'd gotten stuck coming out. At nine years old she admitted this before the priest in Syracuse, stunning him into silence, and later that afternoon she told Gran too. Then Gran smacked her across the ear.

"It was your mother's doing, no one else's," Gran declared.

Maggie was tempted to argue, but she had to be careful. Gran owned the house in which Maggie and her father lived and, although no one ever said as much, Maggie felt certain that if she were to fall from Gran's good graces, Gran wouldn't hesitate to throw them out. The house was right beside Gran's, built for Maggie's father when he gained a wife, and a pregnant one at that, a girl who refused to live with Gran and insisted she have a home to herself. Gran said the girl had showed some nerve, three months out of high school, expecting to be given the Taj Mahal. Even when Maggie was young, she suspected there was another side to the story, but Gran's was the only one she heard. Her father never talked about it.

Gran didn't speak about Maggie's mother so disparagingly when Gordon was around. In his presence she didn't speak of her at all. There was a rule against it, unspoken but as fixed as the other rules in Maggie's life: that she must attend Mass with Gran; that Maggie's father would never come with them; that Maggie was to pray each night for the conversion of Russia and never to read at the table. Gran said only Protestants did that. Maggie wasn't to enter her father's bedroom, either, although this was a rule she'd created for herself. She had made it after Gran told her that he had always wanted a lock for his bedroom when he was a boy, and Gran had refused to humour him, so when finally he'd gotten a house of his own, the first thing he'd done was to install a bolt on the bedroom door. As far as Maggie knew, he never actually used it, but she decided to honour the principle behind the thing.

Another rule was that on Friday nights and no others, Maggie and her father ate dinner at Gran's. Those evenings Gordon never spoke unless his mother addressed him first, and then he responded with the fewest possible words. The rest of the week he didn't set foot in his mother's house and Gran didn't enter theirs, though the homes were separated by not even a fence, only a shallow, grassy depression that lay dry most of the year. If Gran needed to talk with him, she telephoned. This she did at least once a day, and although she was the only person who ever called,

Maggie's father always said hello as if he didn't have the foggiest notion who it could be. It seemed the case that as long as his mother was out of sight, he forgot she was a few yards away. He forgot that she owned his house, that she had gotten him his job. He seemed truly to believe there was just him and Maggie in the world, along with the ghost of his dead wife knocking about in the unlit rooms.

Sometimes Maggie liked to think her mother had merely run away, and that one day on a long car trip across America, Maggie would come upon her singing in a lounge or serving hamburgers at a diner. The problem with this fantasy was that Maggie could remember the first day of her life. She remembered lying with her mother at the hospital, the bright lights above them and the antiseptic reek from the floors, the apple-cheeked nurse hovering in her bleached uniform. Maggie remembered the soft scratch of the blanket around her and the warmth of her mother's hands. She even remembered the exact moment when life passed from the fingers and a cold stiffness settled in. Gran told her this was nonsense and foolishness; no one could remember that far back.

"Your mother was a selfish, stuck-up girl," said Gran. "And the mouth on her! Never when Gordon was around, mind you. In his eyes she could do no wrong. She had him right beneath her sticky little thumb."

Her father thought otherwise. He said her mother was a cherub and an angel. But he and Gran didn't have this argument in person, only through Maggie and the opinions she reported to each of them in turn, passing from house to house with her cargo of second-hand speech. She ran between her father and Gran like an electrical cord, crackling and throwing sparks, thrilling at how the things she said could make the two of them come alive.

"My mother wasn't selfish," Maggie told Gran one afternoon. "She was an angel and a cherub!" It was so easy and pleasurable to be contrary when Maggie was articulating someone else's thoughts. If they were her own, she'd never speak with such recklessness or conviction.

Her father had stopped going to Mass after her mother died. Gran disapproved of this decision, if that's what it was, but Maggie accepted its wisdom. For her quiet, introverted father to stay away from that place, with all its words and people, seemed natural, even necessary. She was sure that if he was ever forced to go, some disaster would strike from which he'd never recover.

Maggie told her father only once about remembering her birth. As she spoke, his expression grew glazed and terrified. For this man whom she loved more than anything, the loss of his wife was still a scabless wound. Seeing it plainly on his face, Maggie slaughtered her mother once more, this time in her mind, and silently vowed never to mention her again.

When she arrives back at the farmhouse, she's still trying to decide what to tell Fletcher and Brid. If she reports her encounter with the two girls, Brid will probably say she's a prude and needs to loosen up. She doesn't want to tell Brid and Fletcher about the priest and his sister either. They'll want to know why Maggie entered the church in the first place, and they won't believe it was only because of the rain.

She's halfway up the drive before she notices the mud-spattered truck parked by the house. It bears the logo of a gas company, and for a moment she feels a sense of relief, until she spots Fletcher on the porch, shirtless, arguing with a bald man in a blue uniform. As she draws nearer, she makes out a crest on the outfit that says his name is Frank. He has a slumped, wizened face with bloodhound eyes, and he keeps his forehead lowered in Fletcher's direction like a bull preparing to charge.

"I told you, thirty bucks," she hears Frank say. "I've got overhead."

"You're kidding me," replies Fletcher. "There's no way I'm paying more than fifteen."

"You want me to unfix that leak?" the man says.

As Maggie reaches the porch, Fletcher gives her a look, and she knows she should stop to take his side, but she passes by him into the house. Upstairs, she grabs her purse and counts out bills, then flies back down and pushes them into Frank's hand. He examines her for a moment, making her realize what a sight she must present. Her wet skirt is as filthy as his truck, the broken strap of her top tied together in a clumsy knot.

"Hippies," says Frank with a shake of his head. He waits for a rebuttal, but neither Maggie nor Fletcher obliges him. "Bet you're Americans too," Frank says. Fletcher crosses his arms and stares at the money in the man's fist. At last Frank grunts and sets off down the porch stairs in the direction of his truck.

As he drives away, Fletcher turns to her in bewilderment. "Why did you pay him?"

"You looked so helpless," she replies.

He appears about to protest, but then he draws her into his arms. "He would've come down to twenty," he says.

She knows he's right; ten dollars makes a difference. It's good of him to care about such things, especially when he's probably never had to haggle in his life. She's about to tell him so when he tenses against her, fingering the knotted strap on her shoulder.

"What happened to this?" he asks.

"It broke." She can't bring herself to tell him about the church. Not about the girls either. "Where are we at with money?" she asks instead. "It's only been a week."

"We need to talk," he replies. There's an unsettling gravity in his tone.

"Okay. But I need to change first."

When she comes back downstairs, there's no one in the house, so she makes her way to the front lawn where the camper is parked. A stick of incense burns on the dashboard, and Pauline sits at the fold-down table, a daisy chain lopsided on her head, conducting a tea party with her doll. Across from her, Brid in her sunglasses and bikini throws clothes and toys into a burgundy suitcase.

"Heard the gas is fixed," says Brid when she sees her. "C'mon, honey, let's skedaddle." Pauline sets down her cup and saucer with care before climbing out of the vehicle. Brid starts after her, then sighs and pivots back to the suitcase. "Just a second, I haven't taken La Evil yet today."

Maggie frowns, not understanding, even when Brid pulls out a bottle of pills.

"You know, Elavil," says Brid. "Wonderful stuff. Keeps you from sticking your head in the oven. Hard on the eyes, though." Momentarily she lowers her sunglasses. "You thought I wore these just to look hip? Wale calls it La Evil, as in, 'Sufficient unto the day is La Evil thereof.'"

Maggie says nothing while she waits for Brid to swallow her pill, only thinks of what has just been so casually revealed. Then they carry on into the house with Pauline singing ahead of them. When they enter the kitchen, Brid's all jagged cheer, calling out, "Hey handsome!" to Fletcher where he sits at the table. She dances her fingers playfully over one of his shoulders, but he isn't in a playful mood.

"We need a new plan," he says, his voice sounding self-assured even as his hands grip the edge of the table. "The way things are going, we'll never get anything done. We can't spend Morgan Sugar's dough forever."

"It's barely been a week," says Brid. "That's a little quick to have blown the bankroll." She sends Pauline off to occupy herself in the mud room, then sits next to Maggie at the table. "Besides, I thought the whole thing was a stitch-up between you and your father."

"The company still expects to see something for its money," says Fletcher, "and I promised we'd have at least eight working bodies from the start."

Brid stares at him with skepticism. "You get new marching orders from Daddy today?" When Fletcher doesn't reply, her look grows sharper. "So your old man's under the impression that we're here to make his company a profit."

"Technically, that *is* why we're here . . ." He breaks off and looks grim.

There's an ache in Maggie's gut. Gathering herself, she turns to Brid and finds her staring back as though waiting for Maggie's intercession.

"Fletcher's dad understands we're doing things our way," says Maggie, trying to sound measured and reasonable. "He knows eventually we'll buy the place from the company. Until then, though, Morgan Sugar's paying our salaries." She knows very well that Brid has already been informed of these facts.

"Fine, so we'll get the workers," says Brid. "Those draft dodgers from Toronto—"

"I've talked to them," says Fletcher. "They can't come for at least a month."

Brid heaves herself back in her chair. "Okay then, big shot, tell us your plan."

Looking at them with a wary eye, he says, "There's a programme up here. Government run, migrant workers. Pretty easy to arrange."

"You're kidding me," says Brid. "What, Mexicans?"

"Jamaicans."

"Oh, even better." She helps herself to a cigarette from a pack on the table. Maggie has a sense that right now Brid and Fletcher strongly dislike each other. This fact should soothe her somehow, but instead there's an intimacy to the whole thing that's excruciating.

"The workers fly up, stay the season, fly back," says Fletcher. "It's a lot cheaper than local labour. Plus, you know, it puts money into the Jamaican economy—"

Brid smiles an awful smile and shakes her head in disbelief. "You are fucking kidding me."

"It would just be till we're off the ground."

Maggie hates the beseeching way in which Fletcher says
it. Is this why he asked Brid to join them here—to earn her
approval? She doesn't even care about the farm. She's only
come up for the sake of her daughter and her AWOL boyfriend.

Maybe Maggie shouldn't be so judgmental, though. It
isn't like she has spent her own life driven by idealism.
Even now, her urge is to leave the table, take the Super 8
camera outside, and have some time alone. She's already
starting to imagine what that would be like when she realizes Brid is staring at her.

"You're not even paying attention, are you?" says Brid.

"No, I'm listening." She turns to Fletcher, but he only
sits there sharing Brid's quizzical expression.

"So what do you think, then?" Brid asks her.

"I think—" she begins, not knowing what she thinks.
"I don't know."

"For Christ's sake."

"No, wait." She can't just leave it at that. This place
needs to be a success. "We should try Fletcher's plan. I
mean, we wouldn't be forcing anything on the Jamaicans,
would we? They want to work up here. And we could pay
them better than minimum wage. We could even help
them stay in Canada." As she speaks these words, it sounds
like a plausible arrangement, especially considering she's
devised it on the spot. But Fletcher looks troubled.

"Now hold on," he says. "There are rules, for one thing,
and paying them more money kind of defeats the purpose—"

"What is the purpose, though?" she asks. "I mean, I thought we're trying to create something fair and equal here." At this, Fletcher's face darkens and Brid beams. "I know you're trying to do that," Maggie adds hastily. She feels herself sinking. "So if you think your solution is the best idea," she says with a sigh, "we should probably just go ahead with it."

"Oh, Maggie," says Brid. "You were doing so well." Rising from her seat, she turns to Fletcher. "Do whatever you want. Honestly, the only thing I care about is that we buy a TV."

Fletcher laughs without humour until he realizes she isn't joking. "I thought we agreed on no television."

"Sure, except the kid's bored out of her skull. Speaking of which, where's the playroom you promised?"

"I told you, as soon as Wale gets here—"

"Yeah, well, that's the other thing. If he doesn't show up next week, Pauline and I are going back to Boston." In the mud room, she scoops up Pauline and carries her outside.

Neither Fletcher nor Maggie looks at the other. Brid's cigarette burns in the ashtray between them. He reaches out and mashes it.

"Thanks for all your help there." He speaks the words with a smile, but she can see that he's hurt.

"I said we should go ahead with it, didn't I?"

He lowers his gaze, then pushes his chair back and leaves the room. A few seconds later she hears his footsteps on the stairs. She can't believe it. Instead of following, she snatches up a broom and dedicates herself to sweeping the kitchen.

From the second floor there's banging and the scraping of heavy objects. It's too much. Finally she goes up, telling herself she has to vacuum the hall, and discovers he has shut himself in the unfinished playroom where Pauline found the dead birds. He has even taped a piece of paper to the door that reads *PLEASE STAY OUT*. Fine, then; she'll go back downstairs and leave him to it.

An hour passes before she hears the door open, then the sound of his footsteps. When he appears, his torso and arms are speckled with white paint and his face gives no sign of anger.

"Come with me," he says. "I want to show you something."

Upstairs, the sign has been removed from the door. The space inside is empty aside from an assortment of painting supplies, along with a card table in the middle that holds some large, angular object hidden by a bedsheet. Three of the room's walls are still covered in green wallpaper, but the fourth is bright white.

"Why did you paint just one wall?"

"Close your eyes," he says. When she does, she hears him switch off the overhead light, and then a motor grinds into life. When she looks, a beam of light is crossing the room, illuminating eddies of dust. On the newly painted wall is an image of Fletcher, supine in the outbuilding he's taken to calling the barracks, lifting and lowering a barbell above his chest. There's no sound except the clack of film through the projector. She remembers framing this scene through the camera's viewfinder, yet still she isn't quite able to accept its return in colour and big as life.

"What do you think?" he says, arms circling her waist.

"It's your own projection room. Now we can watch everything you shoot. We'll make you our documentarian."

"It's wonderful," she replies, and means it. But then she thinks of Brid and feels queasy. "This was supposed to be a playroom," she points out. "Brid won't be happy——"

"It can be a playroom too."

Maggie's eyes remain focused on the wall, watching the past version of him as he shows Pauline how to make a muscle. When the film ends, Fletcher goes to the projector and flips a switch so that it begins to run backward. He grins as, on the wall, he and Pauline start once more into their motions, now reversed.

"I thought you were angry with me," admits Maggie.

He squeezes her tight. "I'm sorry things have been heavy. You're so good to me. I don't have the means to repay your goodness."

He speaks so softly and with such affection, it takes her a moment to wonder why he shouldn't have the means. She tries to look him in the eyes, but he avoids her gaze.

"Things are never going to work, are they?" he says. "Christ, I don't want to be hiring Jamaicans, but what else can we do? Ask my father to fork out more cash? Maybe Brid's right—I'm just a rich boy playing up here to avoid the war."

"Forget Brid," she replies. The harshness with which she says it seems to disconcert him.

"Oh, it's not her fault. She comes from a really fucked-up family. That sort of thing messes with your head."

"You ever think——" She tries to sound lighthearted. "You ever think she has a crush on you?"

"A crush!" he says, and kisses her neck. "Don't worry, baby, she's not my type."

Maggie puzzles over his response. She seems particularly fortunate to have ended up living with two people so sure they're not each other's type.

On the screen, the film still runs in reverse. Pauline walks backward from the bathroom to the playroom, approaches three dead birds on the windowsill, and points to them. Then she and the camera retreat down the hall, arriving at a place where another dead bird lies broken on the carpet. Eventually, like magic, it leaps into Maggie's waiting hand.

Maggie draws a sharp breath.

"What is it?" says Fletcher.

On the wall, the bird is now in Pauline's cupped fingers and the girl's crying, tears streaming from her cheeks back into her eyes.

"You didn't show this to Brid, did you?" Maggie asks. "I haven't told her about the dead birds."

Fletcher promises not to say anything, and the two of them stay holding each other as the film winds back to its beginning: the sequence of objects left behind, the glimpses of the outhouse and the decrepit living room. Finally the end of the film flaps against the reel and the wall becomes a slate of light. Once he's turned off the projector, they make their way to the bedroom. When they emerge and descend sheepishly to the kitchen, Brid and Pauline are already eating dinner.

"At it again, huh?" says Brid.

After the meal, while Brid's tucking in Pauline, Maggie takes the scissors and Scotch tape from the kitchen to her new screening room, turns on the projector, and runs it until she reaches the scene with the birds. Very carefully she cuts it out, then tapes the remaining film back together. It seems too easy, but when she runs it again, her taping job holds; the film simply moves from the previous scene to the next. She's glad, but somehow she can't quite bear the thought of throwing away the excised strip, so she rolls it up, goes to the bedroom closet, and nestles it in the pocket of her winter coat.

Her first camera was a Kodak Brownie Starflash, black plastic with a built-in flash gun, the socket for the bulb haloed by a silver dish above the lens. Her father gave her the camera for her tenth birthday, even though Gran told him the thing was too grown-up for a girl her age. Thereafter Maggie took revenge on her grandmother by repeatedly skulking through Gran's house and lying in wait until the old woman came into range. Then Maggie pressed the button and a smack of light caught Gran full in the face. Gran shrieked exquisitely every time, her howls of indignation following Maggie across the lawn during the scamper home, the camera on its strap swinging against Maggie's breastbone with a pain she accepted as her due for such wickedness. Each time she thumbed through a packet of newly developed photographs, she took a special pleasure from the shots of Gran's face drained of colour, garish, poorly framed, her expression somewhere between terror and outrage.

The rest of the photographs were always of Maggie's father, because at that age Maggie assumed that photos had to be of people, and because taking pictures of him was so simple and satisfying. Those moments when she held him in the viewfinder were the only times she could look at him without feeling overwhelmed by the melancholy in his eyes.

What the camera never showed was the long scar on his neck from a piece of shrapnel when the Nazis almost got him in the war. Maggie had seen the scar only a few times, and the story wasn't one her father liked to tell, so she'd been left to read about D-Day on her own and picture the invasion, the rough sailing and frigid waters, the hours of bleeding before a medic finally arrived to help him. The history books described it as one of the most important events in American history, yet her father never marched in the Veterans Day parade, and the scar was his only ribbon. He hid it behind high collars or under scarves that made him look like Roy Rogers with a beard. When he went out, people stared; it was no wonder that, except for his job, he mostly stayed at home.

Fletcher was different. He needed to be out among others, even if he didn't always seem to enjoy it. In fact, sometimes in Boston when she sat with him and a group of his friends at a restaurant, watching him fidget and blush with embarrassment at others' joking, she wondered if he'd committed himself to such sociability on a self-made dare. Or perhaps he thought that spending time with people, talking politics and ideas, was expected from a young man of his standing.

She met him on the opening night of *The Go-Between*, when she sat down in the empty seat next to him, a stranger.

They were both on their own. Later he teased her about that, said she must have had her eye on him from the start, but in truth there were no other seats. At that point she often went to the cinema alone, needing an escape from the stress of teaching but not wanting to watch television because it reminded her too much of home. As a girl she had never really gone to movies. Now she discovered they weren't like TV at all. There was no coyness about them; they showed you everything. She had watched *McCabe and Mrs. Miller*. She had seen *Klute* and *Shaft*. She had seen *Carnal Knowledge* and come out amazed that such things were shown in public places.

After the final credits for *The Go-Between*, Fletcher turned to her and asked what she thought of the film. There was a bashfulness about him that made her decide he wasn't a creep, so she replied that she'd liked the novel better, though she admired Julie Christie's performance. When he observed that not too many girls went to the movies Friday night on their own, Maggie told him she wasn't by herself. He was taking her out for coffee, wasn't he? It was the most daring thing she'd ever said.

The first time he invited her back to his apartment, they didn't make it to the bedroom. Afterward, lying there still naked on the couch, he asked whether it was all right if he turned on the television, because there was a show he wanted to see about the *Pioneer 10* spacecraft that NASA was launching soon. He said it would be the first human-built thing to leave the solar system. Maggie said she didn't mind and pretended to watch along with him, but her eyes went around the room, taking in the bust of JFK on the bookshelf, the framed poster that showed Earth from space.

"Hey, look," said Fletcher after a time, and she glanced back to the TV screen. They were showing the golden plaque the scientists had affixed to the side of the space-craft, hoping that one day an alien race would learn about humanity from the information engraved there. It had hieroglyphs detailing the composition of hydrogen and the Earth's location, and then there was a stark, plain image of a man and woman standing a few feet apart. Neither of them wore any clothes. The man's hand was raised in greet-ing, and Maggie tried to imagine being so confident in her nakedness that she could wave at someone like that.

"Maggie, they're us," said Fletcher, sounding pleased at the idea. She looked more closely and saw the woman's hips were as wide as her own, while the long, straight hair was more or less the same. But the man was stockier, more muscular than Fletcher, and he wore no glasses, had no moustache. Although Maggie didn't say it out loud, the couple wasn't them at all. It was only her and some man she'd never met.

One morning not long after their discussion about migrant workers, Maggie looks through the mud room window and sees Fletcher walking back from the orchard with a dark-skinned man in a checkered shirt and an orange woollen cap. Crossing the lawn to meet them, she apprehends that the man's older than they are, maybe thirty-five, with pockmarked cheeks and short hair touched by grey.

"Maggie, this is George Ray Ransom," says Fletcher. "George Ray works a little way from here, at the Beaudoin farm."

"Nice to make your acquaintance," says George Ray. His voice has a Caribbean lilt and a slightly ironic edge.

"We're going to steal him away from his employer at the end of the month," says Fletcher. Turning to George Ray, he adds, "Then you'll stay with us for the rest of the summer, right?"

George Ray nods his assent. From the studied ease with which Fletcher speaks, she can tell that George Ray has made a good impression on him, and that Fletcher is eager in turn to seem knowledgeable and self-possessed. Of George Ray's opinion about Fletcher, though, she gains little sense. When she asks him what he thinks about the place, he looks toward the orchard for a long time.

"Needs plenty of work," he declares. "Three, maybe four seasons before you turn a profit."

"That's a conservative estimate," Fletcher adds quickly. "If we get more people, there's a lot we can do even before next season." George Ray says nothing to contradict him, only taps the ground with the heel of his boot as though to dislodge something from the sole.

When she leaves them and re-enters the house, she finds Brid standing in the mud room by the window.

"Handsome devil," says Brid. "You find out if he's single?"

That afternoon, Maggie goes for a walk along the gravel road, thinking she might glance next door to see what's going on there. She has decided the thin girl's father must own the wrecking yard, and she imagines seeing him out on the lawn with his daughter. She imagines introducing herself, making the girl squirm a bit. It's a silly fantasy, and Maggie doubts she could pull it off without embarrassing herself. When she reaches the gate for the wrecking yard, she turns toward the mobile home only for a second, trying to be surreptitious.

There's no one on the lawn, but in the driveway sits a truck that bears a striking resemblance to the one driven by Frank, the gas repairman. Then a man in an undershirt, jeans, and a baseball cap steps out from the building. It takes Maggie a moment to recognize it's him. From his clothes, and from the unselfconscious way he lets the door slam behind him, she realizes this is his home. Frank is their next-door neighbour. He must be the girl's father, too. Maggie returns her eyes to the road and hurries back toward the farmhouse.

Once she's out of view and can relax again, her bewilderment turns to irritation. If the man lives next door, why did it take him over a week to come and fix the gas? Why wouldn't he introduce himself as their neighbour? Then she remembers: he thinks they're hippies. He must want nothing to do with them.

Just as she's about to re-enter the farmhouse, the camper comes up the driveway behind her and Fletcher steps out, back from his trip to the St. Catharines mall. She descends the porch stairs to greet him.

"You'll never guess who we have for a neighbour," she says.

"Frank the repairman," he replies. She can't believe it.

"How did you know?"

"I just saw him pulling out of the lane next door."

Then Maggie tells him about her encounter with the girls. He nods as if none of it surprises him.

"The daughter must have inherited her manners from the old man," he says. "I bet he doesn't know she and her friends are smoking dope, though."

"You think I should have done something about them?"

"Nah, you did plenty." She doesn't know how he can have such certainty, but it's a comfort. "Let's get inside," he says, kissing her on the forehead. He unloads a large cardboard box from the camper. "I want to show you what I bought."

Fletcher opens it in the living room to reveal a silver television set, the shape of an egg and mounted on a stubby tripod. He says it's one of the newest models from Japan. Juxtaposed with the room's worn-out furniture, the television looks like an alien invader. Maggie thinks about asking how he plans to pay for the thing, but she decides not to risk ruining the moment. He calls in Brid and Pauline to see the set too, and they all wait on the couch while he fiddles with the rabbit ears, coaxing ghostly images from static.

The rest of June passes by on television. During the day they occupy themselves with cutting away the dead limbs of cherry trees and planting vegetables in a corner of the backyard, and on weekends they drive the countryside in search of lawn sales from which to furnish the house and barracks, but the evenings are spent in front of the little metal spaceship with its screen aglow. Whether they watch the local channel or the ones from Buffalo, it doesn't matter, it all seems to be about America: the Libertarian

Party convention, Angela Davis's acquittal, the break-in at Democratic offices. Their country has moved on without them, but television lets them peek back in at their leisure.

Whenever Maggie tries to read the copy of *Middlemarch* she picked up at a yard sale, the sound and images from the TV keep tempting her eyes from the page. It's better when everyone gathers in the playroom to watch the latest film she's shot. Those nights they eat bowls of popcorn, and Fletcher makes shadow puppets between the reels. Maggie hasn't yet figured out how to match the film with the audio-tapes she's recorded, so the four of them take turns doing each other's voices. Afterward, Brid and Fletcher compliment her camerawork, and Maggie's relieved, because each day she picks up the camera expecting one of them will say it's a frivolous thing to do. She wonders how long they'll let her get away with it.

Often, after dinner, Fletcher spends long hours in the kitchen with the telephone receiver cradled under his chin, bribing and cajoling friends into coming up. None of them arrives, and there's no sign of Wale. Still, Brid and Pauline remain at the farm, and nobody mentions Brid's threat to leave. No one asks Maggie about her father, either. She hasn't heard from him again, and she should be glad, but she finds herself contemplating a call to Gran, just to make sure he's all right. She never did send a reply to Gran's letter.

In the last week of June, they watch on television as Hurricane Agnes arrives in America. The storm rains and rains over Pennsylvania until rivers break their banks, levees are overtopped, and thousands flee their homes. Maggie takes in the images, hears the statistics about the dead and displaced, then goes about her business in the orchard sunshine. But that night the storm escapes the television set. Suddenly it's outside the house, rattling the gutters, still raging after many inland miles, vengeful over a crime no one remembers committing. Lakeshore towns nearby are flooded, while the slimy creek at the back of the property swells into gouts of dirty water. The farmhouse roof springs a dozen leaks, everyone scurries for pots and buckets, and hourly Maggie makes the rounds to empty them. When the power goes out, they play cribbage and crazy eights by candlelight. The next morning Maggie stands at the bedroom window, still in her nightgown, and films the wind as it presses the cherry trees toward the ground. By the time the storm has passed, countless branches lie strewn about the orchard, a new multitude of automobile parts spread among them. The outhouse has been flattened, and the vegetables Maggie planted are drowned. It should be considered a disaster. Yet when the rain abates and she steps outside to film the ruins, she does so gladly.

A few days later, George Ray turns up at the door carrying a battered suitcase. Everyone files onto the porch to meet him, Fletcher pumping his hand energetically, Brid giving him a pasted-on smile that makes her reservations clear. Pauline hides behind her mother's knees and refuses to say hello, while Maggie hangs back and listens to Fletcher talk about the damage from the hurricane.

"George Ray, what would you like for dinner?" Maggie asks after a time. For some reason the question seems to fluster him.

"That's kind of you," he says, not meeting her eyes, "but I won't be able to join you tonight."

"He's going to live in the barracks," Fletcher explains, then starts down the stairs as if to flee any questions. "Come on, George Ray, let's get you moved in."

"He isn't staying in the house?" says Brid.

"It was something he decided," replies Fletcher defensively.

"Don't worry," says George Ray, smiling at Brid and then at Maggie. "It's better for me this way."

Brid bites her lip and says nothing more, but at dinner, when George Ray stays true to his word and doesn't join them, she demands that Fletcher explain what's going on.

He shrugs. "A religious thing, maybe? Honestly, it was his idea."

"Well, it looks terrible, him out there and all the white folks in here."

"Who cares how it looks?" he says, tossing his fork onto his plate. "There's nobody here to see it. Let's just be glad we have him."

The rest of the meal passes in silence. After Pauline has been put to bed, the top story on the TV news is Nixon's announcement that no more draftees will be sent to Vietnam. Maggie lets out a cheer, but Fletcher and Brid stare at the screen with ashen faces.

"That's great, isn't it?" says Maggie, confused.

"It's awful," replies Fletcher. "It means no one else is coming up here."

"Of course they'll come," Maggie says.

"Nope, we're screwed," says Brid. She stands with the pillow she's been clutching, then tosses it into Fletcher's lap.

"But things down south are getting worse," insists Maggie. "People know that."

"Sleep well, you two," says Brid, disappearing into the hall. "Don't run off and leave the country before I'm up to join you."

3

Gordon hurries through the jungle with Yia Pao's baby boy wailing in his arms, Xang eight months old and too heavy to let Gordon run very long while carrying him. The trail has grown slick with rain. Again and again Gordon falls, taking the earth hard with his shoulder because he can't let go of the child. When his red bandana slips from his neck and drops to the ground, he doesn't even notice.

There's no one at the waterfall when he gets there, just the stream of water pouring onto ledge rock. Then someone calls his name, barely loud enough to be heard above the cataract, and he sees Yia Pao step out from a hidden place behind the falls. Gordon goes to him and pushes the crying baby into his arms before bending over at the waist to take deep gulps of air.

"I won't forget this," says Yia Pao. He draws Xang close and tries to soothe him. "Did anyone see you?"

Gordon stands straight and shakes his head.

"Your neck," says Yia Pao.

Gordon frowns and reaches up to touch the thick white scar along his throat. "From the war," he says. When he sees Yia Pao's bemusement, he adds, "The one against Hitler." He tucks his chin toward his collar but isn't quite able to hide the scar from sight.

"I must leave," says Yia Pao, and Gordon puts a hand on the other man's shoulder.

"Go with God," he says. Then, as if he can't help himself, he asks, "Why are they after you?"

Instead of answering, Yia Pao draws back. An expression of terror has overtaken him. Gordon has only a moment to turn and glimpse the men in the distance before Yia Pao is pulling him toward the waterfall, into the dark place behind the rushing water.

The chamber is narrow, a wedge of wet air between the falls and a rock face tufted with moss. The light that filters through the water seems to be in motion, running down their clothes and faces.

"Did they see us?" Gordon whispers, but his words are lost in the tumult. Yia Pao is busy with Xang, trying to hush his crying, rocking him almost violently.

There are sounds from outside that could be men's voices. Gordon tries to peer through the waterfall, but a moment later he recoils. On the other side is a human shape stepping onto the ledge rock. The cries of the baby have ceased. When Gordon looks, he sees that Yia Pao has slipped a hand over Xang's mouth, and the child's face is bright red.

In the next second, something pokes through the waterfall at chest level. It's the barrel of a rifle, and tied to it is Gordon's bandana. After a time the barrel withdraws, and in its absence comes a face. It's the face of a man, the skin pale, eyes closed, teeth bared. It's the face of a corpse.

The eyes pop open. They roll in their sockets until they fix upon Gordon. He can't help himself. He screams and screams.

"Peekaboo," says the face. "I found you." It licks its lips and grins.

Maggie has just stepped out from the mud room to smoke a final cigarette before bed and watch the galaxy unfurl above her when faintly she hears a voice from the barracks. It sounds like the red-haired girl from next door. Maggie strains to listen and the voice promptly falls away. There are only the crickets chirring, the radio towers blinking on the horizon. She imagines the two girls out in the barracks with George Ray. He must be more than twice their age. He's probably married. Maggie sets off across the lawn.

Halfway there, she hesitates. No one has declared the barracks off limits since he moved in, but she'll be invading his privacy. Even if the girls are there, it isn't Maggie's business. Then she pictures them at the barracks window, making snide comments as she stands in the middle of the grass. Continuing on, she knocks at the door. George Ray answers in his undershirt and jeans.

"No cameras allowed in here," he says, deadpan. She gives a nervous laugh and holds out her empty hands, palms up. Laughing along with her, he invites her in.

Nobody's sitting at the long dining table in the middle of the room. It holds only a single plate with a few chicken bones on it. Against the near wall are bunk beds, recently installed. There's nobody in them either, and only one has been made up. Above it George Ray has tacked a Polaroid, while nearby a clothesline sags under the weight of underwear and socks. When he notices her looking in their direction, he rushes over to remove them.

"Didn't know there was inspection today," he says.

"Please, don't go to any trouble," she replies. It's horrible of her to have been so suspicious. "I just came out to see how you're managing." She points at the Polaroid above his bunk. "Your family?" He says yes, and she crosses the room to see.

The photo shows him standing in a suit against a backdrop of palm trees and washed-out sky. Beside him, a round-cheeked woman holds a baby and looks harried. A small boy is pulling at George Ray's hand with all his might, as if trying to drag him out of the picture.

"My daughter's twelve now," says George Ray. The information makes Maggie's peering at the photo seem too intimate somehow, and she turns away to gaze at the back of the room. Against the wall are stacks of insulation. Near Fletcher's weightlifting bench, a wide mirror rises from floor to ceiling. She takes herself in, notices the scar of thread on her top's strap, her pale calves below her skirt, her thin-lobed ears peeking out from hair she hasn't cut in

months. George Ray looks at her in the mirror. He has a
barrel chest along with thick limbs, and deep lines run in
parentheses around his mouth. When his reflection waves
to hers, she laughs.

"Did Fletcher put the mirror there?" she says, and he
nods. "It doesn't bother you?"

"Keeps me company," he says.

She murmurs her understanding, but the mention of
company reminds her of why she's here and makes her feel
guilty again.

"I came out because I thought I heard a girl's voice," she
admits. Somehow it's easier confessing this to his reflection than directly to his face, but still it's embarrassing.

He frowns, then gestures toward the counter by the
sink. There's a portable radio sitting on it. "I was listening to that a minute ago. Perhaps—"

Of course. Ridiculous. She's an idiot to have made such
a mistake.

"I'm sorry," she tells him. "It's just because there are a
couple of teenage girls next door. A while back they gave
me a hard time. I thought they might be . . ." But she
doesn't know how to finish the sentence.

"Bothering me?" he suggests, and she nods.

"Paranoid, I know. I guess they rattled me more than I
thought."

"No girls here. I'm a married man."

She remembers Brid's interest in him the first time he
visited the farm. "Is that why you wanted to be out here
by yourself? Because you're married?"

"Perhaps," he says. She can tell from his voice that she's

right. It seems a shame for him to keep them at a distance for such a reason.

"Would you join us for dinner sometime?" she says. "Or to watch TV? Fletcher said he invited you to one of our home-movie nights—"

"Thank you," says George Ray. His tone is polite, unpromising.

"You don't get lonely out here?" When he doesn't answer, she worries it's too personal a question. "Sorry. I should go." She retreats to the door. "You're welcome any time."

Once she's a few yards across the lawn, he calls to her from the doorway.

"Maybe it was the fulfillment of a wish," he says. She has to ask him what he means. "I mean, you thought you heard those teenagers because you worried about my loneliness. You imagined company for me."

The idea only makes her feel worse.

"You mustn't worry," he says. "It's nice out here. I'm learning."

"What are you learning?"

"I'm learning how to be alone."

She goes back to the house feeling ashamed. From now on she'll leave him to himself. But he didn't seem upset by her presence. Why does she feel so guilty? Ahead of her in the house, a bedroom light turns on, and she sees Fletcher's silhouette sail across the blinds.

Maggie has almost reached the patch of grass illuminated by the mud room floodlight when something moves toward her from the darkness. It says her name and she gives a yelp, but it's a voice she recognizes.

"Wale," she says. "You scared me to death."

"Who's that guy you were visiting?" His voice is a low drawl. Though he stands only a few feet away, she can make out no more than his outline.

"Long story," she replies. Then she wonders how he knew there was a man out there at all. "Were you spying on us?"

"Give me a break. I saw him through the window, that's all."

"Have you been in the house yet?" she asks, and he shakes his head. "Where have you been the last three weeks?"

"I had some trouble from the army."

"They caught you?" He starts to reply, but she interrupts him. "Wait, let's get you inside. I know some people who are keen to see you."

As they walk toward the door, he grows more visible to her: his spark-plug frame, the nose that looks like it was broken long ago. On one wrist he wears a silver watch that he holds to his ear, shakes vigorously, then holds up once more. It takes her a moment to realize his T-shirt and jeans are soaked through.

"How'd you get so wet?"

"I swam over from the States."

"Across the river?" She can't believe it, but he nods.

Holding open the mud room door for him, she tells him to go ahead. As he passes through the kitchen and down the hallway, she lingers, listening for what's about to happen. A moment later she hears Brid's shout of surprise from the living room, then Fletcher's elated greeting from upstairs. On the other side of the mud room window, moths patter out their lives against the floodlight. Maggie switches it off just as the house is filled with the wailing of a bewildered, suddenly awoken little girl.

The kitchen in morning light. Brid wears an apron over her bikini as she cooks bacon and pancakes, while Pauline sulks in her booster seat. She says she wants cereal like always, but Brid laughs and ignores her as if it's a joke. Fletcher hunches over the table swallowing mouthfuls of food drenched in maple syrup, and Wale sits across from him with raccoon eyes of fatigue, wearing a tank top that reveals a scimitar tattooed on one arm and a coiled snake on the other. He seems less interested in his meal than in Maggie, who hovers around the table with the Super 8 camera clicking and humming in her hands.

"You with the CIA?" he asks her.

"Shush," she says. "Pretend I'm not here."

"Yeah, don't look at her," Fletcher tells him. "It turns out more natural that way."

Brid leans over the table with the coffee pot in hand. "Come on, babe," she urges when Wale declines a refill. "You didn't get any more sleep than the rest of us." Topping up his mug, she kisses him on the cheek.

"You have to tell your story again for the camera," Fletcher says to him, but he demurs. When his gaze returns to Maggie, she gestures for him to look away. Resignedly, he stares into his coffee. Pauline is still clamouring for cereal; Brid reminds her that bacon is one of her favourites. Then Wale says he's not hungry and he wants to go sleep some more.

"You're not going anywhere," says Brid. "You think I'm cooking all this crap just for Fletcher?"

"It's the big reunion breakfast, we need everybody here," adds Fletcher, nodding toward the camera as if it proves his point. He grins and reaches across the table to punch Wale on the shoulder. "It's great you showed up. The hurricane was a setback, but now the cherries are growing and we've got the barracks almost ready. Plenty of other stuff we can start on too. We just need more people." A strip of bacon flies past his face and lands on the floor. Pauline begins to laugh hysterically.

"She isn't usually so wild," Brid says to Wale, taking Pauline's plate from her. "She's showing off for you." Fletcher gives him another friendly punch on the arm and Brid sets a full plate in front of him, then stands with her arms crossed until he begins to eat.

When the meal is over, Brid asks Fletcher to babysit while she and Wale go upstairs. Fletcher accepts the assignment, but after a few minutes of playing with Pauline on the living room floor he absconds to the couch, leaving Maggie to watch over her as he flips through a newspaper and casts glances toward the staircase.

"You're jealous," Maggie says.

"Don't be silly. I wanted to start working on stuff with him, that's all."

A few minutes later, Brid comes back down looking hastily dressed. She passes along the hall without a word or a glance into the living room, and soon Maggie hears the mud room door slam.

"Trouble in paradise," muses Fletcher with a trace of contentment before returning to his paper.

Eventually he switches on the television to watch *Face the Nation*. As if it's a signal, Wale comes downstairs too and takes a seat beside him on the couch. Pauline's interest in her building blocks vanishes; she knocks them over in the course of running to her father. He offers her an indifferent horsey ride, bouncing her on his knee without letting his eyes leave the television even as she squeals in delight. Brid reappears soon after, sitting on the floor to watch the programme, the voices from the set rendered inaudible by Pauline's cries.

"Daddy's tired, let him rest," says Brid. When Pauline doesn't respond, she adds, "Mommy needs a hug." The girl hesitates, then dismounts and allows herself to be held against her mother's breast.

On *Face the Nation*, all the talk is about the Democratic National Convention later in July. Fletcher cheers when someone mentions how good things look for George McGovern to take the nomination, despite how left of centre he is, while each reference to Nixon brings on a stream of insults from Brid. It isn't long before Maggie flees outside, then makes her way to the far corner of the backyard where the remnants of their garden lie. A week has passed since the hurricane, but puddles still stretch between the rows and there's not a vegetable in sight. Drowned, all of them. Beyond the barracks, the cherry trees are spangled with tiny fruit, while dead limbs sit piled at the ends of the lanes. Towers of crushed vehicles gleam behind the auto wrecker's fence like the skyline of some futuristic city.

"TV not your scene?" says Wale. She turns to see him approaching barefoot through the muck.

"Not the Sunday politics shows. All that arguing tires me out."

"You'd rather be making the pictures than watching them," he ventures.

"You mean the home-movie thing? I'm not really much of a filmmaker."

"Come on, I saw you in the kitchen. You love it. You like hiding behind the camera."

"I don't know about that," she says, hoping it will be the end of the conversation. Turning to the saturated ground, she shakes her head. "Poor garden. Pretty late to start over."

"Mm-hmm." With his toe he traces a figure in the puddle between them. The water soughs and throws the light, the reflected sky vibrating on the surface.

"What happened with you and Brid?" she asks.

His foot halts for a moment before resuming its path. "You mean upstairs? That's quite a question."

"I'm sorry, never mind—"

"It's okay." He's silent for a time. "Same thing happened that always does, I guess. Neither of us likes to be on the bottom."

Her eyes widen despite herself. She starts to say something, stops, then starts again. "She and Pauline are a lot happier now that you're here."

"Is that important to you?"

"Of course it is. Don't you care about it?"

"Sure," he says unconvincingly.

"Brid told me once," she begins, glancing toward the

farmhouse to make sure there's no one in sight, "that you rejoined the army to get away from being a father."

"Bullshit." His toe flicks the puddle and sluices water across the grass. "I signed on for another tour because a buddy of mine enlisted. I thought he needed protection."

"What about protecting Brid and your daughter?"

"Nobody was shooting at them." With his head tilted, he stares at her. "I didn't realize you and Brid were such good friends." She looks away and sights a hawk describing circles high above them.

"I think the idea of this place," she says, "is that we should all become good friends." She shoves her hands deep into the pockets of her overalls.

"How do I get to be your friend, Maggie?"

"Oh, I'm easy to get along with."

"Sure you are. Just don't look at you, right?"

"That's ridiculous."

"Is it? I'm not sure. Want to hear what I think?"

"You don't even know me," she says.

"I think maybe for you, being looked at is like being on the bottom."

Before she can reply, Brid's voice calls to them. "What are you two doing out here?" She's crossing the lawn in their direction.

Quickly, Maggie takes a step back from him. When Brid gets nearer, she flashes Maggie a frown of disapproval before extending her hand to Wale, smiling at him in a way that seems carnivorous and worn out at the same time. "Get back inside, will you, lover boy? I want another go at it."

Brid and Wale entered Maggie's life in December, not long after Fletcher did. On the way to meeting them for the first time, Fletcher explained that he'd been friends with Brid since his freshman year, and that Wale was the father of her kid, though he'd been out of the picture until recently. The guy had served in the army, he'd killed people doing it, and he wasn't much of a talker, but Brid was crazy about him.

Maggie took in this information distractedly. She had just gotten off the phone with her father, who had called with the news that in the spring he was going to leave his job and join a mission in Laos. When Maggie had asked what Gran thought of the idea, he'd replied that she was delighted. Maggie shouldn't have been surprised. Gran had been waiting twenty-three years for her widowed son to do something with his life.

"It will save money for me to live over there," Maggie's father had told her. Then he'd admitted what she already knew from Gran: bad gambles on the stock market had put him on the edge of bankruptcy.

"So you're going over there to save money?" Maggie had asked him.

"No," he'd replied. "To save lives."

At the bar, she only half listened as the others talked. For the most part the conversation was about politics, Brid arguing with Fletcher while leaning against Wale and reaching beneath the table every few minutes to clasp his knee. It was as if Brid's body had split completely from her brain, and each was given over to a different man. As for Wale, each time Maggie glanced toward him, he was staring at her, smiling like they were sharing a private joke, and each time she looked away.

When Brid went off to the bathroom, Wale asked Maggie about teaching. It was the last thing she wanted to discuss, and Fletcher must have sensed it because he came to her rescue, jumping in to ask Wale in turn whether he'd found a job yet. Wale shrugged, then asked Maggie where she was from. Maggie tapped Fletcher on the leg to signal that it was all right and started talking about Syracuse.

Eventually, because there wasn't really a way to avoid it, she came around to her father. It was easy enough to speak about the man she remembered from her childhood. Gliding through the story of her adolescence, though, she found herself running headlong toward describing his return to the Church. Instead of breaking off, she crashed right into it.

"In college, I lost my faith," she said. A funny expression, she thought, as if her faith were something she'd misplaced somewhere, when the experience was more like a wave rolling over a sandcastle. "I took a course in World Religions, and that was enough, just learning about all those creeds with their different gods. Suddenly it seemed arrogant to believe in one true Church." She saw Fletcher nodding and realized it was her first time talking about this with him. "I didn't tell my dad, though. He wasn't a churchgoer, but I thought he'd take it hard. When I'd gone away to college—"

She broke off, not wanting to tell Wale that her father had seemed lonely, that to make him feel better she'd often said how homesick and out of place she felt in Boston, even though in fact she'd liked her classes, liked the city, was happy knowing she could go out whenever she wanted without letting anyone down.

"Then last year, while I was at teachers' college," she went on, "he called me to say he'd started going to Mass. At first I thought he was joking, but he wasn't. I felt so bad, I finally told him about the World Religions class."

"How did he take it?" asked Fletcher.

Maggie shook her head, still dismayed. "He wanted to have a theological debate. This guy who hadn't gone to Mass since he was a boy, suddenly he was trying to argue me back into believing. He went on about Vatican II and all the reforms, the liturgies in English, the Masses at people's houses. He even felt obliged to tell me they have Eucharists of milk and cookies now, because milk and cookies are more relevant."

By the time Brid returned to the table, Maggie was explaining about her father's plans for Laos. Fletcher squeezed her hand in sympathy, while Brid said missionaries were just another kind of soldier. Wale wanted to know if Maggie was familiar with Laos, and she admitted she'd never even seen it on a map. He said it was a squiggly turd of territory between Vietnam and Thailand with its own special brand of Communists, the Pathet Lao, fighting against the royalists. He said officially it was a civil war, but everybody had their fingers in it. The North Vietnamese were backing the Pathet Lao; the Thais and U.S. were helping out the royalists. There weren't any American troops on the ground, though. Instead, they had CIA agents train the local mountain people, the

Hmong, to fight the bad guys. It hadn't been going so well for the Hmong. Nowadays their typical soldier was a twelve-year-old with a machine gun. Wale said the only upside of Laos was that they'd legalized the opium trade, so you could make a lot of money if you didn't mind being shot at.

"Not that you'd know anything about it," said Fletcher with a laugh, but Wale looked at him with a blank expression, and Brid seemed less than pleased by the comment too, because a second later she steered the conversation toward how well Wale was getting along with Pauline.

The next evening after work, when Maggie stepped through the front doors of her school, Wale was waiting for her. At first she didn't register him, because she was still suffering her daily wave of post-class recrimination, remembering the inanities she'd uttered, the moments when one second-grade delinquent or another had spoken back, refused to follow directions, or in some other way reduced her to a wheedler and a nag. The Christmas break was a week away and she still hadn't wept in front of the students. It was her only success as a teacher.

The prospect of a stiff drink was beckoning when she noticed Wale ahead of her. Though it was ten degrees, he had nothing on his head or hands, and he was stamping his feet to stay warm.

"Thought I'd surprise you," he called out.

"Well, you did," she said, trying to sound unflustered. She almost asked how he knew where she worked until she remembered telling him at the bar. It had just been small talk. Now she considered making some excuse and turning back into the school, but no, he was just an odd duck. She was grown-up enough to handle him.

"Got time for a beer?" he asked. When she told him she was late to meet Fletcher downtown, he seemed undaunted and said he'd ride there with her. On the way to the subway station he asked about her day, as if the two of them walking along together were an ordinary thing. At the station he offered to pay her fare and she told him not to be silly, thinking it best to give no sign of encouragement.

On the subway, she made a point of bringing up Fletcher, and there was relief in seeing how the mention of his name made Wale's eyes lose their gleam. She said that without Fletcher she'd have quit her job already. She said how surprised she'd been to find herself dating him. Teaching had made her such a wreck, she couldn't imagine being attractive to anybody. But that was the wrong comment to make.

"There's your problem," said Wale, the gleam returning. "You don't see yourself like other people do." She didn't know how to respond to that. "For example, the way you listen. Last night you asked me all those questions. Most people don't bother doing that, especially with a vet. You pay attention, though. It's a turn-on."

She wanted to point out that she'd barely asked him anything, and that asking questions didn't mean she was into him; it only meant she found it easier than talking about herself.

"You know, your dad will probably be okay in Laos," said Wale out of the blue. It was disconcerting to have the matter raised so unexpectedly, and she had to shunt away a sudden feeling of despair.

"Probably he won't go," she said. "He's never even left the Northeast."

"If he does, will you join him?"

"Why would I do that?" But as she said it, she knew why she would. Guilt about leaving him had already sent her back to Syracuse summer after summer. How could she let him go to Laos on his own?

"Last night you made it sound like you two are close," said Wale. "Or you used to be, at least. Maybe you'd want to look out for him."

Maggie didn't reply.

"Well, if you do go, tell me," said Wale. "I might come over and look you up." He grinned at her, and she decided he was probably insane.

In silence they exited the train and rode the escalator to the surface, Maggie worrying the whole way up that he was going to say something else she'd have to deal with. It was a relief when they reached the cold air outside, but Fletcher was nowhere to be seen.

"He said he'd be here," she explained, unable to hide her unease, needing to be out of Wale's company. He seemed to think she was only concerned about Fletcher's welfare.

"You're really stuck on this guy. It's not for his money, is it?"

Even though he said it jokingly, Maggie scowled. She often worried about the Morgan family's wealth, not because people like Wale would think she was a gold digger, but because her father might feel self-conscious about his own money problems.

It was only another minute before Fletcher arrived. He seemed taken aback to see Wale with her, and she found herself saying that the two of them had run into each other on the subway. Wale winked at her, and immediately she regretted the lie. As he said goodbye and started away from them, she could imagine him growing ever bolder with her, not caring what Brid or Fletcher thought, until there was some confrontation and Maggie got blamed. The next time she and Fletcher met up with Brid, though, Wale wasn't there. He'd re-enlisted and shipped out to Vietnam, beating her father to Indochina by a good four months.

Between the hours of gardening, cleaning, and making dinners, Maggie retreats to her camera. She films George Ray atop a ladder as he tends the trees, a transistor radio in his shirt pocket piping music to him through an earphone. She captures Fletcher and Wale on the farmhouse roof with their hammers flashing. From the creek bank a mile downstream, she films them and Brid swimming in a shady pool beneath an old concrete dam, while water passes over the edge in a smooth, clear stream and an empty bird's nest bobs in an eddy. Across the road, the church's steeple pokes up from the horizon, scratching a human presence into the sky. Pauline sits cross-legged on the bank in her pink swimsuit, collecting pebbles for a tiny, slowly growing cairn.

By now Maggie has recognized that when the others are conscious of the camera, they each have their reactions. For Brid, to be filmed is an affront, as though someone has called her a dirty name. Wale tries to escape, so that often there are only blurred glimpses of him quickening away like a sasquatch. George Ray is almost as elusive, cloistered in the barracks when he isn't working. Those times she does catch him out, he acts embarrassed. By contrast, Pauline squirms her way into every shot she can, dancing and hamming. A camera appears and the world rearranges itself in response. Fletcher alone changes not a bit, as if he's been exposed to cameras all his life.

With each person, it's the private moments Maggie's after. She doesn't want self-consciousness; she doesn't want performance. In daydreams she imagines aerial shots that would let her study everyone at her leisure, unobserved, but in practice she's limited to filming from ground level, so she stays on the periphery and wills herself to be part of the landscape, carrying the camera even when it's turned off, hoping others will become less sensitive to its presence.

It would be easier to blend into the scene if more people were around, but no one else arrives. Even Frank and the girls next door remain absent from the lawn in front of the mobile home when Maggie walks by. As the middle of July approaches, Fletcher's optimism about the farm starts to dwindle.

"A hundred thousand draft dodgers in this country and we can't get one of them," he complains. He stays up late watching television, feet on the coffee table, pulling at his moustache while twin quadrilaterals of light reflect in his eyeglasses. He has never drunk much beer, alcohol being long shunned by his family, but now as he watches he always has a bottle in hand. When the Democratic convention begins, he takes up near-permanent residence in the living room, and no one bothers to chastise him for not working. At the dinner table he speaks less often about his plans for Harroway and more about the failings of the party leadership. On the convention's last night, they all sit together to watch McGovern take the nomination. By the time Eagleton's declared the running mate, though, Brid and Wale have given up and gone to bed.

"I still can't believe Ted Kennedy refused to stand," says Fletcher. Maggie knows that he and his father once went fishing with Ted Kennedy.

It's almost three in the morning when McGovern makes his acceptance speech. Maggie's lying with her head against Fletcher's thigh, wanting to luxuriate in this propinquity, the stillness of the night, everyone else asleep and his hands resting in her hair, but she can't get comfortable. There's a tautness in his muscles; the speech has got his attention. She hasn't even been listening, but now she tries to focus on the words. Through the stupor of her tiredness she sees McGovern as a mass of light distinguishable only by eyebrows and sideburns. Then a phrase hooks her.

"From secrecy and deception in high places, come home, America." Her heart begins to thud. "From military spending so wasteful that it weakens our nation," McGovern says, "come home, America." She glances at Fletcher, but his face is unreadable. "Come home, America. Come home to the affirmation that we have a dream."

Gently, Fletcher lifts her head from against his leg, and she thinks he's going to kiss her, but instead he gets up and turns off the television, then says he's going to bed.

Upstairs in the dark, she lays her arm across his chest.

"You know, we can go back if you want," he says.

For a while she doesn't answer.

"Do you want to?" she asks.

"No, I don't."

"I'm happy here," she tells him.

"That's good," he replies, kissing her on the eyelids. "I am too."

It isn't long before she hears his breathing stretch and deepen. Before she joins him in sleep, she marvels at the fact that although she was prepared to lie, her words felt like honest ones. It's the truth of Fletcher's response she can't quite take for granted.

Wale stares into the camera as if daring it to look away first. A window behind him reveals the cherry orchard's rustling leaves. He seems to have dressed up for the occasion, wearing a collared shirt and black denim pants.

"All right," he says, sounding a little bored, "where do I start? Well, maybe the kookiest thing about the whole story is that I served my time in the army back in sixty-five. I wasn't in college, so of course they drafted me right off the bat. Yeah, I'm not a spring chicken like you and Fletcher. The kicker is, back then I didn't even go to Vietnam. The army found out I had certain, what do you call them, aptitudes, so I was with Special Forces in other places." He produces rolling paper and tobacco from his pocket. "I'm not going to talk about that stuff, okay?" The camera closes in on his hands, perhaps to ascertain what the fingers of someone in Special Forces look like. The knuckles are a bit knobbly, and there are fine dark hairs on the bottom joints.

"I did my time, then got out. After that I started rapping with guys who'd been in Vietnam. Some of them were hanging out with SDS types. That's how I met Brid." Once the cigarette is rolled, he flicks his lighter. "Then last December my buddy enlisted. He'd hit some hard times and wasn't thinking straight. The two of us grew up together, and back then he saved my ass more than once, so I figured I'd join up and watch out for him. Brid was pretty pissed off about it—but I guess you know that."

There's a cut, a change of angle. Now his face is visible from the other side.

"What can I tell you about Vietnam? It was a good gig, all right. For most of the guys it's their first time out of the States. They get to Saigon and suddenly they're in this whole other world with banana palms and two-buck whores. They love it. Lots of them think that with the nice weather, the drugs, and the easy pussy, they'll just stay there to open a hotel once their tour's done. Our boys don't want to fight, they want to be Bogie in Casablanca." He takes a long drag on his cigarette. "Who cares if the locals live in hooches made out of Coke cans? Uncle Sam feeds his boys pretty well. Every night at dinner the chaplain says the same prayer, 'Forgive us any harm we may have done today,' and you tell yourself that's goddamn magnanimous of him. You repeat that little prayer before you go to bed and you think America's doing a pretty decent thing." He covers his mouth to cough. "You meet some pretty interesting people, too." At this he gazes past the camera intently.

"Then they load you in a truck and send you down Highway One. It's a real nice stretch of road: no jungle, no villages, because they've all been ploughed under to fuck up snipers. Just mud and rubble on either side, and any slope dumb enough to be out there is target practice." Another change of angle, this time back to the frontal view. As Wale talks, the camera moves in on him. "It's right about when our boys are being driven down Highway One that they start thinking of some mighty convincing reasons not to be there. Because people who look American aren't supposed to be fighting anymore, right? If you're sent out on patrol, it's only because ARVN has fucked up again. And the guys humping it in the jungle with you are a real choice bunch. Either they're the ones who avoided the draft till now and are pretty freaked out at the idea of being shot at, or they're the nut jobs who keep re-enlisting and somehow aren't dead yet."

His gaze drops and he leans forward in his chair. "You tell yourself all sorts of things. You grease a woman by accident and think, well, she won't get raped now. You grease a nine-year-old boy and think at least he won't have to grow up in this place." He closes his eyes. "You figure they don't even mind dying the same way Americans mind it, because most of their family's dead and their rice paddies are bombed to hell and there's nothing to look forward to but more of the war, so how could they see death like we do?"

Maggie speaks in the background, and Wale shrugs.

"You said you wanted to hear it all, didn't you? I'm only talking about this stuff for you." He reaches up to touch the dark forest of his beard. "At least I know who I am. Some people, they'd rather wait all their lives to be told whether they're in the red or the black. I know what I deserve."

The camera's tight against his face now, so that even his chin is out of view. At a turn of his head, the shot becomes disorienting. There's a cutaway to the trees in the orchard through the window. When the camera returns to him, he has stubbed out his cigarette.

"I pissed off some people by refusing to do more Special Forces stuff, so they wouldn't even let me serve in my buddy's platoon. You don't want to piss off the boss men over there, Maggie—you're liable to take some friendly fire in the back of the head. That's when I decided to split. It involved certain evasive strategies I learned in sixty-five. Like I said, I'm not going to talk about that." His free hand goes back to rubbing his beard. "Spent a bit of time hiding out—maybe sometime I'll tell you more about it—but long story short, I made it to a pay phone in Saigon, called Brid, and she told me about your little plan for reinventing Paradise up here. The way things had been going, that sounded pretty good to me, so I aimed to catch the next freighter back to America." He starts rolling another cigarette. "The night before I was going to ship out, though, I got a bit sloshed. Bad timing, because that's when the army caught up. Somebody at the bar must have ratted. When they found me, I was out cold, shit-faced in the john." He fumbles with the rolling paper and tobacco spills across his lap. "Fuck!" Angrily, he wipes it from his jeans. "Even once they had me, I wasn't too worried, figured I'd find a way to bust out. Except then they stuck me in the hole." He shakes his head as though this was a humorous turn of events. "You know about the hole, Maggie? No, well, maybe you can imagine.

"At first, they said I was looking at five years of hard labour. Turned out worse than that, because then someone checked my file and connected me to a certain guy from Special Forces, somebody who'd gone freelance and started running opium. He'd made a reputation for himself leading a merry band of rip-off artists all over that part of the world, mostly with CIA approval, but somebody in the army must have had enough of him, because they put the squeeze on me. The interrogating officer was a real son of a bitch." His voice drops in pitch and volume. "He worked me over pretty good." Wale touches a place near his belly, smiles, and tries to laugh, but his throat seems to close on him. His hands fold into one another; the fingers twitch. When he resumes speaking, the camera has caught him at a different angle and there's something drained from his words, as if a part of him has gone and not come back.

"By the time they transferred me, it was the end of May and I'd seen better days. Just me in a jeep with a couple of MPs, but I wasn't in shape for any fancy tricks. No court martial either. They were moving me to a place where they could spend some more time with me, private-like." He takes a long pause. "That guy who worked me over, he said he was going to be there. He said he'd see me again." The leaves on the trees through the window are still now, and shadows are beginning to creep along the wall.

"When we stopped for gas, it was pissing rain. Made them sloppy. They took turns guarding me while the other one used the can, and I guess they thought they were being careful, but the smaller one ended up with a good knock on the head. After that, it was just a lot of running. The other guy couldn't go after me with his buddy out cold, and over there the army has better things to do than chase after deserters."

He talks more easily now. "Next day I was on a container ship to San Francisco. Once I got there, I hitched to Buffalo, thinking the whole time about ways to cross the border." He grins to himself. "Had all sorts of crazy schemes, but turns out I just swam across the river. Not even half a mile, not much current, no patrols. The water was warm." He sounds baffled by the ease of it. "It was weird, swimming in the middle of the night. There were all these stars reflecting around me like I was in outer space." He squints as if seeing it again before him. "I'll tell you, I've crossed some borders in my time, and this was no border." He reaches out toward the camera. "Then my hand touched something solid"— he draws it back with startling speed—"and I screamed. Scared the bejesus out of me." He laughs. "Turns out it was the shore. I'd made it across and not even realized it. I walked the rest of the way." He speaks these last words and falls silent, seeming once more in the thrall of the river's darkness. Eventually he looks back to the camera.

"So that's it," he says. "Now I'm a family man up here with the Eskimos and beavers and you college-educated types." He raises himself a few inches from his seat. "How's that for you, sweetheart? Got everything you wanted?

"Oh, right, my buddy in Vietnam. Far as I know, he's still over there. Last I heard of him, he hadn't even seen any action. Apparently he was having a real good time."

At first, as Wale speaks, Maggie isn't listening properly. She's concerned that Brid will turn up to watch, and that by making comments she'll ruin the whole thing. Maggie keeps an eye out for her while worrying over the composition, the changing light, the angle of the next shot. It's only when he breaks off that he draws her full attention.

"What is it?" she asks. "Don't stop, you're doing great."

"I'm talking to a machine. I want to talk to you."

"Oh. Okay." A part of her can't bear the thought of just sitting there, but when they start again, she tries to react visibly to his words. Then she begins to hear what he's saying about the war, about killing women and nine-year-old boys, and she grows more certain that she doesn't want to listen. To distract herself, she fiddles with the zoom, trying to concentrate on matters of technique. When he speaks about how the Vietnamese treat dying, though, she bursts out, "You can't really think that."

A moment later he has his head in his hands and the cartridge has run out. For a second she wonders whether she should go to him or reload. Then she's putting her arms around him, but it feels like a mistake. Not knowing what else to do, she keeps holding him and finds herself taking the measure of his back, his different scent, comparing his muscular torso with Fletcher's lanky one. There's something wrong with her. She isn't a good person.

"I don't think we should film any more," she tells him.

"No, it's all right." For a while they sit there hanging their heads. There are distant voices that sound like Pauline and Brid in the orchard. "Come on," says Wale, pointing to the camera. "Let's get this over with."

Reluctantly, but also with relief, she goes back to load a new cartridge.

He talks of his desertion, his capture and escape, his journey to the farm. When he finishes, she turns off the camera, the cassette recorder, and the lamp she has used to light his face, then gathers the cord for the microphone. There are half a dozen cartridges scattered on the floor where she dropped them. She collects them into a paper bag.

"What will you do with those?" he asks, still sitting in his chair.

"Don't know. What would you like me to do?"

"Whatever you want. I don't care."

By herself in the playroom later, as she arranges the cartridges with the others to be dropped off at the Virgil grocery store for development, his question returns. What's she going to do with them? And not just with them, but with all the reels she has accumulated? Remembering the editing machine that Fletcher bought, she decides she needs to start piecing them together into a longer film before they become too unwieldy.

There's a certain pleasure at the thought of lodging herself in the playroom with the machine and bringing order to things. Probably Wale would say it's just another version of her hiding behind the camera. But she remembers his composure while he talked, then his racked body in her arms, and she realizes that if some people hide behind the camera, others hide in front of it.

They travel through mountainous forest, a line of them with Yia Pao and Gordon in the middle, three Lao men ahead of them, and two white men behind. Yia Pao has been blindfolded using a strip of cloth torn from the garments of his son, while Gordon's eyes are covered by his red bandana. Both men's clothes are filthy from stumbling and sliding, Gordon's hands having been bound in front of him while Yia Pao's hold the child. The baby cries, falls silent, cries again. Their captors seldom speak, and they walk with their eyes on the ground.

As darkness approaches, they reach a place high up where the trees are stunted, the ground cover sparse, and a pair of tents has been pitched next to a campfire circle. The hard-eyed Lao guard removes the captives' blindfolds; his companion from the riverbank enters one of the tents. After a time it grows luminous, and he returns holding a kerosene lamp that emits a low hiss alongside a stammering light.

The two white men stand off to the side, conferring with each other. One is tall and gawky, a feather poking out from his mane of dirty hair. There are patches of reddish soil on his cheeks that once might have resembled war paint but have since been smeared so that they look like the rouge of a circus clown. The other man is shorter and older, with grey hair cropped to a brush cut. Occasionally he casts a glance at the captives, who stand silent while Xang whimpers in Yia Pao's arms. The man with the brush cut finally points to Yia Pao and orders him taken away. The Lao men march him into the forest carrying his son.

"Where are they going?" says Gordon.

The man with the brush cut ignores the question. "So you're a missionary," he says. His voice has a Southern twang. "Since when did missionaries grab people's kids?"

"The baby was in danger," Gordon answers.

"Danger?" says the man, sounding affronted. "It wasn't the baby that had our money."

"I don't know anything about your money."

"Yeah, you're innocent as grass," says the man. "Just like every American over here." He chuckles, then turns to his gangly companion. "Isn't that right?"

"Sure, Sal," says the other man without conviction.

"You aren't getting out of here unless we say so," the man called Sal says to Gordon. "You wouldn't survive the jungle, and nobody's coming for you. I had a word with the priest before we left the mission. If anybody asks, he's going to say you and your buddy went to Ban Den Muong. And if we hear he's been telling people otherwise, we'll pay him a visit. You understand?" Gordon nods. "Now, you're going to write a letter. A nice personal one, so people will know we've got you and we're not just making it up."

"If I write it," says Gordon, "will you let Yia Pao and his son go?"

Sal punches him in the stomach, and Gordon doubles over. "This isn't a negotiation," says Sal.

"I'll write the letter," says Gordon, coughing. "I will. But Yia Pao—" He has to take another swallow of air before he can finish. "He doesn't have your money."

"Sweet that you're such good friends," says Sal. "I might believe you if you hadn't snatched his kid for him." He pats Gordon on the back as he coughs again and spits into the dirt. "That hurt? It was just a taste, okay? Remember that."

He disappears into one of the tents. Gordon straightens while the other man watches, shaking his head as though disappointed with him. After a minute Sal returns with a pen and spiral notebook.

"You got money?" he says to Gordon. "Rich friends? Rich old man?"

"I have debts," says Gordon. "My mother's a widow. Missionaries don't get paid."

"Well, you better hope the Church ponies up for you." Sal circles behind Gordon and kicks his feet out from under him, toppling him. Gordon lands with a cry of pain.

"Sit up," says Sal.

Slowly, Gordon gets himself into a cross-legged position. The Lao men return from the forest without Yia Pao or his son and take up a position on the light's periphery.

"The baby needs milk," says Gordon.

"My friends and I need money," Sal replies.

"If the baby doesn't get milk, it will die," Gordon insists.

"If we don't get our money, you're all going to die. My friend and I here retired early from the army, so we're short on our pension." He drops the notebook and pen into Gordon's lap. "Don't be a hero. Just write what I tell you."

When they've finished, Sal gestures for him to be taken away. The third Lao man, older than the guards from the riverbank, steps forward and drags Gordon to his feet, then leads him down a trail to a place in the forest where a narrow pit has been dug. Beside it is a pile of heaped earth. Gordon pulls up short at the sight, and the guard speaks to him sharply in Laotian. Yia Pao's voice comes from the bottom of the hole.

"It's all right," he says. "He isn't going to shoot you, Gordon. He wants you to lower yourself in."

Gordon sits down at the edge, slides his body forward until finally he drops. At the bottom it's pitch-black except for a purple square of sky ten feet up. The silhouette of a head appears above them and whispers something before vanishing.

"What did he say?" asks Gordon.

"Tomorrow he will try to bring milk. He is Hmong, he will help us if he can."

"I told them you didn't take their money," Gordon says, then adds, "I didn't lie, did I?"

"I don't have it," Yia Pao replies. "I promise you."

"They didn't believe me."

"Perhaps not. If they were certain I took it, though, they wouldn't have brought us all this way. They may wish to ransom you now, but you weren't part of their plan. These men are drug runners, not kidnappers."

"How do you know?" Gordon asks, and Yia Pao doesn't answer. "All right, then. Tell me why they brought you here. Why not kill you or let you go?"

"Because they think I might have their money after all."

"What about Xang? Why haven't they killed him? Could it be there's some decency in them?"

"Perhaps they think that as long as he lives I will try to save him by revealing where the money is."

"Is he all right?" asks Gordon. As if in response, the baby cries feebly. Gordon offers to hold him, and Yia Pao hands him over.

"We'll get out of here," says Gordon once the child is settled in his arms. "If it comes to it, I'll give myself for both of you. I won't hesitate."

Yia Pao gives a low laugh, and Gordon's voice turns gruff. "What is it? What's so funny?"

"I think you have been waiting a long time for this moment."

"I don't know what you mean."

"You have wanted a chance to surrender yourself," says Yia Pao. "Tell me, what crime did you commit to require this self-sacrifice?"

"It's not what I did," Gordon replies. "It's what I never did." Before he can say more, there's the sound of something smacking against the wall of the pit between them.

"Climb the rope, Yia Pao," says Sal's voice. "Leave the kid with your friend. It's your turn for a talk."

After Yia Pao is gone, Gordon coos a lullaby to the child. A few minutes later, when Yia Pao starts screaming in the distance, Gordon breaks off from the song and begins to pray.

part 2

CHILDREN

of

PARADISE

4

One evening in the middle of July, a sedan pulls into the driveway bringing unexpected visitors. Dimitri and Rhea are in the front seat, their two little boys asleep behind them. Maggie rises from where she has been sitting beside Fletcher on the porch step and calls into the house for Brid and Wale, then asks Fletcher in a whisper whether Dimitri told him they were coming. Fletcher shakes his head in wonder.

Dimitri climbs out of the vehicle in a pair of cut-off jeans that separate his pot-belly from slim, strong legs, the two halves of him so disparate that he looks like both a horse and its rider. Rhea, not more than five feet tall, has the same powerful thighs and high-bunched calves. Brid has referred to these two as the Centaurs, and she has made it clear she doesn't much like them. But today she greets them with a smile before lifting Pauline to the car window and pointing out the boys, Judd and Jeffrey, as if they're a rare species of animal. After Rhea rouses them, Pauline turns shy and buries her face in Brid's chest, while Wale nods a hello from the porch.

When the vehicle's back doors are opened, a flash of silver grey leaps out and tears across the drive on four legs, disappearing behind the house. Dimitri gallops after it, shouting, "John-John! John-John!" The two boys call out too, even while Rhea chastises them for opening the crate in the back seat. Over the next hour everyone helps in searching for the Centaurs' cat, without success.

To Maggie, it's a disquieting arrival, but in this feeling she's apparently alone. That night after dinner, once the boys have been placated with candy bars, the adults talk and laugh with a celebratory air, even though Dimitri soon informs them that he and his family have come here only for the rest of the summer. He says rumours about Fletcher have been flying around Boston. Some people are saying he's had a nervous breakdown; others swear he's going to run for Congress. Last week Cybil called Dimitri to ask if Fletcher had really joined the Weathermen. Maggie watches Fletcher's face as he hears this news and perceives no sign of displeasure. For his part, he gives a sanguine history of their settlement on the farm, even managing to mention George Ray without eliciting any comment, only a quick, dour look between Dimitri and Rhea that Maggie takes to mean trouble.

After dessert, there's a rush to change the sleeping arrangements. The Centaurs and their boys are given

Pauline's room, while she's moved in with her parents. The new configuration delights her but leaves Wale less than happy.

"So much for fucking," he announces.

In the morning, the men go to work harvesting cherries with George Ray. The fruit they carry back from the orchard is blighted, and much of it is already starting to rot. Maggie stays in the house preparing lunch, then dinner, her inter-actions with Brid and Rhea limited to sightings from a dis-tance as they watch over the children, looking bored and conspiratorial by turns.

A few days later, as if the Centaurs have begun a trend, a green Beetle full of teenagers and aromatic smoke appears in the drive. They have heard about Harroway from the draft dodgers in Toronto, and they wanted to check out the scene. Fletcher can't believe the good fortune of it. When he puts them in the barracks with George Ray, Maggie worries they'll make the place unbearable for the man, but for the most part they stick to the house, toking up, eating all the food, and doing no work at all.

After a week, they leave just as stoned as the day they appeared, but others begin to arrive. An earnest-looking couple named Sarah and Jim turn up from New Jersey speaking to each other in baby talk and offering to read people's palms. A thick-bearded man calling himself Luther rides in on a motorbike with a low-slung saddle, his clothes too small for him and smelling as if they haven't been washed in months. Someone named Ralph calls from the St. Catharines bus station asking to be picked up, though nobody has heard of him and they can't imagine how he got the number. Upon his arrival he says he saw the farm in a dream.

Suddenly there are too many people to eat in the dining room all at once, so they migrate to picnic tables in the back-yard, and when it rains, they carry their plates out to the barracks. Each day more people arrive, some driving cars, some hitching; others leave abruptly without even saying goodbye. It gets to the point that Maggie can't remember all their names. Most of those who join in the cherry harvest spend more time eating the fruit than picking it, and by the end of the month Fletcher has delivered only a few dozen baskets to Morgan Sugar's processing plant in Toronto. Instead of seeming disappointed, he orders more bunk beds for the barracks and devises sign-up lists for chores. When people complain that the bathroom is always occupied, he talks enthusiastically of building a washhouse.

Most of the new arrivals aren't travelling from the States as he imagined. Rather, they're on their way back there, Americans no longer afraid of the draft, young men and women who say they're fed up with the cold winters, the lack of jobs, the complacency of this little country with its inferiority complex and superiority complex at once. More than a few want to campaign for McGovern, even though Eagleton has had to withdraw from the ticket and they agree it's all over, Nixon will get back in for sure. Fletcher still gives them room and board, hoping to convince them of the good life they could have if they stayed. Those who help out for at least a week are put on the Morgan Sugar payroll. A group of them excavates a drainage ditch along the south fence, and another lays the foundations for a drive shed to hold the tractor Fletcher plans on buying. Some don't help out at all, but Fletcher says it doesn't bother him. Maggie's the one who resents the dirty sheets and bare refrigerator shelves, the cooking and cleaning for people she doesn't know, the absence of time with those she does. For the most part Brid and Rhea stick to minding their children, leaving Maggie to herself. Every time she visits the barracks, it seems Wale is there playing cards with someone. She worries about him and the newcomers out there taking George Ray from his solitude, keeping him awake at night with their idle talk and singalongs.

She doesn't see that much of Fletcher, either. He stays up long hours reading books with titles like *Tender Fruit Husbandry* and preparing financial reports for Morgan Sugar. Late one night, looking over his shoulder at the kitchen table, she sees a blank form for the migrant labour programme.

"Still going to apply?" she asks, and he says he isn't sure. After all, they have people now, right?

"Not a very reliable bunch," she replies, surprised at her own sourness. It occurs to her how much she wants this whole venture to succeed. "What about getting locals?"

"I've talked with some of them in town. People around here don't think much of what we're doing. To them we're cowards for leaving the States, or we're imperialists taking over their country."

"Maybe send in the form just in case," she says.

"Maybe." He looks at her with beseeching eyes. "Don't tell anyone, okay?"

In bed, he sleeps peacefully, like a baby, and it's Maggie who's insomnious. Why should she be offended by all the comers-and-goers? Maybe it would be better if her friends, not Fletcher's, were the mainstays. But she doesn't really have any friends. Through college she had classmates and roommates, acquaintances who came and went with the changing of majors and dormitories. Then, as she slogged through teaching, there was simply Fletcher.

Now half their nights are taken up by meetings in the living room to discuss the future. Sarah and Jim from New Jersey suggest a meditation circle, while Dimitri expounds on the need for study groups. Fletcher responds that it's a farm, not a seminary, and what they need are dedicated work hours. Maggie sits smoking one cigarette after another, fearing she might be called upon to speak. Other times she makes herself unassailable by bringing the camera. As the others discuss their hopes and ideas, she records the play of light through a wine bottle or a baby asleep in its mother's arms.

One night after the meeting has ended, she finds Fletcher by himself at the kitchen table, writing something on a piece of foolscap he's too embarrassed to show her. The next morning she wakes up to discover he's stapled it to the porch door.

Principles for the Pursuit of Happiness
1. *We are all human beings.*
2. *Technology is not an end in itself.*
3. *True happiness requires company.*
4. *We must not mortgage the future of Spaceship Earth.*

It goes on in the same vein, most of the lines recognizable from the previous evening's discussion. That afternoon she finds Brid by the door, eyeing the page skeptically.

"'*We are all human beings*'?" Brid reads. "What else could we be—wombats?"

"I think he means we each deserve dignity and respect," replies Maggie. "Anyhow, he included the one about the planet's future. That was your idea."

Brid glowers at her. "You're just smug because he used '*God is not an American*.' Which, as I pointed out last night, is Judeo-Christian propaganda. It makes it sound like God exists in the first place."

"Like I explained," Maggie begins, careful in choosing her words, "it doesn't have to be a Christian God. Most people agree there could be some higher power—" But she can tell Brid isn't listening, so she tries another tack. "Brid, are you okay? How are things with Wale?"

"Why, hasn't he told you?" says Brid. The bitterness in her voice makes Maggie pause.

"We haven't talked for a while." She thinks of their interview and his coolness toward her since. There's been little more than strange looks from him in passing and half smiles that could be leers. "I don't think Wale gets close to anyone," she says. Realizing how that might sound, she quickly adds, "Except you, of course."

"Yeah, well, next time you see him, remind him of that." A certain resignation has entered her voice.

"I know things have been chaotic," Maggie says. "There isn't as much time for being alone together. But this is what we wanted, right? People working as a community."

"To be honest, I liked it better when it was just us and Wale." Brid returns her attention to the piece of paper on the door. Without another word, she rips the sheet from its nail.

Involuntarily, Maggie's hands curl into fists. But she doesn't mention the incident to Fletcher, and at dinner, when he asks if anyone knows what happened to the page, she and Brid only exchange a long glance.

At the end of the day, drained of all energy, Maggie watches television on the couch with half a dozen others in the living room. A body passes before the screen, and she realizes it's Brid coming to sit down next to her. There's meaning in this, she suspects, but she's too tired to grasp it, she's almost asleep, and a few minutes later she discovers she's no longer watching television, she's just dreaming of it. When she wakes up, an old Bette Davis movie is playing and Brid's head is heavy against her shoulder. Maggie can hear her breathing; she can feel the hitch at the end of each exhalation that summons another ream of air.

In the morning, when she enters the kitchen, she finds Brid feeding Pauline breakfast. No one speaks until Fletcher comes in looking cheerful.

"Did you hear?" he says. "They've picked Sargent Shriver to replace Eagleton."

"Who?" says Brid, sounding annoyed.

"You know Sargent Shriver. The guy who founded the Peace Corps."

"He's married to a Kennedy," adds Maggie. She could also add that he went to Yale with Fletcher's father.

"Oh, that guy," says Brid. "Sorry, but I'm officially not giving a shit about the election. No longer my country, no longer my problem."

"Well, I think he's fantastic," replies Fletcher. "God knows the Democrats needed some good news."

"They're still dead in the water," says Brid.

"Not everyone's as cynical as you—" Fletcher begins, but Maggie can't stand to hear any more.

"Why don't you two cool it?" she says. Brid and Fletcher turn to stare at her.

"What, we can't argue about politics now?" says Brid.

"You're not arguing about politics." Maggie takes her coffee mug in hand and starts for the door. "I don't know what you're up to."

With everyone settled into work, pouring concrete for the drive shed and scything long grass where they intend to plant more trees, Maggie feels obliged to join them. Whole days go by without a cartridge being loaded. Where does the watching Maggie go? Sometimes, when she's in the middle of watering the garden or emptying ashtrays, she has a sudden sense of being observed and turns to find precisely no one there, just the shadow of another self taking her in. The few occasions she does remove the camera from its bag, she's unsettled by the comfort it brings. Eventually she stops resisting and spends her days with her eye against the viewfinder.

By experimenting, she learns the art of cinematography fifty feet of film at a time. She figures out how to bounce light so as to soften it on skin. She learns that everything becomes cool blue if you take the UV filter off the camera outdoors, and if you leave it on inside, it casts the room in an orange glow. She starts to open and close f-stops, making reality seem more real by stealing light or occluding it. For interior shots during the day, a supplemental lamp makes things clearer, but she prefers scenes illuminated by a single source because the shadows look more natural. In the afternoons she waits for the soft, slanted sunlight that comes through north-facing windows.

Then she discovers the time-lapse function. At a single frame a minute, the clouds race over the orchard, shadows wheel, and dawn changes to dusk in thirty seconds. It's the way the cherry trees themselves must look at things, abiding while the world hurries. Her films gain angles, too. She shoots from her knees, through windows, experiments with slow motion, and becomes fascinated by the ability to zoom. For a while all her shots move from detail to sprawl or sprawl to detail.

Once a week, everyone gathers in the playroom to watch the latest developed film. A hush rises as the lights go down, and Maggie thrills at the whoosh of the projector's fan ploughing air past the lamp, at the chatter of the machine taking hold of perforations in the strip. She's less enamoured of the grainy Super 8 film stock, which is easily marred by scratches, spots of dust, and eyelashes jigging onscreen, but no one else appears to mind. They don't even seem to notice the imbalances of composition, the shadows intruding where she wanted light. They clap and catcall, laughing at the showboats and the camera-shy

alike, demanding certain reels be played again. There
are gasps over the footage of the hurricane and hooting
at Pauline's antics during the staged tour of the house.
When these latter scenes play, Pauline hides her face in
Brid's lap, overcome by all the staring adult eyes, though
whether she's embarrassed by their attention to her or to
her image, Maggie can't tell.

One night they watch a sequence Maggie shot in the
orchard just after dawn. Sunbeams splay through the
branches almost horizontally, while the trunks are split by
light and shadow, their bark silvery purple in the main
but turning lichenous green toward the roots. There's
no movement, no human presence, and Dimitri makes a
crack about artistic pretension that Maggie decides not
to hear. Then Jeffrey calls out, "It's John-John!" Maggie
has viewed this clip several times before, admiring the
hues and textures, but until now she has never noticed
that perched up in a fork is the outline of a cat. Although
she shot the footage a week ago, the Centaurs' boys want
to see right away if John-John's still in the tree. A search
party is dispatched, returning without success. At each
subsequent screening Maggie's obliged to replay the clip,
every projection eliciting new tears from Judd and Jeffrey,
until Rhea complains that they show more attention to
the cat now than they did when it was around.

Another much-requested sequence begins with a shot
of an inflatable wading pool. Pauline leans forward to
dip her fingers in the water and shrieks at the sight of a
daddy-long-legs floating on the surface. Judd and Jeffrey
run past in their underwear to jump over a lawn sprinkler,

Judd kicking up his feet as he goes, Jeffrey doing his best to follow suit. At the barbecue pit, Fletcher presides over the sizzle of hamburger patties while people sit nearby eating and slapping at mosquitoes. Two teenage girls in halter tops pass a Frisbee back and forth across the lawn, seemingly unaware of the young men watching from the picnic tables. The shot pans back to Fletcher.

"Thirty people," he says, smiling into the lens. "Can you believe it? Two months and already we have thirty people. Just today we planted half an acre of trees. We're doing something incredible here." His voice is declamatory, his enunciation precise, as if he's speaking to a bigger audience than just the person behind the camera. "With our sweat we're making a living for ourselves. There's a wholesomeness in it, a sense of well-being—" He pauses as though trying to remember a line. "There's a decency here. We're new to this place, but somehow it feels like it's always been ours. It's a young country; we're going to help make it grow."

A second later, Wale appears from nowhere, a flash of sinew and tattoos, grabs Fletcher by the waist, and carries him to the wading pool, Fletcher struggling and laughing at once. When Brid spots them coming, she pulls Pauline from the water. Wale plants his feet behind Fletcher's and in one smooth motion twists and falls, dragging him down. Water flies in all directions; there's a pop like a gunshot. The two men are a tangle of drenched limbs engulfed by sagging plastic.

At this moment during screenings, the residents of Harroway cheer. Afterward, when Fletcher makes unsubtle hints about Maggie excising the clip, she tells him she needs to keep a comprehensive record. Privately, she has her own concerns about why the clip should be so popular, but still, she's pleased with the reaction it gets. Some proud, reckless part of her thinks everyone is more together while watching her footage than at any other time. The only person never in attendance is George Ray, whom she imagines stretched out on his bunk as the reels are playing, glad to have the barracks to himself. She can almost imagine joining him out there, sitting at the table and sharing the silence, but she takes too much pleasure from the screenings to abandon them.

The films are still more rudimentary than she would like. The camera always trembles. Shadows turn faces into blots of darkness, or lens flares splash them with light. In one sequence she has too many close-ups, while in another she has stood too far away. And there are many things she can't properly capture: the porch step always on the verge of snapping underfoot; the air near the wrecking yard after a rain, heavy with the smell of motor oil; the screeching of raccoons at night as they fight and fornicate on the roof.

Maggie decides that what people are seeing at her movie nights is merely the rough draft for something else. After screenings she stays up late selecting the sequences that garnered the best reactions, and she starts to edit them together. The card table in the playroom grows littered with egg cartons holding rolled-up bits of film. Sometimes the cutting and splicing seem like the wilful destruction of what gained life on the screen, but in her mind there's a greater film waiting to be realized, along with someone waiting to watch the thing. When she tries to apprehend who it is, she realizes it's her father. Strange to find him still abiding there after so much distraction. Three months have passed since he wrote. By now anything could have happened to him. But surely Gran would call if something was wrong; Gran wouldn't pass up a chance to make Maggie feel guilty.

What would her father say if he saw the film? No doubt the believer of the last few years would condemn it, accuse them all of worshipping false idols. But she can imagine the younger man, the one done in by a desk job and his mother's sanctimony, being attracted by the promise of their life. She can even picture him joining them up here.

It was at Christmas that he gave her the Super 8 camera. She had gone back to Syracuse and told him how much she hated teaching, how she couldn't get over her stage fright and the daily humiliations at the hands of eight-year-olds. Admitting such things seemed easier than talking about his plans to become a missionary. Before she knew it, though, he was telling her he had the answer to her problems. She should come with him to Laos and work at the mission.

His enthusiasm for the idea was so heartbreaking that she didn't say no right away. She didn't mention Fletcher, either, because they'd only been dating a few weeks and somehow she sensed her father wouldn't be glad to hear she had a boyfriend.

Christmas morning she sat with him in the living room and unwrapped the box he handed her, discovering the camera within. She should have said thank you right away, but there was no gratitude in her, only confusion. She had never expressed the slightest interest in such a thing.

"How much did it cost?" she asked. Had he borrowed from Gran? He always hated doing that.

"It shoots in colour," he said, ignoring her question. "And it has a zoom."

"It's too much," she told him, but that wasn't the response he wanted.

"You remember your Brownie Starflash? You loved taking pictures."

"I was a little girl then."

"You could bring it to Laos. You could film our work there, show people back home what it's like."

Suddenly she realized what was inside her along with the confusion. It was anger, a white-hot rage she'd never felt before. The camera wasn't a gift, it was a bribe. Did he think she could be swayed so easily? Did he think she had nothing better to do than take pictures of him?

"Dad," she said, "I'm not going to Laos."

How strange it was to call him that. When she was a child, she'd had no need of any name for him, because whom else could she have been addressing?

The camera went back into its box, and when Maggie returned to Boston, she didn't take it with her. Her father never said a word. He was still hoping she would change her mind, hoping she would bring it with her to film life in a foreign country. It's what she has ended up doing, too, if not in the country of his choice. She tries not to feel too guilty about the pleasure and solitude that filming brings. The time alone may not be in the spirit of a commune, but the camera is one thing she doesn't want to share.

The bathroom door's ajar when she knocks on it, the camera in one hand and the tape recorder slung from a shoulder. She can see Rhea sitting on the toilet with the lid down, reading a magazine and watching over Judd and Jeffrey as they bathe in the claw-footed tub.

"All right if I film in here?" Maggie asks.

"Go ahead," says Rhea. "There's no shame in these parts." She has a tinkling voice that gives each word its own particular tone but lays emphasis on none, like a pianist running through scales. Turning to the boys, she snaps, "Jeffrey! I saw that, young man." Her dress is practically a sack, and with her pageboy haircut, her thin face, and her small body, she seems rather like a child herself, yet she's lordly and indomitable in the humid air, commanding the boys to soap and rinse. After tucking away the magazine and adjusting her dress, she cranes her neck to glance in the mirror by the sink, while Maggie kneels and frees her hands to hold the camera by squeezing the microphone between her legs.

"Can I ask you a few questions?" she says to Rhea, focusing on her through the lens.

"Film us! Film us!" shouts Judd. Jeffrey joins him in the chant, but it's quelled by a maternal glare.

"She's always filming you," Rhea tells them. "Right now she wants to talk with Mommy." Brightening as she shifts back to Maggie, she folds her hands in her lap. "So what do you want to know?"

"Why don't you tell me what it's been like for you up here?"

Rhea sighs. "The boys have pink eye. Yesterday Dimitri burnt his elbow." She pauses and laughs. "There I go again! My sister always says to me, 'Rhea, you've got to stop defining yourself by other people's crises.'"

"Where does your sister live?" Maggie asks.

"New York. Fashion writer, no kids. Rest of my family's in Lexington."

"You miss them?"

"Nah, it hasn't been long enough. You miss yours? I heard about your father—" She makes a face as if she has given the wrong answer on a game show.

"I'm all right," says Maggie. "Go on, tell me how you've found it here."

Rhea thinks a bit before she answers. "Well, I guess things are mostly the same. There are little twists like the accent, and the store clerks are so rude. I don't expect them to be just like Americans, but they could at least be nice. Right, Judd?" She speaks in the direction of the bath. "You should be nice to people?" Maggie pivots to capture the top of Judd's head nodding.

"I can't imagine living here permanently," says Rhea. "I want the boys to grow up with their grandparents and aunts and uncles around." She peers past the camera. "You're not really going to spend your life here, are you, Maggie? For God's sake, whenever I leave my toothbrush by the sink, somebody else uses it." She wrinkles her nose.

"Maybe I shouldn't say this, but there are plenty of spongers, too. Not naming any names." Suddenly she stares straight into the camera. "You know who you are!" she booms, then laughs. "It's a nice old house, at least. You think it was really part of the Underground Railroad? I don't believe it, but you never know."

"That's great," says Maggie, drawing away from the viewfinder.

"What, is that all?" Rhea sounds disappointed.

"I'm out of film," Maggie explains.

"Oh—good," says Rhea without much enthusiasm. "Now we can really talk." In a friendlier tone, she asks, "How are you doing?"

"Why, what have you heard?"

"Oh, nothing. We just never seem to chat, do we? It's Brid's fault. You can't get a word in edgewise." A second later there's a geyser of water from the tub and a high-pitched cry of pain. "Judd, don't kick," she orders, then waits for peace to return before she speaks again.

"Fletcher has got quite the set-up here," she continues. "It isn't much of a commune, but it's cute how straight he wants things to be. Some folks think he's only slumming it here after Cybil Barrett dumped him, but that's just silly, right?"

"It better be," says Maggie, laughing uneasily. She wonders who has been saying such things. To change the subject, she asks, "You really can't imagine staying up here?"

"Not if Dimitri gets his job back." Rhea looks at Maggie intently. "You knew he was fired, right?"

Maggie shakes her head. Fletcher only told her that Dimitri was in between things.

"Well, it wasn't a surprise," says Rhea. In a lower voice, she adds, "Did you know he got into speed?"

Maggie says she didn't.

"He had me trying it, even," says Rhea. "He had me trying a lot of things." She glances back at the boys, whose attention seems focused on some unseen aquatic phenomenon. "I figured out pretty fast I wasn't into that stuff, but Dimitri had some people in his life who were bad influences."

"The dragon lady!" exclaims Judd, looking up at her. For a moment Rhea appears horrified. Then she gives a sigh.

"The dragon lady," she agrees. Leaning toward Maggie, she says, "One night he came home so strung out he couldn't remember the kids' names. I told him that was it, no more drugs, no girls, or else. So he went cold turkey, tried Zen, spent three weeks in a field near Hartford building a geodesic dome. Fine, I thought, whatever works. But in June I spotted the tracks on his arms, and a few days later so did his boss."

It's Maggie's turn to glance at Judd and Jeffrey.

"Oh, I don't care if they hear it," says Rhea. "They need to know their father isn't the Almighty."

"Are things better up here, at least?" Maggie asks, and Rhea's overtaken by a look of gloom.

"I wanted them to be. We'll see. He goes out a lot." Seeing Maggie's puzzlement, she adds, "Not in the car, just walking. He says he's looking for the cat."

As if she's just remembered something, she stands and strides over to the tub, picks up a wet washcloth, and begins to wipe at Jeffrey's neck.

"It's cold!" he shouts, enraged and ducking. "I don't like it!" Rhea dips the cloth into the bath, wrings it out, and reapplies it.

"It's no fun for me either," she mutters, scrubbing hard. In a brighter tone, she says to Maggie, "I hope you won't mind me saying something."

"No, of course not," Maggie replies, still trying to wrap her brain around what Rhea has already told her.

"The problem with Fletcher," says Rhea, "is he's too hard-headed."

Suddenly Maggie realizes she does mind. She wants to say as much, but Rhea doesn't give her the chance.

"Fletcher never listens at meetings, he only talks. All that stuff about the bourgeois machinery and the repressive state apparatus—the rest of us hashed that out years ago. We were going to teach-ins when Fletcher was on his parents' yacht every weekend. Now we've moved on. Hold still, I'm almost finished," she instructs Judd. To Maggie, she says, "I know he's trying to show his father he can run a business up here, but he's too uptight. You know what I mean?" Maggie nods absently and Rhea smiles. "Of course you do. You're a good listener. Fletcher could take a page from your book."

Maggie's still kneeling on the floor. She remains silent long enough that Rhea glances over at her.

"Rhea, I want to be your friend," says Maggie. "If you have something to say about Fletcher, though—"

"What? I can't hear you." Rhea sets to work smoothing down a cockscomb of hair on Jeffrey's head.

"I said, if you want to complain about Fletcher, you should talk with him yourself."

As soon as Maggie speaks the words, she gathers the camera and audio recorder, then stands to go, already regretting what she's said. But as she turns to apologize, she discovers that Rhea's attention is fixed on the tub. Judd and Jeffrey are flexing non-existent muscles for their mother, and exuberantly she praises their physiques. When Maggie says softly that she'll see them later, Rhea waves without even turning around.

That night, Fletcher's mouth refuses to move in time with his voice. "Punch me," he says a second before his lips purse. Sitting at the card table in the playroom, Maggie rewinds the film on the editing machine and cues the audiotape again. Synchronizing the sound with the images is the most difficult part. There's equipment that can do it more efficiently, but already she feels guilty enough about the expense of all the cartridges. "Punch me," says Fletcher, half a second too late. She rewinds once more. "Punch me," he says. He has his shirt off and the lighting's good enough for her to see his abdominal muscles tighten perceptibly as Pauline wallops him in the gut. It's a solid swing, producing a short, insuppressible grunt, but one that comes too soon, just before the little fist makes contact.

"Three-thirty," says a voice not on the soundtrack. "You should be in bed."

Turning from the editor, Maggie sees Wale standing by the door. Against the backdrop of the lit hall, he looks naked. Then her eyes discern the white of his underwear, and she glances away. By day she's seen him in swimsuits, but still, he must know he's embarrassing her.

"I'll go to bed soon," she says. "I just want to finish this." He doesn't leave as she hopes, though. "Punch me," says Fletcher on the audiotape and viewer, finally at the same time.

"You ever think your man tries too hard?" says Wale. He has come up behind her, and he bends over her shoulder to look more closely at the viewer. "You know, to compensate for all his father's dough." Hot air rolls along Maggie's neck, carrying the scent of skin and sweat.

"Fletcher's spending that dough on you and me and this place," she says.

Wale only laughs. "Right on, defend the guy. I know you've got your ideas about him." He pauses, giving her room to retaliate, but she holds back, so he adds, "Hell, you're only up here because he is."

She can't help herself. "That's bullshit."

"You've got quite a mouth," he murmurs into her ear.

She wrenches her chair around to face him, but having completed this manoeuvre, she finds her eyes level with his underwear, so she stands and folds her arms across her nightgown.

"Fletcher's not the only one committed to this place," she says. "Coming up here was my idea." And then, lest he should hear some regret in this admission, she adds, "I was right, too."

"You're a real visionary, Auntie Maggs."

"Don't call me that."

"What, a visionary?"

"No—Auntie Maggs." It's too late in the night for arguments. This must be payback for filming him; he's out to lay her open in turn. Well, she won't have it.

"You really want to live like this?" he asks. "With all the rich kids chasing after satori?"

"If you think they're such phonies, why are you here with them?"

"Sometimes I wonder the same thing." There's a hardness in his voice. She studies his face to see if he's kidding, then waves him away.

"I almost believe you. The way you treat Pauline—like you couldn't care less."

"Pauline," he replies in a flat voice, "owes her life to a broken rubber."

"That's a horrible thing to say." Yet immediately she's sure it's the truth.

He moves into the circle of light from the lamp beside her, a shadow deepening across one side of his face even as the other gains texture and detail.

"Let me tell you something I've learned about myself," he says. "The heart of me is a lump of selfishness. Concern for other people is just a ribbon tied around it. I wish it were otherwise, Maggie, but at the core I'm this piece of petrified shit. It's a fact that has kept me alive, at least, and it never goes away. It'll stick around longer than this place."

"What do you know about it? You don't even come to meetings. You're always playing cards. If you paid more attention, you'd know we're going to be here for years and years."

Wale shakes his head. "People have been setting up communes for decades. They all think they'll work twenty hours a week and live like kings. It never happens. Brook Farm, New Harmony, the Oneida Community—all gone. You know why?"

"Because people have hearts made of shit?"

He chuckles and nods. "But it's nice you think otherwise." Then he adds, "In some ways you're a lot like your father."

Maggie scowls at him. "How would you know? You've never even met him."

"I met him in Laos."

At first Maggie assumes it's a joke, but he isn't laughing.

"It was in May," he tells her. "While I was on the lam."

"You were in Laos?" She doesn't understand. It's impossible. He must be lying.

"Hardly any white people over there," he says. "They tend to run into each other. It's like in Africa with Livingstone and what's his name. Your dad and I, we met at Long Chieng, the big CIA airbase. The reds were on the offensive, so half of Laos had hunkered down there. I was on my way back here, and your dad was heading to some refugee camp."

As he speaks, Maggie feels a growing anger. "Why didn't you tell me before?"

"You broke off contact with him, didn't you? I figured you weren't interested."

But she knows that's bullshit too. He's been playing with

her, waiting for the right moment to spring the news, a time late at night with no one else to interrupt.

"You really talked to him?" She can't help asking it. "How was he?"

"We only spent a couple of hours over beers, but he seemed happy enough." Then Wale's brow knits as if he's rethinking it. "No, not just happy. Maggie, he was radiant. It freaked me out. I mean, Long Chieng isn't Disneyland. I figured your dad had to be working an angle."

"Angle? What angle?" The question carries an energy with it, as though if Wale could give her the answer, it would let her feel better about the situation. But he only shrugs.

"I asked him that, flat out, and he said he was there to make something of his life."

Her chest tightens. It couldn't be so simple and piteous. "He went to Laos because he was broke, and because he didn't have me at home to look after him anymore."

Wale raises an eyebrow.

"Did he tell you about the things he said to me before he left?" she asks. "Did you even tell him you knew me?"

"Sure I did. Then you were all he wanted to talk about. Whatever happened between you two, he was feeling bad about it."

"What did he say?"

"He said he had a hard time when you left for college."

A pain of remembrance shoots through her.

"Hey, I sympathized," says Wale. "If I had you all to myself and you split, I'd have a hard time too."

She remembers Wale in Boston, the intensity of his gaze at the bar, the way he seemed to be mapping her inch by inch. He's looking at her like that now, and it's no less alarming than it was then. What did she do to merit such attention? He reaches out to clasp her by the elbows. "Don't," she says.

"You really see something in that guy?" He's looking over her shoulder at the editing machine. When she turns to it, she realizes that the image of Fletcher being punched in the gut still glows in the viewer.

"Don't," she says again, shaking free of him and flicking off the editor. A low electric hum disappears that she didn't notice until the moment of its vanishing.

"You haven't written your dad lately?" says Wale. "You haven't heard from him?"

"Why do you care?" It's impossible to stay here; she has to leave. "I'm going to bed. Turn out the lights, will you?"

She starts for the door, wishing there were something she could say to let them speak of more trivial things in the future. Instead, she ends up asking, "Did you really meet my father?"

"You don't believe me?"

"I don't believe you just ran into him. It's too much of a coincidence."

"What do you think happened?"

She doesn't reply because she doesn't know.

"Good night," she says, worried he'll call after her and wake everyone. The trip down the hallway seems to take forever. When she makes it to her room without hearing his voice, it feels like a lucky escape.

In bed, unable to sleep, she remembers the father she once had, the one unwilling or unable to change his life. Gran always thought the solution was for him to marry again. She said a man in his thirties was still young. Besides, she insisted, playing her trump card, Maggie needed a mother. Gran always said this in a patronizing tone Maggie loathed. "I don't," Maggie wanted to say. "My father's all I need." But she never spoke the words aloud. It wasn't until she had been accepted for college and was on the verge of freedom that she decided she could say whatever she liked.

"You don't really want him married," Maggie told her then. "You'd rather have him to yourself."

By that point she was too old to be grounded or sent to her room, so Gran's only response was a hurt silence. Maggie should have felt guilty about it, but after a childhood assuming it was a requirement to love her grandmother, she had realized she didn't even like her very much. All through Maggie's years of high school, Gran had taken every opportunity to tell her how to live her life, her favourite topic being the sacred temple of a girl's body and the dangers of young men. It was ridiculous of her to dwell on it, because Maggie never dated anyone. She knew she needed to win a scholarship if she wanted to attend college, and she told herself she didn't have time for boys.

For that reason, it surprised her when, in the spring of 1966, Peter Leggat asked her to the senior prom. All year in Latin class she'd sat behind him, admiring the back of his head and growing weak in the knees when he conjugated verbs. They'd barely spoken to each other, though, and she was so startled by his invitation that she wasn't able to feign indifference. Right away she blurted out a yes.

Afterward, she made up for it by not telling Gran or her father. On her own she bought a pair of pointy blue shoes and a chiffon dress with cape sleeves and an over-skirt that the saleslady said would twirl nicely in a waltz, leaving Maggie distressed because she had never waltzed in her life. Once she'd snuck the outfit into her closet, it seemed quite natural to say nothing to anyone until the night itself.

That evening, while her father watched television down-stairs, she put on the dress and shoes, then crept into his room, never before having entered it on her own. Her mother's dressing table was against the far wall. Maggie had often peered at it from the hallway when her father wasn't there, studying her reflection in the mirror. Now, drawing close, she examined the things spread across the table's surface: the pots of cream, the perfume bottles and lipsticks, a wooden jewellery box embossed with metal hearts. In a small pewter frame was a photograph of her mother at seventeen or eighteen, sitting on a bicycle with her hair pulled back, wearing a long grey coat that hung past her knees, smiling at some secret thought.

Maggie picked up a tube of lipstick from the table and removed the cap. She had already put the stick to her lips when she realized it stank foully, and she fled to the bath-room so she could wipe the stuff off.

Downstairs, she waited by the edge of the living room until her father turned to see why she was lingering. He took in the chiffon dress and the pointy shoes, and suddenly she apprehended just how preposterous she must look.

"Tonight's the prom," she told him. "Peter Leggat's taking me." She said it with an air of confidence, but it didn't sound right, even to her.

"Who's Peter Leggat?"

"Just a boy," she replied. "I don't know him very well." Realizing how that might sound, she added, "He's Catholic, I think." But that sounded no better. She waited for her father to tell her she couldn't go.

"I can see your knees," was all he said.

"You can't," she insisted.

"I can almost see them, then."

"You want me to put on something else?" It was a stupid thing to say, because she had nothing else to wear. She almost added, "You want me to stay home?" If he said so, she'd do it gladly. Anything was better than the look spreading across his face, one she'd never quite seen before. There had only been a hint of it those times she'd asked him to let her attend a slumber party or an overnight school trip. From those hints alone she'd learned to avoid situations where he might gain the forlorn expression he wore now.

A vision came to her of how it would go if she went. Every dance, Peter Leggat would step on her toes and stick his tongue in her ear, and afterward he'd drive her to Green Lake so he could slide a hand under her dress while they sat on the beach. She'd be so worried about her father that she'd barely perceive the movement of Peter's fingers, tentative as he waited for her rebuke. She wouldn't say a word because her mind would be back in the house, imagining how it would have been if she'd stayed behind to watch

Gilligan's Island, and she would barely be paying attention until Peter Leggat reached the wet centre of her.

When he appeared on the doorstep, clutching a pink corsage with his parents' car running in the drive, Maggie told him her father was ill and she couldn't go. It was a surprise to her when Peter looked relieved. She should have been glad, but it made her furious, and she almost changed her mind. Had he invited her on a bet? Probably his mother put him up to it. On the spot, Maggie decided that Peter Leggat was a scrawny, pimply, ninety-nine-pound weakling. What had she been thinking?

After he drove away, she stormed into the living room.

"I'm not going," she declared. "I hope you're happy." She couldn't quite escape upstairs quickly enough to avoid seeing her father's stunned expression.

In her room, she entertained a fantasy of Peter Leggat driving wildly around Syracuse, overcome by regret, then returning to beg her forgiveness. When a knock came at her door, for a second she believed it was him. But it was her father, head down, staring at the carpet.

"You know, it's all right for you to date," he said.

"I know," she replied, although she didn't believe he meant it.

"I want you to see the world," he told her. "I want you to have a career." It was the first time he'd said any of these things. "Maybe you'll be a teacher."

"A teacher?" The idea had never occurred to her.

"You'd be good with children. Also, it would give you the summers to travel."

She found it strange to hear him talk of travel. He

subscribed to *National Geographic* and liked telling her of
the places he read about, but he never talked of visiting
them, either by himself or together, and she didn't mind.
The idea of travelling with him didn't seem right. She
wanted to do it by herself one day.

But what she said was, "You'll come with me."

"I couldn't afford it."

"I'll pay, then. I won't leave you by yourself." She hoped
it was what he needed to hear, but he only looked more
dejected.

"You're leaving in the fall," he said.

She gritted her teeth. So that was why he'd mentioned
travel. She should have known.

"Boston isn't so far," she said, as if he didn't know where
Boston was. "I'll come home on weekends." At this, he only
shook his head.

Suddenly his presence in her doorway was too much.
She needed him to be downstairs in his easy chair. She
wanted to be wearing her normal clothes and sitting on
the couch. "I don't have to go," she heard herself say.
"Maybe I could still get into Syracuse."

He didn't look up from the carpet. "You need to see the
world. I've been a selfish father."

Did he want her to go or not? When she went to hug
him, she felt him shiver. Why was her father shivering? He
shook like a little boy who knew a terrible secret.

"I should have sent you off on trips," he said. "I should
have made you get some distance."

A year later, in Boston, she had a chance encounter with
a girl from high school, someone whose name Maggie had

already forgotten. The girl told her Peter Leggat had burnt his draft card and moved to San Francisco with flowers in his hair. This bit of gossip was followed by a long, sly look. Not for the first time, Maggie wondered what Peter had told people to explain his inviting her to the prom. Perhaps in San Francisco she still had a walk-on role in the stories he related. Maybe, as he told it now, she was the last girl he'd tried before giving up and heading west. Perhaps she played the same sort of crucial, casual role in his personal history that he seemed to play in hers.

Maggie thinks of telling Fletcher about her encounter with Wale in the playroom but decides he already has enough to manage. Each day seems to bring him into conflict with people on the farm. Those on the payroll begrudge the chores he assigns them, while those who aren't being paid don't bother with his labour schemes at all and entice the others to movie matinees in St. Catharines or the beach at Port Dalhousie. In bed he complains to her that Dimitri's the main culprit, setting a bad example with his truant walks in search of John-John. Fletcher complains about the garbage everywhere, the mud on the floors, the noise from record players and car stereos, the shouting and laughing downstairs that make it hard to sleep, until he and Maggie end up arguing over which of them should go tell people to be quiet. In the mornings, there are often bodies asleep in the hall, and many residents of the barracks don't get up until noon. Fletcher starts going out to the building before breakfast, rapping on the door and hollering hellos, poking people awake.

His shortwave radio goes missing, then his welding torch. She tells him not to take it personally, but it's no good. At meetings, he battles with Dimitri, who hasn't lost interest in debating. While Fletcher sits with pens and sheaves of notes laid out on the coffee table like weapons, Dimitri takes equine strides around the room and sweeps the hair from his forehead. He wants a credit system to apportion the work more fairly. Fletcher wants to ban drugs and set a nightly curfew. The number of Fletcher's supporters shrinks with each meeting, and half-jokingly Dimitri takes to calling him Captain Morgan. Brid, whose vote cannot be depended upon by either man, rolls her eyes a lot. It makes for compelling film but is hard on Fletcher's nerves. He vents his anger watching TV coverage of the Republican convention. One night Maggie catches him before the bathroom mirror speaking to invisible assailants.

"Get lost," he says. "Why can't you leave me alone?"

She steps back from the door with a pang, glad nobody else is there to see him. Her period's a week late, and she has been wanting to tell him about it, but when he's in such a state it seems unfair to burden him. She's been late before to no consequence. It would be easier on the pill, except the pill didn't agree with her, and anyhow they're so careful—always the diaphragm or a condom. Probably it's just stress. She hasn't been eating well.

The next morning, he awakens her, already in the middle of a rant. When she asks him what's wrong, he flings a piece of paper onto the bed.

"A complaints letter! I found it under our door. They can't write me a complaints letter—it's a fucking commune! Dimitri's behind this, I know it."

She looks over the page. "Some of these things might be reasonable."

"Like what?"

"Like not enough vegetarian meals—"

"That's Rhea. Goddamn Rhea and Dimitri. Why do we have all those meetings if they're going to bitch behind my back? I swear, they only came here to ruin things. Dimitri's got a chip on his shoulder the size of Cape Cod."

Maggie thinks of asking him what he knows about Dimitri and speed, but she only rubs his back and tells him it will be fine. She says everyone's trying to make the farm better. She tells him to focus on the happy things.

And she's right, too: in some ways it isn't so bad. The lettuce she planted after the hurricane is flourishing. The pumpkins have begun to spread tendrils beyond the borders of their allotment. On warm evenings after sunset, she and Fletcher walk hand in hand down the orchard's central lane, and sometimes through the fading dusk they see pairs of bodies lying together under the trees. There's the luminescence of bare legs, the undulation of a head. At first she's startled by such sights, even as part of her stirs, but she comes to take them as propitious, signs that together all of them have created something good.

The last week of August has arrived when one morning she goes upstairs to find George Ray standing there in his orange toque, knocking on her bedroom door. As far as she knows, he has never set foot in the house before, and he looks uncomfortable standing in it now.

"Sorry to be a bother," he says. "I was hoping to speak with you. Will you come outside?" She nods and follows him down to the porch. After glancing in all directions, he continues onto the lawn before turning to her.

"Top secret, huh?" she says, trying to sound light-hearted, but he doesn't smile, only keeps his eyes on the house as he speaks.

"I had an encounter last night," he says. "Near midnight, in the orchard."

She frowns, confused. "What were you doing out there?"

"Taking a walk. I do it most nights before bed."

Maggie thinks again of the others in the barracks. "Are the people out there too loud? At a meeting we agreed on no noise after eleven—"

"They're fine. The walk is good for me." He doesn't sound as if he's being honest, but she can tell he's not interested in arguing the point.

"So what happened in the orchard?" she says.

He speaks in a low voice. "Some time ago you told me about a pair of girls next door." She nods, remembering.

"Last night I met them out there. They were by the wrecking yard wall, smoking up with a man from this place."

"Who?" Her first thought is that it was Fletcher. No, it couldn't have been. He was lying beside her all night.

"You have to understand," says George Ray, "I didn't wish to intrude on them. It was dark and I stumbled upon them before I could turn back."

"Who was it?" she repeats.

"I promised not to tell. The man was very worried about people finding out."

"So why are you telling me?" She's unable to keep a hint of frustration from her voice.

"Because I'm concerned," he replies. "A grown man with a couple of girls." He looks at her without blinking. "It could cause problems."

She nods. Whoever it was, if Frank Dodd found out, he could get the police involved. They might use it as an excuse to raid the farm, and with all the dope around, God knows what would come of that.

"They were just smoking up?" she asks.

George Ray takes a moment to consider his answer. "The thin one was sitting in his lap."

All manner of debauchery begins to run through her mind.

"How did they act when they saw you?"

"The man was ashamed, the girls less so." George Ray smiles wryly. "The red-haired one has a sharp tongue."

Maggie remembers well enough. She tries to picture going next door and confronting the two of them about what happened but can't quite manage it.

"So what do you want me to do?" she asks.

He shrugs. "You know this man from last night better than I do."

"But you won't tell me who it is."

"I promised," he repeats. But he adds, "I will only say that those girls should not be out late with a married man."

"Dimitri," she says, and his eyebrows lift enough for her to know she's right.

"I don't wish to cause trouble," he insists.

"Of course." Then a thought occurs to her. "Why tell me? Why not Fletcher?"

George Ray's face grows pensive, as if he has asked himself the same question. "Because you seem to care about the farm's success," he replies. "And because Fletcher might overreact."

He seems embarrassed saying it, but she knows he's right. Fletcher would make a stink, and it could backfire on him. She doesn't particularly care if Dimitri and Rhea leave, but she doesn't want half the people on the farm going with them.

"Thanks for telling me," she says. "I'll think about what to do."

He looks her in the eye and nods, and she feels a vibration go through her at what he's shared, at the fact of his sharing it. As he walks off, she realizes she doesn't want to speak with Dimitri. It will only lead to no good. She'd rather keep the matter between herself and George Ray. And suddenly it seems to her that Dimitri isn't the only one in the wrong.

At that night's meeting, Fletcher wants to talk about people who crash at the farm and don't contribute anything, but Dimitri says they have more important things to discuss. He says they should start a public seminar on organic farming. They should organize a parade through Virgil in solidarity with the Quebec liberation movement. Everyone seems to recognize he's just stirring the pot, because nobody bothers to respond. It's as though they have turned up only to watch him and Fletcher argue.

Then Dimitri announces that what they really need to talk about is their exploitation of black people.

"For Christ's sake," says Fletcher, "you mean George Ray?"

"Some of us marched on Washington," says Dimitri. "Anyone here feel strange having this guy as our personal slave?"

Hands go up around the room. Jim and Sarah from New Jersey, Rhea, Brid. Maggie can't believe Dimitri's gall.

"Is George Ray even Jamaican?" Dimitri says. "He doesn't talk like it."

"He's not going to speak in patois with a bunch of crackers like us," says Fletcher. "Look, he isn't a slave. He gets paid. He chooses to be here."

"But that's a problem too," says Rhea. "He's only here for the money. I thought we wanted everyone committed to each other." Maggie wonders if Dimitri has asked Rhea to take his side or if she's just doing it instinctively, unaware of what she's abetting. Either way, Maggie can't let it go on.

"We shouldn't talk about George Ray when he isn't here," she exclaims. Everyone turns to look at her. She meets Dimitri's gaze and glares at him until he drops his eyes.

"Maggie's right," says Fletcher, standing. "I'll go get him." He sounds glad of her support and eager to have another ally in the room.

"That's right, massa," says Dimitri. "You fetch him for us. It's how your family got rich, isn't it? All those plantations."

Fletcher gives Dimitri the finger but sits back down.

From the kitchen comes the ringing of the phone. Nobody moves, apparently unwilling to miss whatever's about to happen next, so Maggie gets to her feet and runs to answer. As she goes, she's thinking she'll find George Ray herself and ask him to join them. When she picks up the receiver and says hello, the voice at the other end gives her a start. It's Gran.

"I'm sorry for calling," Gran says. "I know you don't want to be disturbed."

"What's up?" Maggie asks, wondering how Gran got the number, thinking it must have been the operator. They should have asked for an unlisted number.

"I'm worried about your father," says Gran. "Has he been in touch with you?" Maggie says he hasn't. "He said he'd phone me Monday from a town near the mission, but he never called."

Maggie tries to suppress a feeling of alarm. "Maybe his ride got a flat tire," she suggests. "Maybe the weather was bad. If you're concerned, you should call the head office in Laos."

"I did. They said they'd look into it."

Maggie tries to think of how to reply. Whenever she talks with Gran, she feels adulthood slip away until once more she's the little girl who argued with her every chance she got. Then she remembers her conversation with Wale in the screening room.

"Gran, did Dad ever mention meeting a friend of mine over there?"

"What sort of friend?" Gran sounds suspicious.

"Just a guy here at the farm. His name's Wale."

"I don't think so. Why?"

"Never mind. It doesn't matter." Maggie takes the telephone cord and winds it about her hand. "Listen, don't get uptight about the missed call. I bet Dad phones next week and says he just slept in or something."

"He never sleeps in," Gran retorts, then goes quiet as if waiting for further reassurance. From the living room come the sounds of voices shouting at each other.

"You'll tell me if it turns out something's wrong?" Maggie asks, and Gran says she will. Maggie edges down the hall, unlooping the cord from her hand as she goes, trying to make out what's being said in the living room.

"Are you all right up there?" Gran asks.

"I'm great. I'm very happy. Hey, I even went to church a while back." Why is she telling Gran that? It's the last thing she wants to be talking about. "The farm's a big hit," she adds quickly. "You should come and see it for yourself." But that's no better; she can't believe what she's saying, and it seems Gran can't either, because there's only silence at the other end.

"Yes, well, I'm sorry for bothering you," says Gran finally, then bids her goodbye.

Maggie puts down the phone, telling herself it's ridiculous of Gran to get worked up over one missed call. Her son is in a war zone. What did she expect? This is what she gets for urging him to go, as if it were heroic, not stupid and dangerous. Now she wants Maggie to fret along with her just because he hasn't been in touch as planned.

But there could have been a bombing raid. He could be laid up with malaria. Maggie tries to put the images out of her head. This is why she doesn't want to hear from him at all. It isn't right to make them worry like this.

She returns to the living room only to find people passing into the hallway. When Fletcher emerges, he murmurs to her, "I'm going to kill him, I really am." He continues onto the porch and lets the screen door slap shut behind him. Maggie waits in the hall until Dimitri appears. Rhea is with him, but Maggie doesn't care.

"I know what you're doing," she tells him.

"Of course you do," he says, seeming unperturbed. "You're a real bright chick." Putting his arm around Rhea, he heads upstairs. It's only for the briefest of moments that Maggie could swear she detects a nervousness in his face.

She decides to wait until morning before talking to Fletcher about Gran's call, but when she wakes up, he's gone. After searching the house, she pokes her head out the mud room door and hears the sound of an axe falling in the orchard. On a hunch she starts toward it, the dry grass of the back lawn scratchy under her bare feet. Upon entering the trees, she walks by piles of branches gathered at the ends of the lanes, newly cut limbs thrown on top of debris from the hurricane. The strike of the axe grows louder until she sees Fletcher chopping at a tree, the ground beneath him littered with wood chips, twigs, and bark. His axe hitting the trunk has a hollow, unsatisfying ring.

"Look at this," he says, bending down to the place where the blade has done its work. He rips away a handful of mealy wood. "Rotten right through."

"Wouldn't it be quicker with the chainsaw?"

"For some reason, I find this more gratifying."

"It lets you exorcise your demons," she suggests.

"What demons? There aren't any demons." He takes another swing with the axe. "Richard Nixon, maybe. Spiro fucking Agnew." He's wearing khaki shorts with a leather belt and she notices he's missed a loop, but she doesn't mention it. "My father phoned this morning," he says between swings. "He wants to sell the farm."

The shock keeps her from replying right away.

"But he promised we could buy it, didn't he?" she finally exclaims.

"He says it's different now that no one else is being sent to Vietnam. He doesn't want me up here anymore." Letting the axe drop to the ground, he begins to push on the cherry tree. It seems to struggle against him, until finally there's a snap like a bone being broken. He retrieves the axe and starts to work on the branches.

"What if we asked him to visit?" she says. Then she remembers proposing the same thing to Gran and decides she should have her head examined. Neither Gran nor Fletcher's father would be persuaded of anything if they saw this place. More likely it would only confirm their fears. Fletcher must be thinking the same thing, because he makes a face.

"I'm sick of it all," he says. "I'm sick of the way he tries to call the shots." Picking up the end of a branch, he drags it down the lane. Maggie grabs another and pulls it after him. "I'm sick of all these people. I go downtown and the storekeepers chew me out because some idiot's been shoplifting again. I'm sick of the slobs and the layabouts, and the ones who hate me because of who my father is. They don't complain about taking a ride on his money, though, do they?" He heaves his branch onto the nearest pile, then bends to snatch up a hubcap from the ground. "Fucking car parts. You know, I bet Frank Dodd throws this stuff over the fence just to piss me off." He hurls the hubcap toward the wrecking yard, but it falls short of the fence. When Maggie embraces him, he stands stiffly in her arms.

"You should have seen my dad in March," he says, his voice now little more than a whisper. "When I told him about dropping out of law school, he looked scared. I'd never seen him scared. Did I tell you that?"

"You didn't," she says, holding him tighter.

"At first I figured it was about the draft, but then I realized it was worse. I was killing all his plans for me. Partner at a law firm, politics. The old man was panicking. I realized I could ask him for just about anything right then and he'd agree, so long as it involved some kind of future for me."

"Fletcher, we're going to make this work," she tells him. "We got a rough start here. Your father will understand. I'll talk to him if you like." She says this even though it's the last thing she wants to do. "We're not leaving. You said next year we could grow enough cherries to start making a profit, right?"

He seems unconsoled. His moustache tickles her forehead as he kisses it, while a squirrel rebukes them from a nearby tree.

"Come on," she says. "Let's not worry about it right now. Let's just go inside." She takes his soft, blistered hand and with slow steps leads him back toward the house.

"What if——" he says in the bedroom. "What if we filmed ourselves doing it?"

He's been undressing her, but her thoughts haven't been on sex. Instead, her mind has drifted to her father, picturing him lost and hacking his way through thick jungle.

"Why would we do that?" she says.

"Because it would be exciting." He runs a hand gently down her side.

"What, and then we'd show it to everyone?"

"Of course not. We'd watch it by ourselves. You know, some other time, as a turn-on."

Maggie doesn't think it would be a turn-on. She finds no pleasure in the thought of watching herself. She wants it to be just her and him with nothing added, no distance, only the press of their bodies. The camera is for the rest of the world.

"What about developing the film?" she says. "Someone at the lab——"

"Nobody watches that stuff. It's done with machines."

"I don't know." But he's set on it, she can tell.

"Remember in Nantucket, when we did it in front of the mirror? It would be like that." She hated the mirror. When she doesn't reply, he sits on the edge of the bed. "Never mind, it was just an idea."

She tries to think of some compromise. "What if it's just

you?" she suggests. As she says it, the notion seems reasonable enough. But Fletcher gains the same lonely, hangdog look as in the orchard. "All right," she says. "Fine, let's do it."

Feeling nauseous, she takes the equipment from the closet and sets up the tripod she recently acquired at the St. Catharines mall. He stands behind her, kissing her neck while she adjusts the focus.

"The settings are all messed up," she says. "Have you been using it?" He shakes his head. "Well, somebody has. Honestly, this place. Everyone's always in your stuff."

She senses that he wants to disagree but has decided it isn't the time for an argument. Instead, he goes to the mattress and waits while she continues to make adjustments.

"The light isn't very good," she complains. "Maybe we should move the bed."

"It doesn't have to be perfect. Just get it going."

On her hands and knees, her face toward the lens and Fletcher behind her, the room is a jumble of shadows and angles. It would be better if she were underneath him, not having to look at the camera. Her skin tingles in the places where she feels watched: the stretch marks from her growth spurt, the legs she hasn't shaved in weeks. The camera's clacking is the only sound in the room other than the soft slap, slap of flesh on flesh. The hands holding her are invisible; she can barely feel them. Where has Fletcher gone? Reduced to a guiding, pounding force. The fear creeps into her that someone will open the door, and every few seconds she turns her head to check.

"Nobody's going to bother us," says Fletcher, sounding impatient.

The noise from the camera stops.

"It's out of film," she says, pulling away.

"Already? Hold on." He gets up and crosses the room, removes the cartridge from the camera, then reaches for another and tries unsuccessfully to tear open its foil envelope.

"Let me do it." She doesn't want him to touch the equipment. After he hands her the cartridge, he flops back on the bed, posing like a model. He seems free of cares, of self-consciousness.

Retrieving the first cartridge from the dresser, she lifts its plastic tab, then begins to pull out film by the handful.

It's amazing that so much can be contained in such a small space, her body and Fletcher's connecting thousands of times over, destroyed in an instant as she yanks them into day. At some unseen level, chemicals are going crazy. On the bed, Fletcher vamps a while longer before he realizes what she's doing.

"Hey, why are you—"

At that moment, she reaches the end of the strip. "I changed my mind," she says, tugging hard and snapping the final length of film in two.

"What's wrong? Didn't you like it?" He sounds genuinely confused. "I must be pretty ugly if the idea of watching me is so horrible."

"Don't be silly. It's just not my style."

Going to him, she tries to smooth out the wrinkles from his forehead. Then his eyes widen as though he has just gained some deep and sobering knowledge.

"Maybe I understand," he says. "I can't take a leak when someone's in the room. Is it the same kind of thing?"

Despite herself, she starts to laugh.

"What? What is it?" he asks, smiling too. "What did I say?"

"Yes, I think you're right. It's probably the same kind of thing."

That night, she tells him it's too hot and she's going to sleep downstairs. It's easier than saying she wants some time alone. When she arrives in the living room, it smells of weed but blessedly lies vacant. She collapses on the couch and tosses for an hour, snatched from the brink of sleep half a dozen times by creaking floorboards and noises from outside.

It's after two when she hears someone come downstairs. Through the doorway, she glimpses the distinctive profile of Dimitri, his pot-belly overhanging his slim legs as he canters down the hall. At the sight of him she has a ludicrous, uncontrollable impulse. After listening for the sound of the mud room door opening and closing, she gets up to follow him.

From the back of the house, she can see a flashlight's beam passing over the ground toward the orchard. She slips out to follow. The barracks is dark and silent. When she reaches the trees, there's enough moonlight for her to make her way while keeping Dimitri well ahead of her. At the wrecking yard wall in the far corner, he comes to a halt. Taking a few more steps, she perceives his outline along with that of the thin girl from next door. They're pressed together in a kiss.

For the first time, Maggie thinks she should have stayed inside. A second later she snaps a branch underfoot. The two bodies separate, and suddenly the flashlight's beam is blinding her.

"What are you doing out here?" says Dimitri in an accusing tone.

"That's the one I told you about," Maggie hears the girl say. "The one who got heavy with me and Jacqueline."

Feeling brave, Maggie steps toward them, shielding her face until Dimitri turns the flashlight away from her. "Hello again," she says. The girl wraps her arms around herself and doesn't reply. "Just you tonight?" Maggie asks her. "Where's your friend?"

"Dead," says the girl sourly. "From smoking that joint last month. It's your fault for not stopping her. Thanks to you, my best friend is dead from a pot overdose."

"Knock it off," Dimitri tells her. To Maggie, he says, "It was her cousin, visiting for the summer. She went back home today."

"Tell her everything, why don't you," mutters the girl.

"Lydia, maybe you should go home," he says.

"What, because of her?" says the girl, gesturing to Maggie. "We just got here." Dimitri stares at her until she gives a humph. "Fine, then." Bending down, she picks up something that has been lying at her feet and hands it to him. Squinting through the night, Maggie realizes it's an aerosol can. "You can explain this to her." Before Dimitri has time to react, the girl kisses him on the lips, then turns and passes Maggie without looking at her.

"What does your father think of you coming over here?"

Maggie asks. "I thought he didn't like hippies." She's determined not to let the girl have the last word.

"My father's an idiot," says the girl. "Tell him everything if you want, I don't care." She turns back to face Dimitri. "If you decide to stop being so square, let me know."

She walks off, following the curve of the wrecking yard wall. Maggie waits for the sound of her footsteps to disappear before addressing Dimitri.

"So that's what you call looking for your cat?"

"I've been doing that too," he replies.

"Are you sleeping with her?"

"That what George Ray told you?"

"George Ray?" She does her best to sound confused, glad for once of the darkness. "I was on the couch tonight and heard you going out."

"So you followed me."

She isn't going to let him make her feel guilty. "How old is Lydia?" she asks. "Fifteen?"

"Sixteen. So yeah, screwing her would be legal up here, if that's where your mind's at. But we've just been hanging out."

A thirty-year-old man hanging out with a teenage girl. He must think Maggie's an idiot.

"What's in that?" she asks, gesturing to the can he's holding.

"Spray paint," he replies, throwing it to her feet. "She brought it. I don't know why." Maggie waits, until he heaves a sigh and says, "The other night I made a joke about writing something on the wall. Maybe she thought I was serious."

"Kids are impressionable," she agrees.

"Oh, fuck off."

Then Maggie remembers her conversation with Rhea in the bathroom and grows angrier. "I can't believe you're doing this under Rhea's nose."

"She isn't wife of the year, you know."

"And trying to get George Ray sent home. You're such an asshole."

"He did tell you, didn't he?"

She doesn't reply. Instead, she says, "If someone found out about the girl and you're still seeing her, you're certifiable." Then, although it would probably be better not to, she adds, "Are you back to sticking needles in your arms too?"

"Rhea told you, huh?" There's a wistfulness in his voice.

"She's worried about you."

"Sure she is." Maggie tries to imagine what he and Rhea have been through for him to speak the words with such sadness and incredulity.

"Does Lydia know you're married?" Maggie asks, and he gives a bark of laughter. "You doing drugs with her?"

"Nothing hard." In a softer tone, he says, "Listen, if you've talked to Rhea, you know things have been tough for us."

"So now you're making things tougher?"

"I know I'm messing up." There's an ache in his voice. "Maggie, I'm hanging by a thread."

"Okay," she murmurs.

"Promise you won't tell anybody about tonight," he says, and she hesitates. George Ray made the same vow, and what good did that do?

"You'll stop seeing the girl?" she asks. It doesn't feel right to bargain over such things. But Dimitri promises, and all at once there seems nothing else to say.

They start back toward the house together. As they go, she has an urge to extract something more from him, a promise to stop arguing with Fletcher, to drop the complaining about George Ray. It would practically be blackmail. Is that what's necessary to keep this place together?

They're almost out of the orchard when Dimitri stops and grabs her arm. "You smell that?"

She inhales and gets a whiff of something awful. "Smells like shit," she replies.

"Cat shit. John-John. That little bugger's around here somewhere." He peers into the branches overhead.

"How do you know it's him?"

"Because he's a vegetarian cat. Their shit smells different."

"A vegetarian cat," repeats Maggie with dismay.

"Yeah, I know. It was Rhea's idea."

"I'm starting to understand why he ran off."

As Dimitri goes through the trees whispering John-John's name, she can hear his hopefulness. She joins him in the search, but they find nothing. When they take up their route back to the farmhouse, it occurs to her that all those times he skipped out on work claiming to look for John-John, he was actually doing it. Probably it's how he came to meet the girl. Maggie has this apprehension and doesn't know whether to think more or less of him for it.

The next morning, she finds George Ray alone in the barracks and tells him she has taken care of things, then provides a cursory account of the night's happenings.

When she says she didn't betray his confidence to Dimitri, he seems pleased. It's only after she has returned to the house that she reflects on George Ray's warm eyes, his grateful smile, and thinks again about the fact that he told her rather than Fletcher the story of his encounter. Probably it's as simple as he said: he didn't want Fletcher overreacting. Yes, that must be it. She barely lets herself consider that maybe she wasn't the only one glad to share a secret between them.

5

When Maggie enters the grocery store in Virgil, the checkout girl asks if she has brought more film to be developed. Obligingly, Maggie hands over a paper bag, then gets herself a cart and pulls out her shopping list. She has gone some distance along the first aisle before she looks up to find the way forward impeded by Wale, slouching in a leather jacket. Beside him is the priest from the stone church. He has a golf cap perched on his high forehead, and his eyebrows look thick enough to be painted on with grease.

"Miss Dunne," he says, sounding genial and cautious at once. "Is good to see you again."

"You two know each other?" she asks.

Wale and the priest exchange a glance, as if to confer about a proper reply.

"We just met," says Wale.

"This friend of yours, he is telling me about your father's work in Laos," says the priest. "Your father sounds like a remarkable man." His eyes narrow when he sees Maggie's irritation, but he presses on. "I wish you to understand, at church you are welcome. I am happy for you to be there—" He stumbles for the words. "—in different arrangement from past time."

"I'm apostate," she says.

"But already you go to church once," he observes. "Something draws you, no?"

"The rain," she replies, and he smiles as if accustomed to recalcitrance.

"Rain is good beginning." Looking at his watch, he announces he must depart, then raises the wire basket he's holding, with its still life of bundled carrots and a single lemon, as if to prove the matter's urgency.

Once he has disappeared down the aisle, Maggie turns on Wale. "Why were you telling him about my father?"

"Just small talk," he replies.

She doesn't believe him. "So this is what you do now? You gossip about my family in grocery stores?"

"Father Josef's not so bad. I think you should give him a chance. He could help you with your hang-ups around your dad."

She doesn't need Wale telling her what her hang-ups are. "My father and I got along fine until he found God. Then we—" Abruptly she stops. An old woman in horn-rimmed glasses is pushing an empty cart toward them. "Look," says Maggie more quietly. "There was something I wanted to ask you."

She tells him about her conversation with Gran and the news of her father's missed call. As she speaks, Wale's face seems to freeze.

"What day was your father supposed to call?"

When she tells him, he falls silent. Finally she slaps the handle of her cart so hard her shopping list goes curlicueing to the floor. "I only told you about this so you'd say everything was all right."

"Sorry. Yeah, of course. It's probably fine." He doesn't even try to sound convincing.

"His ride must have run out of gas, right? Or the phone lines went down."

He studies her face. "You really haven't heard from him? Nothing at all?"

"Like I said, not since May." But that sounds worse than it is. "It's only because I asked him not to write. He's talked with my grandmother plenty of times."

"I'm going to call some people," says Wale. "See if they've heard anything." A look of unease hasn't left him.

"Wale, when you met my father, was he in some kind of trouble?"

"All of Laos is trouble. The place is full of bad cats."

"But my father wasn't mixed up with any of them," she insists.

"He didn't strike me as the type." He avoids her gaze as he says it. "Honestly, if I was worried, I'd go over myself and bring him back with me."

She stares at him a moment, trying to discern if he's serious. "You wouldn't. Your heart's made out of shit, remember? You only do things that are in your interest."

"It would be in my interest," he says with a glint in his eye.

Maggie blushes and looks away. "Don't talk like that. Just call those people and tell me what you hear."

She offers him a ride back to the farm, but he says he has things to do and heads off down the aisle. On her own she continues through the store, cursing when she realizes she's lost her shopping list. She gathers ketchup, buns, and napkins. At the checkout counter, the girl working the till asks her if she's stocking up for tonight's party at the farm.

"You know about it?" Maggie asks.

"Sure," says the girl. "That Fletcher guy you're always with has been inviting everyone in town."

Once the groceries are rung through, the girl reaches for the cigarette case, but Maggie declines the offered pack. She's three weeks late. She still thinks it must be stress.

"Cold turkey?" the girl asks, and Maggie nods. "Yeah, I figured as much. To be honest, right now you don't look so good."

When she returns to the farmhouse, the sun hangs low in the sky and there are a dozen unfamiliar vehicles parked in the driveway. She should be glad of them; drawing new people was Fletcher's whole reason for suggesting a party at the start of the Labour Day weekend. But there's too much to do: groceries to deliver into Rhea's hands, food to prepare, and the projector to set up so people can watch the film Maggie has put together. It's a single movie, not quite the one she has imagined but a version of it distilled from all the summer's footage, a mammoth thing four reels long, each twenty minutes except the shorter final one. And thanks to the checkout girl, who remembered them at the last moment, now Maggie has three more spools of processed film to add, though she'd forgotten all about them. She worries they'll spoil whatever shape and order she's managed to give the thing, but the new footage will have shots of newcomers who aren't in the rest, and people will want to see themselves.

As she carries the grocery bags past a group drinking beer on the front lawn, she sees Fletcher talking to a pair of men who sport aviator sunglasses and Robert Redford haircuts. She has met them before: Karl and Lambchop, friends from Fletcher's boarding school days. Changing course to meet them, she realizes they're in the middle of an argument. When Karl spots her, though, he breaks off to greet her as if she's the surprise visitor and he's the one long settled on the farm. It turns out he and Lambchop are only up for the weekend.

"Did you get the burgers?" Fletcher asks her. "Rhea's waiting—"

"Here," she says, handing him all the grocery bags except the one with the film spools. "Tell her I'll be there soon. I have to start up the projector."

Approaching the porch door, she spies a piece of paper on it that at first she takes to be a new version of Fletcher's principles for the pursuit of happiness. Steeling herself to be embarrassed, she draws closer and sees the words are different.

Give us your tired, your poor, your huddled asses. We accept
dodgers, deserters, and dissidents. We also accept peaceniks,
beatniks, cowlicks, and New York Knicks. We do not accept
American Express.

It could be worse. Looking back, she finds Fletcher still
on the lawn, waiting for her reaction, so she gives him
a thumbs-up and he smiles with a relief that makes her
ashamed of herself. Behind him, the sun has been swallowed by a cloud, the pink edges damming a great reser-
voir of light that looks on the edge of bursting. It would
make a good shot, but for tonight she's decided to leave
the camera in its bag.

Upstairs, the playroom is empty of people though
crammed with chairs, the rest of the house denuded of
them earlier in the day by Fletcher, who said he wants her
to have the biggest audience possible. Moving down the
crooked space between the rows, she reaches the corner
where the editing machine has been tucked away on its
table. With a sloppy taping job she appends the new footage to the end of the final reel, doing it quickly because
she'd rather not think about how inferior the unedited
footage will seem after the rest. Then she winds it by
hand from its old spool onto the new one. As she does, she
remembers her interview with Wale. At first she thought
she'd include it. She hasn't finished synchronizing the
sound, so tonight the film will run silently, and it struck
her as innocuous enough to show a few minutes of Wale's
face at least. When she watched the interview with the
volume down, though, it seemed even more exposing: the

way he doesn't look at the camera, the way his expression grows rigid like it's all he can do to keep himself in check. No one who sees him in that footage could ever look at him again in quite the same way.

Then there's the other clip, the one that has been bothering her awhile.

On an impulse, she goes to the closet in her and Fletcher's bedroom, where she retrieves the curl of film with Pauline and the dead sparrows. Probably Fletcher's right and Brid won't find anything wrong with it. Maybe she won't even see it. Hurriedly, Maggie adds the clip to the reel as well. It's out of sequence, but as finales go, it should do fine.

Loading the first reel onto the projector, she starts up the machine, watches the camper van travelling along the road, and is tempted to linger. She remembers the day at the start of June when she filmed the shot, standing on the shoulder while Fletcher, indulging her, drove back a quarter mile to be recorded going by. There's a comfort in viewing a scene watched many times before, one thing following another in an expected way. Next come the shots of the bedroom with its trash-filled drawers and the crack in the ceiling that still hasn't been fixed. There are so many things to do before the cold weather sets in: insulation for the attic, new mats and coat hooks for the mud room. She ticks through the list in her head before assuring herself that every item is already on paper. Then she forces herself out of the room and downstairs.

In the kitchen, Rhea greets her without disguising her annoyance at Maggie's lateness. There's a handful of people drinking and chatting around the table, but apparently as far as Rhea is concerned their idleness is sacrosanct and only Maggie's work is necessary. All week Maggie hasn't spoken with the Centaurs. Dimitri has stopped making an issue of George Ray, so she has decided to leave things be, not wanting to play Dimitri's chaperone. Lately he and Rhea always seem to be ill-tempered, though, and yesterday at dinner they just smiled coldly when Fletcher called tonight's party a farewell bash for them. Now, as Maggie works alongside her, Rhea stays silent except to order her around. After fifteen minutes of it Maggie excuses herself to change the reels.

During her absence from the playroom, a number of people have discovered the film, some sitting on chairs, some leaning against the wall. Onscreen, there's a row of neon signs she shot in Niagara Falls, which means only a few more seconds remain before the reel ends. When it does, she replaces it quickly to keep the audience from losing interest. Nobody speaks or moves, as if they've gone blank with the screen and will be reanimated when the projector starts again.

By the time she arrives downstairs, people are lining the hall, smoking and talking with one another. Usually by this time in the day the place smells of sweat and dirt, but tonight the air's scented with perfume, beards have been trimmed and faces scrubbed. The living room shades are drawn, leaving the space patched with a darkness that would be hell to film. In the corner, the television sits unplugged, looking sad that no one's watching it. Somebody has turned on the record player, and she can

hear Joni Mitchell above the layers of conversation, singing about pieces of paper from the city hall. It seems just
what Fletcher has envisioned, yet as Maggie pours herself
a glass of lemonade from a pitcher on the coffee table, the
fragments of speech she overhears make it doubtful the
night will produce new residents as he hopes. They all
seem to be talking about the election, going over the day's
Olympics results, or speculating about an amnesty for
draft dodgers. From the dining room comes a high-pitched
voice appealing for a ride across the border.

Passing through the kitchen to the mud room and
onto the lawn, she finds the sun vanished. September has
brought cooler weather, and most of the people outside
are dressed in sweaters or jackets, seeming more adult,
less profligate than before. Fletcher, overseeing the barbecue pit with Karl and Lambchop next to him, is the only
one with bare arms. He grimaces in response to something
Lambchop says, and when serving a hot dog to a little boy,
he doesn't even smile. It's a shame for him to be unhappy,
especially when the party was his idea. It must be Karl and
Lambchop's fault, whatever they're laying on him. When
Karl sees her heading their way, she could swear he elbows
Lambchop and whispers something. Promptly the two of
them sidle into darkness.

"Shouldn't you be filming?" Fletcher asks as she draws
near. The question grates on her. Why should he assume
shooting movies is always what she wants to do? She
doesn't like his wilful innocence either, as if there isn't a
history between them with the camera now.

"What were you talking about with those two?" she asks.

"Nothing much." The way he says it makes her worry, and she waits for more. "They just wanted to know how long we're staying here." He seems embarrassed by her puzzlement. "They've been talking to my father," he adds with some reluctance. It takes a moment before it clicks.

"He sent them to talk you into coming home, didn't he?" Fletcher says of course not, but she's having none of it. Then she remembers the film and checks her watch. Already another twenty minutes have elapsed. Telling Fletcher they'll talk more about it, she hurries back inside. Upstairs, people are filing from the playroom.

"Wait, there's more!" she exclaims, rushing to the projector and fumbling with the reels. Most of the chairs are still occupied, the audience content to chat during the intermission. A few more people whom she caught at the door return to positions along the wall.

The next reel begins with footage from her time-lapse experiments. The audience seems enthralled, and Maggie can't help but be glad. She'd love to film their faces now, their preoccupation with the screen. She should go back to Fletcher, but she stays to watch a little longer, worried he'll only impart bad news: that they've run out of money for good, or that his father has made a final decision to sell the farm. If he told her that, she's not sure what she'd do. All she knows is she couldn't leave now. It isn't because of the people or the work they've done on the house. It isn't because of some political principle. Foolishly and simply, she realizes, it's because of the film. After all the energy and time she's put into capturing the place, framing and editing it into shape, she can't imagine bidding it farewell.

The room continues to fill, people entering loudly but growing quiet as they're arrested by the images on the wall. They doff hats, stifle coughs, settle into seats. Rhea's there in the front row with her boys, waiting for the ritual glimpse of their lost cat. George Ray is there too, his orange toque for once left behind, and she's pleased that finally he's watching something she has filmed.

Then Maggie sees the girl from next door, Lydia, standing by herself at the back. She seems bony and prepubescent in her slip of a dress. Dimitri can't have invited her; he wouldn't be so stupid. Is she here to cause trouble? Their eyes lock briefly, and Lydia's expression reveals nothing. Maggie wonders if the girl knows that Dimitri's wife and children are sitting a few feet from her. She seems less sure of herself than the other times Maggie has encountered her, slouching and straightening against the wall by turns, tugging her dress down over her knees.

Maggie considers confronting her, but then she notices the woman near the projector. Her features are so pale as to be ghostly; only a dark mole on her chin anchors her to the world. Something about her is familiar, and Maggie stares at her until she realizes who it is: the woman from the church. The priest's sister, Lenka. Her beehive has been let down so that her hair flows over her shoulders, but it's her.

The priest could be here too, then, maybe in this room. Wale must have invited him at the grocery store. When the reel comes to an end, Maggie sets to work changing it, conscious of her proximity to the woman. The beam from the projector cuts through the smoky air like a solid thing Maggie could reach out and touch.

"Margaret Dunne," says a voice, the accent unmistakable. A jolt goes through her. How does Lenka know her name?

"Actually, it's Maggie," she replies without looking up.

"Maggie." Lenka pronounces the name awkwardly but with a hint of enjoyment at its intimacy.

"Did your brother come too?" Maggie asks, and Lenka nods. "I didn't think this would be his kind of scene."

"Josef is here because he wants me to come," says Lenka. "We are still new to country, and is quiet in rectory all day. Priest's sister, she meet people easy, but is hard to make friends. You go to house for dinner and people are— what is expression?" Maggie shrugs, but Lenka finds it. "On best behaviour!" She lifts the wineglass in her hand, whether to toast her own vocabulary or the hospitality of local parishioners, it isn't clear. With stern, drunken eyes she looks at Maggie. "Josef says you do not like talking of father. Fine, relax, I do not talk of him." Maggie flicks the switch on the projector while Lenka takes a mouthful from her glass, then tips down the dregs. "Come to Mass, do not come. It doesn't matter to me. But church is trustworthy, Maggie, in way you cannot trust people." She pauses, frowning. "I do not speak properly for making friends. Pardon me, please. I drink too much tonight."

Maggie says it's all right and excuses herself, not knowing where she's headed. The house has grown hot with bodies and makes her dizzy; for a moment, going down the stairs, she worries she'll be sick. On the ground floor a current of cool air steals along the hall, carrying Fletcher's voice from the porch as he holds forth about Sargent Shriver. Tonight she has no stomach for Sargent Shriver.

In the kitchen, she glimpses Wale just about to slip through the back door. When she calls out to him, people at the table look up, hearing the edge in her voice. He turns and she sees his beard is gone. She has always thought that men who shave their beards regain a measure of their youth, but Wale seems older than before.

"You invited the priest, didn't you?" she says as she crosses the room, speaking loudly enough that conversation around the table halts. Wale doesn't become defensive, though. Instead, he gazes at her with something like fondness.

"Maggie, where's your camera?" He's wild-eyed, but she doesn't think he's drunk; maybe some other drug. "My kingdom for a camera! United States of a Camera. Ha!" He begins to sing out of tune. "*O Camera, we stand on guard for thee . . .*" Abruptly he breaks off and speaks in a stage whisper. "You should see the way you look now. The light on your face. Really lovely." Without warning, he leans in as if to kiss her, and she ducks away. There's a titter from someone at the table. "You know, I didn't come up here for Brid," he tells her.

"Don't say that."

"I wanted to spend time with you. You must have figured out that much."

"You're stoned."

"You don't even realize, you make me—" He hesitates, and she scrambles to say something so he'll stop, but he gets there first. "You make me want to be better."

"I don't believe you." She's sure that all the eyes in the room are on them now.

"I swear, whatever kind of guy I am, I never meant for anything to happen, okay?"

The words create a feeling of vertigo in her. "What are you talking about? Have you heard something about my dad?"

"Just remember what I'm telling you. I promise you, I'm going to look after things." Before she can respond, he steps out the door to the mud room, and she sees there's a rucksack in his hand.

A few seconds later, a shriek comes from upstairs, followed by peals of laughter. Her first thought is that word is already spreading about his attempted kiss. Then someone calls down, "You've got to see this." The people at the table start out of the room and Maggie finds herself abandoned, her mind still on Wale's rucksack.

It isn't long before more partygoers come in from the backyard to investigate the ruckus, and she's swept along with them toward the second floor, trying to imagine what has happened. Maybe Lydia's making a scene with Rhea. Or maybe Brid is watching the film and has viewed the dead bird in Pauline's hand. Maggie's legs grow heavy, but there are more bodies in motion behind her and she's compelled upward.

Everyone is ascending the stairs except a lone pair making their way down. It's Frank Dodd dragging Lydia by the hand. His bald head is beet red, his eyes angry slits, while Lydia's skin is bloodless. Frank sees Maggie ahead of him and looks as if he might strike her.

"You people," he seethes. "You people are sick."

A second later they have passed by her and Lydia turns to flash her a helpless, desperate look.

Whatever has happened, it isn't over, because upstairs the hallway is packed tightly with people pressing toward the playroom door, straining to look in. Maggie has to push past them to get inside. When she finally enters the room, everyone is staring at the wall and what's projected there, and with horror she realizes why.

Beyond the backs of heads and wisps of smoke is a shot of her and Fletcher's bedroom. The camera's steady, as if mounted on its tripod. Sunlight pools on the floor, revealing a castaway pair of men's underwear and a single brown sock. The comforter on the bed has been pulled down. Fletcher lies there on his back, not quite centred, his body sprawled across the sheets, naked, the light falling across him such that his ribs are individuated, countable. His legs are straight out, one foot hidden beneath a corner of the comforter, the other cut off by the frame. He faces the camera with a contented demeanour, head propped on a pillow, one arm flopped across the bed as though forgotten. With the other hand, he strokes his penis.

Fingertips run down the shaft, then squeeze and push up over the foreskin. Testicles hang one a little lower than the other, each disturbed by the hand's motion, the skin that encloses them bright pink in contrast with the baked brown of the torso and the bleached thighs, the genitals so brightly coloured they're almost not part of the body but an alien thing tugged at in a lazy effort to remove it. The fist works its way up and down. His hips lift from the bed to reveal the cleft of buttocks and a momentary wedge of darkness beneath them that collapses and vanishes as they compress upon the sheets.

The camera's focus is there at the root of him. His face is slightly blurred, subtleties of expression lost to the low resolution of the film stock, which registers only a kind of growing studiousness and flickers of pleasure that come and go with the flash of teeth. Maggie waits for a cutaway shot, a pan, a dissolve. Briefly a bird's shadow flits through the square of light on the floor. The camera doesn't flinch.

The soundtrack is whispers and guffaws. She dares not look around. Why does no one act? It's as if they're waiting for something. The comments grow louder, the laughter more raucous. Are Rhea and the boys still here? The priest's sister? Someone says it's disgusting and they should shut it off already, but Maggie seems to have lost a connection to her limbs. The image of Fletcher on the wall wavers. Squiggles of light dance in front of her. He tugs with more energy now, over and over, as though the film's being rewound and replayed. She can't get herself to move.

"Lucky Maggie!" says someone in the crowd. "He's hung like a horse."

Somebody else says, "If he doesn't come soon, I'm going to."

On the wall, he's smiling and talking to the camera. What could he be saying? She fears that soon she's going to see herself step into the frame, her pasty backside moving to straddle him, but they never did such things with the camera there. His expression is awful, so blithe and unaware of his audience. She looks around the room in a panic, wondering where he could be.

"Oh, Maggie, hi," someone says, noticing her for the first time. Others turn toward her.

"The director!" someone else calls out. "Nice flick."

Stumbling into the person beside her, she realizes it's Dimitri. The scene on the wall has been happening forever. Pushing off him, she lurches toward the projector. Before she gets there, though, all sound drops away. It's no longer her they're watching. She knows what has happened, and she wants to call out for him to leave. A moment later someone greets him with a friendly, mocking cheer.

He hasn't even realized what it is. In the doorway, he grins like it's a surprise party. He's about to make some remark when he notices what's on the wall. Maggie watches as his face dies.

He takes a step back as if pushed in the chest. A few people snicker. When Maggie recovers herself enough to start for the projector again, the image on the wall has changed: a group is playing baseball in the backyard. Clouds graze blue sky, and the long grass bristles in the wind.

"When does the next show start?" says Dimitri.

Fletcher seems not to recognize him. "Get out," he says. No one moves.

"Hey, relax—" Dimitri begins.

"Get out!" Fletcher cries. With arms extended, he rushes at the other man, grabs him by the shirt, and tries to drag him toward the door. Dimitri's beer bottle flies from his hands, spraying its contents across the carpet. People on all sides step back as the two men clutch each other, the tendons in Fletcher's neck taut, his jaw clenched in effort. Dimitri is heavier and more powerful; it isn't

long before he has Fletcher pinned to the floor. "Get out!"
Fletcher screams. When he finally stops struggling, Dimitri
releases his grip, stands, and adjusts his wrenched shirt,
while Fletcher remains on the floor, panting and shouting
for them all to go.

After Dimitri leaves, others follow, a few nodding at
Maggie with the sympathy of downcast eyes.

"I don't see what the problem is," she hears one of them
whisper to another. "Everybody jerks off."

Once Fletcher and Maggie are the only people left in the
room, he's the one who speaks.

"I want them gone," he declares, then shoots her a
savage look, as if it's she who has betrayed him. A moment
later he's in the hall shouting at people, ordering them off
the property. Gradually his voice diminishes; she hears
automobile engines starting up. From below there's the
sound of something heavy hitting the floor, glass breaking, and more shouted threats. On the projection wall the
baseball game comes to an end, and the film of Pauline and
the birds begins to play.

Maggie watches until the screen is white. Afterward, she
goes about putting away reels in their canisters, moving
the projector to the corner, and folding up chairs. The air
stinks of smoke, though the window is open as far as it will
go. The carpet is wet with beer and wine. She heads to the
bathroom for paper towels and finds the door open but the
room occupied.

It's the priest and his sister. He sits on the radiator by
the toilet in a turtleneck and corduroys, looking not much
older than Maggie. Next to him, Lenka kneels over the

toilet. Her mascara has run down her cheeks. He's holding her hair gently in one hand, while with the other he rubs the small of her back.

"Sorry," he says to Maggie when he notices her. "Something she ate, maybe." The words are spoken without conviction or any need to be believed. Maggie nods and closes the door to grant them some privacy.

The porch and front lawn are deserted. Most of the cars are gone, including the camper van. Where could he have driven? Bottles, potato chips, and paper cups lie scattered across the hallway floor. In the living room, candles and incense still burn, while the coffee table has been tipped on end, its glass top smashed. Carefully, she begins to gather the shards. It feels urgent to clean everything up without delay. Then, as she snuffs candles, a long, anguished cry from the kitchen prickles her neck. She moves toward it without wanting to know its source.

At the table, Brid is slumped holding Pauline, who clings to her mother's neck and stares into the distance. Neither of them acknowledges Maggie when she sits beside them.

"He's gone," Brid mumbles. "He's gone again." A short handwritten note lies before her on the table.

Maggie remembers the rucksack and doesn't know what to say. She wants to offer comfort but can't quite do it. Something is telling her that if she speaks, Brid will blame her for Wale's leaving.

"Did he say where he's headed?" Maggie finally asks. A horrible thought has occurred to her, one that somehow she's sure is the truth. Wale has gone to Laos, and it's because her father truly is in trouble. "Did he give any hint?"

Brid shakes her head and holds Pauline more tightly. "Your father is a bastard," she whispers to the girl. "He's such a big, big bastard."

As Maggie sits there, another idea comes out of nowhere. No, it's been brewing in her awhile. She hasn't wanted to think about it, but there's a lingering question about the shot of Fletcher on the bed. A technical question, simple and disastrous. All of a sudden, knowing the answer to it seems like the most pressing thing there is.

"Brid," she says, "were you upstairs?" Brid shakes her head. "But you heard what happened? Brid, I don't know how to say it—"

"Spit it out," Brid growls, and somehow this animosity allows Maggie to speak what's on her mind.

"Someone had to be running the camera."

Brid looks at her with bemusement. "What—you think it was me filming him? Is that what you think?" She laughs in a way that sounds like a cough and holds Pauline even more tightly. "Go find your boyfriend and ask him."

For hours, Maggie cleans and tidies, the lights burning in every room. Occasionally a person crosses her path, hurrying on at the sight of her or hesitating so that she has to ward off conversation. Through the kitchen window she sees human shapes passed out on lawn chairs. At some point the Centaurs trundle in from the barracks, each with a sleeping boy over a shoulder, and make their way upstairs. When she checks a few minutes later, their door is closed and the light off.

At two o'clock, sitting at the kitchen table with an empty mug, she hears a vehicle pull into the drive, then the front door opening and closing. Eventually there's a clang above her. It happens again as she climbs the stairs. When she reaches the top, Dimitri emerges from his bedroom in pyjamas, bleary-eyed and dishevelled.

"Go back to bed," she tells him. "I'll take care of it." The playroom terrifies her now, but there's a muttering from within that she recognizes as Fletcher's voice.

He sits in the middle of the carpet with a film strip lying all around him. It's off its reel, hundreds of feet long, twisted, knotted, and tangled about chair legs. The white projection wall is gouged where he has flung the reel against it. He isn't wearing his glasses. What happened to them? He shouldn't have been driving without his glasses.

"Where is everyone?" he says.

"Gone," she answers, "or hiding in the barracks."

Without a moment's pause, he says to her, "You humiliated me."

Her sympathy drops away. He can't accuse her of such a thing. Has he been thinking it all this time? "I didn't see it till the rest of them did," she says. "How was I to know what was on the reel?"

He looks unbelieving. "But you always watch them first. Always."

"I was busy, there wasn't time. I just stuck it on." She's talking fast, searching for lines of defence, and recalls the start of the evening. "You! You were hurrying me along, remember? So I could help Rhea." She waits for him to relent, then lapses into even darker thoughts. "You must think I'm an idiot," she says, not hiding her bitterness. He seems surprised by this statement, but not as surprised as she would like.

"What are you talking about?"

"On the film, you were speaking to someone. Who was running the camera?"

He remains quiet. She thinks she can hear movement in the hall. Anybody could be listening. Well, let them.

"It was only me," he replies. "I was talking to you." He shakes his head. "You thought I was with somebody else? Jesus." The little smile he gives her makes him seem even more distant. "I meant it as a surprise for you, when you were putting together the reel." The smile gives way to a look of despair.

"But then—" She doesn't know how to finish. What kind of a surprise could he have intended? "Was it supposed to be a joke?"

"I—I thought it would turn you on."

"You thought it would . . ."

The time in bed with the camera returns. Doesn't he remember it? Wasn't he there?

"Anyhow, it was your idea," he continues. "You're the one who said it should just be me."

"My God," she breathes. He's never seemed so far away. Even his attention has drifted to another place. When it returns, his eyes are hardened with some frightening certitude.

"I can't stay here anymore," he says.

Can't stay. It's a marvel how the words stab her.

"Don't say that," she tells him. "Because of the film? Fletcher, what happened is awful, but you can't—"

"I need to go away," he insists, then sits there in some unfathomable contemplation.

"For how long?"

"I don't know. A while."

"I see." There's a long silence. "And what about me?"

He blinks a few times, as if until now he hasn't considered this detail. "You can come too." He says it with no enthusiasm, only tosses it out like a coin.

"That's very kind."

"I didn't mean it like that—"

"Where will you go?" It's not her voice that asks the question; it's some other person's.

"I don't know. Back to Boston, I guess." He doesn't protest that she has referred only to him, not both of them.

"After all the work we've done? There are so many people here now."

"Bunch of jerks," he mumbles. "Most are leaving anyhow."

She can't believe what he's saying. "But I don't want to go. I want to stay here—with you."

This thought seems to overwhelm him. "Didn't you see this?" he shouts, grabbing loops of film and thrusting them toward her. "Of course you did. Everyone saw it!"

It's too much. Backing away, she escapes to the living room, hoping he'll follow. On the couch, she weeps and wills unconsciousness. It's cold, she should get a blanket from the closet, but she has no energy to move. Her thoughts buck against her exhaustion until at some point she starts awake and realizes he's standing over her. Through the window is the blue bruise of the pre-dawn.

"I'm sorry." His lips touch her cheek. "It'll be all right. Come up to bed."

"Don't leave," she says.

"I won't," he tells her. "I promise, I won't go anywhere."

In their room, he's the only one who sleeps. Maybe it won't be so bad. A few days of teasing, perhaps a few weeks. Dimitri will be the worst; he'll never let it go. To hell with him. He and Rhea will leave soon anyhow. And what of Wale? He couldn't really have gone to Laos. He'll be back tomorrow—and even if he isn't, so what? He and Brid were never really close, except in some toxic, mutually degrading way. Maggie wonders how many women there have been for him since Pauline was born.

Her shoulders and hips work themselves into the bed, casting a mould of her body in the mattress. The ticking from the alarm clock maddens her.

At sunrise, she goes to the playroom, where the un-spooled film still lies spread out like skein-work. She winds it back onto its reel, trimming the torn ends and taping them together. Once she's finished, she can't help herself; she places the film in the editor and finds the beginning of the scene, then plays it back. Eventually Fletcher enters the frame, removing underwear and socks before lying on the bed. She watches, telling herself she's finding the end so she can cut out the whole sequence. When she reaches it, though, a tremendous fatigue comes over her and she returns to their room. For an hour she sleeps beside him, until nausea awakens her and she hurries to the bathroom, making it just in time.

A few inches of fetid water at the bottom of the pit prevent Gordon and Yia Pao from sitting down, forcing them to lean against the muddy walls when they want a rest from standing. Gordon's beard is a tangle, and his skin is clean only in rivulets where sweat has washed away the earth. Yia Pao is worse. There are scabbing cuts all across his face and a gash on his forehead that won't stop bleeding. In his arms he holds Xang, the baby's clothes so stained as to have lost their former colour altogether. The little boy's skin is jaundiced, his face covered in mosquito bites. Gordon yells in a rasping voice for the guards to come, while Yia Pao takes a piece of banana into his mouth and chews it, then removes a bit of the mush with his fingers and tenderly feeds it to his son.

"They must be dead," says Gordon. "I'm going to do it."

"Wait a little longer," says Yia Pao.

"They're gone. It's been a day."

"It could be a test," replies Yia Pao. "They could be waiting up there to beat us."

Gordon looks at his companion's forehead. "They haven't needed excuses for that." He squints up toward the edge of the pit. "If we wait any longer, we'll be too weak."

"I'm already too weak," says Yia Pao. "It could be miles to a village."

"They must get their supplies from someplace close," Gordon observes. "What if they don't come back? Xang needs milk."

"He won't get it from the jungle," says Yia Pao. But he holds Xang out toward the other man. "Take him. Take him and go."

"Don't be ridiculous," replies Gordon. "You're coming too."

"You'll move more quickly without me."

Gordon doesn't budge, so Yia Pao pulls the baby back to his chest and offers a forefinger for Xang to suck on. "I want him to live. There are no more men in my family. My father, all my brothers, my cousins are gone. Xang's the only one left."

"You're left too."

"You don't understand, Gordon. I wasn't a good husband. I wish to be a good father."

"You were a fine husband," says Gordon. "You loved your wife, didn't you?"

Yia Pao nods. "But when I returned from Vientiane to marry her, I had been to school, I had lived in the city. I thought myself better than her or my parents. I laughed at things she said. Then a bomb struck the village and took her."

"Yia Pao—" Gordon begins, but he isn't listening. Moisture beads and falls from the tip of his nose.

"Gordon, it was the work of your God. He was teaching me a lesson."

Gordon is about to say something but only purses his lips.

"I didn't learn the lesson right away," says Yia Pao, "so the next bomb took my parents too. God is a stubborn teacher." He lifts his head and stares at the white scar on Gordon's neck. "Is it really from a war?"

Gordon flinches and averts his gaze, staring into the pool of water at his feet. A moment later he reaches up to put his hand on a thick black root protruding from the earth just above his head. With the toe of his boot, he begins to kick into the wall of the pit. Once he has created a secure foothold, he hoists himself and starts to kick another. Yia Pao watches him rise. The only sounds are Gordon's grunts as he labours toward the top, struggling to keep hold of the slick walls, and a rain of muddy earth falling into the water at Yia Pao's feet. At last Gordon reaches the edge of the pit and lifts himself from view.

Yia Pao rocks the baby and stays silent. After a time, a shadow passes over his face. Then a length of nylon rope tumbles into the pit with a towel tied at the end to form a sling.

"I don't see them anywhere," says Gordon from above. "But they left the fire going. We have to hurry. Send Xang first, and then I'll pull you up."

The afternoon sun lords over the farm. A pair of jack-rabbits grazing on the front lawn dart across the grass as Maggie returns from her walk. She has gone all the way to Virgil and tramped every street in the village without really taking in anything. She told Fletcher she would be an hour; it's been over two, but she doesn't care. She needed the time alone.

From the wrecking yard comes the rumble of heavy machinery and the screech of rent metal. Ahead of her, near the porch, Lambchop and Karl sit in a red Alfa-Romeo convertible looking impatient. As she approaches them, Fletcher steps out onto the porch with a pair of suitcases in his hands.

"Where were you?" he calls out. "You missed lunch."

"I told you, a walk," she replies, still focused on the suitcases. "What's going on?"

"Karl and Lambchop are heading out."

"Those suitcases are yours, aren't they?"

Suddenly his attention is caught by a line of crows on a telephone wire near the road.

"I'll come back soon," he tells her. He says it like an apology.

Maggie stops in place. In her peripheral vision, she apprehends Lambchop and Karl easing out of the car, then disappearing around the corner of the house. Fletcher descends the porch stairs and walks over to her before setting down the cases.

"You were going to leave without telling me?" she says.

"No, of course not—"

"What were you going to do? Phone from Niagara Falls? From Boston?"

Fletcher refuses to look her way. "I want you to come with me. You could go back to school, start teaching again—"

She kicks at the ground and feels pain shoot through her toe. "Fletcher, you can't do this. You can't try running off and then ask me to join you."

"I need some time to think. Don't you see? Everybody else can stay, and—"

"Have you already checked with your father? Does everyone else know too?" None of what's happening seems real. "I don't understand what I've done for you to treat me like this."

Fletcher stands blinking with his face toward the sun. "It's not you. It's that film! The whole place is poisoned now. I can't stay, really I can't." He takes off his glasses to scrub at a lens with the corner of his shirt. Then he notices Karl and Lambchop hovering at the side of the house and waves them toward the convertible.

"I'm sorry," he tells her. "I'll be back, I promise." When he moves to hold her, she shrugs him off, so he picks up the suitcases again and starts for the car.

"Wait!" she says. "Why do you have to leave right now? This isn't the way to say goodbye!"

"Karl and Lambchop need to be back in Boston tonight. Please, Maggie—"

"Then drive yourself tomorrow in the camper. Don't go now." Karl and Lambchop are already in the car again, watching her. "You know," she says to Fletcher, "I'm three weeks late."

It takes him a few seconds to comprehend what she means. Behind him, Karl lays on the horn, and Fletcher yells at him to knock it off.

"It's probably just stress," he tells her. "You shouldn't worry—"

Maggie kicks the ground again. "You're heartless, you really are."

"Christ, how can I be heartless when I'm asking you to come with me? Please let me go. Don't you see? If you care about me at all . . ." His voice falls apart, and he bows his head.

Maggie gazes across the lawn, wanting to tell him every-thing at once, all she has kept from him lately to make his life easier: Wale meeting her father; Gran's phone call; Dimitri and the girl.

"All right," she says. "If you have to go, go."

He's slow raising his eyes. "Really?" Some barrier in him gives way. Dropping the suitcases, he moves to hold her. "I'm so sorry, I really am, but—"

It's the last word that makes her break free and rush toward the porch. Even when he calls to her, she keeps on going. Inside the door, she stops and hears Lambchop say, "You told her you're coming back, right? Why's she acting like such a baby?" With that, she runs for the stairs.

Sitting on their bed, she wraps her arms around herself, while from the drive come the sounds of the convertible being loaded. At one point Karl laughs. On an impulse, she leaps up and opens a drawer in the dresser. It's empty. So is another, and another. She turns and notices an envelope lying on the windowsill. Before she can go to examine it, the car's engine starts and there's the crunch of tires on gravel. A line of reflected sunlight travels like an arrow across the bedroom wall. The noise slowly fades and vanishes.

6

"You okay?" asks Brid the next morning when Maggie enters the kitchen.

She nods, trying not to pay attention to the nausea that woke her, and pours herself coffee while Brid sits at the table brushing Pauline's hair. A minute later, Maggie's stomach leaps. She covers her mouth and flees the room.

It's half an hour before she makes her way into the orchard. Long-fallen cherries lie squashed and puckered underfoot, crawled upon by yellow jackets. The brush piles wait for her at the ends of the lanes. Reaching the first one, she bends low to light a match. The flames spread quickly, and soon the air is plumed with smoke. She moves along a beaten-down path in the grass until her matches are exhausted and half a dozen piles are aflame.

From the barracks comes George Ray, running and shouting like a madman. "What are you doing? The whole orchard could go up."

"It was on a list of jobs that Fletcher left," she replies.

He shakes his head vehemently. "Too early. Everything's tinder." Even as he says it, sparks begin to meander into the trees. From one of the piles there's a rifle shot of exploding bark. Above the crackle she hears the chorus of geese calling to each other, a phalanx of dark dots moving south.

George Ray enlists her help in dragging a hose across the orchard, then begins to spray down the piles. She stands watching him, fearful and curious. When the water meets the flames, there's a hiss like static through giant speakers.

Eventually the flames abate and he takes up a place beside her, sweating in the cool air as the doused mounds smoulder.

"I'm sorry," she says. "I just wanted to get it all done."

He pats her on the shoulder and tells her not to worry. When she returns to the farmhouse, Brid's waiting at the mud room door in her bikini top, one of its straps askew to reveal the sear of a tan line. She smiles and extends an arm to draw Maggie inside.

"Good idea, kiddo," she says. "Burn the place down."

It takes an hour of seclusion in her room before Maggie thinks that she should have filmed the fires. There's still time for her to record the ashes, maybe even a whiff of smoke, but when she goes for the camera, it isn't there. Then she discovers it isn't just the camera; all her reels are missing, including the one with Fletcher on the bed. She searches the house and finds nothing. He'll have destroyed the film by now. It isn't right. Those reels weren't his to take.

Twenty-four hours and no phone call from him. There's just the single page of writing he left for her in the envelope, a list of instructions laying out in legalistic prose what to do while he's away. George Ray Ransom's contract is to be extended until the thirty-first of October, and only Margaret Dunne and Brigid Garland shall continue in the employ of Morgan Sugar. Fletcher listed dozens of farm chores too, with no suggestion of when he might return.

At lunch, Maggie breaks the news that there's no more money forthcoming. Dimitri says it doesn't matter because he and Rhea are heading back to Cambridge anyway. Everyone else is furious; almost unanimously, they vow to pack their bags. Jim and Sarah won't even look Maggie in the eye, as if it's her fault. They don't seem to care when she tells them Fletcher will be coming back soon.

Most go that evening, the rest the next day. Nobody expresses regret or concern for her well-being, and no one asks her to accompany them. Their hearts are already bent on some other place. Part of Maggie wants to cry out, "Wait! I could be pregnant," but they're a pack of mutineers. After each round of goodbyes she circles through the house picking up relics forgotten or forsaken: clothes, books, homemade jewellery, toys. In the playroom, she stares at the blank wall, waiting for it to present her with some revelation.

The Centaurs are the last to go, Rhea with her makeup on, Dimitri freshly shaved, Judd and Jeffrey in their good shoes as if they're heading off to church. It's Labour Day, exactly when Dimitri always said they'd leave. Maggie expects him to be triumphant in the wake of Fletcher's desertion, but he bids her farewell without any evident emotion. She wonders whether he has bothered saying goodbye to Lydia. When Maggie waves from the porch as they drive off, none of them returns the gesture.

Only Brid and Pauline stay. Maggie half wishes they'd go too, but Brid expresses no interest in leaving. A few minutes after the Centaurs' departure she starts doing calisthenics in the living room, jumping in place and shaking out her arms, while Pauline lies on the couch watching TV with her doll.

"Cheer up, babe," Brid says to Maggie. "You've still got me, at least. We'll be a real pair here, sitting in our rockers all day."

This is an image to chill Maggie's blood, yet at dinner Brid's too preoccupied with Pauline to bother with Maggie, wiping her daughter's nose and cutting up her food as if she's a baby. Maggie considers asking about Wale but thinks it safer not to mention him. After Pauline has been put to bed, the two of them watch television without speaking. Onscreen, people are talking politics; it turns out that Canadians are having their own election soon. Maggie's too distracted by the day's departures to be interested. Until Fletcher returns, this is how things are going to be: just her and Brid, alone together for hours. What is Brid thinking and feeling as she sits there? Might she too be waiting for the phone to ring? Maggie imagines Wale on his way to Laos. No, it's impossible. He wouldn't go there just because of one missed call. Even Wale isn't that deranged.

"Brid," Maggie can't resist asking, "did Wale ever mention my father to you?"

At Wale's name, a ferocity comes into Brid's eyes. "Why would he do that?"

"He said he met him in Laos, when he was on the run from the army."

Brid laughs harshly. "Wale's a bullshitter."

"So he never mentioned my dad?"

"He never even mentioned Laos. When he called after he'd gone AWOL, he told me he was in Saigon."

Then Maggie notices the silver watch on Brid's wrist. It's too big for her and hangs loosely, the skin beneath looking irritated. Before Maggie can turn away, Brid catches the direction of her gaze.

"Yeah, I stole it from him," she says. "Figured he might cut out, so I grabbed a souvenir. I'm not proud of it." She waits for Maggie to challenge her, then replies to an unspoken allegation. "Some people give you zilch. If you want anything from them, you have to take it for yourself."

The next day, Maggie wakes up determined to make the best of things. For breakfast she eats dry toast and tries to ignore the nausea's return. Afterward, with Fletcher's account books open on the kitchen table, she begins to make her own lists: bills to pay, jobs to do, vegetables to grow next summer. Brid comes upon her going over figures and offers to help, though Pauline tugs at her to play outside. Maggie says she'll manage on her own, then at lunchtime bolts down a sandwich before Brid and Pauline can turn up. When she's finished, she heads to the barracks for a talk with George Ray, taking with her a list of questions about the orchard. Since the incident with the burning brush piles she has spoken with him only once, to confirm the extension of his contract. Then he told her Fletcher had already raised the subject the morning he left. It must have been the busiest hour of Fletcher's life, packing, scribbling orders, and telling everyone but her that he was leaving, all while she was out on her walk, imagining how the two of them might go on together.

At the barracks door, George Ray greets her with a welcome that seems at once thankful and anxious, as if someone's pressing a revolver to his back. When she steps inside, she finds Brid sitting at the table. There's no sign of Pauline.

"Where's—"

"Napping," says Brid.

Maggie nods and surveys the barracks. As if by magic, the place has been rendered immaculate, all traces of other inhabitants removed. She thinks of George Ray stripping mattresses, clearing the fridge of other people's mouldy leftovers, desperate to reclaim his solitude.

"We were just talking about George Ray moving into the house," says Brid casually, as though this notion has been circulating for a while. A glance at George Ray confirms it isn't his idea. "It would make things easier on all of us," Brid continues. "For one thing, we could share the cooking."

"We settled this back in June," Maggie replies. To George Ray, she says, "You'd rather have your own space, right? It's fine if you want to stay out here."

"Maggs, you're such a wet blanket," says Brid, then flashes a smile at George Ray, who's avoiding her gaze. Her smile wavers, and Maggie worries about what's at stake for Brid in all this. Judging by George Ray's expression, he has a similar concern.

"It's a very kind offer," he says in a diplomatic tone. "I think, though, I'd prefer to remain where I am. Wouldn't want to cause any botheration."

"Don't like us?" says Brid, pushing back from the table so that the chair legs grind against the floor. "Fine, then."

"Some people need peace and quiet," says Maggie, trying to sound lighthearted but earning a scowl.

"My wife wouldn't approve," adds George Ray, looking hopeful that this will put an end to things.

"Wife, schmife," mutters Brid.

Then Maggie has an idea. "What about—" she begins, trying to think through the consequences before saying it aloud. "What about having dinners with us?"

Brid looks unimpressed by this suggestion but holds her breath and waits. For a time George Ray ponders the idea, then nods.

"Dinners," he agrees, and Brid rolls her eyes.

"How romantic." Brid stands up from her chair. "All right, then, see you at six for pork and beans." With that, she starts toward the door. Maggie hasn't had a chance to talk things over with him as she'd like, but Brid lingers at the threshold waiting for her, so Maggie bids him goodbye and heads out too.

In the living room, they have set up TV trays to hold their plates as they watch the Olympics, Brid and Maggie from the couch, George Ray from the armchair. What they find when they turn on the television isn't what they expected. Dead athletes, masked men with guns. An anchorman wearing a yellow blazer sits in a Munich studio recounting what has happened so far. At her mother's feet, Pauline watches not the picture but George Ray, who occasionally glances back at her and sticks out his tongue, then smiles in a friendly manner. Pauline looks to her mother as though scandalized and expecting that Brid will put a stop to such behaviour, but Brid's too focused on the television to notice.

The telephone rings and Maggie hurries to the kitchen, trying not to hope it's Fletcher. When she snatches the receiver from the wall, she discovers it's him after all. Right away she asks him where he is.

"My parents' place," he says. It's where she guessed he would go.

"You see what's on TV?" she asks.

"The hostages? Yeah, it's crazy."

"They've been at the airport for hours now."

"Hell of a publicity stunt. Those guys have the whole world watching."

"Publicity?" she says, incredulous. "They've killed innocent people."

"They've also got people talking about the Palestinians."

She tries to relax her shoulders. "Four days without calling, Fletcher. You want to argue about the Middle East?"

"No," he replies. Then he says, "Rhea called today. She said everybody has left but Brid and Pauline."

"And George Ray. Things are under control, don't worry. Your instructions were very helpful." She doesn't bother to disguise her resentment. "Listen, what happened to the camera and all the film?"

"I took them with me." He offers no further explanation. "You want them back?"

"Of course I do! The camera's mine."

"I know. I wasn't thinking very clearly." She worries it's a bid for sympathy and doesn't want to pay it heed, but she can't help it.

"How are you?"

"I'm okay," he replies. "The last couple of days have been hard. To distract myself I started volunteering for McGovern."

All pity in her vanishes. "You're kidding, right?"

"Just at the local campaign office. A few hours a day."

"What about the farm? Aren't you coming back?"

"Right now?" He says it like it's unthinkable.

"You said you couldn't face people, remember? Well, now there's no one left to face." With the phone tucked under her chin, she goes to the cupboard, pulls out a plate, and imagines throwing it against the wall.

"I need a bit more time," he says.

"How much?"

"Two weeks." He says it as if expecting an argument.

She takes a breath and slides the plate back onto the shelf. "Fine," she says.

"Thanks for understanding." Then abruptly he asks,

"You going to keep watching TV now?"

"I doubt it." Already he's bringing the conversation to a close. Is he so eager to be rid of her? "Fletcher—"

"Hey, did you pay the electricity bill?"

"Yes, I've looked after everything."

"Thanks. Listen, I'll call you again soon." His voice is tentative, as though he knows what he's getting away with.

"Sleep well," she says wearily.

"You too. Bye."

In the living room, George Ray seems to relax upon her return. Brid says there's good news: the TV people have received a report of the Israelis freed and the terrorists killed. Neither she nor George Ray asks who was on the phone, but once Maggie has settled onto the couch and they're all waiting for more details to be announced, Brid remarks offhandedly that she just remembered Maggie's granny called earlier. She wanted Maggie to know that her father went upriver to some village and that's why he didn't get in touch. With closed eyes, Maggie thanks her for the message.

Friday morning, she feels nauseous again. It has been almost a week since Fletcher left. She should see a doctor. Opening the medicine cabinet, she hunts for something to settle her stomach and finds a stockpile of other people's sanitary towels, nail polish, eye drops, and deodorants. Everything but what she needs.

In the camper van, she drives through Virgil without stopping, loath to run into someone who was at the party, and continues a few miles to Niagara-on-the-Lake. There she goes into a pharmacy for some Gravol before finding a hardware store that sells bathroom scales. A construction detour on the way home leaves her lost among side streets with her stomach so bad that she's forced to pull over at a park beside the river. Sitting at a picnic table, she gazes out across a beach cross-hatched with driftwood logs to the place where the river meets Lake Ontario. An old American fort with a watchtower stands on the far side, hemmed in by garrison walls. Incredible how close it is. She could return so easily. Just a few miles' drive to the nearest bridge, and she could be in Boston by nightfall; she could make Syracuse in time for lunch. What would she say to Gran if she turned up at her door? The news of Fletcher's departure would seem only to justify her grandmother's warnings.

Back at the farmhouse, Maggie goes upstairs with her purchases, steps on the scales, and finds she has gained four pounds. It's surprising that Brid hasn't said anything; surely she's the type who would notice. In an old medical manual among the books on the living room shelf, Maggie looks up the symptoms. Dry skin—yes, but then that's always been a problem. Cramped legs—well, of course, she's on her feet all day. The indigestion and constipation—they could just be from stress. But all of these things together, and a month late? With the phone book in front of her, she calls the only doctor listed for Virgil and is told he can see her in a week.

The next day after dinner, Brid cajoles George Ray into staying a little longer and watching the Olympics with them again. It's the last day of competition, but there's still a miasma hovering over the events. Once more they play clips from the memorial service earlier in the week, and Maggie can't believe they didn't send everyone home already. George Ray's beside her on the couch, while Brid takes up the armchair with Pauline on her lap. Half an hour earlier than usual, she announces Pauline's bedtime. The girl bawls in protest, but Brid's unrelenting and carries her upstairs. Eventually she returns alone with a bottle of red wine.

"Just grown-ups now," she says, squeezing between them on the couch. To Maggie's surprise, George Ray accepts the offer of a drink. Maybe he's warming to the idea that he has gained the attentions of an attractive woman far from home. Brid treats his assent as a victory, then turns her focus to Maggie, urging her to have some too. Reluctantly she agrees, thinking she'll just swish it around and nobody will notice. When Brid leans over to pour herself a glass, Maggie glimpses her small breasts swinging freely within her blouse.

After that, Brid gives up all pretence of watching television. She asks George Ray about Jamaica, claiming it's for the sake of intercultural understanding. But when he starts talking about the country, she shows little interest in what he says, seeming more attentive to the way his lips move. Every so often she makes a little hum of encouragement and reaches out to touch his knee. Maggie worries she should be protecting him, but he's married and a decade older than she is; he must have learned by now how to deal with the Brids of the world. Before his glass is even half empty, Brid refills it, and she glares when she realizes that Maggie has barely had a sip.

"C'mon, sweetie, let your hair down." With flashing eyes, she reaches over to undo the first button on Maggie's blouse, then laughs at her own trespass. To George Ray she says, "Don't you think she should let her hair down?" Brid's caftan rides high on her legs as she crosses and uncrosses them. Her nails are painted red but nibbled short. Beside her, George Ray leans forward to glance across the couch. Giving Maggie a sad smile, he points out that her hair is already down. Brid laughs as if this is the funniest thing she has ever heard.

She tries to draw them into conversation, at some points putting an arm around both at the same time. George Ray seems no more comfortable than Maggie, but Brid is dogged. Maggie resists an impulse to retire for the night, half curious to see how it will end, unsure whether she's staying to prevent a seduction or to abet one. Maybe she's a little jealous.

Through the news she sticks it out, but once Johnny Carson comes on, she declares she's going to bed. George Ray stands promptly and says the same. Adopting a smile, Brid gives Maggie a long hug and a lingering kiss on the cheek that feels like it leaves lipstick. She's on her fourth glass of wine.

"Are you sure?" she says. "You can't stay a bit longer?" She offers to walk George Ray to the barracks and grows testy when he demurs. "I'll come out anyway. I need a little fresh air."

Maggie can't help herself. "Jeez, Brid, give the guy a break." She tries to make it sound humorous, but Brid's eyes narrow.

"Relax, Auntie Maggs," she replies. "You've got one back in Boston."

Upstairs, Maggie is sleepless. Too hot; she opens the window and shivers at the chilly air that blows in. Her mind slips over to the barracks, to George Ray's broad shoulders and Brid's freckled breasts. Maggie couldn't stay here with the two of them like that. The bed is lumpy, enormous. Finally she goes to the kitchen and puts the kettle on. Before the water has boiled, there's the distant slam of the barracks door and Brid's voice shouting.

"Fine, you fucking prude!"

Silence follows, then a muttering that grows closer. When Brid appears in the mud room, she's talking to herself, unaware of Maggie's presence. "A bitch," she's saying. "God, I'm such a bitch."

Maggie wants to hide under the table before Brid's eyes fall on her. Once they do, she waits for the assault to begin, for all the woman's spite to be heaped on her, but Brid looks through her as if she isn't there.

"Don't worry," says Brid in a wavering voice. "Everything's going to be fine." Maggie stands and moves toward her. "What about Pauline?" says Brid. "She didn't wake up, did she?"

Maggie tells her it's all right, but she might as well not be speaking, because Brid rushes upstairs to her daughter's room. A few minutes later, Maggie goes to peek in through the door and sees both of them asleep, sharing the bed peacefully with their two golden heads of hair dimly radiant across the pillows.

After Maggie wakes up, she stays in bed awhile, listening to the silent house, wondering how long she could remain here before someone comes to check on her. All morning, probably. Brid and Pauline must have gone out; maybe they've left for good. Eventually she hears the telephone ring and makes her way downstairs to answer, thinking it could be Fletcher. It's a woman's voice on the other end, though, telling her in broken English that she has a collect call. The operator says it's from Wale. With a sense of trepidation, Maggie accepts the charges and hears a click. The line gains an underlying flow of static.

"Wale?" she says. "Where are you?"

The voice through the static is murky and phantasmal, but it's him.

"Bangkok," he replies.

"Bangkok?" In the background is the sound of car traffic. Jesus. He really is going to Laos. "I can't hear you very well. What time is it there?"

"Dunno. Dark. Dark o'clock. Half past dark."

He sounds wholly drunk. Maggie glances toward the hall, worried that Brid will come in and find out who's on the line.

"You want me to get Brid?" she asks.

"No, honey, it's you I want." The way he says it makes her flush. There's a burst of crackling before the line clears. "I've been dreaming about you," he says, but she doesn't want to hear about his dreams. Nervously, she looks up again to see if anyone is there.

"You aren't really in Thailand. You're putting me on, right?"

With slurring words, he affirms he's really and truly in that country, and she asks him what the hell he's doing there.

"Going to Laos to check on your dad." At this response her stomach knots up further. It's impossible. No, it's not. Wale's insane. He's gone halfway around the world to prove it, and to make her crazy too. He waits on the line as if expecting more questions, but she refuses to play the game.

"You ran out on us," she says.

"Ran out? I'm trying to show you I'm not so heartless after all."

She isn't going to be made responsible for his lunacy. "You're not over there to impress me."

"You think I'm a goon. A thug who shoots little kids."

"I don't think that." In fact she does, but only because he's made himself out to be one.

"You're right, I'm a piece of shit. Some of the things I've done, I know I can't make up for them."

"Wale—"

"You have to believe me—your dad, if I'd seen anything coming . . ."

"Wale, would you listen to me? There's nothing wrong. If you'd stayed here, you'd know. I heard from my grandmother, he's fine, he just went over to a village—"

"You talked with him? You heard from him?"

"I told you, I got a call from Gran—"

"But you didn't talk with him?" The way Wale says it makes all her relief fall away. She wants to hang up the phone and call Gran. "If I thought it was safe, I'd have asked you to come with me. I miss you, Maggie. It's been a long time since I missed somebody."

He's interrupted by a voice shouting what sounds like abuse in another language. She says his name, but he doesn't answer. Then suddenly he's back and speaking in her ear.

"I'm off my face, aren't I? The beer here is piss." There's the clonk of an empty bottle dropped onto pavement. "It's so goddamn lonely. You know?" On the other end, a car passes playing a Simon and Garfunkel song. "Maggie, I wanted to tell you something. What was it—"

"You were dreaming about me," she says feebly.

"No, something else." There's a noise like a long belch, then another voice in the background. "Shit, my ride's here. I'm flying to Long Chieng in a couple of hours."

"Wait, let me get Brid—" she says, but once she finishes speaking, she realizes he's already gone. Out of the corner of her eye she catches a glimpse of movement: Brid and Pauline coming in through the mud room door.

"Who was that?" asks Brid.

"Wrong number," Maggie says, and she hangs up the phone.

No, honey, it's you I want. That's how real confession goes. Not in the church with the priest levying penance; not in the network studio with the cameras rolling. It happens in a phone booth by the roadside late at night when you've had a few too many, shouting down the line to someone on another continent. It's a good thing Wale's ride showed up. Whatever else he had to say, she's pretty sure she didn't want to hear it.

She's also sure she doesn't want to call Gran. How would she explain her worries without sending the woman into a panic? The barest description of Wale would leave Gran thinking that Maggie has involved herself with degenerates and crooks. Returning to the telephone, she dials the number, unsure of what she'll say. The phone rings and rings without an answer. At last, a little thankfully, she puts down the receiver and goes back to bed.

It turns out Brid and Pauline are leaving too. There's no explanation, just one stark sentence during lunch. Maggie nods as if the reasons are obvious. She doesn't try to argue Brid out of it, only expresses concern about them making the trip to Boston in one day on their own. Even this statement she saves until they're on the porch with the Toyota loaded and Pauline buckled into her safety seat, her uncombed hair standing up in a bright flaxen frizz. Brid says she'll be all right, but she looks wan and keeps removing her sunglasses to rub at her eyes. From the car, Pauline's wailing that she doesn't want to go; she wants to stay with Auntie Maggs. This is a surprise. When did Pauline ever like her?

"Just so you know," says Brid, "I'm not clearing out because of the Jamaican. Last night was nothing, okay? I'm going because I'm a mess, and because I know you don't care whether I stay."

"That isn't true," Maggie protests.

"You're sweet to say it. Anyhow, good for you, not needing me. You're tougher than I thought." She sounds hurt that this should be the case. "I'm sorry, I'm just fed up with it all." Looking out over the front yard, she dwells on the place as if seeing it for the first time. "Maybe a few years ago we'd have stood a chance, but people got worn down by everything. I thought maybe up here we could relax and try something new. Oh well."

In her voice there's at once a lassitude and a confidence, as if she's been formulating this elegy for some time. Yet something doesn't sit right. It couldn't be that simple. There's a vital element she's missed, but there's no time to figure it out: she seems ready to depart.

"What will you do now?" Maggie asks.

"Stay with my brother, I guess. God, I hate him. It's going to be a train wreck." She looks over at Maggie with concern. "What about you? You'll be okay?"

Maggie nods, pretty sure that Brid's just asking to free herself from obligation. Still, there's a compulsion to provide some kind of self-defence, to articulate the thoughts she's been mulling over in her head.

"I couldn't go back now," she says. "Anyhow, I prefer it on the farm. You know, working the land—"

"You don't prefer it, sweetie," says Brid with an earnestness that surprises her. "You think you do, but you don't. I've watched you. You've been so unhappy here."

The words strike Maggie to the quick. There's such assurance in them. But if that's what Brid has been thinking, why didn't she say anything till now?

"Will you look up Fletcher when you get there?" Maggie asks.

Brid seems unprepared for the question. "You want me to?"

"No." She says it without hesitating. The idea of them together in Boston while Maggie waits for him here is unbearable.

"Don't worry," replies Brid as if she has read her thoughts, "he was never interested in me, even before he met you. Not that I didn't try." The comment is made with such nonchalance that Maggie almost doesn't register it. Before she has a chance to respond, Brid has already moved on. "Hell, forget it. Can't let the past fuck up your perspective, right?"

Maggie thinks of the kinds of things one is allowed to say just before parting. She wants to share something in return, something to make Brid stay a bit longer. Not Wale's phone call; she couldn't bring herself to mention that. Her late period, perhaps. No, to tell Brid would make it too real.

"Goodbye," says Brid, giving her a squeeze. Into Maggie's ear she says quietly, "There was a time, I think, when we might have . . ." But she seems not to know how to finish, and she laughs in a self-defeated way. "Oh, never mind." She pulls back. "It's no big deal. Goodbye!" She gives her a kiss on the cheek, then a surprising look of regret.

Maggie didn't know regret was something Brid could feel. Regret rests on hopes and dreams, an ideal you reach for and fail to find. Regret's about living in the shadow of an inner gleaming you that Maggie's never quite found in herself. Until now she hasn't thought of Brid as someone with a self like that either. People are different from each other, though. It seems like some kind of breakthrough to apprehend this simple fact, but Maggie doesn't feel much wiser than before. Why that look of regret on Brid's face just now? It's too late to ask. She's ensconced with her daughter in the Toyota, and the two of them are disappearing down the drive.

Monday morning, Maggie tries calling Gran again. Again she gets no answer. One more day, she thinks, and she'll drive to Syracuse to see what's going on. To distract herself from the thought, she begins to clean, compelled by the idea that at last everything in the house can go where she wants it. From now on, each speck of dirt will be her dirt, the mess no one's but her own. She tries to focus on the cobwebs hanging from the ceiling and the scum in the toilet bowl, even while she feels a building anger with Fletcher, with Brid, with all those who have left these tasks for her. Cleaning, always cleaning, since the first day she was here. Her body grows sticky with sweat and dust even as the house becomes pristine.

Just before lunch, there's a knock at the front door. By the time she gets downstairs, the mailman's pickup truck is pulling out of the driveway and a parcel sits on the porch, the size of a shoebox and wrapped in brown paper. Even before she identifies her name above the address, she recognizes her father's handwriting. The paper seems to take forever to remove.

Inside is a cardboard box, and in the box is a letter along with a little statue made out of fired clay. Maggie turns the figure over in wonder. It's a long-haired woman eight inches tall, muddy brown and unglazed, mounted on a short pedestal of rough cement. The limbs are stubby, the body shaped in such a way as to suggest the woman's wearing a robe. Thick lips have been painted on her face, and there are black dots for eyes, while a hairline crack runs around her waist. The thing looks crudely made, and Maggie's surprised that it survived the journey intact. Setting it down, she turns to the letter and begins to read.

August 13, 1972
Dear Maggie,

Enclosed is a gift for you made by a friend of mine, Yia Pao the potter, whom I mentioned the last time I wrote ("Yia" is an honorific given to Hmong men when they become fathers, in keeping with the race's respect for parenthood). I fear he is at risk of falling in with bad company, so I have taken him under my wing. I like to think it due to my influence that he has begun to fashion the likenesses of saints. I told him Saint Clare was your favorite when you were a girl, because she was the patron saint of television, so he made you a statue of her. I hope she brings you comfort.

I know I was wrong to leave for Laos in anger as I did. I should have seen sooner that you're no longer a girl but a woman leading her life, and that your life is not with me. Now I am trying to make amends through service. "By their fruits you shall know them," we are told. We're all His vessels, sealed up in ourselves and opaque to each other but transparent to Him.

Some would take the happenings in Laos as proof there is no God. I've seen the little moments, though, the generosity of strangers, the love of families, and find recurrent proof that God exists. In America we put our faith in technology and progress, but there are things that modern life doesn't apprehend, a beauty not created by human hands, beauty that persists even when it can no longer be perceived.

So much has happened since I wrote in May. I'd like to tell you about it, but I don't wish to impose. I received no response to my last letter, and I have given up hope of a reply, concluding that you were telling the truth when you said you wished no correspondence. Indeed, Gran has mentioned that you said the same to her. However, she did provide the address to which I'm mailing this parcel. I hope you will forgive both her and me.

With love,

Your "Yia" (Dad)

The first time she reads it, she's barely taking in the words. Then she checks the parcel and sees it's postmarked August 14, a week before his missed phone call to Gran. So the letter proves nothing about whether he's all right. There's no hint of anything to come, no mention of trouble, unless she counts the reference to Yia Pao falling in with bad company.

Carrying the letter and clay figure to the kitchen, she sets them on the counter and dials Gran's number. A man picks up. It's Uncle Morley, and he turns sarcastic when he realizes it's her, calling her the prodigal granddaughter.

Then he says Gran has been sick. Just a stomach bug, but she got dehydrated. She'll be out of the hospital by tonight, and the family is taking good care of her; Maggie shouldn't worry her little head about it. He asks if she wants to leave a message, and she says no, desperate to get off the line. She'll try again tomorrow when Gran's back home.

With the phone returned to its hook, she picks up the statue and takes it to the living room. When she was a girl, she and her father had a ceramic likeness of Saint Clare atop their television set, because it was said that placing one there was supposed to improve reception. Now she tries perching the clay figure on top of the silver TV. It takes some time before she can get the balance right. If Brid were here, she'd make some remark about hopeless superstitions, or perhaps she'd simply say that whatever gets them PBS is fine with her.

That evening, George Ray doesn't come to dinner for the second night in a row. Looking out from the mud room door, she can see his silhouette pass back and forth across the barracks window. She should tell him that Brid has left, that it's safe for him to enter the house, but she stays inside and eats cold cereal standing up, then returns to cleaning. When she goes to the bathroom, she begins to close the door behind her before realizing she doesn't have to. Leaving it open, she keeps an ear out for the telephone or a car in the drive. Right now Fletcher might be with Cybil. They could be eating at some fancy restaurant. He might be sleeping with her. Maggie should go and make a pass at George Ray to get even. No, it's a petty thought. Besides, why does she think she'd have any more luck than Brid?

It's midnight before she gets into bed. Her chest hurts, her skin's clammy, and she needs a cigarette. Sleep comes not as a drop into oblivion but as a glass plate slipped over consciousness, distorting the world. Something left undone—she can't remember what, and she's panicked at forgetting. A voice in the attic, low and hostile. What did it say? A train about to leave, too many people, her baggage lost. Searching on a beach littered with stranded fish. The train disappearing across the sea.

When she wakes, it doesn't feel like waking because it hasn't felt like sleep. Her forehead's slick with sweat. She tries to stand and her stomach revolts, her legs buckle; she just makes it to the bathroom in time. Stumbling back to bed, she pulls the sheets around her and shivers. It's hours before she floats to the fever's surface, and this time she has only reached the hall when the sickness overtakes her. Somehow she has the energy to clean it up. Then she sits in the bathroom and shakes awhile, weeping for herself, for her reduction to the status of a suffering thing. She should call somebody, but whom? George Ray? No phone in the barracks, and she couldn't make it out there on her own like this. Fletcher. What could he do? It's the middle of the night. There's no one.

Twice more she tries to rise, and each time nausea sends her into heaves, trying to expel something that isn't there or can't be dislodged. Her throat burns, and there's a film of bile on her teeth. This is what it means to be alone. No one nurses you. No one finds your body till they come to read the meter. Then Fletcher will have to return and deal with the aftermath.

The first light of morning slices through the blinds. Someone knocking on the front door. A dream? There it is again, faintly penetrating the fever's gauze. She tries to call out, but her voice fails her. Pray, Maggie, pray. All the nuts and oddballs turn to prayer as a last resort. She doesn't need a miracle, just a bit of strength; it doesn't seem too much to ask. Even God must lose patience, though, with those who call only in their hour of need, not to worship but to bargain, despite their bad credit, proffering devotion in return for His love. It's her father she wants. Not the man from the last months, intimate only with God. She wants the father from her youth, who stayed home from work when she was ill and sang to her. He's the one who should be next to her now.

As if in answer, she hears a noise. Footsteps on the stairs. Imagined saviours and tormentors approach her bedroom door. Brid or Fletcher, or Lydia Dodd and her red-haired cousin. In the end, it's George Ray who speaks her name.

"I'm sick," she tells him.

He comes to the bedside and places a palm on her forehead. "How long have you been lying here?" he asks, but her throat is too parched for her to reply, and besides, she isn't certain of the answer. When he goes to leave the room, she reaches for him, afraid he won't come back. A minute later he returns with two Aspirins and a glass of water. He helps her to sit and feeds the tablets to her, tilting the glass carefully to her lips. Then, after another trip to the bathroom, he lays a wet face cloth over her brow and sits next to her until she falls asleep.

When she awakens, it's the afternoon, the face cloth is newly cool and moistened, the water glass refilled, and the fever has broken. She thinks of God. She didn't actually pray, she wants to tell Him. He can't claim any credit for this. She can't be held in hock for the mere invoking of a name.

Still too woozy to get up, she stays in bed. At some point she sees George Ray in the doorway, and with a heavy arm she beckons him. He enters with porridge and juice on a wicker tray.

"Sweet of you," she croaks, trying to sit up.

"What else could I do?"

"I'm not very hungry," she warns, but she manages a few bites. The cold juice stings and soothes her throat at once.

By the time it's dark again, she feels well enough to be bored. He helps her to the living room, holding her elbow on the stairs, then brings down her bedding so she can lie on the couch and watch television. The Olympics are over. She ends up dozing on and off through an interview with the prime minister about the Canadian election. Every so often George Ray stops by to sit with her.

"Brid's gone," she says to him at one point. "You and I are the only ones." He nods. "Fletcher will be back next week." At this he nods again, if more slowly, and she wonders what he's thinking, though she can't bring herself to ask.

Eventually he leaves and television too grows dull. On unsteady legs, she enters the kitchen to find him bent over the cast iron skillet on the stove. The smell of frying liver turns her stomach.

"Don't worry, it's not for you," he says, seeing her face. "Your dinner's still to come. This is for him." He gestures to the table. At first she doesn't see anyone, but then there's the flick of a tail and she perceives the slate-grey body sitting on one of the chairs. It watches the stove intently with two black and yellow eyes like blots of dark vinegar in oil.

"Is that John-John?" she says, amazed. The cat doesn't move at the name's utterance. She has only ever seen John-John streaking from the Centaurs' car, and later among the grainy shadows of her film. This cat looks rougher for wear than the one she remembers; the tip of its tail is bald like a rat's, and when it jumps down to rub against her, it favours one of its hind legs.

"Don't know any John-John," says George Ray. "I call him Elliot."

"Where'd you find him?"

"He found me—scratched at the barracks door two nights ago." George Ray gives the liver a stir.

"I doubt you need to cook that," she points out. "He'd eat it raw."

"He likes it better this way." George Ray removes the skillet from the stove, cuts the liver into pieces, and deposits it on a plate. The cat meows loudly as it's set before him. Maggie's unable to take her eyes off the creature and resists an urge to pick him up. When she looks back to George Ray, he's dicing an onion.

"What are you doing?" she asks.

"Making your dinner."

"I can do that," she says weakly. She doesn't have the energy to protest as she should.

"You're sick. Sit and talk to me if you like."

So she sits and they talk, although George Ray does most of the speaking, as if he knows it will be easier for her just to listen. He tells her of the skunk he saw scuttling around the corner of the barracks yesterday, the first one he has seen after seven summers working in this country, although he's smelled the creatures often enough. He talks about how the knots in the trunks of cherry trees remind him of faces, so that he thinks of them as people living in the orchard, from the crone near the wrecker's wall to the little boy in the back corner. Maggie's still too lightheaded to take in properly what he's saying, but it's pleasant listening to him. He doesn't make any allusions to Fletcher's absence. He doesn't lay bare his neuroses, demanding to be accepted. He doesn't dump his troubles on her, whatever they may be with a wife and children a thousand miles away. She catches the scent of the garlic he's frying and bursts into tears.

"I'm sorry," she says, wiping at her eyes with her sleeve. "It's just that you're being so nice to me. I can't remember the last time someone was so nice." As she says this, she thinks of the day Fletcher presented her with the projection wall in the playroom. It seems like years ago.

George Ray offers her his handkerchief. "You should remember I'm getting paid," he says. As far as she can tell, there's no irony in the statement.

"Please don't say that. You shouldn't diminish it, especially when—when I know you prefer it on your own."

He stays silent awhile, and for the first time with him today she feels awkward. It's as if her words are floating between them, material things he's inspecting for their stress points and defects. She doesn't like it.

"Do I prefer it on my own?" he says. "I don't know. It goes with living here."

A motion across the kitchen catches her eye. The cat has licked its plate clean and lazily walks away, stretching its legs one by one.

"You told me you were learning to be alone," she says to George Ray.

"Yes. It's a long lesson."

"Has it been so bad, all these years?"

He shrugs. "At the Beaudoin farm there were a dozen men. I was almost never on my own."

"Wouldn't you rather be with them?"

For this question he needs no time to consider the answer. "Sometimes on Saturday nights I still go with them to St. Catharines, watch them drink and get chatty-chatty with the girls. That's enough for me. My wife worries about Canadian women, but it's living with a lot of men that ruins you." At the mention of his wife she thinks she detects an uneasiness, as if he has suddenly remembered where he's standing.

From the other side of the room comes a retching sound. Elliot, né John-John, is hunched over, neck outstretched. He brings up a stream of undigested liver. George Ray makes a face like it's to be expected.

"He did the same this morning."

"Poor thing," she says. "Maybe it's because he's vegetarian."

George Ray gives her a quizzical look, then goes over

to pick him up. Elliot seems unconcerned by what has just transpired, and he tolerates the attention only a few seconds before pushing himself away. George Ray sets him down and retrieves a rag from the sink to clean up the mess.

"Too much throwing up today," he says.

He feeds her rice with peas, her stomach handling it better than she feared. After dinner he goes back to the barracks and the cat mews at the door to be let out. She's tempted to keep him inside; what if he should disappear again? There's no litter box in the house, though, so reluctantly she opens the door and watches him trot off, tracing the perimeter of the backyard by slinking next to hedges and fences until he reaches the barracks. Eventually the door opens, and perhaps it's only her imagination, but as the cat's admitted, it looks as though George Ray steals a glance to see if anyone else is there too.

Abandoned by both of them, she thinks of calling Gran. It's too late in the evening for that now. When she tries to read, her mind keeps drifting to the barracks. What does he do out there with his evenings? For her own part, she's still only halfway through *Middlemarch*, and she can barely keep her eyes focused. The lines turn to caravans stretched across the white desert of the page. What kind of marriage must it be for George Ray and his wife, sleeping so far apart for months every year? What would he say if Maggie told him she was pregnant? She forces her attention back to the page.

Finally she gives up and turns on the television to let the ions flow over her. The familiar intonations of reporters and news anchors on the U.S. channels are a solace, though all they have to tell her is bad news. No wonder the people up here have their little left-wing haven with its free health care and its pacifism; every night they can study the States on TV and learn what not to do.

She watches until they play the national anthem. When she turns off the set, its picture condenses into a white pearl occupying the centre of blackness. In contrast with the departed TV studios, the house seems shabby, a hodgepodge, poorly lit. She staggers upstairs but can't sleep. The walls creak, and something scurries across the roof. Finally she decides the only thing left for her is to seduce herself. She thinks of Fletcher and, at the end, of George Ray.

In the morning, she has forgotten about it until Fletcher calls. Then it returns and shames her into silence. When he asks how she's doing, she says she's fine. Sounding tired, he explains that things have gotten complicated, that he needs another two weeks in Boston. Reluctantly she acquiesces, thinking it will serve as some kind of expiation for her. Before he hangs up, she says she loves him. It may just be the bad connection that produces a slight delay before he says he loves her too.

Yia Pao carries the baby as he and Gordon follow muddy paths up and down the side of the valley. Sawtoothed mountains loom on either side while monkeys scream from the trees. Rain drums on the foliage overhead, striking them in fat, heavy drops, and orange worms stretch across the trail, their spiny backs slick with slime. Gordon flicks them out of the way with a long stick. Whenever he and Yia Pao reach an open place, he searches the sky.

"No one's looking for us, Gordon," says Yia Pao.

"But we still might flag down a plane."

"We need to keep going, or it will be Sal and his men who find us."

The rain lessens, then stops, and a thick fog settles in, reducing visibility to a few feet. Eventually they arrive at a clearing where the trees are shattered, trunks snapped in two and branches flung everywhere, the ground pocked by craters filled with water. Tadpoles wriggle at the borders of the pools. Leading the way, Gordon trips over a jutting length of metal. It's the tail of a jet. The wreckage is spread across the clearing and covered in vines.

"This is a bad place," murmurs Yia Pao. "A ghost place."

Gordon gazes into the fog. From somewhere in the jungle comes the deep-throated call of a bird.

"It isn't Christian to believe in ghosts," he says.

"Have you never seen your wife's ghost?" asks Yia Pao. "Mine visits me often." His tone suggests the visits aren't happy ones.

Gordon takes a few more steps through the blasted clearing. "Not her ghost. She used to come in dreams. She'd plead with me to die too."

"Gordon, I'm sorry." They pause beside a crater, and Yia Pao soothes Xang in Hmong.

"I told her I couldn't because we had a daughter," says Gordon. "My wife wouldn't give up, so I started to take sleeping pills at night. They made her go away for a while."

"Did she bring you to Laos?" asks Yia Pao. "Did you come here to die?"

Gordon frowns and doesn't respond. "I leaned too hard on Maggie," he says after a time. "She went to college and it nearly finished me." A few seconds later, he brightens. "That's the thing about God. You can lean on Him as much as you want."

Yia Pao turns to survey the plane's wreckage, the shredded trees and torn earth. He passes Xang to Gordon and bends to massage his own calves. "Is God in this place? I would like to lean on Him now."

As if in answer, there's a low whine that grows louder, and the men raise their eyes. The jungle reveals only a small area of sky, so that the plane is almost right above them before they see it, bright white, propeller driven, flying low. Gordon shouts at it but is drowned out by the engines. A moment later the plane has passed out of sight. The men listen as its roar fades.

"He didn't see us," says Gordon dolefully.

"Wait," says Yia Pao.

The noise from the engine grows louder again. Yia Pao pulls off his shirt and whirls it above his head. The baby is crying, but Gordon whoops.

When the plane reappears, it's even lower than before. The men are yelling and waving for it. Then there's a clap of thunder. The earth falls away. A tidal wave of mud carries them across the clearing, while a ball of flame roils over the treetops.

Lying on his side with Xang still in his hands, Gordon

tries to shield him from the debris showering on them. The air fills with a dirty, suffocating smoke. The baby starts to cough, but when Gordon gains his feet, the smoke grows thicker and he falls to the ground again.

When he looks up, he sees Maggie striding out of the jungle. She wears an iridescent blue dress untouched by mud and rain. The smoke melts away as she approaches, even though the trees around her are on fire.

Smiling at her father, she spreads her arms wide. Gordon reaches to take her hand. She vanishes just as she's about to touch him.

Xang coughs and cries against his chest. For a time Gordon weeps with him. Finally he struggles upright, looks himself over, examines the baby. They're both filthy but seemingly unhurt. He turns in search of Yia Pao and sees him getting to his feet a few yards away.

"You all right?" he says, and Yia Pao nods. "So are we. It's a miracle."

"He had terrible aim," says Yia Pao. He points toward the smoking crater on the other side of the clearing.

"Why did he bomb us?" says Gordon.

Yia Pao shrugs. "They do whatever they want." He makes his way over to Gordon, takes Xang, and kisses him on the cheeks. Then he starts toward the trees and gestures for Gordon to follow. "We must hurry. Before he returns to finish us off."

The doctor in Virgil is squat with buckteeth and tufts of white hair sprouting from his ears. In the examining room, as Maggie lies on her back, her feet in stirrups, he prods her without much interest.

"Five weeks late, you say? Temperature's high."

"I've been ill. I had a fever."

The doctor tuts as if this fact is medically uninteresting. "Have there been mood swings, headaches? Cervix feels a little soft. No spotting, but morning sickness, you said. Well, the chances are pretty good. Don't worry, we'll sort it out soon enough." He draws a vial of blood and dispatches her to the bathroom with a plastic cup, saying it will be a week before the results come in.

When she exits the office, there's a cluster of people just outside beneath an awning, watching as rain pours down before them in a solid sheet. Few vehicles pass by, and no one speaks. They all stand and wait, their numbers swelling with more patients from inside. When a man in a suit rushes down the street into the awning's sanctuary, drenched from head to toe, those already gathered smile in sympathy, and the newcomer smiles too as he wipes himself off. Above them, a swallow perches on a strut, silent and unmoving.

Eventually the rain abates. One by one, at some sign known only to themselves, people begin to depart and continue on their way. By the time Maggie leaves, a patch of sun is poking through the clouds.

7

When the little blue Volvo comes up the driveway, Maggie's first thought is that it's Fletcher. She's on the porch beating out rugs and George Ray is working close by, humming tunelessly as he plants saplings along the edge of the lawn. She's not expecting Fletcher for another ten days, but he must have bought another car and come back early. The silhouette behind the wheel doesn't look like his, though, and when the driver exits the Volvo in his golf cap, she sees with a sinking heart that it's the priest from the stone church.

"Pardon intrusion," he says, ambling up the steps. "Lenka tells me I must call first, but telephone is its own intrusion, yes?"

Maggie agrees that it is.

As the priest reaches the top of the stairs, he hands her a brown paper bag. *"Buchty,"* he says. "Lenka makes it for you."

Maggie takes the bag and thanks him, worried about what kind of obligation she has just accepted.

"Is very quiet," says the priest, turning to take in the property. On the lawn, George Ray's hammering a stake into the ground, while the moon hangs just above the orchard, tiny and pale in the afternoon sky like an egg laid in the treetops. At first Maggie assumes the priest's being sarcastic, given the hammering. Then she figures out his implication.

"Yes, most people have left," she says. She can't bring herself to admit that everyone has gone.

"Is nice man from grocery store still here?" asks the priest. He means Wale, she realizes, and she laughs at the idea of Wale as a nice man. The priest seems puzzled by her reaction.

"That man abandoned his girlfriend and his daughter," she tells him. His expression falls, and he asks how the woman and the girl are doing. Maggie merely says they're back in the States now. She doesn't feel like talking about Brid and Pauline with him.

"I must tell you," says the priest, "I come as courtesy to your grandmother."

"My grandmother," Maggie repeats.

"She writes nice letter to me asking how you are." The priest sees her look of incomprehension and goes on. "You tell her you come to church, so she makes inquiry about this parish and discovers my address."

"I didn't tell her——" Then Maggie remembers what she said to Gran on the phone. She can imagine Gran's excitement at the thought of her attending Mass.

"Your grandmother writes nice letter," says the priest. "She has great worry for you."

"Well, you didn't need to come. Gran and I talked on the phone last week."

The priest nods as though he's up to date regarding contact between her and Gran. "She says you do not tell her very much of yourself," he explains.

"We've had other things to talk about."

"Yes, she tells me that too. Your father. She writes me that they are finding out if he is in village upriver. You have had more word?"

She shakes her head. "You know as much as I do. Maybe I should be asking you for news." For a moment she mulls what would happen if she told him that the nice man from the grocery store has gone to Laos.

"Is dangerous, the mission work," says the priest. "Your father has great courage. He is like the Jesuits in this place many centuries ago."

"I didn't want him to go over there," she replies. "I didn't want to be worrying about him. If it's okay, I'd rather not talk about it. Thanks for coming over, though. You can tell Gran I'm fine."

The priest looks disappointed. Probably he thinks she's a selfish, ungrateful child.

"Before I leave," he says, "Lenka asks me to tell you that she wishes to see you again. But she is embarrassed from night of party."

Maggie remembers Lenka kneeling at the toilet with her brother beside her. Suddenly the brown paper bag brought by the priest seems less like a demand and more like penance.

"She shouldn't be embarrassed," Maggie says. "It was something she ate, right?"

The priest looks at her as though to ascertain whether she's being serious. "You must understand," he says, a certain fatigue creeping into his voice, "before we come here, our parents are taken. They are dissidents, yes? Lenka, she is almost thirty, but she lived with them. Is difficult. She is not great lover of life here." His face grows troubled awhile before it brightens. "She asks that I invite you for the Sunday dinner. Will you give us this honour?"

Maggie tries to picture herself alone in a dining room with the priest and his alcoholic sister. He appears to have forgotten that the first time he saw Maggie, he accused her of stealing from a poor box. No, it would never work. Still, standing before her with golf cap in hand, he looks hopeful, almost needy. And what else does she have going on?

Then she remembers George Ray. He's acting as if busy with a length of twine, but from the tilt of his head she suspects that he's been listening all this time, that he's waiting with the priest for her response.

"I'll come if I can bring him," she says, nodding toward George Ray. She says it thinking George Ray will appreciate the gesture, but upon the words leaving her mouth, she worries he'll consider it patronizing.

When the priest turns to look, George Ray waves at him. She takes it as a good sign.

"Our hired man," she says. "George Ray." Tentatively, the priest waves back. "He's Jamaican," she adds, not quite knowing why. The priest raises an eyebrow, whether at the

fact or at the oddness of her mentioning it, she can't tell.
"Of course," he says. "Hired man is very welcome too."

The rectory is a small bungalow clad in aluminum siding
and sufficiently tucked away behind the church that all the
times Maggie has driven past she's never noticed it. Now,
arriving at the front door, she stands with George Ray on
the little concrete stoop, she in her nicest dress, he with
a bottle of wine in hand. There's only a moment of panic
that the whole thing is a mistake before Lenka answers,
carefully made up and wearing a necklace of thick wooden
beads. She greets Maggie with a kiss on the cheek, and
then, as she leans in to kiss George Ray, he chooses the
same moment to thrust forward the wine. She hops back
in surprise and laughs.

The priest acts pleased to see them too. The sweater he's
wearing seems meant to draw attention from his priestli-
ness, but his collar serves as a reminder that he's still not
quite one of them. Behind him on the wall is an oleograph
of Jesus prying open his chest to reveal his flaming heart.

While Lenka disappears into the kitchen, the priest
leads them on a tour of the rooms. There are two bedrooms, a sitting room, and a small dining area, its table
laid and waiting. As Maggie takes in the place, she realizes it's the first dwelling other than the farmhouse she's
entered since the spring. She finds herself admiring the
spotlessness of it all. Nowhere are there gouges on the wall
or haphazard furniture with torn upholstery. The kitchen
gleams as though nothing has ever been spilled or burnt.

The effect is heightened by the priest's obvious pride in the place. He explains that Lenka's bedroom was a study when they arrived, and that the rectory is usually for one person but for them an exception was made. This is all the two of them need, he says. It's bigger than their parents' apartment in Prague.

At dinner, George Ray sits next to Maggie, and Lenka serves them all a noodle soup, which is consumed with obligatory compliments to the chef but without any conversation, only noisy slurping by the priest. Then, after Lenka has brought the sirloin and dumplings to the table, suddenly she begins to talk, as if it's a Czech custom to withhold discussion until the appearance of the entree. While she speaks, the priest watches her as he might watch a child playing a violin piece he has taught her.

"We come four years ago, yes? Is not by choice. Josef and I are sheep, we keep opinions to ourselves, we hide in flock." Her brother murmurs as though she has hit a wrong note, but Lenka shushes him. "After parents are arrested, is dangerous to stay. People say Canada is good for Czechs. We joke it is Siberia but colder." George Ray gives a sympathetic laugh, and Lenka beams. "Now, in one more year, we are citizens. When we arrive, we talk no English. Today we are not too bad, yes?" Maggie and George Ray agree they are not too bad.

"What about your parents?" asks Maggie.

Lenka adjusts the napkin on her lap. "Some gulag," she says. Maggie expects the priest to offer a word of commiseration, but he only sits gazing at his plate.

"You ever think of going back?" she asks.

"Back?" Lenka repeats it as if the possibility would never occur to any reasonable person. "No, there is no back. We come here, Josef puts heart into church. We pretend we are in paradise and not in exile." The priest makes a face to suggest he's familiar with this viewpoint but not approving. "Is hard on priest here—not many Catholics. There are Mennonites everywhere, you notice? Women in the black dresses, men with the buggies. People think they are nice. Josef hates them." At this, the priest speaks sharply to Lenka in Czech, and she responds with equal severity before resuming in English. "He denies it, but I fear he is on path to becoming—jaded? Is that right? Yes, jaded. Once he has great hopes for life in America. Canada is always letting him down."

"Is not true," says the priest sulkily, but he offers no further rebuttal.

"What about for you?" Maggie asks Lenka. "What's it like here?"

"In Czechoslovakia I train as legal secretary. Here, degree is worthless. Cousin in Toronto, she promises to find me a nice Czech man to marry, but I tell her I am old, I will settle for a Canadian. If I have too high standard, I will spend all my life cooking for Josef." She smiles at the priest, who's still sullen.

"Did you have a boyfriend in Czechoslovakia?" asks Maggie. As she does, she recognizes something too personal in the question, but it's too late. The priest lowers his head, and Lenka gives him a glance that he doesn't return.

"Long time ago," says Lenka. Then she gets up to fetch something from the kitchen.

Maggie wonders what George Ray must think, listening to all this. He's already finished his meal, unhampered by speech because no one has asked him a thing. Should she try to draw him into the conversation? No, it's better not to expose him like that. When Lenka returns, though, it seems she's had a similar thought, because the first thing she does is to ask him what part of Jamaica he's from. The question is puzzling. Why does Lenka care? For a moment he doesn't respond, and Maggie feels a nervousness on his behalf. There's a compulsion to rush in and reply for him, though she doesn't know the answer.

"Little place called Newcross," he says. "Up in the mountains, not more than twenty houses, mostly farms. There's a dry goods store and a church. Anglican," he adds apologetically, directing this information to the priest. Josef shrugs as if to say it can't be helped.

"You spend all the summers working in this country?" asks Lenka, and George Ray nods.

"Each time I go back, my children say I sound like a Canadian, all speaky-spokey."

"You have children!" Lenka exclaims. "But is so long away from them! If I am prime minister, I make rule, I do not let fathers come."

"The Canadians like fathers best," George Ray replies. "They're more likely to go back when the contract is finished."

"But is hard work, no? And pay is not so good?"

Again some time passes before he responds, as if he's weighing up how much to tell her. "Most places it's minimum wage, ten-hour days. Rain or shine outdoors. You sleep eight or nine to a room. I don't complain, though. Do that and the boss sends your backside home. Plenty more in Jamaica to take your place." He speaks with a wry, amused tone that loses some of its humour as he goes. Then he turns to Maggie and sees her look of horror. "It's not so bad where I am now."

She tries to smile at him but can't. She should have asked him about such things a long time ago. Perhaps she was afraid of what he'd tell her.

"Soon you will be home?" Lenka asks.

"Five weeks," he says, and again Maggie's taken aback. Only five? Yes, of course. He must be counting the days, eager to see his family. Perhaps next year he should come for less time. But less time is less money; surely he wants more of that. And by then Maggie could have a baby. They'll need George Ray to look after the farm.

Now Lenka's asking him about his wife. It's another thing Maggie hasn't discussed with him. She starts to feel an irritation with the questions, as if they're meant to make both her and George Ray uncomfortable, but he seems not to mind. He says his wife's name is Velma, and Lenka asks what it's like for the two of them to be apart so long.

"Oh, Velma is a jealous woman," he replies with a grin. "She says no messing with the white girls. Black girls neither. I tell her there aren't any black girls in Canada. She says don't sound so sad about it."

The priest and Lenka laugh, while Maggie begins to plot how she and George Ray might make an early escape.

Then Lenka turns to her and asks if she's all right. From the start of the evening Maggie has been resigned to the idea that eventually the conversation will shift to her, and she has expected a quiz from the priest about her father, but to a simple query about whether she's all right, she has no answer whatsoever.

"Yes, thanks," she manages. "It was a wonderful meal."

It feels like the beginning of something but turns out to be the end; Lenka merely acknowledges the compliment and starts to clear the table, promising dessert. Bewildered, Maggie rises to help. Have their hosts agreed beforehand not to ask her questions? Following Lenka with a load of dishes, she grows annoyed at the thought that they're handling her with kid gloves.

When the two of them have reached the kitchen, Lenka glances back toward the dining room. Once she seems assured that no one else will join them, she speaks in a low voice.

"You are pregnant, no?"

Maggie can't hide her shock. Looking down at her stomach, she observes no change.

"Is not belly," says Lenka. "I hear from doctor's secretary." In response to Maggie's expression, she adds, "Is horrible, I know—forgive her."

Maggie's not thinking about forgiveness; she's thinking of the implication. "She's seen the results? They haven't called me with them yet." Twice this week she's phoned the office and received no satisfaction. Lenka could have misheard; there could have been some problem of language.

"This is what the woman say," Lenka insists.

So flustered is Maggie that she doesn't immediately

comprehend Lenka's next words, spoken in the same low voice as before.

"You know, with doctor's permission the abortion is legal here."

Slowly, Maggie grasps what has been said. It's outrageous. Lenka can't tell her this news and then suggest such a thing in the same breath. How could she? A priest's sister! Is it a kind of test? But she thinks of Lenka's near whisper and realizes this is something about which the woman hasn't consulted her brother.

"I tell you because is harder to get in other countries," Lenka says. "And some women here do not know the rules." She says these words very precisely, so that Maggie has a glimpse of something, like a phrase on a poster in her peripheral vision, and it leaves her not knowing how to respond. There's been too much all at once; she never asked to be told such things.

"I'm going to have the baby," she says.

Lenka looks surprised. "You are sure? What of father?"

"He's coming back."

"I see." As Lenka meditates on this, her silence is freighted and intolerable.

"Really, he is," Maggie tells her, irritated by her own insistence. She fumbles to picture how things will go: her belly like a watermelon, Fletcher pacing outside the delivery room. Something in her needs Lenka to affirm this vision or refute it, to tell her she's a fool and he's never coming back. It doesn't happen, though. Lenka's thoughts have already passed on to some other matter.

"So is not George Ray's?" she says.

Maggie feels herself blush. "Of course not. We're just friends." But this last assertion sounds too defensive, and it might not even be true, because who ever said she and George Ray were friends?

"I forget to ask him whether he wishes coffee," says Lenka, as though there's no more to be said, and without any further comment she starts back toward the dining room.

Maggie lags behind, still trying to make sense of what has been revealed to her. Right now she couldn't stomach coffee. She needs to get home and phone Fletcher with the news. No, first she needs to call the doctor. What if that secretary answers the phone? Maggie doesn't know what she'd say to the woman.

Instead of reclaiming her seat, she lingers at the edge of the dining area and announces that they have had a lovely time but should be going. George Ray takes the hint and rises while the priest turns to Lenka accusatorily, seeming to recognize that something has transpired. Maggie doesn't want to think about the discussion those two will have once she and George Ray are gone. Then the priest is all smiles again and stands to show them to the door. Lenka remains behind him, saying nothing. She doesn't have to speak; there's an invisible thread running between her and Maggie now. *Harder to get in other countries.* To distract herself from the phrase's implications, Maggie studies George Ray putting on his shoes and realizes that tonight he has changed for her as well. What is she to do with his village in the mountains and his resentment about being here? Only the priest, with his sanctimony and hard stare, has stayed within himself, and in that respect she's grateful to him.

"Was that okay?" she says to George Ray on the drive home. "She asked you a lot of questions."

"Not too many."

The radio towers blink on the horizon, starlike in their fixity. When Maggie speaks again, she feels detached from her words.

"In the kitchen, Lenka told me I should have an abortion." She keeps her eyes on the road as he turns to her.

"I didn't know there was a baby."

"There might not be. Fletcher thinks I'm just stressed."

George Ray ponders this information while scanning the dashboard as if scrutinizing lines printed there. "Why would she suggest abortion? Because you aren't married?"

"Actually," she replies, "Lenka seemed more concerned that you were the father."

He gives a surprised laugh that stutters into silence. "You must be glad your man is returning soon," he says finally.

"Yes." But she doesn't hear gladness in her voice. "And soon you'll be home. You'll get to see your family."

To this he doesn't respond.

At the turnoff for the road to Harroway, there's the noise of the tires transferring from pavement to gravel. A minute later Maggie steers them up the farmhouse driveway. Once the camper's at rest, she and George Ray exit on their separate sides. As they cross over in front of the vehicle, she makes herself busy rifling through her purse.

"Good night," he says.

"Oh! Right. Good night." They stand facing each other until awkwardly she puts out her hand. He shakes it with an exaggerated pump. "Sleep well," she says, starting up the porch stairs. At the top, she turns to find him in the same place as before. "You okay?"

"Yes. I was just thinking."

"Do you want to come in for tea? No, of course. Sorry, I shouldn't—"

"It's just that it's late."

"Yes."

"Maybe one cup," he says.

She smiles, fumbles to get her key in the door while he climbs the stairs. When she gestures for him to enter, he hesitates.

"What is it?" she says.

"Nothing." But still he won't go in. Finally she reaches up, takes his head in her hands, and turns his face to meet hers.

"Hello," she says.

"Hello."

As if in response to their greetings, there's a meow. They look down to see the grey cat circling their feet and brushing against their ankles. George Ray bends to pick him up and rocks him against his chest. When she goes to pet him, Elliot pushes his cheek into her fingers.

"You take him tonight," says George Ray.

"No, it wouldn't work. I've tried. He just yowls to go outside. He likes you more." She glances back into the house. "Will you—"

"I should go," he says, setting Elliot down. "You know?"

She swallows before putting on a smile. "Sure, of course. Good night, then."

She watches until he has disappeared around the side of the house. Then the cat bounds down the porch steps and sets off after him.

The next morning, she tells herself she didn't do anything wrong. If she confessed it all to Fletcher, he'd only praise her for being sociable. It isn't true, though. He wouldn't be glad to know about her holding George Ray's face, feeling his cheekbones, and taking in those sad eyes. For that matter, what did George Ray think of it? During breakfast, she sits by the window watching the lawn. When she spots him, she hurries out to ask if he'll be eating dinner in the house tonight, trying to make it sound like an everyday, ordinary question. He answers that he will be and he seems relaxed, but it doesn't stop her worrying.

She calls the doctor's office at nine, only to be told by the secretary that the results still aren't in; there's been a problem at the lab. Probably they won't need a retest, but it could take another week. "So why are you telling people I'm pregnant?" Maggie wants to ask, but she can't bring herself to do it. When she steps on the bathroom scales, they say she's gained another pound.

She spends the morning in the garden among the pumpkins, less because they need tending than for the sake of a distraction. Her hands and knees grow slick with muck, while her feet bang around in her rubber boots until they blister and the blisters pop. For a long time she watches the bird feeder near the house, which has become an airport for chickadees, each one winging in and pecking for its seed before bursting away to eat in a private place. There's a desire to record them that she regrets, because such wishes take her back to the box of Super 8 equipment sitting someplace in Boston.

No sign of George Ray. Perhaps last night was too much for him and he's left for good—except he has no car and presumably no money, so until Morgan Sugar pays for his ticket home next month, he might as well be a captive here. And what of her? The camper van is Fletcher's, and the money in the bank is mostly his. Next week October will arrive and he'll return. He'll help her harvest the pumpkins, which should bring them some cash, and he'll be impressed by how little she has spent since he left. By that point she'll have heard from her father, too.

She thinks she hears the phone ringing. As she runs toward the farmhouse, the popped blisters make her wince. Then the ringing stops.

Maybe Lenka's right. Maybe she should have an abortion.

Yia Pao and Gordon lay huddled on the ground with Xang between them, besieged by rain. They have covered themselves with banana leaves, but all three are shivering. Yia Pao gives loud, hacking coughs, and every few seconds Xang whimpers.

"Can you sleep?" asks Gordon. Yia Pao says he can't. "Neither can I. Let's keep going."

They continue on through knee-high mud. After a few miles Yia Pao takes off his boots to inspect his feet. They're covered with bruises and pus-filled pockets of infection. Gordon raises his pant leg and finds half a dozen leeches fixed to his calf. When he tries to pull one off, the body elongates, then snaps, while the mouth remains dug into his flesh and blood streams from the wound. Yia Pao gestures for him to keep moving.

They hear the river before they see it. The water runs high and coffee brown through a narrow gorge, the banks rocky on both sides. At the edge, they fall on their knees to drink, Xang crying on the ground behind them. Then Yia Pao scoops water into his palms and brings it to his son's mouth.

"If we can get to the other side, they'll have a hard time tracking us," says Yia Pao. But the river is too deep and quick to ford, so for a mile they follow it downstream until the track dead-ends. The water is calmer here, and someone has strung a thick rope from one bank to the other. Still, the current looks powerful.

Gordon offers to carry the baby across. He points out that he's taller than Yia Pao and in better health, but Yia Pao insists that he's the father and will take responsibility. Finally Gordon relents and starts for the other side. The rope is slimy, and he gasps that the water is freezing. A few feet out, it paralyzes him. Yia Pao has to urge him onward.

In the middle, he stumbles and loses his footing. His head submerges; the noise of the world is reduced to an underwater roar. When he comes up sputtering, Yia Pao shouts to him from the bank, and he calls back that he's all right, clinging to the rope in the same way the leech stayed fastened to his skin.

After dragging himself onto the far shore, he looks back and sees Yia Pao is already more than halfway across, the water up to his chest, holding Xang with one arm while hooking the rope with the other. It seems he'll manage it on his own, but as he draws near he gives a shout, and Gordon rushes back into the water. He tries to reach for the baby while still grasping the rope. Yia Pao tips forward and pushes Xang into Gordon's chest. The force sends Gordon underwater once more. When he comes back up, he's holding on to the rope and infant at once. But Yia Pao is gone.

Gordon turns to see him being swept down the canyon by the current. Yia Pao's head bobs and disappears, re-surfaces. The river pins him against a rock, and Gordon can see his scrunched eyes as the water pounds him. Then he's sucked back into the water and carried away.

On the bank, Gordon struggles for air even as he checks the silent baby. Xang is breathing but stupefied, too sickly to complain about his near drowning. He only stares into the treetops as if he has been waiting a long time for a decision to be made about his fate and is resigned to wait-ing for a long time still.

Gathering himself, Gordon discovers there's no path on this side of the river either. The bank on which he sits is crowded by jungle. He couldn't chase after Yia Pao even if he had the strength.

He sits until the mosquitoes begin to circle and he has

to shoo them from Xang's face. Finally he rises and starts into the jungle with the little boy in his arms.

When Maggie walks out to check the mail that afternoon, she sees an unfamiliar object at the end of the driveway: a placard not more than two feet across held up by thin metal poles. The sight of it sets her stomach grinding, but the sign is oriented toward the road, so she has to wait until the last moment before the words become plain.

FOR SALE.

The bastard. He didn't even warn her.

To make sure it isn't an error, she phones the realtor listed on the sign. Then she calls Fletcher at his parents' house. It's his father's doing, it must be. If the man answers, she doesn't know what she'll say to him. But it's Fletcher who picks up.

"How are you?" he asks. The line whispers overtop of silence. "What is it? Are you all right?" She hates the way he says it. He's never coming back, she can tell just from his tone.

"Somebody put a For Sale sign out front today." On the other end there's an exclamation of surprise. "You didn't know?"

"It must be a mistake." He sounds genuinely upset. A month ago she would have taken him at his word. "I'll talk to Dad. We'll get it sorted out."

"Why don't you let me speak with him?"

"You mean right now? I don't think he's here." He says it too hastily.

"You knew about this, didn't you? Or was it your idea?"

"Really, he didn't say anything." He clears his throat before continuing. "All he told me was that if I couldn't show him a viable plan, he wouldn't be able to defend continued ownership."

She hates the way he lapses into his father's business-talk. "So you showed him a plan?"

"First I wanted to talk with you. I don't know whether things are feasible."

She hates words like "feasible." He doesn't call unless she badgers him. He lets her live on his father's money to salve his conscience while he lounges in Boston, and all because he was crazy enough to think she'd be turned on by that film.

Maggie still hasn't told him about being tested; she hasn't even reminded him about her missing period. Until now she has thought it would be unbearable if he were to come back early for the sake of someone who isn't born yet, a mere hypothesis, when he's decided not to return for her.

"Fletcher, I got tested," she says. "I'm pretty sure I'm pregnant."

At first she wonders if he has hung up. Then his voice comes over the line again.

"Why only pretty sure?" He sounds anything but loving.

"It's a long story. The results aren't official yet."

"Shouldn't we wait until they are before we get worked up about it?" He says it as though the results are a credit card bill that doesn't need paying until the end of the month.

"The doctor's secretary said it was positive! I told you I

was late three weeks ago, but you didn't take me seriously. You just ran away."

"It wasn't like that," he begins before cutting himself off. "All right," he says in a clipped, low voice. "Tell me what you want to do."

As the statement sits there between them, a buzzing starts in her brain.

"You think I should get rid of it." Part of her is impressed that she can be so forthright. Fletcher seems surprised too.

"I didn't say that, I just . . . It's a bit of a shock, that's all. We never talked about a baby."

"What do you mean? We've both said we wanted a family."

"Not this way."

He doesn't even ask her to come back to Boston anymore. He'd rather keep her hidden in this attic of a country. Suddenly she has never felt so dedicated to the place.

"I'm going to have the baby," she tells him, "and I'm not leaving this house." Before he can reply, she adds, "Thanks for the support." After rushing the receiver back to its cradle, she goes to the living room and turns on the television.

It takes him an hour to call. When he does, he says he's talked with his father and there's good news: he and Maggie will be allowed to keep working the farm. He says he'll be up in a week, as they planned. Sounding pleased with himself, he asks her when the results of the pregnancy test are going to be confirmed.

"They said maybe a week," she mumbles.

"Okay." He sounds unsure, as if it might be a point to argue. "Call me if you hear."

She says of course she will. Then a thought occurs to her. "What if it's negative? Will you still come?" He says he will, but she doesn't believe him. "What did your father say about the baby?" He doesn't answer. "Did you even tell him?" She isn't playing this game right, slashing about when she should be conciliatory, but she seems impervious to her own good advice. "Fletcher, I swear, you leave me here, I'll make this place such a success . . ."

"Jesus, you're keeping the farm, you're having the baby, I'll be there soon. What else do you want?"

Isn't it obvious? She wants him to want all these things too.

Afterward, she starts to see it in a better light. He's coming back in a week, and if he wasn't thrilled about the baby—well, she couldn't expect that right away.

She imagines how it could be: the warm bundle in her arms, then eventually a walking, talking child. They'll have a household of just three, with George Ray to help keep up the farm in the summers. She'll paper the walls in the playroom to make a nursery but leave the white wall as it is, and one day she'll screen her films again, this time for their child. Her father will return from Laos and visit them. Perhaps he'll even stay for good. So taken is she by these thoughts that she almost doesn't let it bother her when at dinner she and George Ray barely speak.

In the morning, she wakes up shivering and sees her breath in the cold air. Once dressed, she descends to the dirt-floor cellar and tries to start the boiler. There are

minutes of silence, then a terrible clanking as if someone
with a wrench is thrashing the pipes, before finally the radi-
ators start to hiss.

Out among the cherry trees, she finds that overnight the
landscape has transformed. The world is aflame with golden-
rod in flower and bushes bearing red, poisonous-looking
berries, while tiny butterflies swirl through the air like bits
of paper and grasshoppers take wing to thwack against
her leg. The earth seems sharper, more brittle than before,
infested by burrs, thistle, and bone white twigs. The air is
rank with the urine smell of rotting leaves. Abandoned
ladders, scythes, and bushel baskets litter the ground, and a
wagon lies covered in a black tarp that flaps in the wind like
a sail. The creek is a trickle of water through scummed rocks
and dried cress. She kicks through leaf drift worrying that
when Fletcher returns he'll expect her to have raked it all
away. After lunch, driving past a yard sale on the way to
Virgil, she spots an old-fashioned bassinet and buys it without bothering to haggle.

For the next few days, those times it isn't raining, there's
a grey gloom that makes her wish it would. The house
acquires a pervasive musty smell. When she tries to start a
fire in the living room hearth, the room ends up filled with
smoke, and there's the sound of a bird panicking in the
chimney. As she scrambles to open the windows, the creature flies into the room and darts about, leaving streaks
of soot on the walls before escaping. In the kitchen cupboards she finds fresh mouse turds. She sets traps, and in
the night the snap of their springing startles her awake.
When she goes to check the next morning, she finds two

tiny furred bodies pinned in the same mechanism, their necks broken and their noses touching.

There's no more word from Gran, but every night Fletcher phones dutifully, and Maggie spends much of the days anticipating his calls, totting up the things she has done and seen, trying not to let it faze her that each night he asks about the test results. Finally she tells him about her father, and he reassures her it will turn out all right. He says he'll see if his dad knows anybody over there who might be able to give them some answers. He tells her if she still hasn't heard anything in a couple of weeks, he'll fly over to Laos with her and they can go find her father together. It's foolish bravado, and it makes her angry. Fletcher has spent all this time away, yet now he's willing to travel across the world for her? He's the same as Wale.

Each time she hangs up the phone, solitude hurtles in on her. After all the hours of keeping busy, the night undoes the work of the day. She retreats to the television and watches *Truth or Consequences*. She watches *Search for Tomorrow* and *Mary Tyler Moore*. She watches *All in the Family*. One afternoon, finding nothing on the Buffalo stations she can bear to sit through, she resorts to watching a hockey game on the Toronto channel. The Canadians are playing the Russians in Moscow, the last game of a series she hasn't been following. It's the final period and the game is tied. When one of the Canadian players scores, there's jubilation among his teammates, but Maggie isn't really paying attention to them. Her eyes are on the thousands of Russians in the stands, dressed in suits and ties or dark woollen jackets. The few times the camera shows them, their faces are unblinking and forlorn. They have the look of children at Christmas who were promised one thing and given another.

That evening, George Ray doesn't appear in the kitchen to dine with her, and she doesn't go to check on him. There's a long list of things to do this weekend before Fletcher returns, but she can't bring herself to start any of them. Instead, she watches TV and takes in the people on the local news crowing over the hockey win. One of them says God must be a Canadian. She shakes her head and watches late into the night, while the clay statue of Saint Clare stares back at her from the top of the set. The next morning, when Maggie passes by the living room, she glances in at the television with contempt, as if the two of them have shared an ill-advised tryst.

Rain falls hard on the jungle, striking the canopy and collecting into giant drops that crash down on Gordon and the baby. Gordon's clothes are waterlogged, his hair plastered to his head, while Xang's little hands are shrivelled from the damp and a stream of yellow mucus runs from his nostrils. He breathes in time with Gordon's footsteps, the jolts producing wet little whispers of air. Below them, the river tumbles down the gorge, appearing and disappearing through the trees. Sometimes Gordon stops to stare in the direction of the water, but there's no sign of Yia Pao and little evidence of any life, only a pair of rats at the trailside, both of them enormous with matted black fur, indifferent to him as they gnaw at the innards of a rotting monkey.

The trails Gordon follows are no more than the pathways of animals, criss-crossed with fallen trees and clogged by branches that tear at his skin. A few times he has to stop and set Xang down to clear a way forward. Finally he reaches a place where it seems that a while ago someone went through with a machete, and he's able to walk more freely while resting Xang against his shoulder.

A hundred yards later, the path jogs. As he completes the turn, he stumbles over something, barely keeping his feet. At the same time there's a lash of movement, quicker than the eye can follow, and a sound like the flight of an arrow. An unseen force propels him backward, pinning him against a tree.

He doesn't move, only groans in agony. Slowly, his eyes travel down to his midriff. A long piece of bamboo presses against him there, the end of it neatly sawed off. A spike of metal sticking through it has pierced his body to an unknown depth.

"Oh God," he says. "Oh Jesus."

Raindrops stipple the surface of a puddle beneath him. When he tries to shift in place, blood spurts from his body and he stiffens. Xang starts crying, but Gordon doesn't comfort him, can't speak. For a long time he stands there, one arm around the wailing child while the other hangs at his side. The blood flows from him until it has soaked his shirt and begins to stain the puddle at his feet.

"Hush," he whispers at last, then he tries to sing. "Hush, little baby . . ." He repeats the words before falling silent again.

Branches around him droop under the weight of the rain. After a few minutes Xang gives up his crying. A black rat crosses the path and sniffs the air, looks Gordon in the eye, sizes up the baby.

"I promise," Gordon murmurs. "I promise, Xang, I won't let go."

It's getting darker. Xang whimpers a little, falls into sleep. Eventually the puddle at Gordon's feet overflows its edges, and a trickle of pinkish water starts making its way toward the river.

Monday morning, Maggie awakens at sunrise and goes straight to the kitchen for coffee. It's the second day of October, and there are only twelve hours until Fletcher arrives. At nine she's tempted to call the doctor's office, but already she has made herself a nuisance there, and they've said they'll contact her when they know. What else to do? In the orchard she finds George Ray mending the wire fence that keeps out deer, and she asks him if he has any jobs for her. He shakes his head but suggests they eat lunch together when it's time. This is a surprise. They almost never have lunch together, and all week they've maintained their distance from each other. Perhaps he's trying to distract her from the waiting, or maybe he's realized it will be their last chance to share a meal on their own.

After she hears the mailman's truck turn in the drive, she walks out to the box. There's a letter there, the address written in a hand she doesn't recognize, the stamp from Laos. Opening the envelope, she finds two sheets folded inside, coffee-stained and rumpled as though stuffed in a pocket for some time before they were mailed. The handwriting on them is cramped so as to get everything in.

Dear Maggie,

Yesterday I finally reached the mission. Traveling takes longer here now that Air America is pulling out. The mission's a charming little place, with tents and fish ponds and a big fucking crater in the yard. The people aren't much into talking, at least not to me or my loyal interpreter (sweet guy, one-armed, probably Pathet Lao), but I can be persuasive when I want to be.

That morning in the grocery store when you told me about not hearing from your dad, I got worried, so I called a friend in Laos, and it turned out I was right to be. Sorry for cutting out like I did, but I figured the sooner I got over here, the better.

See, there's this guy I know named Sal. I mentioned him in that film of yours. Used to be in Special Forces with me—now he's a drug runner. When the army caught up with me in Thailand, they accused me of being in his gang. They were wrong, but as luck would have it I'd just seen him in Laos.

You might remember me saying I met your dad at Long Chieng in May. What I didn't tell you is that I was there because of Sal. He and his buddies were running a good racket in Laos, stealing opium from farmers and selling to the CIA. After I went AWOL I bumped into him. He and I were on a bender in Long Chieng when we met your dad and his buddy Yia Pao.

I have to admit, right from the start I had a bad feeling. Your dad said where they were headed and Sal got this look in his eye. But we were pretty drunk and I figured nothing would come of it. Forgot about the whole thing until that morning in Virgil at the grocery store when you said your dad hadn't been in touch. Then I got a hell of a jolt. I should have known. Sal doesn't believe in coincidences, and he doesn't let chances go to waste. He probably spent the whole summer wondering how he could make use of those two guys.

When I called my friend in Laos, he didn't know anything about your dad or Yia Pao, but he knew Sal had a deal going down with a bagman at some refugee camp. Plan was for the CIA plane to drop off the money, then for Sal to pick it up the next day. The CIA doesn't like dealing directly with the banditos, because it looks bad to the natives. Apparently when Sal turned up, though, the bagman said the money hadn't come in. So Sal checks with the CIA, and of course they said the bagman's story was bullshit. They didn't ask Sal what he'd done about the bagman. That isn't how things work over here.

I'm pretty sure your old man wasn't wrapped up in it. The priest at the mission figures it was just Yia Pao. But he says that after Sal and his boys turned up, they took your dad along with Yia Pao and his baby.

Sal's not stupid enough to go killing Americans. I bet he's thinking he can cover his losses by getting a ransom for your father.

Anyhow, I'm sorry for breaking the news like this. There's no phone here. Also, I don't want you jumping on a plane or getting the State Department involved to fuck things up. I can handle it, Maggie, I swear. By the time you get this, everything will be sorted out. Hell, maybe your dad is there beside you. He can tell you how good old Wale saved his ass. I'll find him, I promise.

Thought I was doing the right thing by going to the farm. Thought I could be a proper father and put this part of the world behind me. You can't just move on, though, can you? You drag your shit with you like a parachute till it snags and you have to start sawing at the cords. I have my knife out now, Maggie. I'm hacking with all I've got.

Sorry for going on like this. There's been too much time to think this week. Hardly anyone here speaks English, and the opium's cheap. You spend a lot of the day in your own skull.

I keep dreaming about you, and it's always the same dream. On the phone you said you didn't want to hear about it, but it's not dirty like you were probably thinking. In the dream we're out in the garden behind the farmhouse again, only it's full of fruit and vines. Then Brid comes looking for us like she really did that day, but this time we run into the orchard and hide from her. It's a nice dream. The last few nights I've fallen asleep hoping I'll have it again.

A couple more hours at the mission and then I'm going upriver. I know I told you not to come, but I wish you were here. Yeah, that's right, I want you in this hellhole with me. I'd trade your comfort and well-being for a bit of company. Wouldn't even hesitate. I told you I'm a bastard. Have you figured that out yet? You understand now the kinds of people there are in the world? Real nice folks who'll break your arm before they say hello. Assholes who can't even look in the mirror.

Wale

After that there's a postscript, but it's been scribbled out, hard enough to poke through the paper.

She checks the envelope again. The postmark is too blurred to discern the date. It must have taken the letter at least a couple of weeks to get here, yet in all that time there was no news about her father from anyone. If what Wale says is true, surely someone must have found out something by now. She has to call Gran and let her know what Wale has written.

Once more she reads the thing. He was probably high when he wrote it. Maybe he's not even in Laos anymore but in Bangkok or Hong Kong—or Buffalo, for all she knows, sitting in a bar and having a good laugh.

As her outrage grows, she realizes she's angry not just with Wale but with her father. Didn't she tell him it wasn't safe? All along she said that, yet he talked like the only protection he needed was her, like if she didn't go with him, any worrying she did would be her fault. Now look where it has gotten him.

As she walks back up the driveway and steps onto the porch, the phone starts to ring. It's Wale, she thinks. It's the doctor's office. It's her father calling to say he's all right. Rushing through the house, she snatches the receiver just at the dying of the bell and finds it isn't any of them. It's Fletcher. Maggie looks at the clock and frowns.

"Where are you?" she asks.

"Still in Boston."

"What happened? You should be through Albany by now—"

"Something's come up. We're having problems with the Brookline voters list."

If he's joking, she doesn't see the humour in it. "I thought you were done with the campaign."

"I want to be, but I was assigned this thing a while back. I feel like I should get it finished." He speaks as if everything he says is reasonable and has to be accepted.

"Fletcher, that's crazy. Let someone else do it. I need you up here." Then she hears a woman's voice at the other end of the line. "Who's that talking?"

"Nobody. Just someone at the campaign office."

"Fletcher, what's going on? You're waiting to hear about the baby, aren't you?"

"No, of course not." But he goes silent.

"Fletcher, my dad's been kidnapped. You hear me? Some drug dealer has taken my father." Saying it aloud sends her into a panic, and she tries to control her breathing as she waits for his reaction. He doesn't speak, though. There's just the woman talking again in the background, then Fletcher replying to her, their voices muffled as if he has covered the receiver with his hand. Still, Maggie can hear his tone, supportive and slightly exasperated at once. She recognizes it well enough. All month on the phone he's used the same one with her. "Sorry," he says, his voice returning to full clarity. "Things at the campaign office are a bit hectic. I'll call you back after lunch, okay?"

"Didn't you hear what I said?" she cries.

"Look, I'll make it up to you, I promise. I love you, baby," he says. A moment later there's the click of him hanging up.

The receiver in her hand feels insubstantial. It doesn't matter, she tells herself. He was just distracted and didn't hear her. She doesn't need him anyhow. Maybe she doesn't even love him. No, that isn't right. It's some kind of trespass to think like that. Love might inflate and shrivel, it may be impatient or unkind, but it keeps on going, doesn't it?

When she calls Gran, the line's busy. In a few minutes she'll call again. To distract herself, she turns on the television and flops across the couch. Onscreen, a man in a suit is saying there are only five weeks until the election.

She doesn't want to hear about the election. She's sick of waiting, sick of politics, sick of television telling her that everything important is elsewhere, that her only role is to stay tuned and find out what happens next. From the kitchen, she fetches a pair of scissors.

By the time she returns to the living room, it's as if the deed is already done, and she's glad. In her mind the future's no longer a maze of unexplored passages but a safe, well-lit corridor leading through the years to come: her father's return, her baby a toddler, then growing into a little girl. But it could be a son. Why does she assume it will be a girl?

Crouching behind the silver orb of the TV set, Maggie unplugs it and with one snip of the blades cuts the power cord in two. Immediately she feels the world dwindling. Not for her the Cold War, the hijackings, and the price of oil. Already her life is growing smooth as a stone in a river. Time flows around her. Nothing sticks.

As she stands again, she brushes against the set and her elbow catches the clay statue of Saint Clare perched on top. Before she can do anything, the figure goes tumbling from its place. It lands face up and stares at her accusingly with its black eyes.

"What are you looking at?" Maggie says. She snatches it up and throws it against the wall. Falling to the floor, it cracks in two, the legs neatly separating from the torso.

For a moment it feels like a triumph. Then she thinks the statue could be the last thing her father ever gave her. No, she can't think like that. She can't start feeling sorry for herself or him. Probably he sent the statue less as a gift than a provocation, another way to make her feel guilty.

Crossing the room, she bends to retrieve the pieces. When she touches the top half, she feels its cool surface on her skin, then the rough white line of the fracture.

"Doesn't matter," she says. "Doesn't mean anything."

As she picks it up, an object dislodges from inside. It drops through the air, takes a soft bounce on the floor, and comes to rest by the statue's feet. At first Maggie registers only sheets of paper, greenish-grey, then the rubber band that holds them together. Finally they resolve into a thick wad of bills. She takes them in hand and thumbs through them. They all seem to be hundreds.

The telephone's ringing from the kitchen. Maggie looks from the cracked torso in one hand to the roll of money in the other. Setting the statue down again, she turns, still holding the bills, and hurries out of the room to answer.

part 3

PATRON SAINT

of

TELEVISION

8

Her last night at Gran's, the night before the funeral, she's already eager to be back on the farm. The house next door calls to her dolefully, but so far she has managed to avoid it, instead only looking through the boxes carried over by the auction people and choosing a few things to take with her. She doesn't need physical reminders of him. She isn't like Gran, who has framed photos of him everywhere now. All week Gran has kept referring to his martyrdom, talking about it like something to celebrate, not bothering to ask Maggie a single question about her life. It makes what Gran says over dessert all the more surprising.

"That Fletcher Morgan left you, didn't he?"

Apple crumble lodges in Maggie's throat. Gran doesn't wait for her reply.

"It doesn't matter. You stick it out up there. Show him what a woman can do."

Maggie can't believe what she's hearing. Out of the blue, like a blast of grace, she has finally been granted the grandmother she always wanted. In her astonishment, she blurts out her plans to purchase the farm and work the place herself. Gran shocks her again by approving.

It doesn't last. The next morning Gran is tetchy and caustic, back to her usual self, unable to stop talking about the miracle of her son's death.

At the cemetery, fallen leaves rustle around the headstones while an American flag twists and snaps against the sky. Maggie stands with Gran and a few dozen others near the open grave, keeping her chin tucked low so the brim of her hat obscures her face. While the elderly priest speaks and Gran dabs away tears with a handkerchief, Maggie sneaks glances at those around her. Finally she spots Fletcher near the back in his trench coat. His hair has been cropped, and he's reaching up to tug at a moustache no longer there.

The priest makes the sign of the cross. Soon most of the mourners disperse, but a few stay behind to converse in hushed voices. Maggie doesn't speak much, just accepts the words of others. She's remembering how her father used to call her Opie and announce his return from work by whistling the theme song from *The Andy Griffith Show*. She remembers the two of them pretending to be Topo Gigio and Ed Sullivan, Maggie saying to him in a high-pitched voice, "Eddie, keesa me good night!"

Fletcher waits until everyone but she and Gran has gone before he draws near. He gives Maggie a tentative hug.

"You didn't have to come," she tells him. "I said that on the phone, right?"

Gran glares at him, then says she'll see Maggie at Aunt Harriet's and starts away. Once she's gone, they begin to walk together across the grass.

"It was a nice funeral," says Fletcher.

"It should have been weeks ago," she replies. "There was a lot of red tape getting him back." She grimaces at her own words. Her father isn't back. He'll never be back. "The Church has been making a big deal about him, you know. Reporters keep turning up at Gran's doorstep."

Fletcher says he heard about it on the news. He says it must be hard for Gran.

"Oh, she's loving every minute," Maggie replies. "She and the bishop are thick as thieves. Today she bent over backwards to avoid introducing me to him. She doesn't want the hippie daughter spoiling things."

Fletcher gives her a startled look, and she realizes she doesn't sound like herself. She doesn't care. He can't expect her to be the same as always.

"Gran blames me for his death," she says. "She thinks he wouldn't have been so reckless if I'd written him like he wanted."

"She said that?" asks Fletcher. "Don't listen to her. She's projecting, probably."

They leave the grass and start along a path of crushed stones. After a few steps, he turns and asks if she's still going back to Canada tonight. "Long drive on your own. Maybe wait until tomorrow?"

She shakes her head. "If I have to stay at her place one more night, I'll go insane."

"You've been through a lot," he says, and she wonders what he's thinking of exactly. Then he asks, "Did you tell her about the pregnancy?"

Maggie cringes and pulls up short. "Phantom pregnancy, you mean." She doesn't want to talk about it. "No, I didn't tell her. Why would I? There was nothing to tell." A part of her still worries that he thinks she tried to trick him. She didn't read the symptoms right, that's all. The doctor said anyone could have made the mistake. She still hasn't fully forgiven Lenka for mishearing what the secretary told her.

Fletcher reaches to put his hand on her shoulder, but she shies at his touch. "You're a strange one," she says. "Two months in Boston refusing to come back, only visiting that once after I found out he was dead"—Fletcher starts to object, but she cuts him off—"and then, without me asking, you drive all the way here for this."

He keeps his eyes on the ground and doesn't reply.

"You know, I prayed for McGovern to lose," she finds herself saying. "Back in October, when I still thought we might work things out. I worried that if the Democrats got in, you'd take a job in Washington. I figured if Nixon was re-elected, you'd move back to the farm."

Fletcher stops in the middle of the path, looking dazed. "Why are you telling me this now?"

She doesn't know. It was the first thing that came to

mind, and the part of her that censors speech seems broken. She watches a man and woman in blue rain slickers pass by hand in hand, while a little boy wearing a baseball cap skips ahead.

"George Ray's going home in ten days," she says. This morning she promised herself she wouldn't mention him. "The second extension on his contract is up. He'd have come down for this, but migrant workers aren't allowed to cross the border."

"You're going to miss him," says Fletcher. There's an insinuation in his words that she chooses to ignore.

"He's been a big help on the farm. Most days he's the only person I see. Sometimes there's Father Josef and Lenka. I go to their place for dinner." Fletcher seems surprised. "Don't look at me like that. You think I want to hang out with priests?" Then she adds, "It's hard having a social life when everyone's run out on you."

Fletcher takes on a pained expression. From her pocket she produces a pack of cigarettes and lights one.

"You still stuck on your plan to buy the farm?" he asks.

"I told you I was serious, didn't I? As soon as the lawyer gets Dad's finances sorted out, I'll know where I stand." She has other means now too, but she isn't about to mention them.

"And more Jamaicans in the spring?" he says. "You sure this is something you want to do?" She sets her mouth, stays silent. "I mean, I'll make sure you get a fair deal, but it's company property, I can't just give it to you—"

"Don't worry," she says. "I promise not to make you look bad in front of your old man."

His shoulders slump. "That isn't what I meant. Don't you think you should wait, at least? It hasn't even been two months. You need time to mourn—"

"Fletcher, I don't think you're in a place to judge what I need."

He hangs his head, and she takes a long drag on her cigarette, then flicks it away. A mist has settled on the cemetery lawn and it's begun to drizzle, beading on the brim of her hat.

He points toward the gate leading to the street. "Walk with me to the car? I have something for you." They move onto a paved walkway lined by thick elms with amputated limbs. Halfway to the gate, he stops and says, "Listen, Brid came with me."

"She's here?" Maggie turns back toward the burial site. "Where—"

"Coffee shop a few blocks over. At the last second she decided it would be too much. She's a wreck. Completely broke down last month." His voice slows along with his pace. "She took pills."

"Oh," says Maggie.

"She spent three weeks in a sanatorium—how do they put it?—under observation."

Maggie moves closer and takes his hand, pulls him to a halt and hugs him. "Why did no one tell me?"

"She didn't want you to find out. You had the news about your dad to deal with."

Holding him isn't what Maggie expected. She hoped its familiarity would be a relief, but his body doesn't feel right, doesn't fit. She draws away and resumes walking toward the gate.

"Pauline's been at her uncle's," he says, "and this week Brid stayed at my place. But lately——" There's a hitch in his step. "Well, she's got the idea that she should spend some time on the farm."

"What, now?"

"She thinks you need looking after. I told her you wouldn't want visitors, but when she's got something into her head . . ."

They pass through the gate and onto the street, waiting to let a man go by with three spaniels straining against their leashes, leaping together like one animal.

"She'd be a handful," says Fletcher. "If you don't want her, you should just tell her no."

Maggie tries to imagine Brid back at the farm and remembers her last night there, her fury, her glassy eyes.

"Fletcher, I'd take her, but it's really not a good time." Surely she can't be the answer to Brid's problems. There must be someone else. "What about Wale? Still no word from him?"

"Not since he left the farm. Don't mention him to Brid, okay? To be honest, I thought the sanatorium was wrong to let her out, but somehow she convinced them she was doing better." He pulls a set of keys from his pocket. "Will you come say hi, at least?"

Maggie looks at her watch. "I'm due at Aunt Harriet's——"

"Just five minutes. Please?"

A little way down the sidewalk, he stops beside a silver Bentley. The dented, rusting camper van sits farther down the street, where she parked it. Opening the car's trunk, he draws out a cardboard box. As he lifts it, there's the clang of metal against metal.

"Here," he says. "The camera's in there with the reels." But she can't bring herself to reach for them, and he has to press the box into her hands. "You don't want them?"

"I don't know. For a long time I did." She rests the box on a hip, thinking of what's inside. "You edited out—" Solemnly he nods, and Maggie has a terrible, cruel thought. "Hey, did you show it to Cybil? She might think it's a turn-on."

He only stares at her with pained eyes. "I told you, Cybil and I aren't—"

"I know," she says. "But sometimes I think it would be easier if you were."

In their separate vehicles, they drive half a mile before pulling into a small parking lot with a row of storefronts. Brid sits on the other side of the coffee shop window reading a book. She isn't wearing sunglasses or makeup, and her coat is draped around her shoulders like a blanket. With a wave, she greets them from behind the glass, then frets over a run in her stocking until they enter and she stands to give Maggie a long embrace.

They begin to talk with fragile smiles, and Maggie has a sense of growing distant from herself, observing the conversation from outside. At one point Brid starts up and runs for the bathroom, leaving Fletcher and Maggie to stare at one another across the table. Finally Maggie goes off in pursuit. A few minutes later she returns with Brid on her arm and nods to him. The coffee shop door jingles as they exit. From the trunk of the Bentley he retrieves a suitcase and loads it into the camper. He and Brid hug, exchange a few words, hug again. Then Maggie and Brid get into the van and drive off.

The farmhouse at night. No crickets, moon, or stars. In Maggie's bedroom, all is dark but for a line of light from the hall. A shadow disturbs it and the door swings open.

"You awake?" says George Ray. "I brought company." He has Elliot over his shoulder. When he sets him down, the cat crosses the floor with headlight eyes and jumps onto the bed, starts purring, gently pummels her with his paws. George Ray remains at the threshold.

"You shouldn't be here," she whispers. "We agreed you'd stay in the barracks tonight."

"Don't worry, I came with great stealth." He steps into the room and closes the door behind him. "Are you all right? You want to talk?"

"Later. God, I've missed you. Hurry, get into bed."

He takes off his clothes and lies down next to her. At the edge of the mattress the cat grooms itself. George Ray touches her a long time between the legs until she squirms away.

"Enough," she says. "Inside me." He shakes his head. "Why not?"

"I'm shy," he replies, and she gives an unbelieving laugh. "No, not shy, but, you know—it's a sad time for you . . ."

She climbs on top of him. Afterward, she can't stop crying.

"I'm sorry," she says. "It was just so horrible all week." He strokes her hair. "You think Brid heard?" He doesn't think so. "Is it okay, her being here? She bawled when we crossed the border."

"Don't worry. Only a few more days for me anyhow."

She groans and holds him tighter. He says he wishes they'd met long ago, when he was still young. She asks him if he was being honest when he said he'd liked her even in the summer, and he says it's the truth. Then she starts to question him about his wife. At this, he rolls to the far side of the bed, but she pursues him across it. Will Velma meet him at the airport? Will they make love the first night, or will she make him wait to pay him back for being away so long?

"Do you ask these questions to punish me?" he demands. "Or to punish yourself?"

"I don't care what happens, I'm resigned to it," she says. Turning onto her back, she asks, "You think Velma's had lovers?"

There's a flicker of impatience on his face. "Seven years for me in Canada," he replies, "six months apart each year. Long time to be lonely."

Maggie cogitates on these words. She tells him he should go back to the barracks, and he says he doesn't want to.

"Go," she insists. "Think about your beautiful wife and children."

"Don't say such things. You had a sad day. I want to be with you."

"Why? What can you do?" He tries to hold her, but she shrugs him off. "You should leave. It's good practice for later."

He lets his head drop heavily on the pillow. "All right, if you insist—"

When he starts to get up, though, she grabs his leg. "Wait, not yet!"

And laughing quietly, he falls back to the bed.

That night in her dreams, she's at the Syracuse airport again, waiting for her father's ashes to arrive. The plane lands, and with its appearance her trepidation begins to build. The aircraft taxis down the runway, stopping some distance from her, and passengers start to disembark, a line of tourists in Bermuda shorts along with soldiers in uniform. Maggie hopes that this time her father will appear among them, but there's no sign, only a pair of men in dark suits who wait ominously by the tail. Maggie doesn't want to be here. When she wills herself to turn, something won't let her. She tries to scream and discovers that fear has stopped up her mouth.

A shadow falls across the ground. Someone's standing behind her. His voice speaks into her ear.

"Who are you waiting for, little girl?"

At the moment his hand clutches her neck, she leaps awake.

All morning, Brid doesn't leave her room. Maggie putters in the kitchen while terrible images run through her head, but she's afraid to go upstairs and knock, fearful that Brid will sense the reason. Maggie shouldn't have let her come. Half the time she can barely get out of bed herself; how can she be expected to look after someone else? Brid took pills, for God's sake. In a panic, Maggie goes upstairs and clears out the medicine cabinet.

Afterward, she stands in the hall by Brid's room listening for signs of life. When she hears the creak of bedsprings, she decides she's had enough. An impulse has been growing in her ever since she awoke, but until now she hasn't been able to act. Now she goes to her bedroom and retrieves the Super 8 camera, loads it with film, and carries it into the orchard.

The weight of the strap on her shoulder feels out of sync with the season. The trees around her should be green-leaved, the air sweltering and alive with voices, but there are only dark clouds and a chill breeze promising winter. Hoses have been put away for the year, while the branches of the cherry trees are bare and pruned. The pumpkins were harvested weeks ago. A lone relic remains on the porch, skull-faced and caving in on itself, welcoming costumed kids who never came.

The camera in her hands feels alien and ill-intentioned. For whom would she be filming, anyway? Not for Fletcher. Not for any child of theirs. Not for Maggie's father. He'll never see this place. Her father is buried dust. He's a roll of banknotes. Gran's right: Maggie should have replied to his letters. She shouldn't have let him go in the first place.

Walking up and down the orchard lanes, she looks for things to film. The ground is muddy, and George Ray has laid out planks on which to pass over the worst stretches. As she makes her way across, she thinks about her calls to him this week, the late night whispering down the line in

Gran's kitchen. It was amazing how much solace Maggie took from hearing his voice, when two months ago they barely knew each other.

All she knows about her father's death comes from the priest at the mission. On the phone, he told her that there'd been an opium deal with Yia Pao as the middleman, that her father had been an innocent bystander who was kidnapped when the deal went wrong. The man in the State Department who talked to Maggie after she sent them Wale's letter was unable to confirm the existence of a man named Sal, and he didn't put much stock in Wale's story. He called it hearsay from a deserter.

Her father's body was found miles from anywhere, in a region so depopulated by bombing that news of his death didn't reach the authorities for weeks. A month had passed by the time Gran and Maggie found out. The weekend of the Labour Day party at the farm, her father was likely dead already. There was no coroner's report or police investigation to tell them what happened for certain; death in Laos is too common for that. There has been no sign of Yia Pao, either, and no trace of the gang that kidnapped them. There's only the priest's account of what was discovered: her father, still warm; the infant, barely living. The priest said Maggie's father must have escaped his captors, because how else could he have ended up with the baby in the jungle? She doesn't know, and Wale hasn't surfaced to tell her. No word in two months, nothing since his letter. But somehow he must have been involved in what happened. Maybe he's too ashamed to get in touch, or maybe he's dead and nobody will ever reveal the truth.

No one will tell her what to do with the ten thousand dollars in the statue of Saint Clare.

Maggie hasn't put it in a bank, hasn't spent a dime of it, just hid it in the attic and hasn't breathed a word, not even to George Ray. She can't go to the police, because what if they seize the money and her father intended it for a purpose? It was tempting to tell Gran, if only to disrupt all the talk of holy martyrdom, but Maggie has no desire to tarnish her father's reputation. She wants to believe that somehow he didn't know what was in the statue, that he was smarter than to get involved with criminals and send so much money through the mail. Except he must have known. Maybe he was in on some scheme with Yia Pao; maybe her father double-crossed him. Maybe he felt reckless and didn't care if he was caught.

These possibilities have to be considered, because on her nightstand lies his final letter, now read over many times, damning him with its guile. *We're all His vessels*, he wrote, *sealed up in ourselves*. A hint disguised as theology, spelling out his guilt. Did he want her to spend the money, or did he plan on coming back and claiming it? Sometimes she thinks the only fair thing would be to give it over for the care of Yia Pao's son, but when she wrote the priest at the mission, he replied that he didn't know where the child was, and he warned it would be foolish of her to come searching for him.

The priest's right. What does she know of Laos? That it's cold at night in the mountains where they found her father but tropical and humid in the valleys, hot enough for those who handle the dead to forgo embalming. Instead, they burn bodies on pyres and send the ashes of foreigners back on planes.

If she could do so without guilt, she'd use the money to purchase the farm. There's no other way she can afford it. Her father's debts will gobble up the life insurance payout, even if the company makes good. They're claiming his policy was voided when he entered a war zone. They say it was tantamount to suicide, and maybe they aren't wrong.

She has walked half the orchard without stopping once to film. The camera's strap digs into her shoulder. Ahead of her is the farthest corner of the farm, where the perimeter fence ends and the corrugated metal of the wrecking yard wall begins. Nothing grows along it; the soil is stained rusty orange and reeks of gasoline.

As she gets nearer, she glimpses something she has never noticed before: flashes of scarlet on the wall. Writing done with spray paint. Her first thought is that Lydia Dodd has returned to cause trouble. Then she realizes what the writing says.

In two-foot lettering are the words *DIRTY MONEY*.

They can't be referring to what she fears. Lydia couldn't know what's in the statue. Maybe it's a reference to Morgan Sugar. Maybe it's just an obscure joke.

She starts back toward the house thinking she'll grab a bucket of paint from the cellar. A few brushstrokes and the words will be gone. Then she won't have to speculate with anybody about their meaning. She won't have to imagine someone who knows about the money lurking on the farm at night, seeking to torment her with the knowledge.

Getting rid of it takes half an hour. When she's finished, she finds Brid lying on the living room couch in her nightie, watching *Captain Kangaroo*.

"What happened to the other TV?" says Brid, pointing at the new set. It's plain and boxy, with imitation walnut panels.

"I threw it out," Maggie replies. "Thought I didn't need it." She's distracted by the sight of Brid's tangled hair and puffy face. Could Brid have been the one to do it, sneaking outside late at night to paint the words? Maggie can't imagine why she would, but it seems a strange coincidence that the graffiti should appear the same night as her return. Brid doesn't look in shape for such a venture, though. She doesn't look much in shape for anything.

"I look bad, huh?" she says.

"No, same old you," says Maggie. "But without the sunglasses."

"Yeah, my eyes are better now that I'm off La Evil."

The admission feels like an invitation to talk, but Maggie's mind is still on the graffiti. She wants to check on the money and make sure it's there. To do that, she needs to get Brid out of the house, and right now it doesn't feel safe to send her someplace on her own.

When Maggie asks whether she's hungry, Brid jumps from the couch and proclaims how thoughtless she has been. What would Maggie like? Some tea? A sandwich? It takes a moment for Maggie to accept that Brid isn't being sarcastic.

"Really, you don't have to," she says, but Brid insists. Isn't that why she came? To take care of her? Maggie agrees to tea, though she doesn't want it, and Brid heads for the kitchen. A few minutes later she returns, looking troubled and without any tea in evidence.

"I don't have money," she says. "I can't pay for my keep." She seems genuinely anxious, as if she might be turned out for want of funds. Surely it can't be that heartbreaking.

"Don't worry, stay as long as you like," Maggie says.

"I'm sorry I left," says Brid, bursting into tears. "I'm so sorry." Maggie takes her hand and squeezes it. "God, I'm a disaster. I cried when we crossed the border, did you notice?" Maggie says she didn't. "I feel terrible about your father." Brid sniffles and collapses onto the couch. "Poor Pauline. Poor little sweetie. You must think I'm rotten. I've left my daughter."

Maggie sits down beside her. "You just needed a break. She's being looked after, isn't she?"

"Sure," replies Brid without conviction. "God, she'll never forgive me. I've fucked her up for life."

"She'll be fine," says Maggie, thinking that once Pauline is reunited with her mother, she'll probably forget about what happened. Maybe one day it will come flooding out again in front of some encounter group.

Brid seems to have followed her own unspoken train of thought, because her head is cocked in curiosity. "You're on the pill now? I saw the package in the medicine cabinet before you emptied it out." She says it without any clear intimation. Still, Maggie feels herself blush.

"It keeps my period steady." She thinks of adding that it's a different brand than before, and that so far this one hasn't bothered her, but she never told Brid about her troubles with the pill in the first place. Then she thinks ahead to another night of George Ray sneaking down the hall or of her crossing the lawn to the barracks in the darkness. "Also," she says, "George Ray and I have got involved."

Brid's face drops, and Maggie rebukes herself. She hasn't told anyone; she and George Ray made an agreement. Why start with Brid, the last person who should know? She'll feel passed over; she'll make a scene. Maggie tries to think of an amendment to undo her mistake. *George Ray and I have got involved—with the Kiwanis Club.* No, it's too late. Brid nods as if the news confirms something long suspected.

"His wife doesn't know," Maggie adds. "He's going home in ten days. You'll keep it quiet?"

Before Brid can respond, Elliot slinks into the room and makes a beeline for her. When she spots him coming, she looks surprised.

"Isn't that—" she begins, and Maggie nods.

"Yeah, John-John. We call him Elliot now." Then she adds, "Don't tell the Centaurs."

Brid smiles conspiratorially. It's the first time since the coffee shop in Syracuse that Maggie has seen her smile, but she seems less pleased when the cat begins to rub itself against her shins.

"I'm not a cat person," she says.

"Too bad. He likes you."

"Men," says Brid. "This is always how it starts."

As if aware that he's the subject of their conversation, Elliot amuses them by exploring every cranny of the room, taking fright at a splotch of light on the floor, then attacking

the armchair. Finally he perches on the sill above the radiator, sphinx-like, eyes closing by degrees. Maggie's glad of
his presence. Talk of cats is safe and harmless. It's better
than speaking of Brid's troubles, of George Ray, of the
words painted on the wrecking yard wall. It's better than
talking about pretty much anything in their lives.

All that morning, George Ray doesn't appear in the house,
as though he really does resent Brid's arrival. If he does,
Maggie can't blame him for it. The week in Syracuse took
her away from him with less than a month left together.
Now the final days have been stolen from them too.

When he turns up for lunch, he smells of woodsmoke
and seems congenial enough, even saying hello to Brid
at the table like he's missed her. More surprising still,
Brid greets him with an equal warmth. Surely neither of
them has forgotten the last night they saw each other.
Nevertheless, as Maggie slices bread at the counter, they
talk like old friends, Brid asking him about the orchard's
prospects, George Ray quizzing her on Nixon's re-election.
Gradually Maggie realizes they're doing it for her benefit.
They want to make things easier on her. But by the time
they have finished the meal, her desire to check on the
money is nearly overpowering.

"Why don't you give Brid a tour of the orchard?" she
tells George Ray. "I'll handle the dishes. Show her what
we've done since September."

He gives her a baffled look. It's true, there isn't much
to show.

"Fed up with me already?" says Brid. Maggie starts to protest, but Brid isn't listening. "Come on, Georgie Porgie, let's get out of here." She starts for the mud room, and hesitantly he follows.

As soon as they're out the door, Maggie hurries upstairs. At the end of the hall she unfolds a stepladder, climbs it, and pushes aside the trap door to the attic. Hoisting herself with a grunt, she wriggles forward on her belly.

The air is musty under the sloping roof, and there's little light except what comes through a small window at the far end. Apart from the whistling of air through a crack, it's still and quiet. No floor up here, just rafters with nothing between them but pink insulation and, beneath it, the plaster ceiling of the second-storey rooms. Standing, she curls her toes around the edge of the beam supporting her. The first time she came up here looking for somewhere to stow the statue, it was like that dream she has sometimes where she's back in Syracuse and discovers whole new rooms in Gran's house that she never realized were there. Now the rest of the farmhouse grows faint and distant as she takes in the things abandoned here over the years. A coat rack, a washtub, stacks of yellowed newspapers, jars full of an amber liquid that could be moonshine or maple syrup. There are fishing rods, broken hockey sticks and snow shovels, half-empty cans of motor oil. A tricycle has been propped against the wall with streamers on the handlebars and its front wheel missing. Affixed to a dartboard hanging from the roof is a photograph of Joe McCarthy, his face perforated many times over and barely recognizable. In the corner is one of Maggie's few additions to the place, the bassinet purchased at the yard sale. It's been there a month, yet already it has the same dusty, abject countenance as everything else.

The shelf holding the clay statue is next to the window. Maggie makes her way toward it carefully with arms out to balance. One misstep and she'll go crashing headlong through to the playroom. As she teeters across the rafters, the choice to hide the thing up here seems worse and worse. The little saint seems to taunt her. When she finally picks it up, the statue holds a low heat from sitting in the sunlight. By its weight she thinks the money's still inside, but repeated shaking brings no confirmation. It was a mistake to have resealed the thing; now she'll have to smash it again.

Before she can act on the thought, she hears the groan of the stepladder. She turns and sees George Ray's head pop up through the trap door.

"What happened to the tour?" she asks, quickly setting the statue back in place.

"Brid was worried about you. I agreed to see how you're doing."

Heaving himself into the attic, he approaches across the beams, showing none of her fear or caution. When he reaches her, he picks up the statue from the shelf and turns it over, examining the squibs of dried glue that seeped from the cracks when she pressed the thing back together. She resists a desire to snatch it from him.

"When did it break?" he asks, and she says she can't remember. "Tired of having it downstairs?"

"It—it was painful to see every day." It's not a lie, exactly. "We should go back down."

"Wait. Will you tell me about the graffiti first?"

Maggie feels her face grow hot with blood. "You saw it?"

"Just before lunch."

"But I painted it out."

"It needs another coat." His voice carries the hint of a reprimand, as if she should have told him.

"I didn't want to bother you. It's probably just Frank Dodd's daughter getting up to no good." She explains about the can of spray paint the girl had that night in the summer.

"But why would she write those words?" he asks.

Maggie shrugs, avoiding his eyes.

"Perhaps it was someone else," he says. "You could call the police."

"I don't want to cause a fuss." She finds her gaze returning to the statue in his hand.

"Oh, Maggie," he says softly, "do you ever cause a fuss?"

The statement takes her aback. It's something Brid would say; Maggie doesn't want to hear it from him.

"I don't know what you mean."

"I mean, you lose your papa and you keep it in." His tone is compassionate, but that only makes it worse. "Soon I'll leave too, and—"

"You think I don't care about my father? You think I don't care about you going?"

"I know you do. But you keep in all those feelings."

"We knew from the start that you had to leave." Even to herself she sounds cold, and he doesn't respond, only clutches the statue in a manner that seems possessive. Instinctively she reaches out to take it from him, and instinctively he resists letting go of it. When he pulls the figure away from her, it slips from both their fingers.

Maggie has a vision of it crashing through the ceiling beneath them, tumbling to the floor far below, breaking into a hundred shards and a swarm of paper bills. George Ray reaches for it as it falls, loses his balance on the rafter, flails. Grabbing his arm to steady him, she's dragged forward. They end up pressed together, frozen in place, one's weight countering the other's, arching over the empty space between the rafters.

He starts to laugh, at their good fortune perhaps, and the reverberations run through her. There's nothing but his body to keep her from falling. Slowly, carefully, they ease their way back to their previous positions, her weight shifting from her toes to the balls of her feet again. When she's standing safely once more, she looks down and sees the statue nestled into the pink foam insulation at his feet, perched comfortably above the void.

Brid's still in bed the next day when Maggie rises, so she puts on her coat and rubber boots, thinking she'll spend a bit of time with George Ray. As she steps into the backyard, she starts to imagine telling him about the money, but her thoughts are disrupted by the sound of a vehicle pulling into the drive. Going around the house to investigate, she sees a woman about her age exiting from the driver's side of a cream-coloured car. She's wearing a buckskin vest over her blouse and a paperboy cap atop long auburn hair. When Maggie calls out a hello, the woman returns the greeting and says she's looking for someone named Maggie Dunne.

Maggie wonders if she can get away with replying that Miss Dunne lives three roads over. She confesses to being herself, though, and the woman's face lights up.

"I hope this isn't an imposition," she says, "but I was hoping to talk with you about your father."

Maggie's throat has suddenly gone dry. "I'm not talking to reporters. If you want, my grandmother's in Syracuse—"

"Yes, I've met your family there," the woman replies. "Your uncle gave me your address."

Maggie can't hide her irritation. Uncle Morley wouldn't have had any compunction about doing it, either. Probably he took great delight in selling her out.

"I'm not a reporter," says the woman. "I make documentaries."

A woman filmmaker. It seems strange, after all Maggie's work with the camera, for someone to turn up who does it for a living.

"You're making a movie about my father?"

"I wasn't planning it," the woman says. "I was in Laos shooting another film when I heard stories about how he died." She reaches into her pocket and pulls out a business card. It's still warm from her thigh when Maggie takes it.

"I have a TV segment on him airing in a few days," the woman continues, "but I'd like to do something longer. When I heard he had a daughter living on a commune . . ." She breaks off and peers at Maggie with dark brown eyes so large and penetrating it's like they're cameras already recording her.

"You were in Laos," says Maggie. Other than Wale, she's never met anyone who has been there. For almost two months she's been desperate for information about her father, and here's someone who has been investigating him. The thought makes her both eager and circumspect. "So you know what happened," she says.

"I know what people said. An opium deal that went bad. Your father caught up in it by accident." The woman speaks in such a neutral tone that it's impossible to tell what she believes herself.

"You think it was by accident?" Maggie asks.

The woman squints at her. "What do you think happened?"

When Maggie doesn't answer, the woman looks toward the house as if hoping for an invitation to enter. "You knew him better than anyone. It's why I wanted to speak with you." Her tone offers intimacy and understanding, but it sets Maggie on edge.

"Are you working for the Church? Trying to prove there was a miracle? Or are you out to debunk all that?"

The woman considers her answer. "I suppose I'm interested in symbols." Seeing Maggie's bemusement, she adds, "Your father's a symbol of the war for people now. For some he's a symbol of faith." She says these last words too earnestly for Maggie's liking.

"He was my father," says Maggie, feeling almost petulant.

"He was never a symbol for you?"

"Is that how you see your own father?"

The woman laughs good-naturedly. "Why, yes. When I was a girl, he was a symbol of the life I swore never to lead."

"And what was that?" says Maggie, although she doesn't care to know the answer.

"You can probably guess," the woman replies, but Maggie doesn't bother and the woman doesn't say.

"I'm sorry you drove all this way for nothing," Maggie tells her.

The woman looks about to make some comment, then bites her lip. "I've gone about this poorly. I didn't mean to upset you."

"I'm not upset. It's just that I've lost my dad. You shouldn't take it personally if I don't feel like talking."

"Don't worry about me," says the woman. "I knew how things stood when I came up here. I just liked the sound of a girl on a commune." Maggie can't tell whether she knows everyone is gone. "Hey, do you mind if I look around before I leave? No camera, just me."

It would be easy enough to say yes, but Maggie doesn't want the woman taking in the place with those big dark eyes. She doesn't want her seeing the graffiti beneath its coat of paint.

"I'd rather you didn't."

"Okay." Still the woman waits, as if hoping Maggie will relent. "Listen, will you do me a favour? Will you watch the segment on TV? It airs the first of the month. At the very least, you'll see what the mission looked like." She names the time and channel, and Maggie nods noncommittally. Then, as the woman is about to get back into her car, she turns. "Is it true your father didn't really serve in World War II?"

It's the last question Maggie expected. "Of course he did." Why would anyone ask something like that? "He was wounded in the neck. Talk to people in Syracuse, they'll tell you."

The woman looks at Maggie with her hand shielding her eyes from the sun. "Yes. Thank you, yes, I will."

She's behind the wheel again when Maggie calls for her to wait.

"Your father," says Maggie. "You said he symbolized the life you didn't want. What did he do for a living?"

The woman smiles, turns the key in the ignition, and pulls closed the door. Maggie assumes that's the end of things, and it seems fair enough. A second later, though, the woman looks at her through the driver's window, one eye closed tight, and with a hand she mimes shooting Maggie with a silent camera. Then she grins, waves, and steers the car up the drive.

That afternoon, Brid enters a bad place. She writhes on the bedroom floor and pounds the walls. She left her daughter, she says. She hates herself. When finally she agrees to come down for a meal, she hardly eats a thing. Attempting to distract her, Maggie suggests they try building a chicken coop together, but Brid's eyes are dark hollows slick with tears and she doesn't respond. In the morning Maggie can't find her until she steps out from the mudroom and discovers her standing in her nightie just beyond the door, shivering in the chilly late November air, skin pale as porcelain, lips chapped and bloodless. No longer does Brid make any pretence of being here for Maggie. She scorns all reassurance, rejects Maggie's suggestions that they go for a drive. By the end of the day, Maggie's exhausted. Only after saying good night to Brid does she realize she has gone more than twenty-four hours without reflecting on her father's death. It feels like a betrayal needing atonement. She imagines phoning the documentarian and agreeing to meet, then sitting in front of the woman's camera and telling her about the good memories, the ones from childhood. But when she tries to retrieve the business card, she discovers it has gone through the wash with her jeans and turned to illegible pulp.

She brings Brid breakfast in bed, watches it go uneaten. She doesn't know what else to do except stay close by. They play blackjack. They play Scrabble. In desperation, Maggie suggests that Brid call Pauline. It's a mistake. Brid rends her nightgown and howls, runs to the bathroom and locks herself inside. Maggie pleads for an hour before Brid comes out. Then Brid apologizes and says they should have her committed. Maggie says they'll do nothing of the sort, but later she asks George Ray to remove the lock.

They spend two more days in the same fashion. On the second, George Ray comes in for lunch with trouble on his face. More graffiti, he announces, but he won't tell them what it says, and Maggie feels a deepening dread. As she and Brid cross the property to see it, Brid seems strangely energized, almost cheerful. She asks when they had problems with graffiti before. Maggie says it was a while ago and claims not to remember what was written.

When they draw close to the wrecking yard wall, through the trees she makes out the presence of two newly written words. The trees reveal the second word before the first.

LOVER.

Maggie can guess the first word without seeing it, but still it's a shock when it comes into view.

"Christ," breathes Brid. "You think they have the Klan up here?"

"It's not the Klan," says Maggie. Her thoughts of the girl are nearly homicidal.

In the kitchen, with Brid and George Ray looking on from the table, Maggie pulls out the phone book and calls Frank Dodd's house. Even before the man picks up, she's shaking with anger.

"It's Maggie Dunne from next door," she tells him. "Someone's been writing graffiti on our side of the wall we share with you. We're pretty sure it's your daughter."

There's a long silence. She starts to think he's hung up.

"Couldn't have been Lydia," he says. "She lives in Toronto with her mother now."

"Oh," says Maggie.

"I sent her there in September. Didn't want her growing up beside a bunch of porno makers." The spite in his voice tempts her to tell him a few things about his daughter, but already her thoughts are racing back to the graffiti. If it wasn't Lydia, then who? Nobody she wishes to imagine.

"I'm sorry," she mumbles. "I didn't realize." She says goodbye and puts down the phone, turns to George Ray and Brid. "I was wrong. The girl moved away."

"So what now?" says Brid.

Maggie reopens the phone book, looks up the police, and dials the number.

9

The officer who turns up is skinny and freckled, with a dopey, self-satisfied expression. Maggie explains to him about the graffiti but finds herself unwilling to repeat the words, fearing he'll ask her to speculate about what motivated them. When finally she speaks them aloud, the man seems unsurprised. Maybe everyone in Virgil has been talking about Maggie and George Ray and where they get the money for the farm.

The policeman's interest in the case doesn't pick up until Brid comes down in her nightie. Upon seeing him, she promptly heads back upstairs. Then, in the kitchen, as Maggie introduces him to George Ray, a crinkle of suspicion splits the man's forehead. He asks if George Ray has a visa.

"George Ray has worked in this area for seven years," Maggie protests.

"Never seen him, is all," replies the officer. He has a nasally, hollow voice. Looking George Ray up and down, he says, "Kind of late in the fall still to be here." George Ray stares back wearily and makes no comment.

By the wrecking yard wall, the policeman spends a long time frowning at his notepad.

"You could put in floodlights if you wanted," he says, tugging at the skin on his neck. "That might scare them off." After jotting a few words, he flips the notepad shut and starts back toward the house.

"That's it?" she says. "Shouldn't you dust for prints or something?"

He makes a face to show how naive she's being.

"It could be the Klan," she exclaims.

The policeman shakes his head. "This isn't the States. Probably it's just teenagers being stupid. In town we get this sort of thing all the time. But if it happens again, let us know."

Over lunch, when she recounts this story, George Ray stays silent. Brid is livid. She wants the cop reported. She wants the story in the papers and on TV. She says they should blanket Virgil with pamphlets. All the anger that until now she's inflicted on herself has a new target, and there's a glimpse of the agitator she used to be.

"The cop's probably right, it's just some kids," says Maggie. She doesn't like the idea of publicity while the money remains hidden in the attic. But George Ray sighs, and she worries she's letting him down. "What do you think we should do?" she asks him. "Stay in a motel for a while?" He looks affronted by the idea. "I want you to feel safe."

"They're just words," he says gruffly. "People up here have said worse things to my face." In horror, she imagines what those things could have been.

Then Brid announces she has a plan. Since the pigs won't do their job, she'll do it for them. Tonight she'll stay up and patrol the orchard.

Maggie suggests it might not be the best idea. What would Brid do if the culprits showed up? There could be a whole gang. What Maggie doesn't say is that she'll have to join her out there, and that means there'll be even less time with George Ray.

In the moment she has this thought, George Ray tells Brid he'll patrol with her. Maggie emits a noise of protest before lapsing into silence.

The rest of the day, Brid spends no time in bed. Instead, she stalks the orchard. Near midnight, alone at the bedroom window, Maggie watches the beams from two flashlights bounce and sway down the lanes, sometimes in tandem, sometimes apart, dancing their pas de deux in the darkness. It's one-thirty before George Ray comes to bed, his fingers and toes like ice.

"I do not approve of this climate," he says. She makes a long game of warming him up. Then, as she's drifting off, he remarks, "You know, she thinks it's Wale hiding out there and writing those things."

"She said that?"

Surely Brid can't be so deluded as to believe such a thing. But before Maggie falls asleep, she entertains her own fantasy that it's Fletcher, driving here in the night from Boston to harass her. She knows it couldn't really be him. There's only a small, persistent part of her looking for evidence that he still has feelings for her: if not ordinary love, then at least something wounded and a bit insane.

The diner in Virgil is sandwiched between the post office and a jewellery store, with a neon sign that's never lit and a plate glass window looking in on a deep, narrow space. There are half a dozen stools at the lunch counter, seemingly always occupied by the same handful of men, and a few booths that have sat empty during each of Maggie's meetings with Lenka over the course of the fall. This time Lenka is already ensconced in the one nearest the back when Maggie arrives.

"How was the time with grandmother?" Lenka asks as Maggie settles across from her. "She was horrible to you?" Before Maggie left for Syracuse, she told Lenka a lot about Gran.

"It could have been worse," Maggie replies. "She was too distracted by the funeral to bother much with me."

"You tell her of buying farm?" At their last meeting Lenka decided this was something Maggie needed to communicate.

Maggie confirms that she did, but her mind is elsewhere. She wants to tell Lenka about the money. On the drive over, her thoughts kept flitting between it and the graffiti until her head ached. She's tired of keeping the secret. If she told George Ray, he'd wonder why she didn't share the news with him sooner, and obviously she can't tell Brid. But the last six weeks Lenka has been kind and solicitous, respectful of Maggie's grief, sensitive enough to avoid subjects like miracles and faith. Maggie needs someone who'll tell her the right thing to do.

She glances around the diner. The men perched on their stools present a row of hunched shoulders like vultures on a wire. The waitress approaches to pour their coffee, then retreats. No, it isn't safe. But Lenka seems to sense Maggie's thoughts slipping away and pursues them like a terrier down a foxhole.

"What is it? Tell me."

"I was just thinking," says Maggie. "About money."

"Josef and I, we wonder if you have enough."

Maggie doesn't like the idea of them discussing her. "You encouraged me to buy the farm," she reminds her.

"It is just that we worry about you—"

"You don't need to," declares Maggie. "I have a lot of money. My father sent it just before he died." Lenka's eyes grow wide. "Can you keep a secret? Even from Josef?"

Lenka hesitates, then nods.

Speaking in a low voice, Maggie explains about the clay saint and her father's hinting letter. She tells of Wale's return to Laos and her bewilderment regarding what to do. When she has finished, Lenka asks how much money there is. Reluctantly, as if this is the most private detail of all, Maggie divulges the number.

Lenka gives a low whistle. "What will you do with this sum?" she asks.

Maggie admits it's still sitting where she found it, waiting for her to decide. An expression of understanding crosses Lenka's face. "Ah, I see problem. You think it looks bad for father."

Maggie feels herself bristle. "I don't care about how the Church sees him, if that's what you mean."

"Still, until now you do not go to police." Before Maggie can explain, Lenka says, "Of course, you do not hand it away. It is last thing father sends you. He wants you to have it."

"Maybe he'd rather I donated it to the mission. I did write people in Laos. I tried to find out what happened." More than she'd like, she feels a need for Lenka to absolve her.

Lenka sits there looking ruminative. Finally she says, "I wonder, why you tell this thing to me?" Without waiting for Maggie's reply, she says, "I think if I ask psychologist, he tell me you really want Josef to know. However, you wish not to ruin father's reputation before man of God, so you confess to sister instead. This is right?"

"No, it's not," says Maggie indignantly.

"Maggie, in spiritual matters I must not serve as substitute."

"For God's sake," she mutters. "I just wanted to hear what you thought."

To change the subject, she asks what's new for Josef in the parish. Lenka knows very well that Maggie has little interest in the matter, but obligingly she starts into a story about the church's leaky roof. As she does, the fact of Maggie's sitting there seems ever more preposterous. She doesn't care about the church roof; she doesn't care about anything in this place. It has been foolish of her to imagine taking over the farm for good. Was it only so she could plan George Ray's return in the spring? If his presence is so necessary, she shouldn't be here wasting time with Lenka.

Maggie glances at her watch, and Lenka asks if she's keeping her from something.

"I need to get home," she replies, reaching for her purse. Without much enthusiasm on either side, they exchange a promise to see each other soon.

As she drives back to the farm, it strikes her that there is less consolation to be found in other people than she keeps hoping there will be. Perhaps once George Ray's gone and Brid has returned to Boston, solitude won't be as terrible as Maggie has feared. It could be the making of her. She turns onto the gravel road almost wanting it already.

Upstairs, the door to Brid's room is closed and the silence is unnerving. Steeling herself, Maggie knocks. When there's no reply, she pushes open the door. The air inside is sour with bed smells and burnt toast. A pair of slippers lies askew on the floor, and there's an arm sticking out from behind the bed. No, it's a towel, twisted and flesh toned. Brid sits near the window looking at the orchard, still in her nightie though it's after three, her legs hidden in a plaid sleeping bag she has taken to dragging around the house with her like some larval creature not yet fully free of its cocoon.

"If we cut down some trees, I could see right to the wrecker's wall," Brid says. "Then I could keep a lookout from here."

"Don't you want to come downstairs?" Maggie asks. "Have you had lunch?" Brid gestures to a plate on the windowsill littered with bread crumbs, but Maggie knows it's been there since last night.

"I like it better up here," says Brid. "It's safer."

Ten days ago Maggie would have asked what was so unsafe about downstairs. Since Brid's arrival she sees things like the gas oven and bottles of bleach in a different light.

"You wouldn't have to worry," she says. "I'd stay with you."

"Babysitting, huh?"

"Don't be silly." The truth is she'll end up watching over Brid wherever she is, and there's no pleasure in the idea of lurking by the bedroom door. "Hey, why don't we watch the Super 8 film? I haven't seen it since—well, since the party."

Brid gives her a disdainful look. She's right, it's idiotic to suggest such a thing. Why would Brid want to revisit that time, with all those shots of Wale and Pauline? But then Brid changes her mind and says a screening would be a good idea. She starts out of the room trailing her sleeping bag while Maggie tries to guess what has fired her enthusiasm. Some spurt of masochism, perhaps. Following her into the playroom, Maggie finds her already sprawled across the floor and staring at the wall. Maggie sets up the projector, settles on a chair beside it, and starts it running.

The first image to greet them is one imprinted on her mind from dozens of viewings: the camper van passing down the highway. Then there's a shot of Fletcher talking behind the wheel with the sunlight flashing in his glasses. After the encounter at the funeral, it's a surprise to see him with his moustache and long hair restored, looking like a dime-store disguise. Maybe the clean-shaven version of him at the funeral was the real one all along. She imagines him flirting with a secretary in his office at Morgan Sugar, offering to take her for a spin in his Bentley. He always claimed to love the camper van, yet when he finally admitted he wasn't coming back, he relinquished it to Maggie with a surprising indifference, as if she and the vehicle were to be discarded together.

Next begins the sequence of Pauline leading the tour of the farmhouse. During summer screenings of this reel, Maggie focused on taking in the rooms' appearance, totting up the improvements made to them. This time her attention's drawn to the girl, who cavorts through the frame with a painful innocence. Maggie glances at Brid.

"It's okay," Brid says, her gaze fixed on the screen. "I can handle it." But her face is wretched.

From that point on, Maggie watches each scene imagining how Brid must see it. There's Pauline playing with Fletcher in the barracks, then the breakfast after Wale's arrival, with all Brid's eagerness to please him on display. Until now, watching this sequence, Maggie has only ever thought of Brid as pestering, but there she is making everyone a meal with neither help nor gratitude.

Beside her, Brid is crying. "I was such a bitch," she whispers. Maggie moves to turn off the projector, but Brid tells her not to stop it. "I can take it, really. Come here, will you?" She unzips the sleeping bag and opens the flap as if turning a page. Maggie sits down next to her, and Brid puts an arm around her waist.

With amazing precision, the film matches Maggie's memories from the summer, not just in terms of what she remembers but in the way she recalls it. There are the same jump-cuts and freeze-frames, the same lack of depth and texture. It's as if the contents of her brain have been assembled by her former self while she bent over the editing machine.

Before she's conscious of what has happened, they've reached the crucial scene in the final reel. A second later, just as she expects the appearance of Fletcher naked in the bedroom, she's plunged into a shot of the baseball game. It's what he told her he'd done, yet it's still astonishing.

Then she remembers the final, added clip about to greet them.

"We can stop it here," she says, hurrying to turn off the projector.

"Yeah," says Brid. "I don't know if I could handle that bit with Pauline and the dead birds."

Maggie can't believe what she's hearing. "You've watched it?"

"At Fletcher's last month," says Brid, seeming unperturbed. "He had some friends over to screen the whole thing. You know, for laughs."

Immediately she can picture it: Fletcher in his parents' recreation room with his fraternity pals and Brid, maybe a few Boston debutantes thrown in for good measure, all of them in hysterics from his stories about that crazy chick and her camera, nobody mentioning his own attempt at filmmaking. Maggie slumps across the sleeping bag and lies on her stomach with the floor hard against her cheek.

"He never really cared about this place, did he?" she says. "Or about me. He just wanted to get away from his dad."

"He did care," says Brid. "He was all broke up after the news about the baby."

Maggie hears this and can't suppress her irritation. "Why does everyone say it like that? There was no baby."

"Oh." Brid seems doubtful. "Well, Fletcher thinks there was." Brid sees her confusion and adds, "He figured you had an abortion."

Maggie lifts her head, then lets it fall, the veins in her temples throbbing. "How could he think that?" It seems impossible. "I explained to him what happened."

"You were so sure you were pregnant, and then suddenly you weren't," says Brid.

Maggie scrambles to reconfigure October in her memory. She only ever worried about him thinking she'd faked it.

"He wasn't ever going to come back, was he?" she says. "Even if there was a baby." It's something she realized long ago, but still a gloom falls on her. She remembers the doctor's consultation room, the news of the test result, and the man's pity along with his disbelief. "At first the doctor thought I'd had an abortion too." She winces at the recollection. "I stopped smoking, took vitamins . . ."

"Of course, honey. Nobody's blaming you."

"I never really wanted to be a mother," Maggie finds herself saying. "Didn't know the first thing about raising a child—" Abruptly she realizes how these words might be heard by Brid, and to change the subject she asks, "Did you think I got rid of it?"

"Oh sure," Brid replies. "But I thought you did it because it was Wale's." She speaks in a breezy way, as if there's nothing at stake in what she's saying.

"How could you think that?" exclaims Maggie.

"Look at the movie." Brid points to the blank wall. "The bastard's always watching you. You seem pretty keen on him, too, the way the camera stays on his face."

Maggie sits up and tries not to look away from Brid as she speaks. "Honestly, there was nothing." There's a temptation to say more, but they've reached dangerous territory and she needs to get them onto something else. Still, to her horror, she hears herself ask, "Have you heard from him?"

"Not once since he left." Brid's face grows suspicious. "Why, have you?"

Maggie shakes her head and Brid's attention drifts away. When it returns, there's a plaintive note in her voice. "He liked this place, you know. He was always saying good things about it. About you, too."

Maggie feels her face go red. "I never heard him say anything nice. He only ever made fun of the farm—and of me."

"That's Wale. He finds something he likes, he kicks the tires a lot." Brid smirks in a way that seems to hurt her. "I tried not to be jealous. I was glad, really. Figured he might stay around longer because of you. So much for that, huh?"

Maggie tries to transmit some sort of empathy through her eyes, but Brid appears uncomfortable being looked at in such a manner.

"Sweetie, what are we going to do here?" she says. "You can't just wait all winter for George Ray to come back. Is it a Catholic thing, this devotion to misery?"

Maggie frowns and turns away.

"Say something, would you?" implores Brid. "God, you drive me crazy, the way you just sit there."

Maggie can't help herself. "I drive *you* crazy? The things you say to me—"

"I only say them so you'll respond." Brid flops onto her back, then lies there with her chest rising and falling for so long Maggie wonders if she's gone to sleep. "There were nights," says Brid, breaking the illusion, "awful nights, the last couple of months, when I thought about calling you. A few times I almost did."

"You should have," says Maggie. She reaches down to push Brid's hair out of her eyes, but Brid seems not to notice.

"No, that kind of phone call is like heroin. Do it once and you can't stop. Soon nobody answers and you don't have any friends left to call." Her gaze starts on a wandering path around the room. "Weird being back without Pauline. In the summer I was terrified she'd drown in the creek. At first she cried for hours in that camper van, but I wouldn't let her into the house because of the gas, remember? She thinks my name is Bread. Isn't that funny?"

Maggie wants to be supportive, to leave behind her own petty self and enter Brid's sadness with her, but she can't quite do it. Reeling through her is the thought that Fletcher thinks she got rid of their child. She needs to be alone to deal with it. Looking toward the door, she hopes for George Ray to appear, to save her and Brid from whatever is about to come.

"Don't worry," says Brid. "I'm not going to freak out."

"I wasn't thinking that."

"You were. You're wondering where George Ray is." She seems more resigned than offended. "I wish I could keep it inside like you, with the surface all shiny and perfect, but I can't. I'm like that wall."

She gestures to the claw marks where Fletcher threw the reels. Maggie has always thought of the wall as purely white, but as she studies it now, imperfections reveal themselves: stains and cracks, and a long vertical line where a joist behind the drywall has swollen. She wonders why Brid, who knows her so well in certain respects, who sometimes appears to read her thoughts, should fail to recognize how Maggie might be a bit like that wall too.

That night, Brid beats her fists against her mattress. The world is a rotten place. She wants to kill herself, and she says it's because she watched that goddamned film. Maggie sits at her bedside and responds to every twitch and moan with a hand on her back. After a time Brid calls for Elliot. When he appears, she squeezes him until he struggles away and hops off the bed. Brid reaches after him and gives a hitched sob.

It's close to midnight before Maggie slides into her own bed next to George Ray. They fall into exhausted, muffled sex. A month ago she imagined that making love in these final days would gain an added tenderness, but she's so tired that it feels as though the two of them are strangers.

That night, she dreams she's her father. Or rather, she's in her father's person, lost in the jungle with Yia Pao's son, following the same muddy goat track she has imagined in waking life. Holding the child makes balancing treacherous. Then it comes to her that the baby isn't Yia Pao's; it's hers. Her father took the child to Laos, and now it's in her arms. She looks for chances to leave the trail and save them both, knowing what lies ahead, but her legs are compelled along the path. She starts watching for tripwires while the baby wriggles in her arms, growing smaller until it's no bigger than a mouse and scampers from her grasp.

The telephone wakes her, ringing and ringing with nobody to answer it. George Ray is no longer in the bed beside her. Even though she takes her time going downstairs, her mind still half tethered to the world of the dream, the ringing doesn't stop, so that when she picks up the phone, she's thinking there must be some technical malfunction. After she says hello, a woman speaks to her in George Ray's accent.

"Is this Miss Dunne? Miss Dunne, my name is Velma Ransom. I'm sorry for disturbing you. Please, may I talk to George Ray?"

The voice is calm and civil, knowing no grievance, feeling no betrayal.

"Yes, of course. Wait, I'll find him." Putting down the receiver, she leaves the house and meets George Ray halfway across the lawn. There's a pair of buckets in his hands. "It's your wife. On the phone. She sounds so lovely!"

He frowns, sets down the buckets, and hurries past her toward the house. From the mud room door she hears him talking angrily, almost shouting, louder than she's ever heard him speak, in sentences she doesn't understand.

"George Ray," she says from the doorway, not daring to enter the room, and he looks up as if mystified by her presence.

"What is it?" There's no affection in his voice.

"Call back."

"Why?" He seems bewildered by the idea.

"It's expensive for her to phone here. Hang up and call her back."

"Expensive. Yes," he says, quieter now. "Thank you. That's just what I was telling her." He seems to say it partly for Maggie's sake, partly for the woman at the other end of the line. Then he tells his wife he'll ring her back in a moment. Once he has set down the phone, he calls Maggie's name, but by that time she's upstairs and doesn't answer. Let him come and find her if he wants. She waits and waits, willing his arrival so hard she gets a headache, so hard it's a surprise when an hour has passed and still he isn't there.

IO

Twenty-four hours before George Ray is due to depart, he enters the kitchen to tell them there's more graffiti on the wall. This time it says *YANKEES GO HOME*. Hearing this, Maggie just laughs; the message seems safely impersonal, clichéd. Brid is less sanguine. She vows to resume her nighttime patrols, and she only grows more adamant when Maggie says she doesn't want her in the orchard on her own. Then, after lunch, George Ray tells Maggie he's going to spend the afternoon working. There are saplings that need attention if they're to survive the winter, and he wants to earn his final day's wages honestly. When Maggie suggests working alongside him, he points out that someone has to mind Brid, and reluctantly she agrees, so Brid and Maggie stay indoors playing cards. At one point Brid asks why they can't just spend the afternoon helping him, and

Maggie finds herself replying that he prefers to be on his own. It strikes her as a lie and the truth at the same time.

At least he comes in for dinner. Then it's Brid who's reluctant to join them, saying she doesn't want to get in the way of their final supper together. She has to be cajoled into sitting down. Even after she does, it's a miserable meal, with Brid poking at her lasagna and George Ray idly swirling the wine in his glass.

"Don't drink this stuff in Newcross," he says. "Could be the last till next summer." He downs it in one long swallow. After dinner he insists on washing the dishes and Brid grabs the towel to dry, so Maggie's left at the table blowing ripples across the surface of her tea.

"Hey!" cries Brid angrily as Maggie's in the middle of a sip. At first she thinks it's something she's done; then she sees Brid running into the mud room. "There's somebody out there. Hey!" In her bare feet and nightie, Brid charges into the yard.

By the time they get their shoes on to follow, she's disappeared. Neither George Ray nor Maggie has thought to grab a flashlight, so once they enter the orchard, the way becomes treacherous. They're crossing flat ground, yet it seems to rise like a mountain beneath them. The blinking lights of the radio towers on the horizon have the coldness of stars. Maggie keeps thinking they've found Brid and turns out to be wrong. The kneeling figure is just a propane tank; the person swinging from a rope is a rubber tire.

Before Brid comes into sight, they hear her cursing as she bumps into things. Once they reach her, Maggie hugs her with relief.

"He's out here," says Brid.

Maggie looks around and sees only the farmhouse lights along with a bright blue moon fending off clouds. When she asks who it is, Brid says she doesn't know, and Maggie can't help but feel doubtful. "Just one person? Are you sure—"

"Of course I'm sure."

"Could have been a deer," says George Ray.

"You think I don't know the difference?"

He gazes into the night. "No good being out here without lights. Best call the police."

Maggie agrees and suggests they go back to the house. Brid says she isn't leaving when someone's on the property.

"You're not even wearing shoes—" Maggie begins.

"I'll stay," says George Ray. "You two go inside. If he's here, I'll find him."

Maggie shouldn't be angry. George Ray's just trying to help. But his willingness to sacrifice his last night with her is hurtful. When he starts off through the trees, she has the feeling that this is the true leaving. Eighteen hours from now, the farm will be nothing more than a speck below his plane. He'll be free of Canada and on the way back to his wife.

As soon as Maggie's in the house, she wants to set out again and find him, but she dares not leave Brid alone, so they watch television and Maggie fidgets. After a few minutes Brid turns to her.

"Go," she says.

Maggie's unsure of what she means.

"Go out to him," says Brid. "I'm sorry, I should have said it sooner. I'll be fine."

Maggie studies her face to see if it's some kind of trick.

Then she stands with a grateful smile, drapes an afghan over Brid's shoulders, and heads back to the orchard, this time with a flashlight. She finds George Ray sitting on a stump near the wrecker's wall, his hands shoved in his pockets and his collar turtled over his ears.

"Come inside," she says. "What are you doing out here? It's our last night." Her tone is more imploring than she'd like.

"I've been praying," he replies.

Praying. He has never talked about doing such a thing. Why would he pray now? They still haven't spoken about Velma's phone call yesterday.

"Pray later," she says, tugging on his sleeve in a way she hopes is humorous. "You'll always have God, you won't always have me."

He only draws his chin further down and mumbles into his collar. "You don't want me in there. You want the place to yourself. I've seen the way you're getting it ready—tidying up, making it how you like it."

The words strike her like a slap. "That isn't what I'm doing. I'm just trying to cope with you leaving."

He doesn't seem to register what she has said. "What happens if you find some other fellow this winter?" he complains. "What if your man Fletcher turns up? Probably he'll tell you not to hire Jamaicans anymore."

Is this what George Ray has been thinking? "I'm going to bring you back," she insists.

"You say that now."

"Why are you acting like this?" The pain of it is nearly physical. "We both understood how things were going to be. It's what you wanted."

"How do you know that? Never asked me. You make all the decisions yourself." His words have a growing unreality. "You haven't even farmed before. By the time I'm back here, you could bankrupt the place."

Why is he talking about money? Could he know what's in the statue? Maybe she should just give it to him. She's had this thought before but figured he would never touch it if he knew its origins. That's the kind of person she has understood him to be. Right now she isn't so certain.

"I'm the one being left," she says. "You'll go home and have someone in your bed."

"I know what will happen. In the spring you'll pay the men too-high wages and think you're doing them a favour. You'll feel good about yourself for living off the land while they break their backs to grow your fruit. Then you'll run out of money and have to send everyone home."

She doesn't know how to respond. The shock isn't just in his saying it but in the possibility that it could be true. She hasn't asked him for advice, assuming she needs to work out for herself how to manage until he returns. And he hasn't breathed a word of criticism; he's just let her go on indulging her fantasies while he's built up this resentment.

"Canada, the land of plenty," he mutters. "I got plenty of things from Canada, all right. Got tendinitis, got old, got a wife who sleeps with the neighbour." He looks at Maggie grimly. "That's why Velma telephoned last night. She didn't want a scene at home." Lowering his eyes, he adds, "Doesn't want me coming back at all."

Oh, thinks Maggie. So that's what's going on.

"I'm sorry," she says. "I didn't have the slightest idea."

"Neither did I."

"Are you still going back to Newcross?" she asks, and George Ray nods.

"What else can I do? Work permit's finished. Government doesn't care if Velma takes up with the fellow next door. Besides, I have children." He looks at Maggie with cheerless eyes. "My daughter blames me, you know. On the phone she told me her mama needs a full-time man. How do you think it is to hear your own child tell you that?"

Maggie says again that she's sorry and draws him against her. "You could emigrate. Bring the children with you—"

"Why would they want to come here? They already have a home." He starts to pull away. "Let's go back. We should get to sleep. I have an early flight, remember?"

"Wait, not quite yet. Stay out with me a little more, please? Just for a while?"

He lays his head against her shoulder, and they stand there holding each other, not speaking or moving, while Maggie hopes for some sign to show them a way forward.

In bed beside him just before dawn, waiting for the alarm clock to go off, she realizes why the sick feeling in her gut is so familiar. Seven months ago, she took her father to the airport and said goodbye to him as well. She had returned to Syracuse from Boston in the middle of the week so she could see him off to Laos, hoping that if she made the trip, he'd be more likely to forgive her for not going with him and for planning a move to Canada instead.

The evening before his departure, as they sat in the living room eating dinner from TV trays, it was almost like when she was a girl, except now he was the one who said grace. But the silence afterward was foreboding. When he finally spoke, she fixed her eyes on *Bonanza* and didn't take them off.

"You remember that time I lost you at the Veterans Day parade?" There was the clink of his fork settling on his plate. "You were only six."

"Five and a half," she said, sensing what was ahead.

"You remember what you said when I found you again?" There was a foolish braveness in his voice, an anticipatory regret, a resentment of her for making him say what he was saying.

"I'd been scared out of my wits," she said. "All those old men staring at me . . ."

"You said from then on we should each wear one of your mittens, the ones with the string holding them together."

"I don't remember saying that."

"Father Jean says there are plenty of missionaries in Laos who go as families."

"Dad, I can't—"

"We used to be so close, you and I . . ."

"We're still close." Her throat closed around the words.

"Don't tell lies. It makes it worse."

"Maybe I'll be able to visit—"

"It's not a place for tourists, little girl."

"That isn't what I meant."

"You're sick of me," he said. "You ran off to Boston."

"I went to college."

"As far away as you could."

"You don't think there are farther places?"

"As far as you could go and still satisfy your conscience."

She had been expecting him to say these things for months, years, ever since she'd left Syracuse, but now she had no strategies to deal with them. Although she had thought of him as the one suppressing everything, suddenly it was her anger that came seething out.

"Am I a bad daughter, then? You think just anybody would keep coming back to sit here and be preached at?" She stared at him until he flinched. "You don't even need me, anyhow. You have the Church."

It sat between them for a time.

"You say it like a dirty word." He gave a wounded sigh. "Perhaps for you it is."

A dare, but she refused to accept it. Instead, she fled to her room. Whatever she'd hoped to preserve was gone. They both knew she was the one who'd always looked after him. Who would take care of him now? On top of her dresser sat the box for the Super 8 camera he'd given her at Christmas. It was a selfish present.

When he knocked, her shame wouldn't let her answer. The knocking grew louder. He called to her, his voice irate, then beseeching, while she lay paralyzed on her stomach with a pillow pulled around her head so tightly it was hard to breathe. She waited for him to barge into the room, but he stayed in the hall, begging her to reconsider, imploring her to let him in. She couldn't, because if she saw his face with its desperation and its brokenness, she'd give in to him, she'd go to Laos, and then she'd never be able to forgive him for making her. Better to tell him in the morning that she didn't want any part of the life he'd chosen. No phone calls, no letters. She needed to find her own way in the world. But she would wait until the airport, until she didn't have to spend too long dealing with the look in his eyes.

From the hall, his voice became almost unrecognizable. He was berating her, cursing her, hurling words she'd never heard him use.

She didn't answer, didn't move.

In the morning, he was lying on the carpet when she opened her door, the comforter from his bed wrapped around him, a corner of it scrunched to support his head. He slept there like a careless guard or a faithful dog. She went to the bathroom, washed her face, and tried to pull herself together. Then she woke him and said they'd have to hurry if he was going to make his flight.

The sun swells above the horizon like a blister about to burst. Along the orchard lanes, the water in the ruts has gained a skin of ice, bubble-ridden and darkly translucent. A metal pipe atop the barracks roof issues a thin stream of smoke. Inside, George Ray paces between the table and a set of plywood shelves near his bunk bed as he packs. He's wearing the same buttoned shirt he wore to dinner at the rectory, and his suitcase sits open on the table, straps dangling, half filled with folded clothes. The mattress on his bed has been stripped and turned on its side. A crack from the fire in the wood stove makes him start. Then he stuffs a few pairs of socks into his workboots before setting them in the case. A pair of leather shoes waits for him by the door, hairline creases veining the newly polished surfaces.

From above the bed he removes the photograph of his family and examines it for a few seconds before slipping it into his pocket. Turning to the mirror at the back of the room, he stands straight to inspect himself, combs his hair, adjusts his collar. After a time his eyes catch movement, and he turns to see Maggie standing on the mat near the door with her purse in hand.

"Finished?" she asks.

There's a bob of his Adam's apple as he swallows. He goes to the wood stove and with a fire iron bends low to prod a few chunks of charred wood. At last he stands upright again.

"Finished."

Late that night, Maggie is smoking and watching TV. It's a religious programme hosted by a silver-haired man in a sweater whose accent sounds Canadian. The time and channel are the ones the documentarian named, and Maggie has been watching with trepidation. She didn't tell Brid, just said good night before sneaking back down to the living room, because whatever she's about to see, she wants it to be a private thing.

The man onscreen begins to talk of martyrdom. Martyrs are models for all of us, he says. In their devotion they're contact points between the earthly and the divine. He says he'd like to share a short documentary about one of them, a man from upstate New York doing God's work in a foreign land. It's what Maggie expected, yet somehow she still can't believe it.

The next shot reveals a line of tents in the middle of a jungle. Then there's a low-angle view of canoes on a brown river, followed by close-ups of brightly coloured birds in cages and a fly crawling on an old man's leathery ear. This is Laos, says a woman's voice, the home of ancient peoples and a modern, secret war. Maggie recognizes the voice as the filmmaker's, but the woman remains unseen as the camera reveals the inside of a little hut and a line of items laid out on a table: a fountain pen, a pair of reading glasses, a canteen in a canvas holster. The woman calls them the last relics of Gordon Dunne.

Maggie calls it thievery. They should have sent those things back to the States. She thinks of the box upstairs containing the few items from his house she chose to keep. There's the white shirt he wore to work every Monday. There's his shaving brush, still pungent with a sweet, rich scent that was his scent as far back as she can remember. There's an album of photographs she gave him one by one after taking them with her Brownie Starflash. He never told her he kept them. Two weeks ago, when she came upon the album among his belongings in Syracuse, she wept for a long time.

Now the television is showing two men by a campfire. One of them is Lao, one a white man with a beard. The Lao man extends a boot and nudges a little figure near the edge of the flames. It takes Maggie a second to realize that the white man is supposed to be her father. Around his neck he wears a red bandana, even though her father hated red, and his beard is shot through with grey, although her father never had a grey hair in his life.

She watches as the two men in the re-creation evade a group of thugs with rifles, then encounter a priest and an old woman who bleeds a fluid far too garishly coloured to be actual blood. Was the scene filmed in Laos? Could that be Father Jean? There's no way to know, because Maggie has never seen an image of him. She watches as the man playing her father steals a baby from under the noses of armed teenagers on a riverbank, only to be apprehended along with Yia Pao as he hides behind a waterfall. Maggie doesn't know if it's the real Yia Pao or if any of it is true. No one has said anything about such heroics. There was nothing about a waterfall.

The camera shows Yia Pao with the baby in his arms, marching ahead of the man who is not her father as they are led through mountains that could be Asian or the Adirondacks. Once they reach a campsite high up among stunted trees, her father is interrogated by their captors' leader, a cruel-looking man with a brush cut. When one of the other thugs calls the man Sal, Maggie blanches. Wale wasn't lying, then. Or perhaps the documentarian just heard the same lies that Wale told Maggie. She thinks the interrogation scene is supposed to seem tense and full of danger, but she feels nothing, not even when her father is punched in the stomach, because it isn't him. When he admits to having debts, when he refers to his widowed mother, she doesn't buy it. These are details anyone could find out; they don't say the first thing about him. She watches him write a letter, knowing there wasn't one, then wonders if there was and she just didn't receive it. She watches him huddle with Yia Pao in a deep, narrow pit that must have been lit carefully by the film's crew, because the men's faces are still visible at the bottom. Nobody told Maggie about a pit.

Her father in the film is brave and caring, innocent of any wrong. He offers himself as a sacrifice, leads Yia Pao in an escape, then is the first of them to cross a swollen river. Maggie would like to believe that this is the man her father became in the jungle, but she can't. He sat at a desk or in front of a TV all his life. How natural it would have been for him to stay in the pit as ordered. It probably wasn't courage that drove him out but the sight of Yia Pao clambering away from him with the baby in one arm. It was probably a terror of being left there on his own.

The documentarian has filmed a fantasy, a fake, one that's all the more offensive for having been made with a technical skill Maggie envies. This woman wanted a saint, so she created one; she boiled down the last week of Gordon Dunne's life to a few minutes of action. No wonder she was content to leave the farm so quickly. She had probably come up here hoping for footage of drugs and orgies. How disappointing to discover only a few acres of trees and a single abandoned woman.

Then the scene changes, and the person looking back at Maggie from the television set is Gran, the genuine one, sitting in the parlour of her house in Syracuse, though the room is brighter than usual and Gran looks different too, all made up and her hair newly permed. When did they shoot this footage? Gran never breathed a word about it. Maggie watches and listens as Gran talks about her son, describing a devout boy with his eyes upon the Lord. While she speaks, the screen shows photographs of him as a child, then as a teenager. Finally there's one of him holding a newborn baby, though he looks not much older than a boy himself. As the screen lingers on the image and the voice-over tells of him becoming a father, Maggie realizes the baby is her. She has never seen photographs of herself at that age, because neither her father nor Gran kept any in the house. Maggie always assumed they didn't wish to be reminded of her mother's bad end. Now, as she looks at the photograph, she notices something. Her father's neck. It isn't covered by a high collar. There isn't any scar to hide. But that doesn't make any sense, because Maggie was born three years after the war.

Before she has time to contemplate what this means, the film leaps forward, gaining colour and motion. Onscreen, a young Lao man with an empty shirt sleeve is gesturing down a track of trampled, slimy-looking undergrowth. The voice-over says it's the trail her father took after making his escape. The surrounding forest is darker and more riotous than in her dreams.

In the next shot, they show the trap that caught him. The young man explains the mechanism while a translator interprets what he says. Apparently the trap wasn't set for her father in particular, just for any poor soldier making his way through that territory. They don't even know who set it, whether it was someone from the Hmong army or the Pathet Lao. There's a cut to a shaky hand-held shot moving down the trail, as if from her father's perspective, then a close-up of three barbed prongs driven through a slender strip of bamboo. The voice-over describes the tripwire, the spring action, and the fact that the trap was designed to be so excruciatingly painful as to make freeing oneself impossible. When the screen returns to the hand-held shot, Maggie feels a throb of anticipation. Surely they won't show it. They mustn't. But they do.

She watches a foot catch on a wire stretched across the ground. Then a shot of the camera swinging wildly toward him, as though propelled by some elastic force. A moment later, standing before Maggie's eyes is her father, pinned against a tree. The whip trap has caught him just below the ribs. The baby in his arms looks toward the wound as if it understands profoundly what has transpired. A dribble of blood travels down her father's shirt. The man still has his salt-and-pepper beard, still is not her father, yet somehow now he is. The scene has been lit to resemble certain paintings of martyred saints, all deep shadows and alabaster skin, so that he has an appalling beauty. It shouldn't bother her as much as it does; she already knows most of the details from the priest at the mission. The sight of him is different, though. The sight is obscene.

The shot goes on for hours, as if the filmmaker is determined that Maggie absorb every detail, every nuance of pain and impossible ecstasy on his face, as if she wants Maggie to feel the sensations with him. Finally there's a release that her father was never granted, and the scene changes to a medical office, where a physician testifies that shock must have been what kept Gordon Dunne from moving during those last hours; his lack of struggle must have kept him alive. The doctor says it's highly unusual for a man to survive that long after such a wound. Then the doctor is replaced by the priest from the mission, who says it had to be a miracle, because no power but God's could have kept Gordon upright all that time and still able to protect his young charge.

The documentarian seems out to prove her objectivity, but Maggie isn't fooled. The woman wants to believe in Gordon Dunne's holiness. Now it's clear why she came to visit the farm. She knew he didn't get the scar on his neck from the war, so she wanted Maggie to clear up the mystery, to affirm or sully him, to steer her out of doubt. Maggie wonders what the woman would say if she knew about the roll of bills in the clay statue. Would that be enough for her to lose her faith, or would she think of the money as another miracle?

In the kitchen, the telephone has started ringing. Maggie thinks she'll just ignore it, but then she remembers what time it is and realizes it could be George Ray phoning from Jamaica, already breaking their agreement not to call.

When she reaches the kitchen and picks up, it's Father Josef. He tells her that on television there's a programme she should be watching.

"Yes, I'm doing that already," she says. Stretching the cord back down the hall, she can just see the TV through the living room doorway. It's unnerving to think that the priest has been viewing the same things she has.

"Is touching, yes?" he says.

"I didn't need to be touched."

"No, of course," he replies quickly. "I was only thinking you might wish to know."

She asks him if Lenka's watching too, and he says she went to bed a long time ago. Onscreen, there's another shot of the river that carried away Yia Pao, and the documentarian's voice-over admits that his being swept downstream is only speculation, that no one knows what has become of him since he was kidnapped. The whereabouts of his son are also uncertain. The people who found the baby in the arms of Maggie's father know only that the child was taken to an orphanage somewhere.

The priest has been speaking in Maggie's ear. What is he talking about? With her eyes still on the television screen, she tries to comprehend him. Then she hears him refer to the money. Suddenly he has all her attention.

"You must forgive Lenka for telling me," he says. "She is worried about you."

The treachery runs through her like poison.

"You talk of going to police, yes?" says Josef. "I think this is wise." Is he making a threat? He could have told the police already. She wants to say it's none of his business. "No doubt," he continues, "they will say the money is yours to do with how you wish." But his tone seems odd. It's as if he's trying to hint at some possibility.

"What would you wish me to do with it?" she asks.

"Me? Is not question of my wishes." He waits a beat. "Perhaps, though, is question of your father's."

"What would he want, then?" she says, feeling lifeless.

"Maybe he wants it given to Church."

It isn't a surprise, but still she's unnerved by the gall of it. "You mean given to you."

"No, not to me! It is parish that has needs. Church roof is old, robes are worn and frayed."

"You think my father would want you to have new robes?" She has spoken so quickly that he doesn't understand her words, but the comment doesn't bear repeating.

"You must come to Mass on Sunday," he says. "I know some part of you is wanting this."

"You're wrong. No part of me wants it."

"You are full of grieving. Church can help you."

"I don't know how it could."

The priest goes silent. "In September, you come to dinner that time," he says finally. "Lenka talks to you about abortion, yes?"

Maggie's dumbfounded. Is there any confidence Lenka hasn't betrayed? Maggie wants to be outraged with her, but she can't quite manage it. She pictures Lenka facing another night in the rectory with Josef as her only companion, drinking too much at dinner and blurting out all manner of secrets to him, then apologizing over and over to an absent Maggie, sick from booze and regret while her brother comforts her. The scene is so vivid and dismal that Maggie can almost forgive them both. Almost, but not quite.

"Yes, Lenka and I talked about it," she tells him.

"I do not wish wrong impression," says Josef, "so I must explain, is not Lenka who has abortion, is another girl in Prague. My girl, when I am sixteen. You understand?"

"Yes," she replies. She doesn't know why he's telling her the story. Does he think she's been judging Lenka all this time?

"I do not ask the girl to do this thing. I want big family, yes? But I am no fool, sixteen is too young, so I do not stop her, either. A boy this age, he is frightened easy."

As he speaks, she finds her impatience growing. Maybe this is his way of seeking intimacy, but she has no interest in playing his therapist.

"I don't see what this has to do with you wanting the money," she says.

"I tell you, is not for me! Parish is what matters. I am trying to explain about the needs of others. Surely you understand this. You are the girl who tries to start commune, no?"

The question takes her by surprise. She would never think to describe herself in such a way. It makes her out as more ambitious than she is. It also makes her out as a failure.

"I should go," she says. "It's late."

"But you will consider what I say?"

To be done with the conversation, she says she will.

When she returns to the living room, the television pro- gramme has departed Laos and the silver-haired man in the red sweater has reappeared, now sitting by a fireplace. He says that one day Gordon Dunne could be recognized as a modern-day saint. He says the followers of Freud would have you believe that the age of saints is over, that because we all have unconscious motives, there can be no purity and thus no holiness. But the unconscious of the saint is God. The saint is a projection of God's mercy, a sign of our ability to transcend our fallen state.

Hearing this, Maggie only feels more powerfully than before that her father is lost to her forever.

The next morning, she passes through the farmhouse half a dozen times without settling on what to do. She considers going to the barracks and removing every trace of George Ray, but it would be painful to see how complete a job he has already done. She should check on Brid. She should rake the lawn. She should do anything that will make her feel needed in the world.

When the phone rings, she picks it up and a woman speaking another language asks her a question. Maggie comprehends a single word: "Wale." Not quite believing it, she accepts the charges. There's a click, and then his voice comes on the line.

"Maggie, I'm sorry, I fucked up." He sounds drunk. He sounds as if he has been drunk the whole time since he last called.

"Where are you?" she says. "I thought you were dead."

"I found them, Maggie. I found them both."

"What are you talking about?"

"I was too late for your old man. He'd escaped by the time I got to Sal. We spent days in the jungle looking for him."

"You and Sal?" The idea of it is sickening.

"It's not like Sal's my friend, all right? I've been doing my best to make up for what he did. That's what I'm trying to tell you. I found Yia Pao and his baby."

"What? Where?"

"The kid was in an orphanage right here in Vientiane. Sal told me to watch the place, thinking Yia Pao might show. It was a long shot, but guys like Sal don't give up so easily."

"You were helping Sal?"

"Listen, will you? Today Yia Pao turned up, just like Sal hoped. So I grabbed him and the baby. I didn't hand them over to Sal, okay? I've got them stashed in a safe place."

Maggie can't believe what she's hearing. "Can I talk with Yia Pao?"

"There's no phone where he's staying."

"Then take him where there is one."

"It isn't that easy. Sal has guys out looking for us."

"I'll come to you, then." She's thinking of the money, how she'll give it over for the care of Yia Pao's son. Then she'll have washed her hands of it.

"You can't come to Laos," says Wale. "It isn't safe. Sal has friends all over Vientiane."

"So bring Yia Pao and the baby here." She hasn't thought it over; it simply comes out of her mouth. "I'll wire you money for the tickets." She almost tells him about the clay saint, but she doesn't trust him.

"I can't just put a couple of Hmong on a plane." He sounds unsure, though. "I have a friend here," he says after a time. "He might be able to handle the papers. Give me a few days, will you?"

She's tired of waiting for letters and phone calls. "How can I get in touch with you?"

"You can't. I'll call you."

A suspicion comes over her. "Have you asked Yia Pao about Sal's money?"

"Not yet. I don't want him getting skittish and taking off."

But Wale must assume that Yia Pao hid the cash somewhere; she can't believe he wouldn't ask about it. She can't believe he was really looking for Yia Pao all this time just so he could help him.

"Wale, why didn't you call until now?" she asks.

A hush comes over the line. She knows he's still there because she can hear his breathing grow uneven.

"I couldn't talk to you," he says. "I felt too bad about your old man." There's the sound of drawn air, as if he's taking a drag on a cigarette. "I thought I could get there in time, Maggie. I really did."

A part of her wants to console him, tell him not to sweat it, but she isn't quite big enough. "You should come here too. Brid needs you." There's no way to explain further, though, not with the line crackling and foaming as it is.

"Shit, I can't come back." He sounds desolate. "I couldn't look her in the eyes. You, neither."

Before she can respond, there's a noise from nearby. It's Brid, standing in the doorway between the kitchen and the hall, glaring at her.

"Is that him?" Rushing forward, she snatches the receiver from Maggie's hand and shouts into it. "You asshole! Leave us alone!" She slams it onto its cradle, hard enough to set off the bell.

"It's all right," says Maggie, though it isn't, anyone can see that. "He was just—"

"I don't care," says Brid. "I don't care, I don't care."

Brid slides down with her back against the cupboard until she's sitting on the floor, her knees drawn against her chest. Elliot appears and nuzzles her side, prowling around her, looking for his chance to climb into her lap. It's going to be a disaster. But when Maggie kneels beside her, Brid looks at her with an expression of confusion, not despair, as though wanting reassurance, as if she might be able to accept the giving of comfort. Maggie hopes for the phone to ring, for Wale to call back, but it stays silent. With a deep breath, she puts an arm around Brid and begins to explain.

I I

The house is immaculate. The baseboards have been dusted and the magazines gathered into tidy stacks, while the refrigerator is barren of lists and magnets. Out in the orchard, Maggie puts away a wheelbarrow and picks litter from the creek bed, then returns to the house and sweeps the hall until Brid comes downstairs with her purse and says she's ready to go. After a few minutes, the real estate agent arrives. Brid sits on the bottom stair morosely as Maggie shows the woman around the rooms. The agent voices her appreciation, saying she could tell stories about how some tenants leave things, but Maggie offers her no encouragement. She only puts on her shoes and wishes the woman luck with the open house.

At the diner in Virgil, Brid and Maggie occupy a booth facing one another, each with a book in hand, neither of them turning pages very often.

"You understand it's because I'm out of money, right?" Maggie says after a time.

"Yeah."

"When we're both in Boston again, we'll find a place together."

"Maggie, you already told me this."

"I can drive you there—"

"Don't worry, I'll be fine."

Maggie frowns into her book and doesn't say anything more.

A few vehicles are still parked in the drive when Maggie and Brid return to the farmhouse, so they wait in the camper until only the real estate agent's car is left. At last they go inside, Brid heading upstairs while Maggie meanders around the ground floor. The lights in all the rooms are on, and there's music from the record player. She finds the agent in the mud room, mopping up footprints from a prospective buyer who ventured into the backyard. The agent says it was a promising afternoon.

On either side of the rectory's front door are potted conifers strung with coloured bulbs. As Maggie makes her way toward them from the camper van, she counts the days until Christmas. Fifteen to go. This time last year she was trying to choose a gift for her father. She settled on a pair of woollen gloves. If she had known it was her last present to him, she would have bought him something better.

From within the house comes Lenka's voice yelling

in Czech. Maggie hesitates prior to knocking. There are more shouts, followed by footsteps, before the door is flung open to reveal Lenka with cheeks left glossy by tears.

"I'll come back," says Maggie.

"No, please, is excellent time. Come, help me murder him."

Josef sits at the dining table pressing at his shirt with a napkin, the wineglass beside him upended, another napkin stained red and lying across the table. When Maggie enters, he hurries to rise, then manages an apology before retreating from the room.

"Do not run from guest, Josef!" cries Lenka. To Maggie she says, "He does not let me go to New York for visit. Is expensive in city, he says. Really he is afraid I will not make return. He prefers me to cook the dinners for him. To him I am not sister, I am servant." Calling after him, she shouts, "Father, you can go to hell!"

"I'll come back later," says Maggie.

"No, stay. I am tired of being alone with him." Roughly she grabs Maggie's hand and draws her toward the sitting room, where Maggie claims the rocking chair and Lenka throws herself on the loveseat. "So, why do you come?"

"To tell you I'm going to Laos."

Lenka's jaw drops. "Josef!" she calls. "You must hear this!"

It takes him a minute to enter, looking skeptical and wearing a new shirt that hasn't been tucked in. Lenka repeats what Maggie has said.

"Ah!" He looks puzzled as he joins his sister on the loveseat. "This is fascinating news. Please, tell us more."

Maggie considers how to begin. "You remember Wale? The guy at the grocery store in September?" The priest nods. "He's in Laos now. He's found Yia Pao, the man who was kidnapped with my father. He's found Yia Pao's son too."

"Maggie, this is wonderful!" says Lenka. Josef still looks perplexed; perhaps he's wondering how Wale ended up in Laos.

"I've spoken with the mission office over there," Maggie continues. "They say that if Wale can get Yia Pao and the baby to them, they'll see about flying them to America."

"So why must you go to Laos?" asks the priest.

"Because I haven't heard from Wale since he called last week, and nobody in Vientiane seems to care where he's gone. The State Department isn't interested, and the mission office doesn't have anyone who'll investigate. So I'm flying over on Friday."

"So soon!" says Lenka. "Is safe?"

"There isn't any fighting in the city," Maggie replies. It's a half answer, but it's what she has been telling herself.

"What will happen to man and his son once they are here?" asks Lenka.

Maggie hesitates. "I'm not bringing them here. I've told Fletcher I'm leaving the farm. The place is up for sale."

Lenka gasps, and the priest leans forward. Maggie explains that she has decided to try teaching in Boston again, that she'll handle it better this time. As she speaks the words, she almost believes them.

"What of plans for orchard?" asks Lenka. "What of George Ray in the spring?"

The mention of George Ray brings Maggie up short. "I haven't told him yet," she admits. "But I don't have enough money to rehire him. I spent the rest of what I had on the ticket to Laos. You were right, I can't afford the place, and Fletcher wasn't going to let me stay there forever."

"What of the ten thousand dollars?" says the priest.

"It's going to the baby. If I can, I'll set up a trust fund. I have to make sure I can do it without the money getting confiscated."

The priest looks disapproving. "So much money for one child."

"It's not just a child," says Maggie. "It's the one whose life my father saved."

The priest clasps his hands in front of him and kneads one with the other, while Lenka peers at her as if mystified.

"What does your grandmother think of your plans?" asks the priest.

Maggie frowns. "Gran has nothing to do with it."

She isn't quite telling the truth, though, because yesterday she called Gran to inform her of the coming trip.

"Actually, I found out something from her yesterday," Maggie says, remembering. "Did you notice how, in the TV programme about my father, he had a scar on his neck?" The priest nods. "I always thought he got it fighting in Normandy. But the documentary showed a photo of him after the war, and the scar wasn't there yet. I asked Gran, and it turns out he never went overseas. The war ended just after he enlisted. She says he spent a couple of years in college after that, dropped out, then met my mother and got her pregnant inside a month. Gran claims she still doesn't understand it, but the whole thing's pretty obvious, right? He was trying to get away from her. War, college, a wedding—whatever it took. Then my mother died giving birth to me."

"You never tell me this," says Lenka.

Maggie lifts a hand to signal that it's all in the past and doesn't matter now. But then why is she telling it?

"Gran said he hated me, those first years. She thinks I reminded him of my mother. More likely he figured I was going to keep him living next to Gran. Anyhow, he had a nervous breakdown. Tried to kill himself. She was looking after me next door when it happened. I don't remember any of it."

"Maggie, it is horrible," says Lenka.

"She's the one who found him. The way she described things—it must have been awful." Gran had tripped over her words, leaving long pauses, not finishing her sentences. Gran, whose descriptions of the world were usually so pat and neatly put together. "After that, she never set foot in his house again. I always thought it was because he didn't want her there, but she says it was her decision." Maggie squints up at the ceiling lamp. "It's funny—I used to think I could remember the day of my birth. I remembered what it felt like being held in my mother's arms. This week on the phone, though, when Gran described taking me to visit him in the hospital, I realized that's what I've been remembering all this time. It wasn't my mother, it was Dad."

"You must not blame yourself," says Lenka.

"Do I blame myself?" The idea comes as a surprise. "I don't think I do. Actually, Gran says there was a happy ending, because he changed after that. She says in the hospital he burst into tears when he realized how glad I was to see him. That's a happy ending, isn't it?" She leans forward in the rocking chair with her fingers clutching the arms, then lets herself rock back. "I'm sorry for going on. I don't know why I told you all that."

"Because you do not wish to repeat father's mistakes," says Lenka. "You want to make your own way in the world."

"She makes her way already," Josef says, sounding annoyed. Turning to Maggie, he says, "Do not run to throw away everything you do since you come here."

"You must not listen to Josef," says Lenka. "My brother wants you to be like him, unhappy in this place forever."

They seem on the brink of falling back into the argument they were having when Maggie arrived. She doesn't have the energy to referee. But before she can make an excuse to leave, Josef's expression grows pacific.

"Come, we talk no more of this now. Let us pray to God for guidance." He closes his eyes and bows his head. After a moment, Lenka joins him. Maggie waits for them to finish before she bids them good night.

The next day, she works in the front yard by the mailbox, pruning the lilac bush more than it needs, trying to avoid the house and Brid's unbearable kindness. Maggie expected Brid to punish her somehow for giving up the farm, but it's been the opposite. Brid has taken up the cooking and the laundry, she has sat for long stretches listening to Maggie talk of Laos, and she hasn't expressed any interest in travelling with her or hunting down Wale. It's as though she's doing everything she can to prove that she'll be all right in Boston by herself and Maggie shouldn't feel bad about leaving her. The result is that Maggie spends more time worrying over Brid's future than her own.

Her thoughts are broken by the sound of steps approaching along the gravel road. She looks up and sees it's Lydia Dodd.

The girl doesn't seem unfriendly. Instead, she looks woebegone, and despite her bulky jacket she hugs herself as if for warmth, seeming even thinner than she was three months ago.

"I saw your sign," she says, gesturing to the placard by the road that reads FOR SALE. "Thought I'd say hello before you take off."

"Your father said you were living in Toronto," says Maggie warily.

"I was, but not now." The girl peers across the lawn toward the porch. "I missed your open house. Would you let me take a look around?"

"You mean inside?" Maggie asks, and Lydia nods. "Why?"

"Because my parents and I used to live here."

"Oh," says Maggie. How could no one have mentioned this until now?

"We moved out when I was a little kid," explains Lydia, as though sensing Maggie's disbelief. "If you don't want me in there—"

"No, no. It's just a surprise." Maggie sets down her shears and waves for the girl to come along. As they cross the yard, it seems surreal for the two of them to be walking side by side.

In the house, Lydia doesn't say a word. Passing through the hallway, then the kitchen, she gazes at the walls, the floors, the furniture as sedulously as a patron at an exhibition. Maggie tries not to feel embarrassed when the girl takes a moment to study the broken cupboard door Maggie hasn't gotten around to fixing. She's tempted to ask if it was Lydia's family who bequeathed to her the layers of grease in the oven, the bottle cap glued over a hole in the counter. But they couldn't have; they moved out years ago.

In the living room, the girl runs her fingers along the old side table Fletcher brought up from the cellar in July. Then for a long time she takes in a series of horizontal notches on the door frame, the highest of them just above her waist.

"Anything look the same?" asks Maggie.

"I can't remember. It was a long time ago."

"You moved next door from here?" It seems a strange thing to have done.

"My father did. Mom and I went to Toronto." From the silence that follows, Maggie guesses there are things the girl remembers well enough.

Upstairs, as they near Brid's bedroom, Maggie puts a finger to her lips and motions Lydia past. "My house-mate's sleeping," she whispers. It may not be true, but she doesn't want to spring the girl on Brid, or Brid on her. They carry on to Maggie's room.

Lydia doesn't enter, only remains at the doorway and looks in. The bed has been made, thank goodness. The rolltop desk in the corner is covered in files, and the bulletin board above it has been pinned with sheets of notepaper. Atop the bureau sits a line of books, some puffed out with yellowed pages from being dropped in the bath. The box Maggie brought back from Syracuse with her father's things in it is tucked in a corner, still sealed with packing tape. She doesn't suppose she'll ever open it in this place.

Lydia stares at the room a little longer before turning away. "I remember them yelling a lot. They couldn't make money out of cherries, but it was his family's farm and he didn't want to leave." Speaking more to herself than to Maggie, she adds, "He wouldn't have if I'd been a boy."

"What about the wrecking yard?" Maggie asks.

Lydia snorts derisively and starts down the hallway. "That was his get-rich scheme once he'd sold the rest of the land."

She takes in the empty bedroom at the back of the house, then steps into the playroom and glances at the projector. Maggie half expects some crack about the party, but when Lydia speaks, she isn't sarcastic. She's distraught.

"Dimitri's not here, is he?"

Maggie shakes her head, and the girl bursts into tears. Suddenly Maggie feels certain that the tour of the house was a way for Lydia to find this out. She wanted to see for herself.

"But his wife's here," she says through her sobs. "I've seen her."

"You didn't," says Maggie softly. "They left months ago. They haven't been back."

"I did see her," Lydia insists, and Maggie tries to think what happened.

"Was she blond?" she asks. The girl nods, sniffling. "That isn't her, Lydia. That's my housemate. I swear to you she isn't Dimitri's wife."

"But he told me she was. At the party he pointed her out to me." Lydia's face turns vicious. "He's a goddamn liar!"

A moment later, she hastens from the room. Maggie waits a minute before following, then finds her on the porch stairs, still weeping. As she sits down beside her, Lydia's hand reaches out, palm up. Sitting in it is a rusty key.

"From under the mat," Lydia says. Maggie takes it from her slowly. "Jacqui and I used to hang out here before you moved in. We didn't know you were coming."

Maggie thinks of the peace sign on the wall, the cigarette butts and empty bottles. She remembers her first night in the house and the shadowy figure at the bottom of the stairs.

"The night Fletcher and I got here . . ."

"That was Jacqui. She'd left her stash in the living room."

"She got it back?"

"Not that time. Dimitri grabbed it for us later." After she has spoken, Lydia bends forward and starts to breathe quickly and shallowly.

"Are you all right?" asks Maggie. "You need help?"

Lydia sits up and puts her hands on her knees to brace herself, eyes closed tightly, leaking tears. "I'm sorry about the wall. I'm very sorry. It was Dimitri's idea, in the summer. He wanted me to write those things."

Maggie feels her jaw clenching. "Lydia," she says.

"I thought he was back. It was supposed to be a joke."

"A joke," says Maggie flatly.

"I thought he was hiding from me," the girl whispers. "I thought he was here with his wife." Her face screws up into a mask of hatred. "He's such an asshole!"

Maggie doesn't know what to say. "Your father told me you'd gone to Toronto."

"My father's a moron." Lydia wipes the tears from her cheeks and stares across the lawn with glistening eyes. "I moved back after Halloween."

"So he was lying. Did he tell you that I'd called?"

"Yeah. I promised him I wouldn't do it again." Suddenly Lydia has taken on the contemptuous air that she shared with her cousin in the summer. "Mom's right, he's spineless. He'd let me get away with anything."

Maggie thinks back to her phone call with the man and wonders whether he'd have covered for his daughter if he knew what she had written. A joke, she claimed. Dimitri's idea. How could they have been so stupid?

"You wrote such hateful things," Maggie says.

The girl starts crying again, while Maggie remains motionless beside her.

"He just wanted to stir things up," says Lydia. "He wanted to rile your boyfriend." She turns to Maggie with desperate eyes. "He's messed up in the head. He's a junkie."

"That didn't bother you?" Maggie wonders whether Dimitri told Lydia or she found out some other way.

The girl's shoulders droop and she puts her head in her hands. "I guess I was in love with him."

Maggie doesn't offer any consolation. She isn't going to let herself feel sorry for this person, not after what she wrote. It doesn't matter how young or infatuated she is.

Eventually Lydia looks up with resignation. "If you're going to call the cops on me, you should do it now. Otherwise I'm leaving on a bus tonight." As if to underscore the point, she stands and makes her way to the bottom of the stairs. "Jacqui and I are meeting in Toronto. We're moving to Los Angeles to live with her dad." Then she adds, "It isn't to get out of trouble for what I wrote. We've been planning it forever."

Maggie doesn't believe her for a minute. It's a silly schoolgirl fantasy.

"Have you told your father?" she asks.

Lydia glowers into the distance. "He doesn't care. He wouldn't even try to stop me."

Maggie feels an impulse to march the girl next door and make her tell her father everything. It isn't her job to fix things between the two of them, though. It isn't her job to make sure Lydia turns out all right. Better for the girl to go to California than stay here and force Maggie to keep dealing with her.

"You do what you want," Maggie tells her. "I'm not going to call the cops."

Instead of being relieved, the girl looks disappointed. "Why not? After what I wrote, I should be in jail."

"Sorry, I guess you'll just have to live with it." She can hear George Ray saying how she never wants a fuss. But right now Lydia's practically daring her to make one, and she refuses to give her the satisfaction.

The girl's glower intensifies. She starts down the driveway, then stops. "This is your last chance," she says.

"Go. You're home free."

"You're being an idiot." Lydia sounds almost frantic. "You can't let people get away with things."

"Travel safely," says Maggie. "I hope you have a good life."

The girl's eyes sweep across the house. "I'm glad he sold it," she declares. "I hated living here."

The pronouncement seems to free her, and she starts skipping down the drive as though without a care. Halfway along, she stops once more.

"I really am sorry," she calls out. "It was a stupid thing to do."

Maggie nods, worrying the gesture could be taken for a sign of forgiveness. She holds tight to the house key, feeling its tacky weight on her damp skin.

Once the girl has gone, Maggie's first thought is to phone George Ray and tell him what has happened. Instead, she goes upstairs and peeks into Brid's room. Sleeping, after all. Maggie tiptoes to the bed and strokes her hair. It would be good to film her as she lies there so tranquilly, but lately Maggie hasn't had much desire to use the camera.

Brid stirs under her hand, opens her eyes, then lets them fall closed again. "Hey," she says sleepily. "I love you."

Maggie starts at the words. Does Brid know to whom she's spoken? Already she has returned to sleep, so there's no way to ask. Maybe it doesn't matter. Fletcher used to tell Maggie all the time that he loved her, and look where he is now. George Ray never said anything about love, nor Maggie to him, even though on more than one occasion the words were on her tongue. Then she thinks of Lydia saying she was in love with Dimitri. A stupid teenage crush, maybe, but Maggie isn't about to deny that it was some kind of love. She gazes down at Brid and wonders at such variety.

"I love you, too," she says, continuing to stroke her hair, as if it's only through the stroking that either of them might find any peace.

The next day, when she arrives at Niagara Falls, there are plenty of places to park. It isn't a surprise, for who besides her would think to visit the place on a frigid weekday morning in the middle of December? Only a few other souls stroll the promenade beside the falls. Sitting on a bench with the Super 8 camera in its case beside her, she watches a pair of teenagers walk past, the boy a few yards ahead, the girl dragging her feet, her swollen belly impossible to hide. They don't even bother to look at the waterfall. When the girl catches Maggie staring at them, she gazes back scornfully, and Maggie realizes how abject she must appear, sitting there without even a companion. She wonders if George Ray has ever seen Niagara Falls, and she regrets never bringing him here.

Once the teenagers have passed out of sight, Maggie goes to the railing above the falls. Lifting the camera from its case, she switches it on and zooms in until the frame is filled with cascading water. She tries to imagine how it will look projected on the wall, whiteness tumbling down whiteness, the whole thing silent because she left the tape recorder at home. Mist starts to collect on the lens. She remembers how, after her father brought her here as a girl, she had dreams where she was in the river being swept toward the brink. They always ended just before she reached the edge.

On the drive home, she has turned off the highway onto the gravel road when the first snowflakes of the year begin to settle on the windshield, big fat ones swirling through the air and smearing the glass. It takes a moment before she realizes they're not snow at all; they're ash. Ahead of her, a long pillar of smoke rises toward the clouds. It must be someone burning brush. Only after she has passed Frank Dodd's driveway and arrived at her own does she realize the smoke is coming from the farmhouse.

The source of the plume is a second-storey window. Brid's room. Occasionally a flame flicks its tongue through the broken glass. Otherwise the house has a strange normalcy about it. As Maggie parks the van and starts up the porch stairs, she could almost believe everything is fine.

She's pretty sure that most people would tell her not to walk into a burning house, but it turns out to be a very easy thing to do. The knob of the front door isn't even warm. There's only a thin stream of smoke trickling down the stairs, pretty and harmless. The sounds from the second floor are of a large campfire before it has died down enough for marshmallows. Standing at the bottom of the staircase, she calls Brid's name and hears nothing. There's no one in the living room, just the day's newspaper spread out on the coffee table. She's almost tempted to go and straighten it. No one is in the kitchen. Then she hears a meowing from the mud room and finds Elliot clamouring to be let out. It's odd to share none of his panic. She opens the door for him, and when he lopes away to safety, she wonders whether she can now be credited with having saved a life, whether sometimes it's that simple and ordinary.

Going back into the kitchen, she picks up the telephone, discovers it's working, and is amazed and unsurprised at once. After dialing zero, she tells the operator that her house is on fire.

"You aren't in the building now, are you, ma'am?" The operator sounds concerned. Then the line cuts out, and Maggie decides she had better go upstairs.

Perhaps I'm suicidal, she thinks as she climbs through the tumble of smoke. But she feels no desire to kill herself, only a detached lack of self-regard, a kind of disembodiment. From impossible angles she watches her own ascent, as if this is the climactic scene in a movie that has often been described to her, one she's finally getting to view.

At the top, it sounds like the house is talking to her, wakeful and chatty after years of dozing, keen to tell her all the dreams it's had. Smoke billows from the open door to Brid's room. This fact breaks her out of whatever trance has held her until now. Again she calls Brid's name, hears nothing. After waiting in vain for the smoke to diminish so she can look into the room, she forces herself over the threshold. Her eyes water and a cinder scalds her tongue. The far wall is roiling and shimmering, the wall between the bed and bathroom has collapsed, and there's no sign of Brid. Maggie coughs and retches with the smoke, then makes her way farther down the hall. No one in her room. No one in the playroom. The flames haven't reached these places yet. She isn't really thinking, only following some inner imperative, when she fetches the stepladder. It's not until she begins to climb it that she realizes she's doing it to save the money.

The handle on the trap door to the attic is hot, and the air has thickened to the extent that it won't let her sweat; moisture evaporates on her as soon as it forms. From above comes a high, multi-layered sound like a choir singing. She's wondering how to proceed when the ceiling behind her falls away, throwing her off balance and toppling her from the stepladder to the floor. She lands in a heap with her left leg under her. Her ankle snaps and the pain shatters her, so woozily sickening that some time passes before she realizes the noises she hears are her own screams.

She can't breathe. There's an agony in her rib cage. She can only gulp and heave. When she tries to put weight on her foot, the pain shrieks through her. The hallway is filling with smoke. Maggie looks down the corridor to the stairs and hopes to see the top of someone's head appear, but no miracle is forthcoming. The flames grow higher, blocking her way out, even if she could move. They're different from the coy, gentle flames in Brid's room. These ones are restless, eager to explore the house. They slither up the wall, shattering a picture frame, then move toward her as though they have caught the scent of a curious new plaything.

She starts to crawl along the floor in the direction of escape, which is also the direction of the flames. Every movement tortures her. A yard becomes a mile. When she reaches the playroom, the smoke's so thick that she's choking more than breathing, and the heat blisters her lips. There's only one choice: she drags herself through the playroom door, then closes it behind her and sits against it, as if her weight might keep out the fire. Even while she rests there, though, smoke seeps into the room through the cracks. Taking off her sweater, she wraps it around her mouth. It's a slight improvement. Finally she's thinking of her survival, lame and cornered as she is.

Across the room, the film canisters lie beside the projector on the card table. It's not just the money that will be lost, then, nor only the house and her life, but the film as well. She should smash the window and throw the reels to the ground, then jump for it. God knows how she'll land. But when she tries to cross the room, her ankle only lets her get halfway. From behind the door there's a growing roar, and the air speaks a multitude of languages. Did someone call her name? A voice is shouting, barely audible. She calls back, feeling foolish and forlorn. Then there's a bang behind her, and she turns to watch the door go flying open. Behind it is Brid, come to rescue her.

Brid tries to lift her, but halfway up she loses her grip and sends her falling back toward the floor. Maggie lands on her bad foot and yelps in pain.

"Sorry, sorry," says Brid, grabbing hold again. She heaves her up and starts to drag her out the door with Maggie leaning on her shoulder.

"Wait, the film—" says Maggie.

"Fuck the film," says Brid.

In the hall, the air is filled with drops of liquid heat. The house burns well, as though stocked for that purpose, a furnace of books and wooden furniture. How does Brid think they'll make it? Apparently the same way she made it here in the first place: daringly, and without much sense.

As Brid leads her along the hall, Maggie looks back and sees there's no floor behind them. She can look straight down into the kitchen, where her bed has fallen through and crashed onto the table. The mattress is aflame, yellow and blue. The house roars and puffs. Without warning, something stabs her in the eye. She puts her hand to it and feels hot wetness. Her other eye fills with smoke and tears.

"I can't see," she says.

The sensation in her feet is going; they might be on fire. Brid shouts at her to hurry, and there's another groan from the house. The house is in pain. The house is dying.

They pass under an arch of flame, and there's the smell of burning hair. Hers? The visibility of things comes and goes as the blood runs down her face and smoke pushes its way through the house.

Her hand alights on the staircase banister. The steps buckle, and Brid's voice fills her ears: "Almost there, almost there." Every moment Maggie's curious to see if this is the point where they'll die.

Just when they have reached the bottom of the stairs, there's a tremor that Maggie feels not only through her good leg but also through her teeth and fingertips. Light shears in through her half-open eye to suggest a wall has fallen away. Brid lets go of her, and Maggie crumples to the floor. Then Brid is yelling, "Help her!" Briefly through the blood and smoke, Maggie sees her leaning on the frame of the front door and another body passing by, a wraith-like shape as numinous as night, Maggie's death come to collect her. It lifts her off the ground.

The house seems to sway. As she's carried through the door, the beam at the top splits a few inches from her head. It's close to Brid's head too, because Maggie can make her out still standing there, propping herself against the frame as if the building wants to fall on her. Brid's clothes are on fire, but she doesn't move. Maggie has a feeling of being released into cooler air, and at the same time the wraith shouts at Brid to come away. From his voice Maggie realizes it's Frank Dodd. In the next second the door comes crashing down, followed by an avalanche of bricks.

There's a jolt as Maggie is lifted down the porch stairs in Frank's arms, then another as he lays her on the grass. When she opens her good eye, she can't see Brid, only Frank crouching on the porch and trying to lift beams out of the way. He grunts and throws bricks willy-nilly while the porch roof sags above him.

Finally he pulls Brid free. The body he sets down beside Maggie is limp, and Brid's face is pale, her forehead streaked with blood and ash. Frank hovers over them, blinking, red-faced, dripping with sweat.

"I didn't call for help yet," he says. "I thought you were burning brush. Will you be all right if—"

"Go!" shouts Maggie, as loudly as she can manage, and he rushes down the driveway. She watches to make sure he doesn't turn around before she shifts her attention back to Brid.

In places the heat has grafted Brid's clothing to her flesh. A layer of skin on her forearms has melted away, so that Maggie can see the vulnerable life below, red strings of tendon packed together, twitching and bleeding. It's too intimate and awful to look at for long. Maggie wonders if she should wrap the burns with her own clothing, but she doesn't know first aid. It could be the wrong thing to do. She can only look at her and caress her face.

A second later, amazingly, Brid is awake and calling Maggie's name, convulsing as if she's about to rise.

"I'm here," says Maggie. "Don't move. It's better if you don't."

"Shit, it hurts," says Brid through gritted teeth. She coughs up a bit of blood. Maggie tells her again to hold still. "It wasn't on purpose," Brid tells her. "I'm sorry. I swear, I wouldn't do it on purpose." Maggie tries to move closer and pain shoots up from her ruined foot. It takes her some effort to sit, but she takes Brid's head in her lap and strokes her face, wiping the ash from her forehead. There's a noise that tears the sky, and a section of the porch roof comes down, blasting them with sparks and smoke.

"I was only out for a walk," says Brid. "I didn't mean for it to happen."

"Hush," says Maggie through her coughing. "Hush, sweetheart, it will be all right."

12

Smoke has blotted out the sun, red lights flash atop fire trucks, and torrents of flame gallop through the tree-tops. Then everything is still, and where the farmhouse once stood is a smouldering heap. All that remain are a few brick walls and window glass melted into lumpish sculptures. Nothing seems to be left of the orchard but charred stumps. There are flakes of ash falling softly on the acres of burnt trees, on the seared grass, and on the iron bed frame in the middle of the kitchen. The fire has scoured all colour from the earth, so that the television screen Maggie's watching might as well be black-and-white.

Before the ruins stands the freckled policeman, testifying that he's never seen anything like it. He witnessed a flock of birds, dizzy from the heat, fly into the wavering air above the trees and tumble like shooting stars into the fire. He says you could see the smoke from as far away as Buffalo. There's a shot of Frank Dodd sitting on the back of a fire truck with an oxygen mask over his mouth. The policeman praises Mr. Dodd for his courage in rescuing two American women from the house. Then a reporter's voice states that the women are now at the Hotel Dieu Hospital in St. Catharines with serious injuries. There's a distant shot of someone being lifted into an ambulance, and it takes Maggie a moment to realize it's her.

As the reporter continues to speak, there's another shot of the rubble. Where the living room once stood, a man is kicking through the remains. The reporter's voice identifies him as a friend of the tenants who was hoping to find something that survived intact. Finally the man leans down, pushes away a blackened piece of wood, and retrieves a small figure.

The statue doesn't look the same. It's glazed by the fire, a deeper, richer hue than before. The features on the face have burned away, leaving it without gender or expression.

The figure stays like that for only a second or two. Then, under the pressure of the man's hands, it cracks in half. Maggie watches as he tips the thing and pours out a stream of fine grey dust. His face is out of focus, but she's pretty sure the man is Josef.

Night has fallen outside the hospital. A candystriper in braids enters the room where Maggie lies, asks if she's comfortable, and offers to change the channel. The girl smells of cigarettes and strawberry gum, a combination that nauseates Maggie and at the same time manages to make her crave both things.

The candystriper asks whether Maggie saw news about the fire on TV. The girl has already made it clear that not all patients get a television; it was a special favour on her part to wheel the set in here so Maggie could be entertained by the sight of her home's destruction. The girl tells her that reporters appeared at the reception desk not long ago, but they were sent away. She adds that a priest turned up with his sister, too, and they were told to come back tomorrow during visiting hours. Maggie asks the candystriper how Brid's doing, and the girl says it's hard to know because they're keeping her pretty doped up.

Once the girl leaves, Maggie regains an awareness of the patient who shares her room, an old woman hidden from her by a heavy curtain. She and the woman don't speak to one another except in the form of moans and wheezes. Oddly, the suffering seems to shift between them, as if they're taking turns with it. In certain moments, when the painkillers ebb and Maggie's ankle maddens her, the old woman grows silent. Then, as the agony subsides, the woman begins to cry out. To hear her in this state is an ordeal, but it distracts Maggie from her own afflictions.

Later, the freckled policeman shows up to take down Maggie's account of what happened. He tells her how lucky she is that Frank Dodd came over when he saw the smoke. He says Frank wanted to stop by and wish her well, but his daughter ran off to California yesterday and he's busy working out how to get her back.

"Are you sure she left yesterday?" asks Maggie, picturing Lydia in the farmhouse with a can of gasoline. The policeman says he's sure.

Upon his departure, her eye begins to throb beneath its bandage. The doctor has expressed optimism that it will heal, but he's said they might need to operate on the ankle. The thing is wrapped up sufficiently that she doesn't have to look at it, only feels it pulsing and aching. She can't reflect for any length of time on the house, the trees, her film, her father's belongings—all gone forever. The money, too. And Josef on television, searching for it. She thinks of calling him and Lenka, but she doesn't have the energy. The drugs kick in again to carry her away on their dark, sweet current.

In the morning, she finds that the curtain separating her bed from the next has been pulled back, and the old woman is gone. Lenka and Josef are standing there instead. From the pitying way in which Lenka looks at her, Maggie gathers she must be quite a sight.

"It's never a good sign," Maggie says, trying to smile, "when a priest shows up in your hospital room."

Josef and Lenka laugh. Then Lenka says how horrible it is and how sorry they are. She explains that after being turned back at the emergency room desk yesterday, the two of them drove out to the farm. She says only the barracks and a small section of the orchard have survived. They hoped there might be something to salvage, but they found nothing.

"I know," says Maggie. "I saw Josef on TV."

The priest picks up a brown paper bag at his feet and withdraws the clay figure of Saint Clare. Somehow the statue's in one piece again, though the cement bottom is missing. When Maggie expresses her surprise, Josef says he glued the figure back together. He has done a better job of it than Maggie did, because this time the crack on the exterior is barely noticeable. When he lays the figure in her hands, it feels smoother than before, and it's lighter now that its contents are turned to ash.

"I am glad the money is gone," says Lenka. "For too long it is plaguing you."

Her brother looks about to argue the point, but Lenka insists it won't do to talk further of the matter. For now Maggie must simply get better, and the two of them will look after her affairs. Lenka has already called Morgan Sugar to let Fletcher know what happened; he's on his way. So is Brid's brother, who's bringing Pauline. Lenka asks whether Maggie would like her to contact Gran and George Ray too.

No, she thinks. Gran would only come up and overwhelm her with smug care, as if a fire was exactly what she expected. George Ray couldn't come back even if he wanted to. Thanking Lenka, Maggie replies that she'll call them herself when she's feeling better.

Fletcher turns up that afternoon looking drained and ill-shaven, as though he jumped in the car and drove all night, a romantic thought undercut by the fact that he's had at least eighteen hours in which to complete a nine-hour trip. As he leans over to kiss her cheek, she asks what took him so long, and when he starts to protest, she tells him she's only kidding. It's a poor way to begin.

Once he's sitting on the chair beside the bed, he asks if she's in much pain. She says it's not too bad, then asks in turn whether he has stopped in to see Brid.

"Not yet," he replies. "The doctor says she's pretty delirious. Third-degree burns on her arms, and she broke her back. Apparently she keeps saying how it's all her fault because she left a candle burning."

"She saved my life," Maggie tells him. He nods but doesn't ask for details, as if they'd be an embarrassment because he wasn't around to save Maggie himself. Here he is, finally back in this country, and all he can do is assess the damage to company assets. When she asks whether the farm was insured, he looks uncomfortable.

"I didn't get around to it," he says. She wonders if his father has jumped on him for the oversight or if Fletcher's still bracing himself for that conversation. "Some developer might want the land, at least," he continues. "Maybe that Dodd guy could buy it to expand his wrecking yard."

As he says this, she remembers that he doesn't know what has happened with Lydia. He doesn't even know about the graffiti, and right now she doesn't feel up to telling him. It's hard enough to hear him fall so quickly into talk of business matters, as though she isn't lying in front of him wounded and drugged. He goes on speaking for some time before he seems to recognize she isn't listening. Then he hunches over in the chair and falls silent.

"So here we are," she says.

"Here we are." Slowly his eyes rise to meet hers. He inspects her face before reaching to touch her cheek. She's in too much pain to pull away. His fingers on her skin are soothing. "You look good," he says.

The pronouncement makes the bandage over her eye feel hot and itchy.

"Yeah, I'm a real beauty queen."

"I mean it," he insists, the solemnity in his voice a little disconcerting. "You'll be out of here soon. If you need money or a place to stay—"

She thanks him without accepting. He's only being polite. Still, if she's honest with herself, a part of her feels owed something. She can't go on like that, though, forever demanding reparations. When she looks at him, she finds him staring back with a pained expression. What's he thinking? Could there be recrimination on his part? Some nostalgia, even? Perhaps he's remembering the day they first arrived at the house, just the two of them, with all their belongings and hopes in tow.

"Never thought it would end up like this," she says, and he offers his agreement, his face shaded by a certain wistfulness that surprises her. "Did you really think it might work out?" she asks. "I mean, back in June, did you really think we might live here forever?" It hurts her to see him nod, regretfully and without hesitation.

"Naive, huh?"

"What happened, then?" she asks. Maybe it's the drugs that let her pose the question, or maybe it's the fact that finally she can ask it face to face.

"You know what happened," he says. The sorrowful expression that overtook him the night of the party returns exactly as it first appeared.

"I don't mean in the summer. I mean after that, in Boston. Why didn't you come back?"

He shakes his head in frustration. "I never got together with Cybil again, if that's what you mean." He speaks as though pained that she might think as much. He's always so sensitive to others' judgment, and at the same time he seems to accept it as inevitable.

Upon having this thought, Maggie says something that until now has only occurred to her in a vague, unformulated way. "Fletcher, you ever wonder if you did it on purpose? The film, I mean."

His face darkens and he looks confused.

"You ever think," she says, "maybe you wanted everyone to see it?"

He gives a harsh laugh. "Why the hell would I want that?" His voice is angry, but he waits to hear her answer.

"I don't know. Maybe you were looking for an excuse to go home."

He only laughs again, though in an excessive way. Then he regains a look of concern. "You should come back to Boston."

The words jar her. It's not the sentiment that's surprising but the tone in which he utters it. During the fall, his counsel for her to return always seemed like a way to allay his conscience. Now he offers it with a kinder inflection.

Casting her a sidelong glance, he adds, "You could stay at my place."

Now it's her turn to laugh uneasily. "You're just a push-over for a girl in a hospital gown."

"No, I mean it." He tries to say it in a lighthearted way, but it's obvious he isn't speaking idly. Then he utters something that seems a hallucinatory product of the drugs. "We could try again."

The sentence seizes her. For a second it manages to blot out the pain, before passing through and taking her defences with it, so that her ankle begins to pulse more sharply than ever. For most of October, after the news of her father's death, after Fletcher told her he wasn't coming back, the words he has just spoken were what she most wanted to hear. Then there was George Ray, and her hopes changed.

"Fletcher—" She thinks of telling him about George Ray, except George Ray doesn't really have a bearing on the matter. What she wants to say isn't even clear to her, beyond a conviction that the time for what he's just suggested has come and gone.

It turns out she doesn't even have to say anything. The way she has spoken his name is enough.

"Never mind," he says. "It was just a thought."

He looks about the room as if searching for an exit, then settles his gaze on the blank television set against the wall.

"You watch the moon landing the other day?" he asks, and she says she didn't. "Last one for a while. You know, in high school I was space crazy. Wanted to be an astronaut. Did I ever tell you that? At least until I found out they can't wear these." He taps his glasses with a rueful smile before sinking back to his hunched position in the chair.

He's travelled a long way to be here; she should be grateful for that. It wasn't a journey through outer space, only a trip to a foreign country, but still he's made the effort, even though by now for him this place must be synonymous with disappointment. It's a marvel, really, to think there was a time when he hoped settling here would be a worthy substitute for earlier dashed dreams, when he thought a life with her might be enough. She lies there sensing the presence of another Fletcher somewhere over them, unfulfilled. She imagines him orbiting Earth, his long body wrapped in a silver suit with a flag on the shoulder, suspended in darkness among pricks of light. His face is illuminated by blinking instruments, and he's thousands of miles from home, from family, from obligation and disapproval. As she envisions him like that, there's a pang, because she feels pretty certain the image is similar to one he once invented for himself, and it might come closer than anything else to his picture of happiness.

A certain amount of pleading is necessary before the doctor allows her to venture from the room. Then, as Fletcher helps a nurse move her into a wheelchair, Maggie muffles cries of pain. With her foot propped out front like a tender battering ram, Fletcher pushes her into the hall. The corridor feels ethereal with its abandoned gurneys and strings of Christmas lights. A few yards down, he wheels her into Brid's room. It contains a single bed, the body on it obscured by a jungle gym of pulleys, straps, and struts. Brid's face is scratched but free of burns, while her arms

are wrapped in gauze. On the windowsill is a bouquet
of lilies that produces in Maggie a brief, ludicrous envy,
because no one has brought any flowers for her.

Brid manages a smile of welcome. Once Fletcher has
positioned Maggie's chair next to the bed, he excuses himself from the room, as if it's been arranged that he's to give
them some time alone.

"Sweetie, I'm so sorry," says Brid when he's gone. "I
think it was all my fault."

"It doesn't matter, you shouldn't beat yourself up—"

"But did Fletcher tell you? I lit a candle while you were
out. Then I went into the orchard for a walk. When I came
back, there was smoke coming from the house and the
camper was in the drive, and that chickenshit from next
door was just standing by the porch like a lump. Maggie, I
feel so bad about it . . ."

"I'm the one who should feel bad." She gestures to the
apparatus around the bed. "You saved my life."

"Guess I did, huh?" Brid manages another smile, then
grows sombre. "Listen, I've been thinking."

Maggie fears what's about to follow, but Brid's expression brightens as she starts to speak.

"Let's stay here and start over with the farm," she says.
"We can build a brand new house."

She must be kidding. Except it seems she isn't, judging by
the enthusiasm on her face. Maggie searches for a response.

"The old place was a dump anyway," Brid says. "We can
live in the barracks until the new one's ready. And we'll plant
trees. Not just cherry trees, but peaches and grapes—"

"Grapes don't grow on trees."

"You know what I mean. Anyhow, George Ray will handle that stuff."

George Ray? What kind of fantasy has Brid entered? There she lies in a hospital bed while Maggie sits helpless in a wheelchair, neither of them with any job or income, and she's imagining a whole new farm.

"Brid, I can't afford to buy the property, much less—"

"I'll buy it, then. I'll take care of everything."

Maggie smiles in bewilderment. Not so many days ago, Brid was on the bathroom floor cursing and screaming. Before that, she was confessing her inability to pay for her keep. Now she looks calmer and more certain than at any time Maggie has known her.

"Where will you get the money?" Maggie asks.

"From Fletcher." Brid says it as if the whole thing has already been agreed upon.

"He won't go for that. It's too much, even for him—"

"He'll go for it," Brid insists. "He's already been offering me the moon, he feels so bad about everything. You think he'll say no if I tell him we want to rebuild?" And as she says it, Maggie knows he won't.

"Sweetie, don't get worked up," says Brid in a soothing voice. "Things will turn out fine, I swear. The farm in the summer was a disaster, but this time we'll do it right." She smiles and winks. "For one thing, we'll put the women in charge."

For a while they just keep each other company and Maggie tries to digest what has been proposed. Then she thinks of something else.

"Have you seen Pauline yet?"

Brid averts her eyes, and the contentment disappears from her face. "Fletcher's going to bring her in a minute. I wanted to wait till you were here." For Brid to say this is touching but disconcerting too. Brid seems to register Maggie's worry, because she adds, "You don't have to do anything. Just sit there. That'll be enough."

"Are you ready for her?" Maggie asks.

"I don't have a choice, do I?" Brid reaches over to the lilies and brushes one of the petals with a bandaged finger. "She hates me now."

"No, she'll be glad to see you."

Brid gives a little grunt of disbelief.

A few minutes later, the door creaks and the girl peeks in, clutching her curly-haired doll. Its left arm remains attached to the shoulder by only a few threads; its button eyes have fallen off. Pauline glares at Maggie as though holding her responsible for her mother's condition. Faced with that accusation on the girl's face, Maggie looks away. Then Pauline rushes into the room, halting at the bedside. Probably someone has counselled her to be gentle around Mommy.

"Hello, Pollywog," says Brid. She's trying not to let Pauline see her cry. Pauline clambers up the side of the bed and gives her mother a fat kiss on the cheek. A second later she throws another suspicious glance at Maggie. It seems Maggie can't stay without having an effect on the proceedings, so as quietly as she can manage, she wheels herself from the room.

The specialist who arrives later in the day to examine Maggie's ankle removes the dressing and doesn't like what he sees. Her foot is purple and scarlet, a worked-over bulbous piece of meat. She nearly faints when he touches it, and he orders an increased dose of the painkiller she's on. A few minutes later, she's asleep.

When she regains consciousness, the morning sun shines through the window. Lenka and Fletcher are standing beside the bed, whispering small talk to each other. Beyond them, someone is seated in a chair near the door.

It's Josef, and in his lap is a baby, a boy about a year old with straight black hair over his ears, looking peaceably at the adults before him. Without anyone explaining it to her, Maggie understands that this is Yia Pao's son.

The priest is singing to the child in Czech and smiling. When he sees Maggie's awake, he grins at her with elation.

"Is Wale here too?" she asks. It's as though she has awoken to a different reality, one without any distances, where everyone exists together.

"No," says Josef. "But Yia Pao is."

"You missed the momentous arrival," says Fletcher. "How are you feeling?"

"Never mind that," she says, even as she apprehends the throb in her foot. "Where's Yia Pao? Where's Wale?"

"Yia Pao should probably explain things," Fletcher tells her. "He's asleep in the waiting room. Let me go get him. He's pretty jet-lagged, but he's eager to talk with you."

Once Fletcher leaves the room, Lenka tells her that last night Yia Pao and his son were brought to the rectory by Frank Dodd. Yia Pao had arrived at the farm and found it in ruins. Then he had gone next door and asked Frank about Maggie.

"The boy's name is Xang," says the priest, jouncing the baby on his lap and staring into his eyes with a goofy, wide-mouthed smile.

"How did they end up at the farm?" Maggie asks, and Lenka says they hitchhiked from the Toronto airport. "But how did they get into the country?"

"I'll tell you," says a voice.

At the door stands a short, thin man, only a little like the one she remembers from the documentarian's film. This version of him looks older than the Yia Pao on TV. No, not older, but more worn, rough-faced and ruddy-skinned, with deep scars across his cheeks. He wears rumpled pants along with a white shirt that looks too big for him, as if lent from Josef's wardrobe.

"My God," she says. "It's you."

Yia Pao draws closer and takes her hand. "I'm sorry about your father. Gordon was my good friend."

From Josef's lap, the little boy calls out. Yia Pao goes to him, then returns to Maggie's bedside holding him against his chest, Xang burbling and pudgy-cheeked, showing no sign that he was ever close to death.

Lenka clears her throat and announces they'll leave them for a bit. She offers to take the boy, but Yia Pao says he'll be all right with him. Once she has departed with Josef and Fletcher, Maggie turns to regard Yia Pao.

"Are you all right?" she asks. "Have you eaten?" Her own stomach growls. He nods and says her friends have been very kind.

"They told me about the fire," he continues. "If you need to rest—"

"Don't go anywhere. I have so much to ask you."

But the sober look on his face makes her fearful of what he has to tell her. If Wale isn't here, what happened to him? The pain in her stomach grows worse than the one in her foot.

"Wale," she begins, then is unable to say anything further.

"I don't know what has happened," says Yia Pao. "Did you not hear from him?" She replies that it's been almost two weeks since he last called. "He was supposed to meet me at the airport in Vientiane," Yia Pao tells her. He's about to say more when the statue of Saint Clare on the bedside table catches his eye. His son has seen the figure too, and he reaches for it as though it's a plaything, but Yia Pao doesn't move to oblige him.

"The money's gone," Maggie says. "Burnt."

Yia Pao nods, not betraying any emotion, and she finds herself close to tears, because at last here's someone who knows about the money and might explain what happened.

"It was still in the statue during the fire," she says. "I only knew about the money by accident. My father didn't tell me anything."

She wants to say that she meant to give the money to Yia Pao's son, but what does it matter now? Yia Pao rounds the bed, picks up the statue in one hand, turns it over to examine its hollow core, then lets the baby grasp it for a while. A pained smile crosses Yia Pao's face.

"Perhaps it's for the best," he says, setting down the statue. "It was the cause of such misery."

"Will you tell me?" she asks.

Rather than responding, he drops his chin. "I'm ashamed of many things that happened."

"Tell me anyway."

As he starts to talk, she almost interrupts to say she's changed her mind. She has no desire to hear that her father was a drug runner, a hypocrite, a thief. But she doesn't want to be told of his innocence and purity either. It's an imperfect man whom she loved; the fervent, holy one will always be a stranger. Settling back to listen, she can't decide which of them she wants to emerge.

This is what Yia Pao tells her. He says that in the summer, he agreed to be Sal's middleman. The job was hardly honourable, but he took it out of a desperation to leave Laos with his son. Yia Pao had no other family, no reason to stay. Eventually the Communists were going to win, and everyone knew what would happen to those with Western educations, to the Hmong who had worked for Americans. People like Yia Pao would be the first against the wall.

Even before the CIA pilot arrived at the refugee camp to hand him the money, though, Yia Pao regretted his decision. As soon as the plane took off, he thought ahead to the twenty-four hours before Sal's arrival and was racked with paranoia, certain that others in the camp knew what was happening, that he'd be robbed in the night. Panicked, he placed the bills in one of the clay figures he'd made and sealed the thing. Even then he worried that somebody would divine what it contained. So, in his terror, he made a mistake. Thinking that no one would look for the money in a missionary's tent, he took the statue to Gordon and said it was a gift, telling him nothing of what it contained. Yia Pao said he'd made the statue in the likeness of Saint Clare because he remembered Gordon saying she was his daughter's favourite saint. Yia Pao shared this detail only to make the gift seem better planned. He didn't realize the calamity it would bring.

That night, he didn't sleep a wink. In the morning, when the time approached for Sal and his men to arrive, Yia Pao returned to Gordon's tent, planning to steal back the statue if Gordon wasn't there, but ready to say that it needed a coat of glaze if he was. When Yia Pao arrived, he discovered neither Gordon nor the statue was there. Alarmed, he scoured the camp and finally found his friend bandaging a little girl's toe. Gordon didn't understand why Yia Pao was demanding the statue's return. He explained that he had put the statue in a parcel for his daughter and had just sent it on the supply plane with the rest of the mail.

Yia Pao raced to the landing strip, knowing even before he set eyes on the field that the supply plane was gone. By the time he returned to the camp, he was weeping uncontrollably. It would have been better if he thought Gordon had betrayed him, but he knew it was his own fault for being so stupid.

Sick with fear, he gathered a few things from his tent, preparing to flee into the jungle. He would have an easier time on his own, but he couldn't leave his son to Sal, so he made his second mistake. With Gordon, he went to fetch Xang from the woman minding him near the river. When they arrived, Sal and his men had already landed on the bank.

Yia Pao couldn't tell Sal the truth because the man would never believe it, so in his terror he offered the simplest lie he could imagine: he said the money hadn't arrived. Sal didn't believe that either. Before he led them away on his boat, Yia Pao tried to return Xang to the woman, but Sal said no, bring him along, we'll take good care of the little guy.

During their captivity, Gordon never blamed Yia Pao. Often he went without food so Yia Pao and Xang might have more, and when the chance to escape presented itself, when they entered the jungle without supplies, already half starved, bruised, and bleeding, Gordon was the stronger of them, the one who insisted on carrying Xang. They moved slowly even so, and when they reached the river, Gordon suggested they split up, then meet again at a rock visible in the distance, so as to confuse Sal and his men should they be giving chase. Upon reaching the rock, Yia Pao found no sign of Gordon and Xang.

He waited an hour, backtracked, tried to follow Gordon's path, became lost. Finally he found the river again and followed it downstream until he stumbled into a village, barely able to stand. It wasn't until he was in Vientiane weeks later that he heard of Gordon's death and his son's survival. The rest of the autumn he lay low, searching for Xang, sheltered by old schoolmates and making inquiries through them, knowing that Sal had powerful friends.

It seemed both a miracle and a cruel joke when Yia Pao discovered that his son was also in Vientiane. He wanted to walk straight into the orphanage and claim him, but he knew that if he'd found Xang, Sal might have too. So Yia Pao entered the orphanage in the dead of night, lifted Xang from his crib, and stole out with him.

They were a block away when a man stepped from the shadows. Yia Pao didn't recognize him until Wale reminded him of their meeting at Long Chieng in the spring. Wale said he wanted to keep him from Sal's hands. Yia Pao worried it was a trick, but he knew that if it was, there was no point trying to escape; he'd be shot in the back before he got ten yards.

They ended up at a tiny flat in a rundown building with no electricity, the single room empty but for a roll-up mattress. Wale told him not to leave and promptly abandoned him, promising to come back soon.

An hour passed, then another. Yia Pao grew ever more certain that Wale would be returning with Sal. But if that were true, why would Wale have risked leaving Yia Pao by himself? Doubt and a lingering hope kept him from fleeing into the street.

It was the next morning before Wale returned with food, clothes, milk, and diapers. He said he had spoken with a friend, a former military man, who could arrange for Yia Pao and his son to go to Canada. Wale explained that Gordon's daughter lived on a farm there, and that she wanted to help them begin a new life. When Yia Pao said he had no money for such a trip, Wale said the tickets would be taken care of, that in fact he'd be grateful to Yia Pao for accepting the offer. He smelled of alcohol, and he slurred his words as he spoke, but Yia Pao didn't hesitate. He said yes.

Wale left him there again and didn't come back until the following afternoon, when he stopped by briefly to inform him they would fly out in nine days. After that, he returned only once a day to drop off provisions, never staying long. Yia Pao wanted to tell his friends in Vientiane of his imminent departure, but he dared not leave the apartment or ask Wale to take the risk of delivering a message.

The day before the flight, Wale informed him that a man would drive him and Xang to the airport in the morning, and that Wale would meet them there. The man who arrived wore dark glasses and barely spoke. At the airport, he produced papers and tickets, as well as an index card with the address and phone number for the farm. Yia Pao asked where Wale was and the man didn't answer, only advised him to get on the plane before the wrong people turned up. Yia Pao passed through the airport with Xang and boarded the airplane, expecting to be pulled aside at any moment. When he felt the wheels leave the runway, he couldn't believe it. Then, at the terminal in Toronto, he called the number he'd been given and got no answer. There was nothing to do except make his way to the address on the card.

Yia Pao says he wishes deeply that Gordon were here too. He can't say how sorry he is for what happened. He wants Maggie to know that her father was a fine man, thoughtful and brave, a true friend. The Hmong believe the spirits of one's ancestors remain in this world, looking out for their loved ones. The spirit of Maggie's father must be a powerful one, and she's lucky to have had him in her life.

As Yia Pao tells his story, the pain in Maggie's body grows. She tries to recall the television documentary about her father, wanting to determine where Yia Pao's version of the story differs from it, but focusing is hard. At times the bed beneath her seems to quake, and Yia Pao's voice reaches her ears as if through a long funnel. She remembers that the documentary showed her father snatching Yia Pao's baby under the nose of Sal's goons, then hiding behind a waterfall. The filmmaker seems to have guessed right that he and Yia Pao escaped from their captors, but Yia Pao says nothing of a pit, nothing of being washed down a river.

When he recalls becoming separated from Xang and her father, she feels the tears start down her face. By the time he finishes speaking, they flow easily, without shame. She reaches for the statue and holds it tight against her chest. Not a taunt, after all, nor a tainted inheritance; just a sad reminder of a shared life. For the first time, the little saint seems like something she can love.

"You really don't think my father knew what was in it? I mean, when he sent it to me?"

A look comes over Yia Pao, as if the question is one he doesn't want to consider. Eventually the muscles in his face loosen. "How could he have known?"

A mistake, then. A stupid mix-up. It should be a comfort, but it makes things seem even worse.

"Why didn't you tell Sal what happened with the money?" she says. "He could have contacted me. I could have sent it back."

Yia Pao shakes his head. "Your father made me swear not to tell. Sal would have thought he'd sent the money on purpose. He would have killed us, then come after you. It was better for him to think the money was still in Laos."

She doesn't want to imagine what it meant for her father and Yia Pao to keep the truth hidden, doesn't want to contemplate the scars on Yia Pao's face. It's easier for her to dwell on the escape, the jungle, the search for his son.

"Once you were in Vientiane," she says, "you should have gotten in touch with me." She could have helped him, and he could have told her what had happened.

"I didn't know how to reach you," he replies. "It was dangerous to make inquiries."

It makes sense. It's an explanation. But when she thinks about it, she can also imagine him staying quiet to keep her from knowing about the money. That way, he might hope to find himself in Canada one day, as he is now, with the chance to take it for himself, and Maggie none the wiser.

She shouldn't be so mistrustful. When she told him about the statue burning in the fire, he looked genuinely glad. It doesn't matter anyhow, now that the money's gone. What matters is that this man was a friend to her father, who never had friends, and he's here with his son, alone in the world.

"What do you think happened to Wale?" she asks.

"I don't know." He looks downcast as he says it.

"You think Sal found him?"

"Perhaps he is lying low." But he doesn't sound hopeful.

The throbbing in her leg grows stronger, turns into a screaming. There's a knock at the door and Josef appears with a grin, his eyes already on the baby. As he enters with Lenka in tow, he waves at Xang and the boy laughs. Josef draws closer and waggles his fingers at the child. Then, turning to Maggie, his smile diminished only a little, he tells her that visiting hours are over for the morning and they'll have to come back later.

Maggie's mind grows crowded, even as her foot shrieks. There's so much they haven't talked about. Where are Yia Pao and Xang going to stay? What about their papers? Knowing Wale and the company he keeps, the documents are likely forged. What about Wale? They should be calling the authorities in Vientiane, telling them about Sal, urging them to keep a lookout. Surely not everyone in the place is corrupt. They should be contacting the documentarian, telling her she was wrong and Yia Pao never drowned in any river. But already he's saying goodbye, his voice once more swirling down a funnel. He and Xang are moving toward the door with the priest and Lenka, and Maggie has a feeling that if she lets them go, she'll never see them again.

Lenka must recognize the look in her eyes, because she returns to take her hand. "Do not worry about things. Only rest."

"Where are you going?" asks Maggie.

"Tomorrow we have appointment with consulate," Lenka replies. "There we deal with the serious things."

"What about this afternoon?"

Even as the pain in her foot drags her away, she can see a look of pleasure on Lenka's face.

"Today we have fun," says Lenka, sounding gleeful, like someone younger than herself. "Today we take them to see the Niagara Falls."

13

Already there are shoots coming up through the mud, green stems starting to dot the barren field that was the cherry orchard, though it's still March. At the centre of the editing viewer stands a backhoe next to a pile of uprooted, charred stumps. Pauline runs through the frame in a rain slicker and yellow boots, followed by Xang, who wears a bright red toque and wobbles on stubby legs. Yia Pao holds his hand and tells him to slow down. In the next shot the three of them examine a puddle while Elliot appears in the foreground, leaping to swat at a fly. Behind them, moated by a ring of tire tracks, is the concrete foundation of the new house. A pair of bearded men with tool belts move between the upright timbers that form the beginnings of a frame.

When Brid steps into the shot, she positions herself so as not to block out the construction scene. Despite the season, she's in a short-sleeved blouse, revealing arms that have healed but still look scalded red from wrists to biceps.

"Brid Garland reporting," she says into the camera. "We're here with Father Josef of the Francis de Sales Church in Virgil." Reaching over, she drags him into view. Josef keeps his eyes down and shuffles his feet. "Father, what does Rome have to say about the new farmhouse?"

"Is going well," he murmurs, sounding flustered.

"What about Xang and Yia Pao there?" The camera pans to the man and his son before returning to Brid and Josef. "How are they adapting to life in the north?"

"Going well," he repeats. By now he looks rather ill.

"Riveting commentary. What about you, Lenka?" Brid looks toward the camera and cocks an eyebrow. "Any reaction to the rumour that Yia Pao's sweet on you?"

"Cameraman must not talk," insists Lenka's voice, and the scene abruptly ends.

The reel is miraculous. The sounds that come to Maggie as she sits before the editing machine in the barracks emanate not from an audio cassette but from the film itself. Super 8 has taken a leap forward, leaving the silent era for the age of talkies. No longer will she need to labour at synching voices and images. When Fletcher presented her with the new camera during his last visit to the farm, he was eager to point out this advance, so enthusiastic that she worried it was a sign he still wanted to get back together. Later, she overheard him talking to Brid about the dating pool in Boston and decided it would be all right.

The next shot traces the horizon, capturing buds on cherry saplings planted last summer and spared from the fire, while in the background lie the foundations of the old house, cordoned off by a chain-link fence. The camera moves more slowly than if Maggie were shooting, and at first she assumes it's due to Lenka's inexperience. Then she wonders if Lenka just has a different way of looking at the world, more leisurely, contemplative. At such a pace, what might she notice that Maggie misses? When faced with a shot of herself walking down the driveway to the mailbox, Maggie is forced to study things at Lenka's speed, and to her surprise she discovers that the limp she gained from the fire is barely noticeable now.

Once the reel comes to an end, she stretches and yawns. The others won't be back for an hour, having ceded the barracks to her so she can work at the editing machine for the afternoon. From the direction of the new house comes the intermittent bang of hammers. The walls around her are decorated with finger-painted pictures of eggs and rab-bits in preparation for Easter, and the area near the door is tracked with mud from little boots. Now that the place is in the middle of a construction zone, the floors are never clean, and there are weeks to go before it's over. Two little children and three adults living in one room with only makeshift dividers to mark out separate spaces for them. Even life last summer was uncluttered in comparison. Maggie wonders what George Ray will make of things when he arrives next week.

Not for the first time, she imagines him watching the film she has put together. Could it be that she's hoping to please him with it? Perhaps that's why she lent the camera to Lenka so easily after feeling so possessive of the previous one. Maybe a part of her wanted to be filmed and put up onscreen for George Ray to consider along with the tree buds and other things of vernal beauty.

She shouldn't have such thoughts. He hasn't given any sign that he's coming back to be with her. The one time they talked on the phone, it was to confirm the details of his contract. In his letters, he has told her of trying to work things out with Velma, and he has said that if he could find a job in Newcross that paid half as well, he wouldn't be coming to Canada. But the letters' tone was strangely impersonal, as if someone was reading over his shoulder while he wrote.

She shouldn't waste time mulling it over. Given his situation, she can't expect anything. A married man, a father, one who lives half the year in another country. He and Maggie won't have time alone together anyhow, at least not until the house is finished; they'll be sharing the barracks with Brid and Yia Pao and the kids. But there's plenty of room if one doesn't put much stock in privacy. Even with five of them, they fill only half of the long dining table. Eyeing the vacant end of it at meals, Maggie has sometimes imagined going next door to invite Frank Dodd for dinner. The last few months, she has often seen him shovelling his driveway, but there has been no sign of Lydia, and Maggie wonders whether she's still in California or back with her mother in Toronto. Maggie hasn't forgiven her for the graffiti; perhaps eventually she'll manage it. One day the girl and her father could be sitting there with the rest of them.

It shouldn't seem necessary to fill out the table, though. Whenever Maggie has felt a return of the summer's worry about needing more people, she has staved it off. This time they're going to do things differently. She doesn't know exactly how; she has no grand vision, no great plans. There's only a desire for the people who are here to make a life for themselves, ragtag bunch that they are.

Attaching another reel to the editing machine, she hits the switch, then watches Yia Pao and Lenka as they squat by a wooden pallet that holds a stack of terracotta bricks. Yia Pao is drawing in the mud with a twig, sketching out a diagram of the kiln he's going to build. He traces a curving line to show Lenka how heat will move through the chamber. Then he adds two stick figures beside the kiln and whispers something that makes Lenka laugh. A moment later she apprehends the camera's presence and waves it away.

Yia Pao never appears bothered by Maggie's filming. He neither mugs nor shies from it, seeming instead to take for granted that what they're doing on the farm deserves to be recorded. In the same way, whenever Maggie talks of expanding the garden and selling vegetables at a stand on the highway, he nods in full expectation of success. He doesn't worry that they'll never stop depending on Fletcher's charity and goodwill. He's sure her father's insurance money will come through soon. It would be tempting to attribute his optimism to the contrast between his life now and the one in Laos, but Brid is just the same. Ever since leaving the hospital, she's been manic with industry, confident they're going to make things work. Maggie wonders if she's the only one who worries that all Brid's energy might come with some future cost.

It's a shame to be so doubtful. Brid's happy, after all. She doesn't seem to mind that there has been no word from Wale, no trace, no news of a body to identify in the Vientiane morgue. She never even speaks of him. Sometimes Maggie fantasizes about going to Laos and trying to find him, maybe even travelling to the mission and asking about her father, but it would be too dangerous and she suspects she wouldn't discover anything. Even if she were to see the refugee camp, the river, and the jungle trail with her own eyes, they wouldn't give her what she really wants: a glimpse of what her father was thinking in his last moments; whether his mind went to his family or to God, whether he looked back on his life with remorse or gratitude.

Across the barracks, the telephone starts to ring. When she says hello, she hears George Ray's voice. He has never called before, and she's a little embarrassed by how glad she is that it's him. Then she thinks of the expense and offers to phone back.

"It's all right," he says. "I can't speak long."

"Is something the matter? You're still coming, aren't you?"

He laughs. "You sound as though you are eager for me to be there."

"Well, I am," she says, feeling caught out but glad of it. "I know we're supposed to be professional with one another now, but I can admit that I want to see you, can't I?"

"Yes, of course. I want to see you, too. Why do you think I'm ringing like this?"

"Are we making a mistake?" she asks. "I mean, with you spending the summer here?"

"What mistake could there be?" he says, sounding too innocent by half. "I am coming as your employee. We will be very proper with each other." The wry confidence with which he says it makes the whole scenario seem ridiculous and manageable at once.

"I'm being serious," she says. "You make it sound simple, but everything feels messy."

"Simple and messy," he replies. "Yes, that is just about right."

When he tells her he has to go, she says she understands. He doesn't offer any expression of affection, nor does she. Maggie has the feeling that he's as uncertain as she is about what lies ahead. At this moment in Jamaica, standing there with the receiver in his hands, he might even share the same adolescent thrill from their conversation that's passing through her. One day, she worries, somebody's going to discover that behind her breasts and hips there's a little girl at the helm, frantically pulling levers to keep up the illusion of a mature human being. A week ago she turned twenty-five, and still she has some way to go before she can call herself grown-up.

Once she's sitting at the table again, she removes the reel from the editing machine and replaces it with footage of the construction site she filmed two weeks ago. Putting her index finger on the power switch, she toggles it back and forth a few times, half with indecision, half in playfulness, before flicking it into action. Thirty minutes until the others return—not enough time for any major changes. Just a snip here, a cutaway shot there, enough to try out one or two ideas she's had and make things a bit better than they were before. Already she can picture everyone seated tonight before the white sheet they've hung against the wall, watching what she has pieced together. It will be an easy pleasure for them.

The sun streams through the barracks window onto all the floating dust, making curtains of the air. Maggie returns her gaze to the editing machine's little rectangle of light. Blinking a few times, she feels a brief, unexpected spasm of happiness and gets down to work.

ACKNOWLEDGEMENTS

Thanks to Ema Jelinkova for her expertise on Czech matters, to Grace McGill for details about life on the Niagara Peninsula, and to Marcy and Bruce McGill for reminiscing about television. I'm also grateful to Russell Brown and Denise Bukowski for sharing their memories of moving to Canada during the Vietnam War, and to Susan Sheard and Andy Strominger for talking with me about life on communes.

With regard to the "secret war" in Laos, I'm particularly indebted to histories written by Fred Branfman, Jane Hamilton-Merrit, and Judy Austin Rantala. Regarding the seasonal workers programme that first brought Jamaicans to Niagara farms in 1966, I'm grateful to Vincenzo Pietropaolo, Aziz Choudry, Jilly Hanley, Steve Jordan, Eric Shragge, and Martha Stiegman for their documentary efforts, and to Puddicombe Farms in Stoney Creek, Ontario.

The Harvard Society of Fellows and the Department of English at the University of Toronto generously provided me with the time I needed to write this novel. Natasha Bershadsky, Amanda Lewis, Grace O'Connell, Siobhan

Phillips, David Staines, John Sweet, and Luke Williams were astute readers, while Sara Salih was a brilliant collaborator. Euan Thorneycroft and Denise Bukowski's efforts on behalf of the novel have been extraordinary, and I'm grateful to Dan Franklin for his commitment to it. Finally, thanks to Anne Collins for her marvellous editorial work, and to Fiona Coll, whose acuity and support are daily gifts.